TO HONOR
YOU CALL US

By H. Paul Honsinger

<u>The Man of War Trilogy</u>

To Honor You Call Us

For Honor We Stand

Brothers in Valor (forthcoming)

H. PAUL HONSINGER

TO HONOR YOU CALL US

The Man of War Trilogy: Book 1

47N⬡RTH

Text copyright © 2013 by H. Paul Honsinger

Printed in the United States of America.

Cover Illustration by Gene Mollica
Published by 47North
Seattle, Washington

ISBN-13: 9781477848890
ISBN-10: 1477848894
Library of Congress Control Number: 2013944440

To my dearest wife, Kathleen, without whom this novel simply would never have come into being. Thank you for your incalculably valuable practical assistance in bringing this book to print and, of far more importance, your patience, your endurance of my many faults and thoughtless acts, your encouragement, your advice, your example, your fundamental decency and goodness, and—of course—your insistence in September 2012 that I just sit down and start writing. Thank God for you. You are the light of my life.

Lake Havasu City, Arizona

June 6, 2013

A NOTE FROM THE AUTHOR

For the benefit of lubbers, squeakers, and others unfamiliar with Union Space Navy terminology and slang, there is at the end of this volume a Glossary and Guide to Abbreviations, which defines many of the abbreviations, terms, and references used in these pages.

TO HONOR
YOU CALL US

PROLOGUE

04:13Z Hours, 11 November 2314 (General Patton's Birthday)

Lieutenant Max Robichaux, Union Space Navy, stood in the crowded boarding tube, breathing the scent of fear—acrid sweat from the thirty-four other men he had been able to round up from the USS *Emeka Moro*. With over fifty Krag boarders on his own ship, it seemed nothing short of insane to be counterboarding the enemy vessel instead of defending his own. Except that his shipmates were losing the battle for their own vessel. Except that unless the Krag ship could be disabled and the two vessels separated, the more numerous crew from the enemy battlecruiser would continue to flow into the *Emeka Moro*, overwhelming the less numerous complement of the smaller frigate. Except that unless this desperate gamble worked, his own ship would be taken, refitted, crewed with Krag, and sent back into battle against the people who built her. And of course, there would be the small matter of the enemy brutally killing Max along with his shipmates and dumping their mutilated bodies into interstellar space.

Call it an incentive to succeed.

Max adjusted his gloves, the material chafing his large hands and trapping his own nervous sweat against them.

"Five seconds—brace yourselves!" yelled the engineer's mate.

Every man covered his ears and opened his mouth to help prevent his eardrums from rupturing.

"Three, two, one!"

Just as Max could see that the young man's diaphragm was beginning the contraction that would allow him to utter the word "now," the slowly telescoping boarding tube struck the outer hull of the Krag warship, triggering the breaching charge with a deafening *THOOOOOOOM*, blowing open a nearly two-meter hole, into which the boarding tube penetrated just under an arm's length. Within a second, a polymer collar around the exterior of the tube folded out and adhered to the inside of the hull, making an airtight seal. Just as the seal formed, the door at the end of the boarding tube dropped to form a ramp, and the men under Max's command stormed into the Krag ship, weapons at the ready.

They found themselves in a large cargo hold, at least thirty meters square, full of assorted containers and with a hatch on the far wall. Three men slipped off packs and pulled out three components that they assembled into a device about a meter and a half square, which they activated. Max noted that both the blue and green lights came on, indicating that, for now, the Krag ship's internal sensors and comms were offline until their computer managed to decrypt the scrambling algorithm, which typically took from fourteen to twenty-three minutes. He hoped it would be long enough.

A quick hotwire job by the engineer's mate (what was his name—Tumlinson? Tomlinson? Tomkins?), and the hatch slid open, admitting the boarding party to a corridor. Max was the first one through the door, sidearm in hand. "After me," he whispered hoarsely, and the men followed him at a trot. The Union had captured enough Krag ships, in the more than thirty-year-long war, for Max to know the general layout. So, he had no trouble leading them to the Main Engine and Power Control Room. The boarding party made its way quickly without encountering any Krag for about sixty-five meters, before turning a sharp corner into a short corridor that ended at the entrance to their destination.

They ran into a hail of gunfire. Ducking quickly out of the way of the bullets, Max pointed to three men behind him, then made a fist and a throwing motion, indicating that the three men were to use grenades. They pulled the fist-sized devices from their web belts and yanked the pins while holding down the safety levers, then looked back at Max. He held up three fingers and counted down silently: three, two, one. A full second after the "one," all three men threw their grenades hard against the far bulkhead of the corridor, to land at the guards' feet in a banking shot. The grenades went off about a tenth of a second apart. Max and his men scrambled around the corner, shooting as they came, in case anyone was left standing.

No one was. Four dead Krag lay bleeding near the door, rifles in their hands. They didn't look so threatening, lying there on the deck, dead. Alive was a different matter. Few humans could look with aplomb at a man-sized, bipedal alien with nearly human arms, legs, and torso, but sporting a 1.5-meter-long tail and a head that looked like it belonged on a giant rat with an overdeveloped brain.

"Remember men, once we get in, no shooting. Boarding cutlasses only. There are too many things in there that can kill us all if they get punctured by a bullet." He turned to the engineer's mate. "Ready, Tomkins?" *That* was his name: Tomkins. "Blow it."

Tomkins pressed and held two buttons on the side of his percom. The green light on the small breaching charge he had just stuck on the hatch changed from green to red, and with a sharp *BANG*, the shaped charge shredded the door. Max led the way, his boarding cutlass, sixty-three and a half centimeters of cold, razor-sharp, gleaming steel drawn, his men wading into twenty-five or so Krag engineers who had been manning stations in that space. Spotting the panels that he needed to reach near the far end of the room, Max strode in that direction. Three Krag converged to block him. The closest drew its own sword, a short, straight affair resembling a Roman *gladius* and stabbed at Max's gut. With a powerful downward swipe of his own longer, heavier blade, Max blocked the blow and struck his opponent hard in the snout with the back of his hand. Stunned, the Krag staggered, allowing Max to bring his cutlass back up and chop into the Krag's neck, cutting three quarters of the way through, severing its spine and dropping it to the deck.

The second, more skilled with a sword than the first, held its weapon in front of it like a fencing foil, ready to duel. Max charged, leading with the point of his own weapon as if to accept the Krag's invitation to a fencing match. At the last moment, Max lunged forward and grabbed the end of the Krag's sword in his gloved left hand, pushing the point away from himself while plunging his own weapon deep into the Krag's abdomen and out its back.

Sensing rather than seeing the approach of the third Krag, Max pulled his sword from the second and pivoted to his right to fend it off just as the one Marine Max had been able to find for the boarding party caught it from behind, stabbing into the Krag's right lung with a distinctly nonregulation dirk. The Krag fell to the deck on its back, gasping as its lungs collapsed from the air filling its chest cavity. The Marine silenced the sound with a savage stomp to the Krag's throat. The way to the panels was now clear.

Max took a quick look around the compartment, seeing that all the Krag were out of the fight except for four who were standing back to back, mounting a last-ditch defense. Twenty or so lay dead or badly wounded on the deck, along with seven of his own men. Confident that the remaining boarders would shortly overwhelm the four holdouts, Max reached the panels he sought in three long steps, struggling briefly with the unfamiliar labels on the controls, to verify that they were the right ones.

He pulled a small cylindrical device from his web belt; ripped off a piece of plastic film, exposing an adhesive strip; and gave the end a half twist. Max pressed the cylinder, adhesive side down, to the panel and stepped back. He then repeated the procedure, attaching a second cylinder to a second panel. A few seconds later, each made a loud, high-pitched whine that started out near the top of the musical scale and rapidly ascended beyond the range of human hearing, all the while emitting a brilliant red-orange glow that became brighter as the pitch became higher. When the noise and the light both stopped, all the displays in that section of the Krag engineering deck went dark, the delicate microcircuitry of their components hopelessly fused.

Until the Krag could bypass those units, a process that might take hours, their ship's grappling field was off-line, and its motive power limited to maneuvering thrusters.

"Men, her claws are cut and her legs are broken. Now, let's get away before we overstay our welcome."

Max had often entertained the idea of boarding with a nuke rather than sabotage gear, but the thought of what could happen if the boarding party's exit from the enemy ship got delayed didn't bear contemplation. Being caught inside the fireball of a nuclear explosion might be a quick and painless way to die, but it was also awfully damned certain. Boarders always took or crippled the ship they boarded, but never destroyed it. That was best done at a safe distance from your own vessel.

Max led the men back the way they came, turning into the main corridor only to be met by about two dozen Krag Marines, probably drawn by the sound of the earlier gunfire. Each side fell back from the intersection, too startled by the sudden appearance of its respective enemy to get off a shot. Knowing he had only a second to act before the Krag got the same idea, Max pulled two grenades from his own web belt, one in each hand, extracted the pins with his teeth, and tossed them both around the corner. As soon as they went off, he charged around the corner, his men behind him, the front rank of five men shooting from the hip and taking out about half of the Krag who had not been felled by the grenades.

The two clumps of combatants merged in a close-order melee, shooting at point-blank range with sidearms and hacking at each other with swords. Max shot one Krag through the bottom of the jaw and was turning to meet another when he felt an odd tug at his left arm. Turning, he saw a Krag sword slicing the back of his wrist, just as Ordinary Spacer First Class Fong shot it through the back of the head. As both groups started to thin from casualties, opening up room between the fighters, what had been an even balance between shooting and stabbing turned more and more to shooting, with the advantage going to the slightly more numerous boarding party. The remaining Krag ran, the Union crew shooting at their fleeing backs and bringing down four more. Stepping over the bodies of friend and foe, Max led the remainder of his men, now numbering only nineteen, back into the cargo hold, down the boarding tube, through the airlock, and onto the *Emeka Moro*.

Tomkins pulled a large lever, sealing the boarding tube air-lock, then slapped a red button. A loud *WHUMP* marked the explosion that blew the tube, cutting the near end loose from the *Emeka Moro*.

Max gave himself the luxury of half a minute—five quick breaths—to savor the familiar sights, sounds, and smells of being back aboard his own ship. The boarding action had been a success, with the bonus that Max and most of his men were still alive. There were Navy crewmen left behind on the Krag ship, probably all dead by now, and there they would stay. Sentimental notions about retrieving bodies of comrades had perished in the first weeks of this desperate war for the survival of the human race. But if things continued according to plan, the fallen would receive the most thorough cremation known to man.

Leaning against the nearest bulkhead, Max hit the orange SND/ATN button on his percom.

"Robichaux to CIC."

"CIC," the voice from the ship's Combat Information Center responded over the tiny device strapped to Max's wrist.

"Boarding party is Romeo Tango Sierra," Max said, informing the command crew via his percom wrist communicator that the boarding party had "RTS," or returned to the ship. "Enemy main sublight drive and grappling field disabled for estimated one-hour minimum. Nineteen effectives remaining. Rest are Kilo India Alfa." Killed in action. Dead. Almost half.

"Excellent work, Lieutenant." Max recognized the cool, well-modulated voice of Captain Sanchez. "Make your way to Auxiliary Control with your party."

"Heading for Auxiliary Control, aye." *Auxiliary control? With enemy boarders to be fought?* Fighting the desire to shake his head at the order, he turned to what was left of his command.

"Men, we're ordered to Auxiliary Control."

Down a corridor Max led his men, now laboring to breathe, through the series of access ladders and corridors that would take them to the deck on which AuxCon was located. Then, *CRACK-BOOOOOM!* A sharp blast, followed by a long, deep rumbling, shook the ship. Max knew that sound. It was the detonation of an implosion charge array collapsing a heavy spherical pressure bulkhead. Like the one that surrounded CIC.

Now the order made sense. The captain must have known that the Krag had taken the spaces surrounding CIC and were setting the explosives that, when detonated together, would crush the CIC pressure bulkhead like an eggshell, instantly killing everyone inside. Everyone in CIC, which likely included every officer on the ship senior to Max, was now dead. Captain Sanchez had just issued his last command.

Max and his men poured out onto H Deck and ran toward Auxiliary Control. Dead men and dead Krag littered the corridor. No one was left alive, save one Krag with a shredded right arm, trying and failing to set a breaching charge on the hatch. Setting a breaching charge is a two-handed operation. Max drew his sidearm, a ten-millimeter semi-auto based on the time-proven Browning Hi-Power, and shot it cleanly through the head; he absent-mindedly kicked the body to the side, put his palm on the scanner, and keyed the access code. The hatch slid open, admitting Max and his men to the room from which the ship could be controlled if the CIC were destroyed.

Only two petty officer thirds were manning stations. The rest of the crew who would ordinarily have been there had been sent out to fight boarders. Max threw himself into the seat at the Commander's Station and divided his attention between pulling up the displays he needed and putting people to work.

"Tomkins, Woo, and Lorenzo, take Maneuvering. Adamson, Tactical. Marceaux, Weapons. Fong, SysOps. Montaba, Sensors. Everyone else cover the rest of the stations as best you can—keep an eye on what's going on and go where you're needed. Don't be afraid to sing out if you see anything, need anything, or have a question. You've all got your Comets, so you know how to run every station in the ship, but you've never worked together doing these jobs, so you'll just have to talk to each other, pitch in, and be flexible. Now, let's see about getting the old girl back into the fight."

"Sir, you're bleeding," observed Montaba quietly.

Max looked at his arm. His uniform sleeve was soaked with blood, and he could see deeply into the muscles of his forearm. The slash was deep, and yet Max felt strangely distanced from the sensation of pain. He pulled a first aid kit from an emergency equipment bin, stuffed a volume bandage into the arm of his uniform, and then stuck his whole forearm into a compression sleeve, pulled the cinch, and tied it off. The sleeve inflated to put pressure on the volume bandage and slow the bleeding, while a medication ampule in the bandage was ruptured by the pressure, releasing coagulants and an antibiotic cocktail into the wound. Maybe Max wouldn't bleed to death in the next few hours or die of an infection before he got to a doctor. Just maybe.

This took only about a minute. People were moving quickly but efficiently to their assigned stations, getting their displays tied into working data channels and bringing their controls online. He turned to the man running the Comms Station. "Comms, give me 1MC."

"1MC, aye."

"Attention all hands, this is Lieutenant Robichaux in AuxCon. CIC is gone and I have assumed command. Ship is being conned from here. All DC and Boarder Repel Stations report your status by lights. I need two Marines to AuxCon. Maintain Condition One. That is all." How the Marines were supposed to determine which two were to respond to this command, they would have to figure out for themselves, because Max had his hands full.

Hands full was right. Max had never commanded anything larger than a 350-ton system patrol vessel. Now he was commanding a heavily damaged 25,650–metric ton frigate in combat with a much larger and more powerful capital ship, light years from any hope of reinforcement or support, with virtually all of his officers and much of his crew dead. The expression "in over your head" didn't even begin to cover it.

The crewman at the Damage Control Station sang out, "Getting damage reports, sir. Relaying them to your board." It would take a few minutes before a complete picture developed.

"Boarders?" Max said to Lewis at the Onboard Defense Station.

"Only green lights so far, sir. They are pretty well distributed throughout the ship. I've got a voicecom report from a squad of Marines saying that they just surrounded and took out the five Krag who blew CIC. Maybe we got them all."

"Maybe so." *And maybe not.* Max stabbed the comm button again. "AuxCon to Engineering."

A somewhat reedy but precise voice answered instantly. "Engineering here. Brown speaking."

"Wernher!" Max responded gleefully, relief flooding through his every cell. He gave the name a German pronunciation, even though Engineer Brown's accent was decidedly British. "Do you have any kind of engines working down there at all, or am I going to have to order 'out sweeps' and have the crew row us home?"

"*Lef*tenant,"—the engineer exaggeratedly gave the rank the archaic British pronunciation, contrary to naval procedure— "since your meager training still doesn't encompass reading the Master Status Display, it is my duty to inform you that the main sublight drive is available at up to 39 percent power, but I suggest you endeavor to keep that lower than 25 percent.

Compression drive is available, but no higher than two hundred and twenty c. Again, my strong recommendation is to approach that speed only in grave need—one hundred fifty would be much more prudent. The jump drive is nothing but scrap metal and molten pieces of abstract art. Oh, and if I were you, I shouldn't want to pull anything more than about eight Gs, because the inertial compensators are capable of no more than seven point eight Gs. That is, unless you wish to kill what little crew you have left."

"Understood, Wernher. If anything else of any importance breaks, let me know by comm. Master Status is down. Would be nice if it worked. Of course, it's not like I expect *you* to fix it."

"I shall attend to it in my copious free time. And *Lef*tenant, if you find yourself unable to remember the route to Lovell Station, feel free to ask me for directions."

"I'll bear that in mind, Wernher. AuxCon out." Somewhere between a third and two-thirds of the crew might be dead; one of the two star drives was gone for good; and a vastly more powerful enemy vessel was just meters off the starboard beam, but gallows humor was alive and well in the Union Space Navy. Good thing.

He jabbed the comm key once again. "AuxCon to Casualty Station…Anyone in Casualty, please respond." Nothing. "Anyone up here not insanely busy?" An ordinary spacer second class stepped forward.

"Shaloob, run on down to the Casualty Station, see what's going on down there, and report back from the nearest working comm. With CIC gone, your percom might not work. And we're not sure the ship is clear of Krag, so watch yourself. I want your sidearm *in your hand*, and make sure you've got rounds in it and a spare mag. Or three."

"Aye, Skipper," the man said automatically. He press checked his weapon, popped the magazine and looked at the witness holes, then drew three spare mags from the AuxCon weapons locker before heading out the door, pistol in hand.

"Skipper." Never been called that before, Max thought.

"Maneuvering, open up some range between us and the Krag ship, in case they've got any more ideas about boarding or they get their point defense weapons working again. Get us out to four hundred kilometers. Course and acceleration at your discretion, but take it easy on the old girl. She's had a rough day."

"Aye, sir, four-zero-zero kills, course and acceleration at my discretion, taking it easy," said Tomkins, who apparently was the senior of the three at the Maneuvering Stations—one for yaw and roll, one for pitch and trim, and one for the drive systems.

"Weapons, what's our status?" *Dear God, please let something work.*

"Status on pulse cannon: no lights at all, no response to comms," Marceaux responded. "My opinion is that we should assume forward and rear batteries are out. Number two and four missile tubes are available. Tubes loaded, crews standing by, reloads at the ready. But I've got a red light on the main coils and amber on the auxiliary. The auxiliary coil driver is running at only 5 percent, so it will almost be a dead tube fire. Tubes one and three show red lights across the board, and their crews do not answer." Short pause. "I think the crews are dead, sir." His report was quick and precise, but his voice shook. The adrenalin was wearing off.

"God rest their souls," Max said softly. "Good job, Marceaux." Then, in what the Navy called an officer's order voice, "This is a Nuclear Weapons Arming Order. Arm missiles and warheads in tubes two and four, and target the Krag ship."

"Nuclear Weapons Arming Order acknowledged and logged, sir. Arming missiles in two and four, arming warheads in two and four, and targeting the Krag," Marceaux responded.

"I plan to fire two while holding four in reserve, in case two does not destroy the target or another target presents itself," Max announced.

"Maneuvering, sing out when we get to four hundred kills; then turn to unmask the number two and four tubes."

WHAM! A hammer blow struck the ship, rattling the teeth of everyone on board.

"The Krag just fired one of their projectile weapons, sir," Tactical observed.

"We noticed. Mr. Adamson, give me a read on the projectile's velocity."

"It was just over a thousand meters per second, sir."

"So, about 10 percent. Most of *their* acceleration coils on the projectile weapon must be out. It'll take a hit at the optimal angle for them to penetrate the hull."

"Unless they can zero in on one of our hull breaches," Adamson muttered.

"Glad you thought of that, Adamson. DC, do we know where our hull breaches are, yet?"

"Affirmative, sir; reports are tolerably complete." This from Arglewa. Somehow he had acquired a nasty burn on his shaved scalp. "We have two right together in Frame Three at azimuth two-zero-five and two-one-two and one in Frame Five at azimuth two-two-three."

"Thank you, Mr. Arglewa. Get some burn foam on that shiny head of yours. The glare is distracting me. Maneuvering, do your best to roll the ship to present an azimuth of about…"—he took a rough average of the three azimuths and subtracted it from 360—"seventy-five degrees to the enemy."

"Just passing four-zero-zero kills, sir, yawing to unmask tubes two and four and rolling to present seventy-five degree azimuth," said Tomkins.

"Very well."

Max's comm buzzed. "Robichaux here. Go ahead."

"This is Shaloob. Casualty Station is *gone*, sir. I think the Krag blew the hatch and tossed in a satchel charge. Looks like the place was full of wounded when they did it too. Nothing but debris and body parts now. Nurse/Medic Salmons and Pharmacist's Mate Cho have got a makeshift casualty station set up on the RecDeck. I count fifty-three wounded there; thirty-two look serious. Salmons and Cho are performing surgery on someone right now, so I didn't interrupt them to get more information."

"Good call, Shaloob, and good report. When either Salmons or Cho gets a second, ask them if they can use you there. If so, lend a hand; if not hustle back here."

"Aye, sir."

"AuxCon out."

WHAM! Another Krag projectile slammed into the hull, this one causing two of the panels in the compartment's ceiling to fall to the deck. A prepubescent midshipman, who had appeared in AuxCon without Max noticing, calmly picked up the two panels and stacked them with the other debris he had quietly been arranging near the inoperable waste disposal chute, the look on his face as blasé as if he were policing a park for candy wrappers. The boy had a short-barreled shotgun slung over his shoulder, the powder deposits on his face and hands proving he had made extensive use of it in the last few hours. The boy wasn't shaving yet, but in all likelihood, he had already killed.

Two Marines with blood on their uniforms and fire in their eyes stepped into the compartment. "Lance Corporal McGinty and PFC Nogura reporting as ordered, sir," said the older of the two. Both saluted smartly.

"Thank you, gentlemen," said Max, returning the salute with equal precision. A Marine felt insulted if you gave him a sloppy salute. "Take up station outside the hatch to this compartment. You see any Navy, get 'em in here. You see any Krag, you know what to do."

"Aye, sir." The Marines did a perfect parade-ground about-face and took up their stations in the corridor.

"Tubes two and four unmasked, enemy targeted," Marceaux reported.

"Very well." Max responded. "Mr. Marceaux, enable drives in missiles two and four. Release warhead safeties. Set for maximum yield."

"Enabling drives in missiles two and four. Releasing warhead safeties. Setting for maximum yield."

"Open number two missile door," said Max.

"Number two open."

"Verify missile target."

"Sir," Marceaux responded formally, "missile number two is targeted on the Krag vessel approximately four hundred kills off our bow."

"Very well. Weapons Officer, you have a nuclear launch order."

"Confirmed, sir, I have a nuclear launch order."

"Fire Two."

"Two away." The ship shuddered as the missile was accelerated marginally by the damaged coils in its launch tube and then continued to accelerate under its own power. "Missile on course and homing on target." Marceaux sounded relieved. He probably had never fired a live missile before. "Impact in seven seconds."

There was an optical feed of the Krag ship on four displays strategically located around the compartment. Every eye was glued to one of them as every man silently counted down the seconds, watching as the Krag ship slowly yawed, probably to unmask a just-repaired beam weapon battery and then fire what was likely to be a killing blow on the frigate.

Three, two, one...Right on the mark, all four displays flared into almost painful brightness as the Krag ship disappeared in an incandescent sphere of rapidly expanding plasma, slowly fading from a brilliant blue-white, through the color-temperature spectrum, into dull red and then vanishing into infrared frequencies invisible to the human eye. When the fireball was gone at last, there were only the cold distant lights of the stars set against the infinite dark of space.

"All right, people, the bad guys died. We didn't. Excellent work. Now, let's see about getting the old girl back to Lovell Station."

CHAPTER 1

19:18Z Hours, 20 January 2315

Max hated parties. Particularly *this* kind of party—the kind of party where no one enjoyed themselves. The kind of party that is called a "party" only by long-standing social convention, because there is no better word for a gathering of officers convened to commemorate some worthy event at which food, wine, and liquor are served, but at which no gaiety of any kind is experienced by anyone present.

The refreshments were standard naval issue for events of this kind: finger sandwiches containing various formerly frozen meats from ship's stores, a reasonable variety of only moderately stale cheeses to be eaten with a reasonable variety of only moderately stale crackers, some kind of grilled something on skewers that might have once been meat or might be some sort of textured vegetable protein, exotic garnishes that undoubtedly came out of equally exotic-looking jars, chips freshly uncrated from long vacuum storage—and a naval favorite because they were easy to store and lasted virtually forever: nuts. Lots and lots of nuts. Nuts from different planets. Salted nuts. Spiced nuts.

Candied nuts. Roasted nuts. Fried nuts. Baked nuts. Raw nuts. And of course, no fresh vegetables of any kind. Not more than a thousand light years from the Core Systems. Not when the Task Force had been in almost continuous action against the enemy for nearly a year. Not given how desperately overburdened the Union Naval Supply Service had been since the Krag launched their war of extermination against an unsuspecting and unprepared Union on 26 June 2281.

This particular party was to celebrate the arrival of Vice Admiral Louis G. "Hit 'em Hard" Hornmeyer, replacing Vice Admiral Vladimir I. "By the Book" Bushinko as commander of Task Force Tango Delta. Maybe it would be more proper to say "fill the vacancy of" instead of "replace," because Admiral Bushinko was dead. Spectacularly dead. He had been vaporized along with his flagship and her 10,237-man crew in battle eight days ago. The loss of the admiral and all those men, not to mention a priceless command carrier and the more than two hundred Banshee fighters she carried, sucked the wind out of the gathering and weighed on Max's spirits.

An even bigger damper on Max's mood was that, as far as he could tell, he was the lowest ranking officer present: a lowly lieutenant, though at least not a junior grade one. On the ladder of commissioned officers, he stood only on the third rung, so far down that the top was almost invisible to him. He wouldn't have received an invitation at all except that he was still in temporary, *pro forma* command of the *Emeka Moro*, now that his skipper, executive officer, and the three other ship's officers senior to him were casualties. Unfortunately, the ship that he "commanded" was a ship in name only, an unpowered hulk in a holding area waiting for time in dry dock for a list of repairs longer than the Code of Naval Regulations. She would not go anywhere under her own power for months, if ever. His "command" was so meaningless, in fact, that he had been assigned temporary duty in Signals Intelligence, sitting at a computer console, sorting through and attempting to interpret enemy communications intercepts.

Everyone else at the party held on the recreation deck of the *Halsey*, Admiral Hornmeyer's flagship, seemed to be at least a lieutenant commander, and most were commanders or captains. To highlight his feelings of inferiority, Max could see that virtually every uniform in the room bore the Command in Space Badge, a medallion in the shape of a stylized warship radiating a salvo of lightning bolts. The CSB, Max's most cherished desire since he'd been eight years old, was worn over the left breast and symbolized that the wearer commanded a rated warship, that is, a ship of sufficient power, speed, and range to be sent to meet the enemy without close support from the fleet. And as a mere lieutenant, there was little chance he would be wearing one any time soon.

Still, maybe things weren't so bad. With all the casualties throughout the fleet, he might not remain stuck much longer, pushing electrons down in SIGINT. After all, by luck, good planning, or natural ability (or maybe a combination of all three), Max's service record was unusually rich in actual combat duty. He had been in more battles than many officers could even name, and he was almost always assigned to one of the "fighting stations" such as Weapons, Tactical, Sensors, Countermeasures, Electronic Warfare, and various other functions directly related to taking, killing, harassing, or destroying the enemy. Hell, he had even been wounded in combat. Twice.

Max was itching to get back in the fight, and maybe he had a chance. Rumor had it that several new ships, fresh out of the massive fleet construction yards back in the Union's Core Systems, were en route to join the task force, perhaps with officer billets to be filled from surplus personnel already here. The Navy Cross he had just been awarded for what most people were calling a "valiant boarding action" might give him a leg up in that department. And from there, perhaps he would receive promotion and a chance at a command.

Just as he started to allow himself a smile of hope, his lips curled into a frown of irritation. Someone, visible to him only as a silhouette, was blocking his view of the majestic ringed planet that hung outside the thirty-meter-long window that was the room's only attractive feature. Max strode up to ask him, in the deferential manner appropriate when speaking to an undoubted superior officer, to step aside so that he could see.

The man, sensing Max's approach, turned around to face him, and Max's planned request went out the airlock. First, the man was apparently the only officer in the room with a rank lower than his, lieutenant junior grade, so Max had no need for all the carefully constructed and convoluted language one had to use when asking a superior to do something. Second, he wore over his left breast a medal consisting of a silver star, indicating that the wearer was a noncombat officer. Superimposed on the star was the outline of a wooden stick with a single, entwining snake. It was the Rod of Asclepius, the ancient emblem of a physician. The man was a naval doctor, a class worth their weight in antimatter, meaning that they were pretty much a law unto themselves and, in particular, that under long-standing naval custom and etiquette, this man could block Max's view of the ringed planet all day if he chose. Third—and what really killed his urge to get the man out of his way—was that he wore on his face a look of such profound grief and intense, protracted sorrow that Max could not bring himself to ask him to move.

The man raised his eyebrows in inquiry. Max decided not to say anything about his view being obstructed and hit upon the most obvious alternate pretext.

"Hello, I'm Max Robichaux, Weapons Officer of the *Emeka Moro*. I've gotta tell you, it's a true relief to see someone else here who isn't the exalted commanding officer of some ship or other."

As Max extended his hand, he examined the man more closely. Physically, he was the most forgettable individual Max had ever seen. Medium height, medium build, brown eyes, dark-brown hair, features representing the mixed ancestry that was the heritage of most humans in the twenty-fourth century, in this case mostly Turkish with some European and Arabian. Neither noticeably handsome nor noticeably unattractive, he could pass as a native or a plausible tourist on any human world and would not stand out on any of them.

The man took his hand, bowing slightly as he did so, a custom on many of the more formal human worlds and one that was growing in popularity. "Ibrahim Sahin, Assistant Chief Medical Officer of William B. Travis Station." A wave of deep emotional pain, quickly checked, washed across the man's features. He released Max's hand.

"I beg your pardon. Former. *Former* assistant chief medical officer." Former was right. The whole enormous facility, which was supposedly in a secure rear area, had been blown to flaming atoms eight days ago, with more than fifty thousand dead and only a dozen or so survivors. No wonder the poor bastard looked like he'd just lost his best friend. He probably had. And his second best friend. And his third.

Max struggled only briefly with what to say when faced with an officer who had lived through what this man had endured. He fell back on the time-honored Navy way: minimize the emotional and talk about the facts. "Sorry to hear it, Lieutenant. How did you manage to make it?"

The doctor shook his head slightly, almost as though he were prepared to disbelieve his own story. "I was treating a patient for decompression sickness in a hyperbaric chamber. When the hospital wing was destroyed, the chamber was blown clear. I closed all the pressure valves, and my patient and I lived off the treatment oxygen bottles in the chamber for twenty-nine hours until we were rescued. We had emergency lights for only the first three hours or so. After that, it was dark. Very, very dark..." His voice trailed off. He collected himself and went on. "Well, in any event, the patient lived and is now being evacuated to the naval hospital on Epsilon Indi III."

That made sense. A hyperbaric chamber had to be built like a diving bell to withstand the high-pressure air it contained, so it would survive even if that part of the station were breached. And the things had to be airtight to work in the first place.

"Quick thinking. And a helluva stroke of luck," Max observed.

"You could look at it that way. I'm wondering if I might have been better off if I had been in the corridor or in the head relieving myself when that part of the station went."

It wasn't the first time Max had heard that kind of talk. Max had gone aboard his first warship as a squeaker when he was eight years old, and the Union had been at war for years before that. Now, at age twenty-eight, Max had a lifetime's worth of experience dealing with people who had survivor's guilt. It had to be nipped in the bud or he would soon be reading in the *Naval Gazette* that the Admiralty was saddened to announce that Dr. Sahin had died in a "regrettable airlock accident."

He put his arm around the man, leading him gently away from the window. "Walk with me, Doctor. Let's both of us get another drink." The two made their way to the bar and were waited on right after a short commodore who looked as though he would be better off drinking strong New Lebanon coffee than the Scotch the bartender had just poured for him. Max got another bourbon on the rocks. Dr. Sahin got a glass of Forthian Stout, a dark beer-like brew that contained no alcohol, because Forthian yeast produced no alcohol.

"Been in the Navy long?" It was a somewhat less lame opener than most, anyway.

"Only four years. When I completed my residency on Earth and it was time to go back home, there was no home to go back to. So, I joined the Navy, spent two years at the DeBakey Joint Forces Physicians Training Facility and when I graduated, was immediately assigned to Travis. I've been there ever since."

"No home to go back to, you said?"

"That's correct," Sahin replied. "I'm from Tubek."

Max could only remember two salient facts about Tubek: it had fallen to the Krag about six years ago, and as with most Krag conquests, no one knew what had happened to the people who had lived there. Naval Intelligence believed that they were either killed or enslaved—or some unsavory combination of both. Dr. Sahin had not only just lost everyone he had worked with but six years before had also likely lost his entire family and everyone he had grown up with. There weren't many grief counselors in the Union Navy's Medical Corps, but this guy was a candidate to have one assigned to him full time.

"My God. How're you managing?"

"I manage. I was very busy on the station. Now, here on *Halsey*, with all the combat casualties I'm too busy to dwell on things. Work is good therapy. My patients need me, and there is satisfaction in helping them, although after I treat them, they are evacuated back to the Core Systems or returned to their ships, and I never see them again. Work is what gets me through the day. The nights... the nights are somewhat more problematic."

"I know what you mean. What do they have you doing?"

"I'm one of fifteen combat/trauma surgeons on the *Halsey*. We do all the combat surgery for the casualties from this ship and also get the more difficult cases from the rest of the Task Force. We're operating around the clock. But they keep on threatening to put me on a destroyer or a frigate on detached service."

No one got rid of a naval surgeon, or even talked about it, without good reason. "Why's that?"

"I'm afraid that I am insufficiently diplomatic in my dealings with superior officers. My medical CO, Captain Choi, has a different philosophy on the extent of reconstructive and rehabilitative surgery: what can be economically performed here and what should wait until the patient reaches permanent treatment facilities back in the Core Systems. I am of the view that, so long as surgical resources are available, we should treat the patient to the maximum level of care that our facilities and staff are capable of providing. Dr. Choi, on the other hand, says that the medications and other consumable resources used in these procedures should be conserved in case resupply is interrupted and we need them to save the lives of battle casualties."

Max could see both sides and recognized that Dr. Choi certainly had some good reasons for his position. On the other hand, Max asked himself whether *he* would want to be treated by a doctor who didn't strive to provide the greatest and highest level of care and benefit that he possibly could every minute he was providing it. Not a chance.

Max certainly did not want to get into an argument with this poor, bedraggled fellow. During their conversation, Max noticed other things amiss with Dr. Sahin, particularly with his uniform. His boots were a bit dull; the creases on his trousers were not as sharp as they might be; there were a few faint spots on his uniform jacket; and his rank insignia and other decorations were less than perfectly situated. He would not pass inspection from a taut commander, that was certain. Max's own uniform was parade-ground perfect.

"Well, Doctor," said Max, "I've had my own issues with—what did you call it? Being 'insufficiently diplomatic.'" The doctor's raised eyebrow invited him to continue. "There was the time when I commanded a little PC-4 and Commodore Barber himself—that was before he became the famous-throughout-the-fleet Admiral Barber—ordered me to disengage and withdraw when..." Max was interrupted by a beep from the doctor's percom. The doctor raised an index finger while he glanced at the display of the device strapped to his wrist. From his angle, Max could see the text of the message but didn't know the medical codes, so he had no idea what it meant except that the prefix "PI" meant that whatever it was, it was supposed to be acted on without any delay.

"Pardon me, Lieutenant, I am needed at the Casualty Station. It was a pleasure to meet you. Would you be averse to our speaking again sometime?"

"Sure, my pleasure," Max replied. "You don't need my com-code—I'm the only Lieutenant Robichaux in the whole Task Force. Not many people know how to spell it. It's—"

"I know how to spell it, Lieutenant. I've heard of you," said Sahin. "Until later, then." He turned briskly and strode out of the room in a manner that was both surprisingly inconspicuous and yet extremely fast. Max wondered how he did it. Max knew that he had never been simultaneously awake and inconspicuous for more than two or three seconds at any time in his life.

He finished off his bourbon, paid his respects to the admiral, and walked slowly back to his tiny berth in guest officers' quarters, taking several detours, spending some time on the hangar deck watching the Banshee fighters being fueled and serviced, and stopping at the ship's store to pick up a spare battery for his percom.

When he finally got back, having killed a few hours, he could barely shoehorn himself into the cramped space—and then only if he left the shoehorn in the corridor. By moving slowly and with great deliberation, he was able to take off his ice cream suit (an age-old description for naval dress whites) without banging his hands or elbows on the bulkhead, hang it up carefully in the almost microscopic closet, and change into the royal-blue jump-suit and half boots, known as the Working Uniform, that was the Uniform of the Day today and most days on the Halsey. He had a duty shift in SIGINT in two hours, so he had time to make his way to the Number Five Wardroom, drink some coffee, and maybe shoot the breeze with some of the other off-duty officers. Maybe one of them had an interesting story to tell that was not too obvious a fabrication and that he had heard fewer than a hundred times.

Or maybe not. Either way, it was better than sitting inside this shoebox and staring at the bulkhead or poking around the news feeds on the berth's workstation.

In the habit possessed by anyone who wears a uniform for a living and who cares about not getting negative reports in his anachronistically named "jacket," Max checked himself in the mirror before leaving his quarters. Max had no thoughts of being handsome. Coming from Nouvelle Acadiana, Max was mostly a descendent of Louisiana Cajuns and had the fair skin, prominent nose, dark hair, and dark eyes that sometimes went with that ethnicity. However, whereas pure-blooded Cajuns tended to be short and slight, Max was a tall man, approaching two meters in height, but slender and wiry. As did so many people who were nominally Cajun, Max had some German, Scottish, and Irish ancestors hiding in some of the far branches of his family tree, giving him not only his decidedly un-Cajun height but also a square jaw and high forehead that spoke more of the Gaelic than the Gallic.

Thoroughly unimpressed with his natural appearance, Max made sure that his uniform was unwrinkled and hanging straight on his frame; that the limited badges, decorations, and insignia that went on the Working Uniform were appropriately arranged (especially his new Navy Cross); that the brass belt buckle shined; and that his boots gleamed.

He had gotten out the door and three steps down the corridor when his percom beeped. He glanced at the screen. It read: "PI MX OR W G-894." Although the percom had voice capability, most routine messages were sent by text and used a highly condensed code so that they could be read on the twenty-character, alphanumeric-only exterior screen of the device, rather than on the color graphical screen revealed when the cover of the device was flipped open. The symbols meant "Priority implementation. Message. Orders. Written. Compartment G-894." Or in something more closely approaching normal speech: "Priority, immediate implementation. A message for you, consisting of orders in written form, is waiting to be picked up in compartment 894 of G Deck."

Max shook his head. Fifteen strategically located message rooms on the carrier, and leave it to the Navy to have this message printed out for him in the room at the other end of the ship. At the other end of a ship that was 2,845 meters long. Actually, the more Max thought about it, it could be worse. His quarters were almost amidships, so G-894 couldn't be more than a kilometer and a half away, plus five decks down.

Fortunately, Max was good at learning ship layouts, so he was able to select the most direct route, find the tram that ran the length of the ship down the central corridor, and locate the proper compartment right away. He reached Compartment G-894 just under twelve minutes after receiving the text and stepped in through the open hatch.

He found a desk running the entire width of the roughly three-meter-wide space, manned by a bored-looking petty officer third class, sitting behind a computer-generated nameplate that said "MUCH." The man did not look up when Max walked in, but continued to peck slowly at a keyboard, while keeping his eyes fixed rigidly on a display placed so that the person operating it had to sit with his back nearly to the door. Max stood at the desk for five seconds without his presence being acknowledged. Apparently, no one of any importance ever picked up their messages in Compartment G-894.

"Ahem," Max said softly. Much didn't so much as twitch.

"Excuse me," Max said somewhat louder.

Much didn't budge.

"Petty Officer Much," Max said just a notch louder. He pronounced it like it was spelled, rhyming it with "such."

"That's '*Much*,'" the man replied, pronouncing the "u" as in "duke" with the "ch" a Germanic guttural, as in "ach."

That was enough for Max. "PETTY OFFICER MOOK," Max bellowed in his best drill instructor voice. He knew that he had mispronounced the name. His Cajun mouth was perfectly capable of producing Germanic gutturals if Max so chose. At this moment, however, he was not in the mood.

Much looked up quickly and rotated his swivel chair to face Max. Max glared at him, lips tightly pressed, until the man was sitting at "seated attention," knees together, back straight, head high, making eye contact—the appropriate attitude for an enlisted man being addressed by a commissioned officer while seated at his duty station.

Max lowered his volume but kept his tone as sharp as a razor. "Petty Officer Mook, I have received a text with a PI code stating that I am to pick up written orders at this location. Are you going to place these orders in my possession immediately, or when I fail to implement my orders with sufficient *celerity*, should I cite *your delay in transmission* as the cause?"

Much's eyes widened slightly. Everyone in the Task Force had read Admiral Hornmeyer's First Standing Order, issued when he took command. Rather than the standard blatherations, this standing order contained several pages of clear, incisive, imperative prose, one item of which said that "All operational orders are to be executed with celerity" and that the admiral "would not tolerate and would swiftly punish any repetition of the delays in transmission that were hitherto endemic in this command." Notwithstanding the inevitable fleet joke that half of the Task Force didn't know whether "celerity" meant a famous person or a crunchy vegetable, people got the point.

Much quickly came to his feet and touched an area, set off by a circle a few millimeters in diameter, on the surface of the desk that separated him from Max. A panel silently withdrew, revealing a square green scanner surface about eight centimeters to the side and a numeric keypad. Max put his left hand flat on the scanner and, with his right, entered his twelve-digit ID code. Much then walked over to a printer at his station that had produced one sheet of paper about two seconds after Max had keyed in the last digit. He folded it in half lengthwise, slipped it into a long envelope proportioned for a sheet of paper so folded, sealed the envelope, and handed it to Max, along with a stylus. Max then used the stylus to sign his name on the same scanner that had just read his handprint, creating a signed and time-stamped digital receipt for the message. When he withdrew the stylus, the panel slid back into place. Max returned the stylus to the chastened petty officer, put the envelope in his pocket, and left Compartment G-894, walking straight across the corridor to another hatch marked with a sign that said "G-895 ORDRDRM."

ORDRDRM—try pronouncing that, Max thought.

The Orders Reading Room was a Spartan enclosure, about two meters square, with one standard issue Navy desk chair and a small table. Max sat down in the chair, ripped open the envelope, extracted the paper, set the envelope on the table, and began to read.

23:14Z hours, 20 January 2315
TOP SECRET
URGENT: FOR IMMEDIATE IMPLEMENTATION
FROM: HORNMEYER, L.G. VADM USN, CDR TF TD
TO: ROBICHAUX, MAXIME T., LT USN
    1. EFFECTIVE IMMEDIATELY, YOU ARE RELIEVED AS ACTING COMMANDER AND WEAPONS OFFICER USS EMEKA MORO, FLE 2379. TAKE NO FURTHER ACTION RE EMEKA MORO. NEW TEMPCOM ALREADY APPOINTED.
    2. EFFECTIVE IMMEDIATELY, YOU ARE RELIEVED OF ALL TDY PREVIOUSLY ASSIGNED.
    3. EFFECTIVE 00:01Z 21 JAN 2315, YOU ARE CIG TO LCDR USN WITH ALL THE RIGHTS AND PRIVILEGES APPERTAINING TO SAID RANK.
    4. YOU ARE ADVISED THAT USS CUMBERLAND, DPA 0004 IS EXPECTED TO RENDEZVOUS THIS TASK FORCE APPROX 07:30Z 21 JAN 2315 UNDER TEMPCOM OF HER FIRST OFFICER LT R.T. GARCIA. CUMBERLAND FULLY PROVISIONED AND ARMED WITH STD WEAPONS LOAD. SOME PERSONNEL FROM THIS TF WILL JOIN SHIP AT THIS TIME.
    5. AT 09:00Z 21 JAN 2315, YOU ARE REQUIRED AND DIRECTED TO REPORT ABOARD SAID VESSEL AND ASSUME CHARGE AND COMMAND OF HER SUBJECT TO ALL APPLICABLE LAWS, REGULATIONS, STANDING ORDERS, AND OPERATIONAL ORDERS THAT SHALL ISSUE FROM DULY CONSTITUTED

AUTHORITY FROM TIME TO TIME. SEPARATE
WARRANT OF APPOINTMENT WILL ISSUE.

6. AS SOON THEREAFTER AS PRACTICABLE,
BUT NO LATER THAN 09:15Z HOURS, 21 JAN 2315,
USS CUMBERLAND UNDER YOUR COMMAND IS
TO PART COMPANY FROM THIS TASK FORCE,
ACCELERATE AT STANDARD TO 0.01 C, AND
PROCEED TO NAV BUOY JAH1939.

7. UPON REACHING DESTINATION, YOU ARE
TO IMPOSE COMPLETE EMCON ON VESSEL AND
EXECUTE SEALED ORDERS IN CAPTAIN'S SAFE.

8. KICK ASS AND GODSPEED.

He read the orders again, more slowly. After he finished, Max
realized he had been holding his breath and slowly exhaled, took
in another slow breath, and let it too out slowly.

Max fought to slow down his thoughts and to process what
he had read. He remembered what his old mentor, Commodore
Middleton, had told him: "All operational orders contain good
news and bad news." So, good news: One, promotion to lieutenant
commander, the next step up. Two, his own command. And—a
big three—a new, powerful *Khyber* class destroyer. The class,
although new, was getting a reputation for being a good ship.

Bad news: One, the *Cumberland*, a known "problem" ship
that had turned in a disappointing performance in two fleet
actions (or as Caesar might have said, "She came, she saw, she
ran like hell"), was becoming known around the fleet as "The
Cumberland Gap." Two, her skipper and XO had recently been
relieved, and rumor had it that many of her senior noncoms had
been reassigned to shore duty back in the Core Systems. Three,
whatever problems the ship had, there would be plenty of left-
overs still aboard for Max to deal with as the new CO.

The rest? A mystery until he opened the sealed orders, but there were hints that gave him hope. The orders directed him to part company no later than fifteen minutes after his appointment as skipper became effective, which said that "Old Hit 'em Hard" was in a hurry. And the "kick ass" part smelled like orders for combat. He wouldn't say "kick ass" if the *Cumberland* were going to be assigned to patrol a rear area or escort a hospital ship back to Earth or Alphacen, right?

Max had a lot to do and not a lot of time in which to do it. For the next several hours, he was going to be nothing but assholes and elbows. His first errand, though, was going to be a pleasure— a trip to the quartermaster to draw the uniforms, patches, and, most important, the coveted Command in Space Badges (one for each uniform) and lieutenant commander's insignia that went along with his new posting and rank. Then, he needed to belly up to a workstation to access everything he could learn about the *Cumberland* and her crew.

CHAPTER 2

Max sat in the copilot's seat of the transferpod as it glided across the seventeen kilometers of space that separated the *Halsey* from the *Cumberland*. There was no sense of motion except when the pod was nudged gently every few minutes by short growling burns from its maneuvering thrusters. He would have preferred to pilot the pod himself, but there were things that commanding officers of rated warships did not do: They did not carry their own gear (his gear had been sent over by a different pod and presumably had already been stowed in his quarters). They did not pour their own coffee unless they were alone. They did not shine their own boots. And most emphatically, they did not pilot their own transferpods.

At this distance, and with the fleet moving slowly through the shadow of the tawny fourth planet out from this particular star—a gas giant world boasting a spectacular ring system—not even the outline of the *Cumberland* could be seen, but only the winking pinpoints of red, green, blue, and white running lights and the barely visible white rectangles of the occasional viewport.

Max longed for a good look at his new command, even though Union warships were never very exciting to look at. They were all essentially long, squared cylinders (or long, rounded boxes) with the rounded bluntness of the sensor array on one end and sub-light propulsion systems on the other, with much of everything in between studded with an apparently haphazard collection of smaller cylinders, antennas, weapons ports, point defense turrets, missile launch tubes, field emitters, and other mechanisms that helped the ship find the enemy, elude the enemy, confuse the enemy, or—Max's favorite—blow the enemy to hell.

Even as he drew closer, the lines of the vessel stubbornly refused to resolve themselves. Union warships were jet black, their hulls coated with a polymer that absorbed light and most other forms of electromagnetic radiation so as to make the ship more difficult to detect. With running lights off and viewports shuttered, she was virtually invisible to the naked eye and darned hard to spot even with sensitive instruments. Even now, with running lights on, docking hatches illuminated, and viewport shutters open, the eye could not trace out her shape and lines from the disconnected dots and blobs of light that appeared to be floating in the darkness, unrelated to one another.

The pod was headed toward a green, blinking circle that indicated the main docking port through which he would gain entrance to the ship. The young able spacer second class piloting the tiny vessel guided it with practiced precision toward its destination. When the pod was ten meters from the port, he brought it to a stop and keyed the autodock sequence. Control of the pod transferred automatically to the *Cumberland*, which rotated the pod 180 degrees to bring its airlock in contact with the hatch and extended the docking seal. A slight hiss, followed by two distinct thumps, signaled to Max that the pressures had equalized between the two vessels and that both sets of outer airlock doors—those for the pod and those for the *Cumberland*—had opened.

A recorded voice announced, "Initiating artificial gravity" as the *Cumberland*'s gravity was extended through induction into the pod. Feeling his weight return, Max stood, walked to the airlock, and took a deep breath. *You're on*, he said to himself as he palmed the door mechanism.

Both sets of inner doors slid open, revealing the *Cumberland*'s salute deck, a small, square compartment holding six naval officers in white dress uniforms, an honor guard of six Union Marines in the emerald green of their service's dress uniform, the boatswain in the scarlet dress uniform of a senior naval noncommissioned officer, and one man in the plain black tunic and pants of an officer from the Union Military Intelligence Directorate. Max took all of this in without turning his head or showing any expression.

Almost lightheaded from emotion, he took one precise step from the pod onto the deck—his first onto his new command—and paused, feet together, for a slow count of five as he heard both sets of doors close and the transferpod detach from the airlock behind him. He then pivoted ninety degrees to his left so that he was facing aft and was looking directly at the Union national flag and the Union naval, or Admiralty, flag standing next to one another on flagpoles against the left bulkhead just inside the hatch. He briskly saluted them, then reversed the turn exactly to face an officer, a lieutenant who apparently was the XO, standing in his path about a meter and a half inside the hatch. Max brought himself into a second salute and held it. "Permission to come aboard, sir."

The lieutenant brought himself into a salute and held it while he said, "Permission granted, sir. Welcome aboard." He snapped his hand back to his side. A split second later, Max's hand followed suit. The lieutenant then said, "Attention on deck," and pressed a key on his percom. A chime sounded on the salute deck and throughout the ship, signaling that every word uttered in that compartment would be heard by all hands.

Max reached into the inside pocket of his uniform tunic, the pocket made for precisely this purpose, and removed the formal Commanding Officer's Warrant that had been delivered to him only an hour before. He unfolded the document and read aloud in his best official voice:

"By the Authority of the President, the Assembly, and the Senate of the Union of Earth and Terran Settled Worlds, and by directive of the Commissioners of the Admiralty, I hereby name, appoint, and constitute Lieutenant Commander Maxime Tindall Robichaux to hold and carry out the post of Master and Commander of the Union Space Ship *Cumberland*, Registry Number DPA 0004, the same being a vessel of war in the service of the Union Space Navy. The said Maxime Tindall Robichaux is hereby required and directed forthwith to take charge and command of the aforementioned vessel; to obey all applicable laws, regulations, standing orders, and operational orders that shall issue from duly constituted authority from time to time; and to secure due obedience to the same from all persons lawfully under his command. Let him answer to the contrary at his peril. And for all of the above and foregoing, let this be his warrant. Given by my hand and seal this twenty-first day of January in the year 2315, by Louis G. Hornmeyer, Vice Admiral, Commanding, Task Force Tango Delta."

As soon as the echo of the word "Delta" died, the Boatswain sounded two notes on his whistle and announced in a stentorian tone: "*Cumberland* arriving."

"I relieve you, sir," said Max to the lieutenant in front of him.

"I stand relieved," he replied.

"It is with pleasure and pride that I accept the honor and responsibility of command of this fine vessel," Max said, sounding anything but full of pleasure. "I look forward to meeting all of you and, more important, to meeting and destroying the enemy. Let the deck officer log the change in command. All standing orders to remain in force until further notice. That is all."

Max shook the lieutenant's hand firmly. The man responded with equal firmness and with what seemed like genuine warmth.

"Max Robichaux. You must be Garcia."

"Yes, sir. Roger Garcia. Welcome aboard, sir. Shall I introduce the officers?"

"Later, I think. Old Hit 'em Hard wants us underway with *celerity*." Everyone in the Task Force was taking delight in using that word, which until recently had been a part of practically no one's vocabulary. "What's our status?"

"Well, sir, the ship is ready for departure in all respects. We've got a top drawer chief engineer—really has his thrusters aligned. Sublight drive is on standby; navigational sensors and deflectors are energized; and Engineering is standing by to answer bells. All we need is a course and speed."

"Outstanding." Max was liking this XO already. "Course is one-one-five mark two-six-two, speed zero-point-zero-one c. Destination is Navbuoy Juliett Alfa Hotel one-niner-three-niner."

Garcia spoke into his percom. "XO to Maneuvering, did you get that?"

A voice responded from the unit, "Maneuvering to XO, aye, aye. Course one-one-five mark two-six-two, zero-point-zero-one c, destination Navbuoy Juliett Alfa Hotel one-niner-three-niner. Sir, are we rendezvousing with the buoy?" Maneuvering wanted to know whether he would be required to decelerate at the end of the run and stop at the buoy.

Garcia looked questioningly at Max.

"Negative."

"Negative," repeated the XO. "You are clear to maneuver."

"Understood, no terminal deceleration. Clear to maneuver, aye. Engineering reports main sublight drive ready to engage." A short pause. "Engaging." Another short pause. "Helm responding and ship coming to new heading." With the inertial compensators apparently set for less than maximum, Max could feel the ship start to move and the deck shift slightly under his feet. "Steady on one-one-five mark two-six-two, accelerating at Standard."

From what Max could hear, whatever was wrong with the ship had not affected the really sharp-sounding man at Maneuvering.

"Very well," Garcia said. Then, to Max, "We're under way, Skipper."

"Well done, XO. How long have you had the ship?"

"Only about eighteen hours, sir. I joined her at Jellicoe Station and brought her here."

"I understand." The man hadn't been on board long enough to unpack his gear, much less make his mark on the crew. Whatever kind of order the ship was in, Max could not reasonably hold the XO responsible, and Max's response communicated that understanding. "I'll meet you in CIC shortly."

"Very good, sir. See you there." The two men shook hands again. Max nodded slightly to the remainder of those assembled on the salute deck, and following the route he had carefully memorized (it simply does not do for a new captain to be seen making wrong turns or wandering about lost on his own ship, no matter how new he may be to her), he went to his cabin. Even on a ship as small as *Cumberland* the captain enjoyed a relatively spacious suite, consisting of a combination office, changing room, and dining area known as the "day cabin," with a small attached lavatory; and a "berth cabin" that contained a bed, various lockers for personal effects, a small sitting area, and a full bathroom with shower.

It was in the day cabin that Max carefully removed his dress whites and hung them in his uniform locker, before selecting the correct uniform designed to communicate exactly the message he wanted to send to the whole crew upon walking into his CIC for the first time. After putting it on, he accessed a security-keyed section of the day cabin lockers to retrieve just one more item.

A warship's control center is never perched in a vulnerable position at the top of its command hull or in its bow behind a huge set of windows. Rather, it is locked away like the crown jewels of a particularly paranoid king, nestled near the masses of computer cores and communication gear that allow it to function, deep in the center of the vessel; surrounded by an independent set of armored bulkheads; provided with its own life support and power supply; and accessible only through a single vault-like hatch watched unceasingly by several layers of electronic protection and heavily armed Marines.

Accordingly, two immense privates and one lean, grizzled sergeant, all holding M-88 pulse rifles at the ready and also bearing sidearms and boarding cutlasses, watched carefully as Max placed his palm on the CIC access scanner. It was not until the scanner's readout changed from red to green, and the CIC hatch opened to admit him that they shouldered their weapons, nodded respectfully, and stood aside, allowing him to enter the ship's *sanctum sanctorum*.

Max took a deep breath and stepped into CIC. A midshipman posted by the hatch, barely thirteen by the look of him, spotted Max immediately and piped at the top of his adolescent lungs, "Captain on deck!" Everyone in CIC, except for those personnel seated at critical control stations, immediately snapped to rigid attention.

"As you were." That fast, Max knew something was seriously wrong on this ship. The midshipman's voice, apparently in the midst of changing from preadolescent soprano to something approaching baritone or even bass, broke comically in the middle of the word "deck." Although the boy blushed furiously, no one laughed. Not even a quickly stifled giggle from another midshipman. If even the generally irrepressible boys, who were on the ship to experience the life of a fighting man on a Union warship and to begin their training to become enlisted men and officers, were too cowed to laugh, that was bad. Very bad.

Max knew he had to start turning things around, and he couldn't start any sooner than now. "What's your name, son?"

"Kurtz, sir." The young man's voice broke again, this time yet more comically. The child was, if possible, even more terrified than before.

Max smiled warmly at the boy and said softly, "Relax just a bit, son. Keep that up and you'll strain something." And more loudly, "Very good, Mr. Kurtz. Carry on."

Max started to walk the several steps that would take him from the hatch to the command island where the CO and XO Stations were located. As he cleared the bank of damage control monitors that blocked most of the CIC from seeing more than the top of his head, Max could hear the slight intakes of breath and shifting in place that indicated that people were startled at what they saw.

So, they're startled. Good.

Everyone in CIC was wearing dress blues. That is, everyone except the skipper. Max was wearing his SCU, or space combat uniform. Although dress blues were just below dress whites in formality and were regarded as being one of the snappiest-looking uniforms in Known Space, the SCU was not snappy looking, even in the slightest. It looked, in fact, like a shotgun marriage between a repair technician's jumpsuit and a pressure suit, with just a dash of children's pajamas thrown in as a fashion statement. It consisted of a rugged, royal-blue coverall, with several odd-looking bulges and even odder-looking pockets, and had integrated "booties" that extended over the feet of the wearer. The bulges held two portable oxygen generators, and the pockets held a collapsible zip-on helmet and pressure gloves. This untidy assembly worked together as an emergency pressure suit that could be configured in about thirty seconds to keep the wearer alive for just over two hours in the event of a hull breach or life support failure. He was also wearing his station harness, which would secure him to his duty station if the ship's artificial gravity failed; his Beretta-Browning M-62 10 mm sidearm, along with five 18-round magazines for the weapon; and his 635-millimeter-long razor-sharp boarding cutlass. In other words, whereas the rest of the CIC crew was dressed to impress, Max was dressed to kill.

Max turned to Garcia. "XO, status."

"Steady on course one-one-five mark two-six-two. Accelerating at Standard. No traffic along our trajectory. ETA at Navbuoy JAH one-nine-three-nine is seven minutes. All systems nominal except that when we tested the weapons before departure, we got a flow rate reading in the coolant manifold for the number four pulse cannon that was a little out of tolerance. An engineering crew is tearing down the unit right now."

"Very good, Mr. Garcia. Keep me apprised."

"Aye, sir."

Max stood at the CO station and took a long, slow look around. Everyone seemed to be doing their jobs: the plotters were manually adjusting the locations of ship contacts on the 3D tactical projection; the three enlisted men at the controls of the Maneuvering Station were making tiny adjustments to course and drive settings under the watchful eye of a chief petty officer;

environmental control specialists were monitoring and tweaking the systems that maintained a livable environment on the ship; and so on around the compartment. Everything looked right and yet was subtly wrong.

He took a few minutes to walk around, briefly looking at each display, noting that as he approached each station, the man serving it would tense up, ever so slightly. And though most of the displays showed things in good order, two revealed what Max could see were comparatively minor but subtle problems that the watch stander should either have been addressing or should have announced for others to remedy. That's when he noticed the shine. On everything. All the surfaces in CIC gleamed, even the ones that were unfinished metal when the ship came out of the yard. They gleamed beyond the rigorous level of cleanliness that was normal for a warship—they gleamed as though they had each been polished laboriously, endlessly, obsessively, many, many times over the roughly year and half the ship had been in commission.

Max casually walked over to an emergency equipment access panel and opened it, as if to check the readiness of the reserve oxygen cylinders. Even the *inside* of the access panel was polished. He removed one of the oxygen cylinders. It was polished too, and the rough edges of metal where the two halves of the cylinder were welded together had been ground even with the rest of the tank and brought to a high gloss. It was then that Max noticed that the chief manning the computer core status console was watching him out of the corner of his eye and smiling smugly, as if he were aware his new captain had seen the extraordinary level of spit and polish to which the ship had been brought and was very, very proud.

Carefully maintaining a neutral expression, Max replaced the cylinder and closed the panel. He opened three other panels and found a similar borderline-psychotic level of polish behind each. To top it off, there was no wear of any kind on the deck tiles, even in places where there was a pair of watch stander's feet every minute of every day the ship was not moored. That meant that someone was replacing the tiles at least every few months, which was certainly not the norm.

"XO, ETA to the navbuoy?"

"Two minutes, fifteen seconds, sir."

"Very well. I'll be in my cabin. Notify me as we pass the buoy. I wish to see all department heads in the wardroom at ten hundred hours. You have the CIC."

"Aye, sir, I have the CIC."

With that, Max left CIC for his cabin. One of the perquisites of being the CO is having one's cabin just a few steps away from CIC. It took him less than thirty seconds to get from the CIC hatch to his day cabin. He went directly to the captain's safe, keyed in the combination, and opened the door. Inside, on top of the usual contents, were two envelopes. One was the large, blue, official Admiralty issue envelope with the red seal used for orders, and the other was a plain, cream-colored envelope addressed by hand to "Lt. Commander M. T. Robichaux—Personal and Confidential."

His heart was racing. These orders could be the key to the most exciting days of his life, or they could be the introduction to untold months of unbearable tedium. And in just a few seconds, he would know. He slipped his index finger under the seal but did not break it.

The comm terminal on his desk beeped. "CO here."

"Skipper, this is the XO. We just passed the buoy."

"Very well. Impose full EMCON, all decks, all systems. Steady as she goes." He broke the seal.

CHAPTER 3

09:59Z Hours, 21 January 2315

Max sat at the head of the table, gazing at his department heads and taking his first good look at the wardroom of his new command. Of the group of twelve, four were in SCUs: the XO, the chief engineer, the weapons officer, and the Marine detachment commander. Of course, it was always possible that one or more of these men were already in their combat gear, but Max took it as a sign of support from these critical officers. On the other hand, he did not take the wearing of dress blues by the others as a sign of disloyalty. Not everyone would have heard about his appearance in CIC just over half an hour ago, and not everyone would have had time to change.

As for the room itself, it was less than impressive. In the trid vids about the valiant naval heroes of the Krag War, the jut-jawed, clear-eyed, broad-shouldered protagonists always conducted their meetings in a beautifully appointed conference room complete with walls of computer displays and lavish arrays of high-definition, 3D projections to show the tactical situation from several angles and on multiple scales. *Cumberland* was too small to have a space set aside just for meetings, so the group was assembled in the wardroom, where the officers typically took their meals and coffee. The designers of *Cumberland*'s wardroom had made only two concessions to the compartment's secondary function as a meeting room. First, it was somewhat larger than was strictly necessary to seat the eight or so officers who were the maximum number off duty at any given time. And second, there was only one flat-panel display on one wall, as well one standard-resolution, one-cubic-meter, 3D projector.

It was 09:59, and there were fourteen chairs around the wardroom table, but only thirteen occupants, counting Max. Perhaps whoever set out the chairs had allowed for an extra or someone had counted wrong. Surely, no one would dare be late. At exactly 10:00 to the second by the wardroom clock, Max began the meeting. In the Navy, 10:00 *means* 10:00.

"Good morning, gentlemen. For those of you who haven't met me, I'm Lieutenant Commander Max Robichaux, your new commanding officer. I'll chat briefly with each of you at the conclusion of this meeting. I'm going straight to the point. We've been given a difficult and important mission that could make a significant difference in the course of the war and, not incidentally, restore to this ship the respect and good name that she deserves. Unfortunately, gentlemen, it's a mission for which this ship and her complement are no more ready than a newborn baby would be for a night at an Alnitakian whorehouse. I've been over the after action reports of your last two engagements and the evaluations from your last battle exercise. They can be described in six words." He counted them off on his fingers. "Pitiful. Wretched. Em. Bar. Ass. Ing.

"Your people can't acquire targets, can't track targets, can't hit targets, can't maneuver toward targets, can't evade targets, can't identify targets, and can't evaluate targets. The only thing that this ship seems to be able to do well is *be* a target. Now the strange thing is that there isn't one reason in this whole big, bright galaxy why this crew should perform like a bunch of fuck-ups. According to aptitude tests, this crew should be well over the naval average for ships of this type. In fact, most of the members of this crew were on the tech team that shook down the systems for the prototype vessel for this class. These people are not morons. *You* are not morons. So, the question of the day is why is everyone performing like morons?"

Suddenly, the door to the wardroom door burst open, and—out of breath, bedraggled, and wearing a dirty lab coat over a mismatched assemblage of different grades of uniform—appeared Dr. Ibrahim Sahin.

"Doctor," Max said severely, "you are late."

He bowed. "Apologies. Please accept my profuse apologies. I had difficulty finding the location of this inappropriately named space in this most confusingly arranged vessel. I mean, when I was informed that this assemblage was to take place in the 'wardroom,' I assumed that we were meeting in a space associated with the ship's medical facilities. After all, a 'ward' is part of a hospital or a clinic, is it not?" He gazed searchingly at his audience, expecting to receive a ringing affirmation. Hearing none, he forged on.

"When I was able to find no such room in or near the Casualty Station, I looked around the ship for a sign or guidepost, such as we had at the Military Physicians Training Facility or at Travis Station, to steer me in the right direction. But I am amazed to report to you, sir—totally *amazed*—that there are no such directive signs of any kind *anywhere* on this entire battleship except those pointing to emergency hatches, firefighting equipment, and escape pods. How, sir—*how*, I ask you—are those uninitiated to the construction of this complex warship to find their way through the labyrinthine convolutions of her multibrachiated corridors? I ask you sir, *how?*"

The doctor stopped talking, not so much because he ran out of indignation, but because he ran out of air.

"Doctor, *Doctor*, please calm yourself and take a seat." Max could not help but notice that a few of those assembled were actually smiling indulgently. If the doctor had intended to provide some much-needed comic relief to the proceedings, he could not have timed it better or delivered a more exquisitely crafted performance. "Doctor, this is a destroyer, not a battleship. A different kind of vessel entirely. There are no directive signs because such things would be an aid to enemy boarders. If you are ever lost again, simply ask the nearest crewman for directions, and he will be happy to assist you."

"My thanks to you, sir," said the doctor, plopping into his seat, apparently mollified that the lack of signs was due to some considered reasoning process rather than mere incompetence. "Pray, sir, return to whatever it was you were talking about. I shall review the recording to acquaint myself with what was said before my arrival."

"Thank you, Doctor. As I was saying, why does a crew comprised of men who on paper are so intelligent and able perform like morons? You know, or should know, the answers as well as I do. Three things: Training. Leadership. Fighting spirit.

"First, training. The level of training on this vessel is abysmal. Why? I've looked through the crew activity reports. This crew spends twice the time on spit and polish and half the time on combat training than the standard for type. Priorities are wrong. Hell, someone has buffed, polished, and polymer sealed the washers on the bolts that hold my toilet to the deck. This isn't cleanliness; this is insanity.

"Now, don't get me wrong; a warship must be clean. Scrupulously, thoroughly, immaculately, *militarily* clean. But there are limits, and this shining-the-insides-of-the-air-ducts crap goes out the airlock from this moment. This is a warship, not an admiral's yacht. I don't care if every metal surface gleams. I don't care if the carpets are deep-cleaned daily. I have posted on the ship's general database the cleaning schedule for the last destroyer I served on in a combat zone. I want it adapted to this ship and followed. From now on, training is the priority. I want as much training crammed into the schedule as humanly possible. XO, you're now the training officer. I want a training schedule on my desk at 0600 hours that'll bring this crew to a razor's edge within twenty-one days."

"If I may, sir," interrupted the XO, respectfully, "why twenty-one days?"

"Because, XO, that's all the time we have before we go into combat."

That got everyone's attention.

"Second problem: leadership. The Admiralty got rid of part of the problem for us. Captain Allen K. Oscar and Lieutenant Pang, his XO, are gone. Good riddance. Based on the admiral's opinion of them, they are probably counting comets somewhere in the Zubin Elgenubi Sector. But you can tell just from walking into CIC that those officers didn't take the problem with them when they left. Now, the primary means by which those of us in this room exercise leadership is by naval discipline, and the discipline on this vessel defies explanation: greenies put on report for making mistakes in duties for which they haven't had adequate training; able spacers confined to quarters and even put in the brig for misinterpretation of orders and honest oversights…good God, there's a man in the brig right now who's been there for forty-five days because he *misidentified a sensor contact*. Major Kraft, I want

TO HONOR YOU CALL US

that man—hell, I want *every* man in the brig—released immediately upon the conclusion of this meeting."

The commander of the Marine detachment nodded. "Aye, sir. My pleasure."

Max noticed from some averted gazes and foot shuffling that not everyone at the table was equally enthusiastic about that last order. *Tough shit.*

"And that's going to be the order of the day, gentlemen. Simple mistakes, errors, and oversights are to be rectified by training, not by punishment. On this ship, punishment is reserved for neglect of duty, insubordination, and willful misconduct. And in the case of officers, add to that abuse of subordinates. Make no mistake about that. I will not have the men excessively shouted at, berated, or abused. I know that the Navy is fueled by profanity as much as by deuterium and that sometimes it takes a lot to get a spacer's attention, but there is a line, gentlemen; there is a matter of degree between manly exhortation and abuse. That line will not be crossed on this ship. The Navy is a *hard* service, but it is not a *cruel* service.

"And remember, these men need to be encouraged at least as much as they need to be criticized. You, the men in this room, are their leaders. They'll be looking to you for guidance, for encouragement, for help. Give it to them. Show them how to be good spacers, good crewmen, good warriors. They can't reach behind themselves and pull it out of their asses. They've got to learn it from you.

"Third and last, we need to cultivate a warrior spirit on this ship. Too many of these men act as though they are getting ready for a fleet exercise or an admiral's inspection instead of meeting the enemy in battle to take or destroy him. Until further notice, SCUs are the Uniform of the Day. Officers will carry sidearms and boarding cutlasses at all times. Enlisted personnel will train regularly to repel boarders and be thoroughly drilled in sidearms, shoulder arms, edged weapons, and hand-to-hand combat. Men will practice boarding and repelling boarders at least three times a week, watch against watch, with an extra beer or liquor ration to the winners.

"I noticed that the corridor and CIC weapons lockers have been removed. I want all weapons lockers that were issued to this ship restored and stocked by 0600.

"I reviewed the armorer's log, and there is no record of any officer on this vessel having his sidearm serviced or his boarding cutlass sharpened in over a year. I'll personally inspect the sidearms and boarding cutlasses of every officer when he goes on duty, starting at 0600 tomorrow. That's for all three watches, and I pity any of you who fail. All of this goes for the senior noncommissioned officers as well. Ratings of petty officer first or higher will carry arms just like the commissioned officers.

"Major, what about your Marines?"

"Captain, we're cocked, locked, and loaded for Krag. When on duty, every member of the Marine detachment, including myself, carries an M-88 pulse rifle or an M-72 COB shotgun, plus Model 62 or Model 1911 sidearms, boarding cutlass, eight M-304 grenades, and combat knife. Every man sleeps with weapons within easy reach. Plus—well, sir, being *Marines*, sir…"

"Right. Every one of your men has one or two little personal surprises for any Krag that manages to get on the ship," Max said, grinning. He always liked the Marine approach to warfare.

"You got it, Captain. If they poke their little black noses onto the *Cumberland*, we want to welcome them properly." The major produced a very wicked-looking, six-inch, double-edged dagger from his sleeve, twirled it deftly in his hand, and made it disappear back into his sleeve in less than two seconds.

"We must never forget, gentlemen, that the purpose of this ship is to kill the enemy. Killing is what we're about, and every man and boy on board must be ready and able to kill at any moment. Our entire crew, including the cooks and the youngest midshipman, needs to be reminded continually that they're warriors, not stewards on a passenger liner.

"Because, gentlemen, if we are not ready to kill the Krag, I assure you that the Krag are ready to kill us."

Max let that sink in for a few seconds. Then, he touched a control on the table in front of him, causing a three-dimensional display of the sector to appear over the wardroom table. "Now, our mission. Most of you know that we're now on course for the Charlie jump point in this system"; a blinking circle appeared around one star. "That jump leads to Markeb B. From there, we will make our way, jump by jump, using an indirect route"— circles blinked around nineteen stars in sequence, tracing out a long, irregular arc—"through these uninhabited systems, to reach the Free Corridor unobserved.

"Intel informs us that the Krag have been making up production shortfalls and resource shortages by obtaining substantial war matériel in the Free Corridor. They are buying raw materials, food, machine tools, and some premunition chemicals from neutral systems through human and neutral alien intermediaries, transferring them to their own freighters in deep space, and transporting them back to the Krag Hegemony. The initial sellers never know that this stuff is going to the Krag.

"Our orders: While respecting all recognized territorial space claims and neutral shipping, we are to conduct a war patrol in the Free Corridor, where we are to attack and destroy any Krag vessels of any description or other vessels that we can positively determine to be carrying Krag cargo, as well as any other enemy targets of opportunity that may present themselves, provided that we can engage them with a reasonable probability of success."

Max noticed that a young ensign, a *very* young ensign, was shifting uncomfortably in his seat, as though he wanted to ask a question but was afraid to interrupt. Max turned to the young man. "If you have something to say, Ensign, say it. That's why I called you together here in person, rather than just sending you written orders by email."

"What about resupply? Sir, I don't know if you know this about this destroyer class, sir, but the *Khybers* have short legs. The book says that we have an unsupported endurance of seventy-five days, tops. With twenty-one days to get there, twenty-one days to get back—factor in a week for unexpected delays or if we have to come back by a longer route—that leaves only thirty-three days on station. If they don't send a tender in after us, it's going to be a mighty short cruise."

"You're Ensign Thieu, the supply officer?" The young man nodded. "Good question. Keep asking them. It's probably going to be shorter than that. That seventy-five-day endurance is a pretty optimistic figure, isn't it?" The ensign nodded again. "I've looked at the your stores inventory, and it looks to me more like sixty days of consumption under intermittent combat conditions plus another five or six days of emergency rations. That about right, Thieu?"

"Yes, sir. That's about how I calculate it, sir."

"Fortunately, the Admiralty has thought about this problem. They've prepositioned supplies, including weapons reloads, fuel, spares, and provisions in three separate locations for us in our operational area. The locations are not in any Union database and are known only to me. With what we've got on board and what's been squirreled away for us, we've got what we need for about 180 days of intensive operations. That'll give us all the time we need to learn the lay of the land, scout out what the enemy is doing, find his ships, and blow them and their valuable war matériel to flaming atoms. This ship is going to be doing what she was designed to do, gentlemen: bring the war to the enemy and hurt him where he lives—war production. Questions? None? We're adjourned."

A few minutes later, three chief petty officers sat around a small table in a tiny office for the use of CPOs, known as the "Goat Locker." They were not happy. "Ship's going to hell on a maglev rail," said the first.

"You got that right," said the second. "First thing young Captain 'Row-Bye-Shit' does is stop the crew from doing the one thing that it's really good at. You can't have a taut ship if the men don't have pride in her, that's for sure."

"And discipline's going to go out the airlock, to boot," the third chimed in. "All this namby-pamby nonsense about encouraging the men and not crossing the line and not punishing them for not doing their duty...there'll be hell to pay for it. With this bunch, you've got to be on them every second, and they've got to know that if they don't do their duty, there's more waiting for them than harsh language and being put on report."

"On top of that, this young torpedo jockey is going to get us killed, every man and boy of us. I can feel it. He's reckless. And this deployment is a suicide mission. It's all right out of some third-rate trid vid: resupply caches known only to him, independent operations in the Free Corridor, destroy enemy shipping—all bullshit!" The first one was starting to get worked up. "That's not what destroyers do. We're *escorts*. We operate with other ships. Right in the training manuals, it says that the functions of a destroyer are primarily to screen larger ships from attack by fighters and other smaller ships, scout the route ahead, and operate as sensor pickets for the Task Force, not run around on our own in a distant sector cut off from all support like some overlong tree branch just waiting to get chopped off. There's only two ways this ends. We're all either cold dust between the stars or louse bait in some Krag POW camp."

"Unless we do something about it first," said the second.

"Aye," said the other two.

CHAPTER 4

11:10Z Hours, 21 January 2315

The hand-addressed envelope in the captain's safe had contained confidential remarks from the admiral himself, addressed to Max's attention and for his eyes only. Max sat in the office section of his day cabin, a moderate space consisting of a desk and office chair, a few chairs for visitors, a few other assorted tables and chairs, and a small waiting room outside a door. Max considered the admiral's comments while he waited for his next appointment, due in a few minutes.

As always, the admiral had said a lot in comparatively few words. Max knew he would reread the note several more times before he squeezed all of the meaning out of it. In particular, on top of some very interesting remarks about a few of the officers assigned to him, he found the admiral's comments about his own attributes troubling: "Normally, a Navy Cross means a plum assignment. In your case, however, certain conduct both in space and in the dirt causes me to have serious reservations about your judgment. You know the incidents of which I speak. As things stand now, the prospects of your rising above your present rank are extremely slender.

"Still, you do seem to have a fire in your belly. There is always the *remote* chance that this command experience will be the crucible that turns poor metal into steel. So, against my better judgment, I am giving you this opportunity. It is opportunity mitigated by serious challenges: former CO is a loon; former XO, a sycophantic martinet; ship shines better than it shoots and has performed miserably by every measure; NCOs are likely to try mutiny or sabotage if you change anything; and even the conscientious officers are green and not terribly proficient.

"But it's not all bad. The ship is one of the best designs to come out of the yards in decades. You will find reason, too, to thank me for the officers whom I have recently transferred to the vessel.

"You are being given lemons. Go make lemonade. And kick some Krag ass while you're at it."

The Marine posted outside his door stuck his head in to let Max know that Dr. Sahin had arrived for his appointment.

"Send him in."

The doctor entered, approached Max's desk, did a fair approximation of a salute, and started to take a seat.

"Doctor, wait."

The doctor froze. Sahin was in something approaching combat gear, but his weapons belt had a twist in it and his boarding cutlass was attached to the wrong loop on the uniform. The sleeves were fastened in such a way that if the ship lost pressure and the doctor had to put on his pressure gloves, they would not make a proper seal with the sleeves, so the uniform would not hold pressure, and he would die. "Doctor, first, you need to review the training file on this particular uniform. You've got a few things wrong. And second, military courtesy dictates that you don't sit in the presence of your commanding officer until and unless he invites you to do so."

"I apologize, sir. I have been serving almost exclusively in a hospital for my entire naval career."

"I understand. You're probably going to want to brush up on these things now that you're on a combat vessel."

"Yes, sir."

"Please be seated."

The doctor sat.

"Doctor, you've sure got an unusual background for a chief medical officer on a warship. Undergraduate degrees in philology, theology, xeno-botany, and xeno-herpetology, master's degree in interstellar relations from the University of New Istanbul, second in your class at Johns Hopkins Medical School, residency in the trauma unit of Beijing General Hospital. And according to your record, no one's quite sure how many languages you speak."

"I find it rather difficult to reckon myself, particularly as so many 'languages' are in reality only dialects or variants of other languages. Suffice it to say that I can converse with virtually all of the humans and most of the aliens in the part of space to which we are headed. The only language that gives me difficulty is the particular argot spoken in the Navy."

"As smart as you are, you won't have any problems picking it up. Now, on top of what your records say, Admiral Hornmeyer has notified me unofficially that you have personal contacts in the Free Corridor that might be able to put us on the trail of Krag purchases and ship movements. Now, how in the big, bright galaxy is that?"

"Captain, as you know, I was born on Tubek. But at the risk of sounding like a well-worn literary cliché about Arab and Turkish traders, my father's ancestors for many generations have been merchants and traders from New Istanbul in the Markeb sector."

"I've served on patrol vessels in that area. Any company I might have heard of?"

"The firm was Harun Sahin & Sons, founded by my grandfather."

"That's not one I remember. But I'd remember only the largest ones and the ones who gave us trouble."

"I am certain that our company would have been neither of those. It was in that broad medium tier of firms. We kept something between five and seven ships running all the time, usually about half a dozen charters and the two with family members on board that were owned by the company."

"Well, that wouldn't make it one of the big players, but that's still a pretty good-sized company. What kind of trading—" The comm panel beeped unexpectedly. Startled, Max flinched. He shot a quick glance at Dr. Sahin, who was studiously looking toward the porthole, as though making a point of not noticing Max's reaction, although Max was certain he had noticed. *Damn.* He hit the button to open the comm circuit.

"Robichaux."

"Skipper, this is the XO. We've got a minor power deficit on the forward main deflectors. Brown says he'll get the problem licked within the hour, but until he does, I'd like to transfer some power from the rear deflectors. Regulations don't allow me to do that without approval of the CO."

"Granted," Max said at once. "Let me know if there is any further problem."

"Aye, sir." Max closed the circuit.

"Where was I? Right. What did your folks do?"

"There wasn't any specialty, really. They stayed away from contraband and extremely bulky goods such as ore and grain, but on the whole they simply looked for items in one system that they could buy and sell for a profit in another. It really didn't matter what, although I remember carrying a lot of precision machine tools, gourmet olive oil, and fine art Pfelung glassware. The routes tended to be among the worlds of the Free Corridor and between the Free Corridor and the Union worlds in the Markeb and Tulloi sectors. Because my cousin and I were to take over the business when my father and his brother became too old to run it, we frequently went along so we could meet their business contacts.

"When the Tulloi sector fell to the Krag, my father, his brother, and their wives were all on board the two family ships, along with most of the rest of my relatives, and were never heard from again. I was relieved that my younger sister and two brothers were attending secondary school on Tubek and were not harmed. Of course, Tubek fell a few years later and they are now lost as well. In any event, on many worlds in the Corridor I know people or—at least know people who know people—who are likely to be the people with whom the Krag are doing business. From them we might learn departure times, routes, and other information that will help you find these ships in the immensity of space."

"Quite possibly."

"Am I correct in my understanding that before our departure, this vessel was provided with a Piper-Grumman *Shetland* class microfreighter?"

"It was. The Navy has done us proud too. She looks worn and banged up on the outside, but she's been retrofitted with naval specification engines and weapons that just might get you out of a tight corner or two."

"I look forward to piloting her," the doctor said with enthusiasm.

"Don't think so, Doctor. Able Spacer Second Fahad came aboard an hour before I did. His pilot assessment score is one-eighty-five on that ship and one-sixty overall. He looks enough like you to pass for a cousin at least. He'll be doing the piloting."

"But I grew up on freighters. I can pilot the ship."

"Sorry, Doctor, I've seen your piloting scores. They're barely high enough to let you at the helm of a Vespa-Martin Dragonfly in open space in some of the more lenient systems. No way are they high enough for me to let you pilot a souped-up armed microfreighter in company with a rated warship, much less land on her hangar deck. Hangar deck landings are a specialized skill, and you haven't had the training. I don't want you banging up our new freighter."

"As you wish."

"Have you had a chance to check out your equipment, stores, and personnel yet?"

"I have. That was the first thing I did when I reported on board around 03:00 in response to Admiral Hornmeyer's most exigent directive."

"Exigent directive?"

"Indeed. I was wakened from a sound sleep at 02:10 or so by the admiral himself on voicecom. He told me, rather loudly, to get my lazy, overeducated ass out of my bunk and said that if I wasn't on board the *Cumberland* in less than an hour, with my duffel ready for an extended cruise as her chief medical officer, he was going to play table tennis with my testicles."

"Sounds like you were shanghaied, Doctor."

"Indeed."

"So, is everything satisfactory?"

"For a ship with a complement of 215 men and boys, I find the Casualty Station admirably well equipped and stocked. I have also met the personnel assigned to me, and I find them to be reasonably well trained for their respective positions, although there appear to be some deficiencies in some specific areas of training—areas that I plan to remedy immediately. I also note that the morale appears to be rather poor. My understanding is that the previous chief medical officer was less than stellar."

"He wasn't the only one," Max said. "What about your head nurse—what's his name?"

"Church. The admiral reassigned him from the *Nimitz*, and he came aboard ten minutes before I did. When I got to the Casualty Station, he already had the secured pharmaceuticals locker open, an armed Marine sergeant standing by to guard the drugs, and was taking inventory with the pharmacist's mate witnessing and performing a cross-check. I am favorably impressed. I could not ask for better. There is only one thing more that one could wish for."

"And that would be?"

"A female nurse."

Max smiled. "Yes, that would have its advantages."

"I resent your implication, sir. There are distinct therapeutic advantages to having a female nurse on board, especially if she is attractive. In my experience, female nurses are more tender and sympathetic than the male ones, and injured men seem to be more willing to submit without resistance or complaint to embarrassing and painful procedures administered by a female nurse. Resistance and opposition seem to disappear as if by magic in the presence of an attractive young woman. Whereas I might have to spend precious minutes, even hours, employing sophisticated reasoning and advanced psychological techniques to secure the patient's cooperation, a lovely young nurse need only bat her eyes at the recalcitrant, cantankerous old chief petty officer, and the thing is done.

"It also goes without saying that females are on the whole, by nature, more conscientious, more attentive to details, have better short-term memories, possess higher manual dexterity, and have a greater facility for understanding the speech of injured, infirm, or excited patients who may not be speaking clearly. They employ problem-solving techniques that are identifiably different from those employed by males. In short, they bring attributes to the table that are not present when one has an all-male medical staff."

"Actually, Doctor, I was making no improper implication, and those are the kinds of advantages I was thinking of. You see, I first went to space in 2295, only two weeks after the Gynophage attack, so when I joined my first ship, the *San Jacinto*, the crew was still about a third female."

"But post-Gynophage…"

"Post-Gynophage, it's a different ballgame," said Max.

A different ballgame didn't begin to describe it. The Gynophage was an incredibly deadly viral disease cooked up by the Krag and launched against the Union sometime in the 2285 or 2286. It was carried on board 217 highly stealthed compression drive drones programmed to reach 217 different planets throughout the Union within hours of each other on 12 August 2295, the fourteenth year of the war, and to dispense thousands of atmosphere entry vehicles that spread the virus in the air over population centers.

Although the virus almost instantly infected everyone it reached, most males experienced no symptoms. Women, on the other hand, were subject to excruciating Ebola-like liquefaction of their internal organs and death within hours of infection, at a rate of nearly 99 percent. Those few whom it did not kill, it rendered scarred, brain damaged, and sterile.

As if that were not bad enough, the disease spread rapidly from person to person by virtually every known means of disease transmission. As infected men fled affected planets on private spacecraft, they spread the disease to the remaining Union worlds within days. Only a Herculean effort, involving practically every human medical researcher in the galaxy, costing more than 300 trillion credits, and tying up most of the interstellar communications bandwidth and computing power available to the human race, saved humanity from extinction. In only thirty-two days from day of the attack, the Gynophage Project developed a combination antibody serum and vaccine known as the Moro Treatment, after the head of the project, the brilliant Kenyan physician and medical researcher, Dr. Emeka Moro.

With more than half of the human females in the galaxy dead and the demographic future of humankind in doubt, the Navy withdrew almost all of its serving female personnel, most of whom were of childbearing age, to the Core Systems, effectively making the Navy an all-male force.

"It's certainly unfair to the women who might want to serve, but I don't see any way around it," said Max. "Damn shame. Maybe, once we've won this war, we can bring them back."

"The Casualty Station will be a better place."

"So will CIC. So, Doctor, if that's all—"

"Lieutenant Commander?"

A look of irritation, quickly squelched, crossed Max's face. "Doctor, aboard this vessel, I'm 'Captain.'"

"Oh, quite right. So sorry. I have only limited experience in dealing with combat officers who are actually conscious. The ones I'm used to seeing weren't much concerned with titles when I had my hands inside their chest cavities. In any event, *Captain*, I have a problem that I need to discuss with you."

"What problem?"

"The men continue to insult me."

Max flushed. "*Insult you?* A commissioned officer? Not here, they don't. There will be no insubordination on my ship. Who's been insulting you? What kind of insult? I won't stand for it."

Sahin was taken aback by Max's vehemence, but having broached the subject, he had no choice but to go forward. "There was a pulse cannon coolant leak yesterday, before I came aboard, and several of the men were briefly exposed to the fumes. There were no apparent injuries at the time, but I was conducting a follow-up examination as a precaution—just to be sure that there was no latent pulmonary damage and hemotoxicity. During these examinations, virtually every one of them addressed me in the friendliest and most cheerful tone of voice, you understand, but with the most insulting name."

Max's anger grew. His eyes blazed and he gritted his teeth. In a cold, deadly voice, sounding for all the worlds as though he were ready to toss the malefactors out the nearest airlock, he asked, "And what, exactly, did they call you."

"Captain," the doctor continued reluctantly, afraid of what would happen to the men in question, "I very much regret to tell you that they called me...*Bones*."

The word hung in the ensuing silence for a heartbeat, after which Max shattered the tension by laughing out loud, the clouds of his anger dispersing like a quickly spent summer thunder-shower. When his mirth subsided and he could speak again, he said, "Doctor, oh, Doctor"—he was still gasping for air—"you weren't insulted. Not even close. Don't you know that 'Bones' is a traditional nickname for a ship's chief medical officer? It's short for 'sawbones.' It's a term of respect and affection, going back to the earliest days of our service. You must've done an excellent job or shown them uncommon kindness. Spacers call a doctor 'Bones' only if they like him. It's quite the compliment, especially to have acquired the nickname so quickly after you've joined the ship."

"How peculiar. And 'Bones' seems like such an unflattering name for a physician. Is this custom of bestowing nicknames that go with one's function common in the Navy?"

"Absolutely. There are about a dozen of them that go all the way back to the first UESF ships in 2034. We call our chief gunner 'Dirty Harry'; the youngest or smallest midshipman, 'Will Robinson'; the armorer or weapons master, 'Burt Gummer'; the astrocartographer, 'Galileo'; our midshipmen's trainer, 'Mother Goose'; the communications officer, 'Sparks'; the chief navigator, 'Magellan'; and the chief engineer, 'Scotty.' There's a few more that are less common. We don't know the source for a lot of these names, but they're traditional, and we in the Navy respect our traditions."

"Oh. That is quite different. Very well. So long as it is kindly meant, then I will take no offense. But I continue to be confused and bewildered here. How does one learn all of these traditions, these unwritten rules, these secret understandings that are a part of this fascinating but so very insular subculture?"

"I've never really thought about that. For most, it isn't a problem. More than 85 percent of the crew on most warships have been in space since boyhood. This world is part of our upbringing. The Navy is our hometown and our shipmates are our family. I went to space when I was eight years old, right after the Gynophage took my mother and baby sisters. I hardly remember what it's like to be a civilian, to live in a house, for the weekends to be different from the weekdays, to look out a window and see something other than blackness.

"The average man on a naval vessel went to space at age nine and a half. Don't worry, Doctor. As you live it, you'll learn it. And you're surrounded by crew who'll be happy to help you because they have every reason to seek your favor. No man on this ship wants to anger the ship's surgeon, for obvious reasons. As you take care of them, they'll take care of you. It appears that the men already think kindly of you, and that'll go far for someone in your position."

"That's good to know, Captain." He smiled sheepishly. "And thank you for the advice and for not berating me for my ignorance, as many have done before. I consider it a kindness. It means a great deal to me."

"Think nothing of it, Doctor. You'll find that there's often great generosity in the Navy, except to our enemies. Now, if there's nothing further, I have another appointment in a few minutes."

"Of course, Captain. That is all I have." He rose.

"Oh, Doctor."

"Yes, Captain."

"Before you go back to the Casualty Station, I need you to do something."

"Yes, sir?"

"Go to the quartermaster on C Deck, Compartment 09, tell him that I sent you, and ask him to give you *correct and proper* instruction on the regulation arrangement of that uniform. Tell him to explain it just like he would to the newest squeaker. And let him know that if he practices on your credulous simplicity in any way, I'll use him as a cutlass drill dummy. Use just those words."

"I will, Captain." The doctor's brow furrowed in thought. "Captain, you said that the quartermaster was not to 'practice on my credulous simplicity.' Is that not a quote from *The Pirates of Penzance?*"

"It is," Max said, surprised.

"Ah, yes. I recall the scene. Right after the famous 'Paradox' song. Are you an aficionado of Gilbert and Sullivan?"

"I am. You?"

"I find the libretti utterly ridiculous and the music totally... sublime. I cherish their work as a wellspring of infinite mirth and a fountain of ever-living beauty in a vast, lonely desert of conflict and suffering."

"That's beautiful," Max said in a low voice, strangely moved.

"Captain, may I say that I am somewhat surprised," the doctor went on, oblivious. "One does not expect to find in your position a man appreciative of four-hundred-year-old British comic operettas."

"Doctor, if that surprised you, then you're in for lots of surprises in the Navy. No mold fits all the men we've got. The quartermaster I'm sending you to was, at one time, a famous Gilbert and Sullivan performer. In fact, he played the Pirate King in a command performance for the Union president and the Senate on Earth about twenty years ago."

"It is surprising, indeed, to find such a man in the Navy."

"Not as much as you might think, Doctor. He was with the Rechartered D'Oyly Carte Opera Company of Victoria Regina."

"Really?" the doctor exclaimed mildly, clearly not getting it.

"Doctor, VicReg fell to the Krag in 2298."

"Oh." Long pause. "We should watch a performance together on trid vid sometime, or perhaps sing a duet or a trio with the quartermaster."

"Maybe, Doctor, when this ship's in better order. For now, though, if there's nothing further, you're dismissed."

The doctor gave a salute that was marginally more correct than the first; Max returned it, and he departed.

Max hit a button on his desk. "Lao, is my next appointment out there?"

"Yes, Captain."

"Send him in."

The hatch opened and the Marine guard admitted a beefy man, just over medium height, with reddish-blond hair and a reddish-blond mustache, framing a distinctly reddish and patently jolly face that was doing its best at the moment to affect an expression of severe disapproval.

The man approached Max's desk. They exchanged brisk salutes.

"Lieutenant Brown reporting as ordered, sir."

"Have a seat, Wernher. Coffee?"

"Thank you, sir, but no. I've got about six or seven liters in me. I'm overdriving my reactors as it is."

"How're things shaping up down in Engineering?"

"Reasonably well. I have to admit that I am very impressed by the design of this class. Every now and then BuDes gets one right. The engines are particularly robust. She'll be fast, nimble, rugged, and very stealthy. I just wish she had longer legs. I don't like running around as far from home as we are going to be with so little fuel in our belly."

"Neither do I, Wernher, but it's all a trade-off for her speed and stealth. Listen, old friend, I need you to do something for me, and I need you to do it in your own very stealthy manner."

"You know how I generally feel about 'favors,' old man, but since you saved my tender, pink hide back on General Patton's birthday, I suppose I might be prevailed upon to do something a little bit out of the ordinary."

"Much obliged. I need covert surveillance installed, full angular coverage, on every critical component of the jump drive, the stealth systems, and the atmosphere processors."

"From where do you want the feeds monitored?" It never even occurred to him to ask why the captain wanted the surveillance.

"The Marine Watch Station. And hide the data lines, make them impervious to tapping—you know the drill."

"I do, indeed. Now, if I am going to do this favor, I am going to ask one in return."

"Name it."

"I think it's high time you told me why you call me 'Wernher.'"

"After all these years, you haven't figured it out?"

"It's only been *three* years, and apparently not."

"Three and a half. Okay, I'll tell. Lieutenant, what's your name, first and last?"

"You know very well that it is Vaughn Brown."

"There, see, don't you get it? '*Wernher* Vaughn Brown.'"

"No, I'm afraid that I don't."

"Don't they teach history any more? I guess not. He was an engineer. Brilliant. He headed the team behind the launch vehicle that first took humans to the Earth's moon. You know. *Wernher von Braun*. Sound familiar?" The engineer shook his head.

"I can't believe you never heard of him. Great man. Noble sort of fellow. Very worthy of admiration in every way. Well, except for working with the Nazis in World War II. But a great engineer. You're the best engineer I have ever worked with, and your name sounds like his, so it is only natural for me to call you that. It's a great compliment, you know. Just don't let it go to your head."

"It never occurred to me that it was a joke, particularly one so…feeble. Now, Captain, I've got a jump coming up in less than half an hour, and I would like to get back to Engineering and make sure that everything is shipshape."

"Go ahead. And be sure to let me know when that surveillance is online, will you?"

Brown nodded.

"Good. You're dismissed."

CHAPTER 5

11:26Z Hours, 21 January 2315

"Captain on deck," young Midshipman Kurtz announced, this time managing to hold his voice in the same octave for the entire announcement. Max met the boy's eye and winked his approval, causing a slight grin to appear on his Oliver Twist–like features. He strode to the command island, surveying the CIC with a professional eye.

Although things were not all good, they were, at least, better. Everyone was in his SCU and, if appropriate, was carrying his sidearm and boarding cutlass. Most of those standing watch didn't look as though they were going to pass out from terror if Max said "Boo!" to them. The CIC arms locker, absent just over an hour ago, was restored to its proper place, and Max could see through its clear polymer door that it was chock full of pistols, pulse rifles, and boarding cutlasses as well as a few sawed-off shotguns, machine pistols, and at least two battle axes. Although Max was not himself very good with a battle ax, he liked them a lot. There was nothing like a two-meter-tall Viking-descended farm boy from Nya Sverige swinging a seven-kilogram battle ax and yelling, "*Död till Krag*" to make one of the rat-faced bastards piss its pants.

Max took his seat. "Status, XO."

"We are next in line to jump and are cleared by traffic control on the *Halsey*. Now on second-stage approach to the jump point, proceeding at fifteen hundred meters per second and set to slow to one hundred fifty meters per second at the two-minute mark. I have verbally conferred with the chief engineer, and he has certified that the ship is jump ready. All stations have reported by lights and by comm that they are secure for jump. Jump officer confirms that his board is green."

"Thank you, XO."

"Coming up on two minutes to jump," said Stevenson, the jump officer. "Two minutes...MARK."

"Beginning third-stage approach to jump point. Slowing to one-five-zero meters per second," sang out LeBlanc, the chief petty officer in charge of the Maneuvering Station. "We are in the groove."

"Navigator," said the XO, "verify coordinates of jump point and resend to Maneuvering and jump officer."

The navigator hit a few keys. "Transmitted."

"Received and congruent with previous coordinates. No change," said the jump officer.

"Same here," said LeBlanc at Maneuvering.

"Jump officer, set your clock and synchronize," said the XO.

The jump officer responded, "Set and synchronized."

"Verify destination."

"Destination is Bravo jump point in the Ypres Minor system, coordinates as displayed."

"Very well," said the XO.

"One minute," announced the jump officer.

"Safe all systems for jump," said the XO.

Because jumping had a way of scrambling delicate electronics, most ship's systems had to be rendered inactive. The few systems that lacked complex data processors, such as lights and the maneuvering thrusters that kept the ship precisely on course to the jump, didn't pose a problem, but computers, external communications, drives, sensors, weapons, and environmental controls had to be powered down or put on standby—"safed"—before jumping, which meant that ships emerged from jump blind, deaf, paralyzed, stupid, and helpless.

"Safing," said Stevenson. Around CIC, display after display went offline, until the only data being displayed anywhere were the seconds remaining on the jump clock and a distance reading to the jump point, both rapidly approaching zero.

The seconds ticked down. Max sat silently while the XO and the CIC crew conducted the jump, consistent with naval custom. XOs typically handled nonbattle maneuvers, which was part of how XOs learned to be COs. One of the most important tasks of a commanding officer was to train his XO in the art and science of command so that he could step into his CO's shoes at any time, something that happened, by promotion or sudden, violent death, somewhere in the fleet at least once a day.

"Ten seconds. Nine. Eight. Seven. Six. Five. Four. Three. Two. One. Jumping."

Just as the ship passed through the invisible and unmarked point in space where the lines of metaspacial flux created by the gravitational field of the nearest star combined with the lines of metaspacial flux spun off by the superstring vibrations of the galaxy's dark matter such that both sets resonated in exactly the right metagravametric harmonic, the ship's jump drive bored a hole in the fabric of space-time. This opened a window into metaspace and jumped the ship in a quantum instant from its location to that of its resonance twin, which was, in this case, just over eleven light years away. The *Cumberland* simply vanished from the space it had occupied, reappearing about 30 AU from the class F main-sequence star locally known as Markeb B and officially known by a Union Space Navy Galactic Survey number that not even astrocartographers ever managed to remember.

Human beings experience the jump in different ways. It is, inherently, a strange event for them: the near-instantaneous transfer of their material selves across light years while passing through an *n*-dimensional realm in which the very nature of matter, energy, and existence is fundamentally different from those in our universe; a realm that, although the size of a single geometric point, is somehow in contact with every point in our own universe. Some people became violently nauseated. Some got dizzy or became disoriented. Some experienced profound visions of a transcendental nature. Max Robichaux typically experienced a deep yearning for drink and food, this time a steaming mug of dark-roast coffee and a chicken-salad sandwich. With sliced pickles.

"Jump complete, restoring systems," Stevenson announced, neither nauseated nor dizzy, nor disoriented, nor graced with a transcendental vision, nor craving coffee and poultry on bread. One watch stander at a secondary navigation console was quietly retching into a jumpsick bag. A greenie and a midshipman looked as though they might pass out, but seemed to be recovering quickly.

Screens and displays started to come back to life, a process that took a few minutes as computers reinitialized, sensors powered back up, and other systems reestablished their normal function. Max always hated that interval: even though it was wildly unlikely that there would be another ship out there in an uninhabited system selected as a destination—selected *because* of how little ship traffic went through it—there was always a chance.

He suppressed an urge to fidget. It was all right to be tense, but he must not ever *look* tense.

"Collision lights are on, and forward lookouts report nothing visible in our path, sir," Kasparov, the sensor officer said. The Mark One eyeball, belonging to men picked for good low-light and distance vision while looking out LumaTite viewports in the bow and assisted in some cases by anachronistically named night vision goggles, was always the first system available. Next, there usually came the report about engines.

"Sir, report from Engineering," said Heinzelmann, the petty officer third class assigned to CIC from Engineering, mainly to report and coordinate information from one to the other. "Lieutenant Brown signals that the main sublight drive is available at up to 80 percent. He expects full availability in one minute. Jump drive is available now. Compression drive in thirty minutes."

"Very well. Maneuvering, let's cautiously clear the datum. Ahead on main sublight at 2 percent. Use ship's current attitude as our heading." Maneuvering acknowledged the order. Various other officers at Comms, Environmental Control, Weapons, and all around the horn were now reporting that the systems under their respective observation or control were coming back to life. Max acknowledged them all, but the man he really wanted to hear from was Kasparov, again. He was taking a little longer than he should.

"Captain," it was Kasparov. Finally. "I have EM, grav, mass, and neutrino passive scans out to about two million kills. All clear."

"Very well. Thank you, Mr. Kasparov." Max could relax a little. No enemy in his immediate vicinity was bearing down on him and his new command. "Maneuvering, shape course for this system's Bravo jump point, main sublight at standard acceleration to zero point five c. Give me a rough ETA as soon as you can work one out."

Max still needed to hear more from Mr. Kasparov, and it was very slow in coming. Max knew that there were Union forces in this system that his people should be detecting by now. That department needed a lot of work. The seconds ticked by. "Captain, contact." Kasparov's voice was both louder and higher than Max liked to hear. "Four contacts—designating as Uniform One, Two, Three, and Four. Apparent fighters, bearing two-seven-eight mark zero-two-eight, closing at point one seven c." Max noted silently that Kasparov did not mention the *range* to the contacts, but he could see that information on his own display. The ball was now in Tactical's court.

Bartoli returned the ball, albeit a little more slowly than Max would have liked. "Ships are fighters, sir, in finger-four formation; they are Charlie Bravo Delta Romeo." Tactical read that the fighters were arrayed in the classic fighter formation invented by the Luftwaffe over France and Poland centuries ago, with the ships arrayed like the tips of the fingers of an outstretched hand: one in front, one on each side of and a little behind the leader, and a fourth trailing a little behind one of the flankers. And they were at CBDR, which stood for "constant bearing, decreasing range," meaning that they were headed straight for the *Cumberland*.

"IFF?" Identification, friend or foe. Max was asking the question of the day: Were the ships transmitting the correct electronic recognition signal?

"Not yet, sir." Then the sound of a relieved breath. "IFF received. Fighters are confirmed friendlies. Banshee B fighters, squadron CFS two-six-three-two assigned to the escort carrier *Lake Baikal*. I think their nickname is 'The Krag Baggers.'"

Max snorted derisively. Garcia turned to him. "Heard of these guys, Skipper?"

Kasparov interrupted. "Changing designation of targets to Charlie one through four." He shrugged apologetically. He was *supposed* to say that. As soon as the targets were identified as friendly, they ceased to be Uniforms, which stood for "Unidentified," and became Charlies, which stood for "chicks," meaning "friendlies."

"Everyone in this theater has heard of them," Max responded. "They're famous, in a way. They used to be hot sticks assigned to the *Constellation* in the Forward Battle Area. About nine or ten months ago, the whole Task Force was conducting a huge exercise—three carriers, seven battlewagons, twenty-five cruisers—you know, a really big deal—under EMCON, with ships dispersed over half a sector, no IFF, no voice comms, no nav beacons—just like a real attack. Well, the Krag Baggers were coming back from a simulated sortie, and somehow the squadron leader got a few digits transposed in the rendezvous coordinates. Squadron XO with the check set had turned back with engine trouble, so there was no backup record of the coordinates and no carrier even close to where they thought it should be. Huge, *huge* FUBAR: the whole fighter squadron in the middle of nowhere on comm silence, near the end of their fuel and wondering if they were going to have to call for help and totally tank the whole exercise. Then, some sharp-eyed stud fighter jock saves the day when he spots a carrier with the Mark One Eyeball, pretty as you please, all lit up and about twenty-seven hundred kills away. He does a 'follow me' signal with his running lights and leads them home. Everybody relaxes because their bacon has just been saved, right? Squadron lines itself up in a perfect approach formation, does the standard visual recognition pass, and then blinkers in their request to land. Then, every signal light on the carrier starts flashing like a Christmas tree on stims, frantically giving them the wave-off and telling them to assume a holding formation, null their drives, and put their thrusters on station keeping."

"Why the wave-off?"

"Because, XO, these fighters from the *Constellation* were trying to land on the *Eugene F. Kranz*. They did a visual recognition pass and didn't even notice it wasn't their own carrier. The *Kranz* had to launch two tankers to refuel the fighters and then feed them the correct rendezvous coordinates by blinker. And you can just bet that along with those coordinates, Admiral Turgenov put in a few choice words in his inimitable way. Now, our friends the Krag Baggers are relegated to flying combat-area patrol off a third-rate escort carrier back here in the Tertiary Defensive Perimeter until they can convince Admiral Turgenov that they can find their butts with both hands tied behind their backs."

"Shouldn't we activate our IFF transponder?" Bartoli interrupted, concerned about being fired upon by the Krag Baggers. Just because they couldn't navigate didn't mean that they couldn't shoot.

"Negative. Maintain EMCON. They're expecting us. Kasparov, have someone in your support room put the Krag Baggers on visual and route it to Comms for a recognition signal by lights."

"By *lights*, sir?" Everyone knew the protocols for visual recognition by flashing lights, but they were rarely used. It was like something out of the Battle of Jutland.

"Yes, Mr. Kasparov, by lights. It's in our orders. The Krag have all these systems seeded with stealthed EM probes. The idea is for us to come through here without being heard or heard of. Those fighters have orders not to hail us or talk about us by radio, and if we keep our transmitters shut down, no one will ever know we were in the neighborhood. So, have your man on the optical scanners train one on the fighters and send the feed to Comms."

"Aye, sir." Kasparov was no dummy. He understood the logic behind the procedure and started speaking softly over his headset, giving instructions to the correct man in the Sensor Station's staff support room. Like most watch standers in CIC, Kasparov was backed up by a team of men in a compartment nearby, called a staff support room or back room; there was one for each major CIC station, in a system that went back to NASA's Mission Control in the earliest days of space flight. As the man in CIC could watch only a few displays at a time, there were several—sometimes as many as two dozen—other men in another compartment looking at all the relevant displays with voice, text, video, and data links to the man in CIC. Each of those men, in turn, could pull up additional displays, access computer databases, make inquiries by voice or data link to anyone, anywhere in the ship, and otherwise do whatever was necessary to provide the man in CIC with the information he needed.

That system made the CIC the center of a web of information whose strands extended to every corner of the ship. It had worked well for the people who ran the moon landings, and it had worked very well for the Navy. Apollo Mission Control's legacy of achievement and excellence lived on, three and half centuries later, in the fighting CICs of the Union Space Navy.

Max noted that one of the screens at the Comms Station changed from a transceiver array status grid to a camera feed from outside the ship. Four of the tiny lights against the black background were moving slowly relative to the background of stars. One of the lights blinked blue twice, red twice, green three times, and white once. Comms was already punching up today's visual recognition codes. "Captain, the fighter element has transmitted the correct recognition code for today's date. Shall I transmit the response?"

"Affirmative, Mr. Chin."

Chin then pulled up the little-used touch screen that allowed him to control the ship's running lights, now extinguished except for the collision lamps, directly from his station. He keyed in the sequence, checked it against the code displayed on another screen, and hit EXECUTE. The *Cumberland's* running lights then flashed one green, one red, four blue, and one white, and the tiny dot on the screen flashed two red. "Recognition code response transmitted and accepted," said Chin. The Krag Baggers recognized the *Cumberland* as a friendly and would not fire on her. Then the spot started flashing again, a series of rapid white flashes, some short, some longer. Nearly five hundred years after its invention, Morse code was just too useful to die. Chin watched the flashes carefully and typed letters into the keyboard at his station. He grunted, then pasted a smile on his face and turned to Max.

"Skipper," Chin said, "signal by Morse from the fighter element. Basically, they wish us luck." Something in Chin's voice told Max that he had not said everything. At that moment the red "MESSAGE" light on Max's console, cleverly set behind a set of bevels that made it impossible for anyone but him to see, started blinking. Max hit DISPLAY, causing one of his screens to read: "To CO from COMMS—actual text of message: 'GOOD LUCK STOP YOU WILL NEED IT CUMBERLAND GAP STOP MESSAGE ENDS.'"

That insulting name. Max had never liked it, even when he was serving on the *Emeka Moro*, but it especially rubbed him the wrong way now that those fighter jocks were applying it to *his* ship when he was in the Big Chair. Well, two can play that game. Max started typing: "CO to COMMS—send this by lights: THANKS FOR SINCERE GOOD WISHES STOP GOOD LUCK ON RETURNING TO CARRIER STOP THERE IS ONLY ONE IN THIS SECTOR SO YOU ARE CERTAIN TO GET IT RIGHT THIS TIME STOP CO SENDS PERSONALLY STOP MESSAGE ENDS." *There. That'll throttle back their thrusters for a little while.* He hit SEND.

Max turned to Chin. "Comms, I've prepared a suitable reply to our friends. Kindly send it by lights." When the text came up on Chin's console, a short yip escaped him, quickly cut off. He input and sent the message with a barely visible smile.

Bartoli turned to Max, doing his best not to smile broadly. Max remembered that the Tactical console could monitor most message traffic. His little put-down to the fighters would be known to every man and boy on board, by change of watch—one small blow struck for morale on the *Cumberland*. "Skipper, those fighters have come about and are running back to their normal patrol station. I don't think they want to talk to us any more."

"I can't imagine why, Mr. Bartoli." He turned to his sensor man and inquired amiably, "Mr. Kasparov, have we located their carrier yet? She is, after all, the size of a small planet. If she's been in system long enough, maybe she's got some captured asteroids orbiting her as natural satellites that you can use to help localize her." Kasparov smiled and a few people chuckled, while others stared at their feet, not knowing what to make of the remarks. Having a skipper with a sense of humor took a little getting used to. Max's comments were, after all, slight exaggerations. The ship in question was a *Lake Victoria* class escort carrier, one of the smaller ones. If Max remembered correctly, she was only 1295 meters long and massed something over a hundred thousand tons, which would have made for a very, very small planet.

"Affirmative, sir." His people had detected the carrier a few moments before, and it was being plotted now, a fact that everyone in CIC could see from the tactical plot. "USS *Lake Baikal* is at the L4 for the fourth planet, a gas giant with about one and a half Jupiter masses. Just sitting there for now. She's got four elements of Banshees out flying combat area patrol and three Mongoose SWACS ships out there pounding the system with sensor sweeps. Our projected course takes us nowhere near any of them."

It was hard to hide something that big, but the *Lake Baikal*'s captain was doing his best not to stick out like a sore thumb. The L4 and L5 Lagrange points, also called Trojan points, were nice little gravity wells, one of which was sixty degrees ahead of the planet in its orbit and one sixty degrees behind, that tended to collect small bodies and debris, known as Trojan Asteroids. A ship at L4 or L5 not only conserves fuel by staying in a stable orbit, but it is difficult for enemy sensors to pick it out from all the other objects put there already by Mother Nature. Or Isaac Newton. Or Joseph Lagrange.

"Maneuvering, do you have my ETA to the Bravo jump point yet?"

"Affirmative, sir, coming up now. Jump point Bravo is just over sixty-four AU from our current position. If we top out at our highest stealthy speed of point-five-four c, with standard acceleration and deceleration at each end, our transit time is eighteen hours, fifty-seven minutes."

Even at half the speed of light, a star system covered a lot of real estate. "CIC to Engineering."

"Engineering. Brown here."

"Wernher, I've got a question for you."

"Allow me to hazard a guess. You want to know whether I trust the compression drive on this ship at low c factors."

Max was floored. "I didn't know mind reading was one of your many abilities."

"It is not. But down here in Engineering we do keep a weather eye on the tactical repeater and the status monitors. It's an obvious question, really. A typical skipper on a typical mission would cross each of these systems at about half lightspeed and get to our destination in a few weeks. That same typical skipper would not consider crossing these systems on the compression drive because superluminal travel is illegal in most systems and dangerous at low c multiples because of compression shear. How am I doing so far?"

"Obviously, you're doing pretty damn well, Wernher. But you also know that these particular systems are uninhabited and unclaimed, so there's no law for us to break. And you know that this ship's got an additional set of compression phase modulators to increase control at lower multiples just so it can do this kind of thing. That lets us zip around at low superluminal velocities inside a star system, a capability that no one in Known Space has except for maybe the Vaaach." And getting there faster would give Max and the doctor more time to figure out what the Krag were buying, where they were buying it, and where their ships were, not to mention more time on station before he ran out of food and fuel. "That makes it a realistic option for us. So, what's your answer?"

"Captain, I have every confidence in the stability and safety of this drive at anything over six c. My recommendation, though, is that you do this at ten c. Ten will give you a good compromise between minimizing shear and not packing on so much velocity that it would be easy to overrun the jump point. And even with the extra phase modulators, you need to understand that although velocity is going to be stable, there will be some unpredictability about the precise equilibrium point. Ten c might turn out to be anywhere between nine point three and ten point five."

"Not a problem. Make whatever preparations you need, and notify the XO when you're ready."

"Aye, Captain," Brown replied. Max closed the circuit.

"XO, make preparations to traverse this system using the compression drive at ten c."

"Aye, sir," responded the XO. "Preparing to make intrasystem traverse from present location to jump point Bravo at one-zero-point-zero c." The XO started giving orders to Maneuvering, the CIC engineering officer, and Deflector Control.

Max turned to the sensor officer. "Mr. Kasparov, you're authorized to break EMCON to the extent, and only to the extent, of conducting a narrow beam active scan at high power along our path to the jump point. We want to make damn sure nothing's in our way." Kasparov acknowledged the order and started talking into his headset. He was going to let his back room set up and execute the scan, rather than trying to do it from the more limited set of controls on his console. Smart move.

It took about a minute. "Captain, scan along our route to the Bravo jump point is clear. No ships or obstructions."

"Very well. XO, you may take the ship superluminal when ready."

Garcia sat up straighter in his seat. "Thank you, sir. Deflector control, forward deflectors to full, lateral and rear deflectors to cruise."

"Forward deflectors to full, lateral and rear to cruise, aye."

"Maneuvering, null main sublight drive and take it to standby. Take maneuvering thrusters to standby."

"Null the main sublight and take to standby, maneuvering thrusters to standby, aye," confirmed the chief. He gave the orders to the men at the station in front of him and watched the status lights on his console. "Main sublight nulled and at standby. Ship is coasting. Maneuvering thrusters at standby. Attitude control by inertial systems only."

"Prepare to engage compression drive, set c factor for one zero point zero."

"Aye, sir," Maneuvering responded. "C factor one zero point zero." Ten times the speed of light. About three million kilometers per second. "Green light from Engineering—compression drive is ready for superluminal propulsion."

"Engage."

"Engaging. Compression field forming. Field is going propulsive. Speed is zero point seven. Zero point nine." There was a brief, shrill screech as the ship passed through the lightspeed barrier. As the barrier was known as "Einstein's Wall," the sound was unavoidably named "Einstein's Wail."

"Ship is now superluminal. One point five. Three. Five. Eight. Field reaching equilibrium. Equilibrium achieved. Field is propulsive and stable at ten point zero seven c. Our ETA at jump point Bravo is ... one hour and forty-nine minutes from now."

Not bad. First chance Max got, he would see that Wernher got a promotion.

"Steady as she goes," said the XO.

"Good job, XO, everyone," said Max. Then, to Garcia, "I'll be in the Sensor back room."

The XO said, "Understood, sir." The expression on his face, though, said, "Outstanding idea, sir."

The Sensor back room was around a few corners and down a corridor about ten meters. Max hit the door control and stepped quietly inside. No one noticed him in the darkened room because everyone's attention was focused on two men on the far side of the compartment, their faces lit by sensor displays. One was screaming and one was cringing.

The screamer, a lieutenant JG who looked just a little too old for his rank, also looked a little too red in the face for his own good. "The drive emissions are totally distinctive," he screeched in a voice like fingernails on slate. "Look at the Doppler on the absorption lines. When you correct for relative velocity of the two ships, a greenie could see that the exhaust gas velocity perfectly matches a Banshee. And look at the emission lines themselves. Not *there*, fuckhead. THERE. THERE. AND THERE. What are those?"

The cringer, an ordinary spacer third class, croaked out "Potassium and cesium?"

"*No*, dipshit. *Sodium* and cesium. Standard additives to Union Fighter fuel, not used by most other powers. This Doppler plus these additives give you a solid specident on this contact as Union Fighter. If another sensor can identify him by another means, we've got a dual phenomenology posident, and our man in CIC can tell the skipper what the target is. Got that, or do I need to repeat myself?"

The information was correct, but the way it was being delivered required correction.

"NO. YOU. DON'T!" thundered Max. "Don't repeat a goddamn word. You have said *quite enough*," he continued in a voice that was low but hard and cold and sharp as a boarding cutlass. "What is your name, mister?" Mister was a correct but less than complimentary way to address a junior officer.

"Goldman, sir." The man's face was going from red to purple.

"*Mister* Goldman, who is your relief?"

"Ensign Harbaugh, sir."

Max scanned the room for the person next in rank after Goldman, quickly finding a chief petty officer first class, whose service stripes proclaimed he had been in space long enough to have served with John Glenn and Gordo Cooper. He was looking at Goldman with poorly concealed hatred, a look that confirmed the impression Max had already formed of this officer.

"Chief, please tell Ensign Harbaugh by voice comm that he is to report here on my order to take over as senior officer in this compartment. Immediately." The chief hit a comm button on his console and started talking into his headset.

"*Mister* Goldman, I'm relieving you as sensor SSR commander and reducing you in grade to midshipman second, both effective immediately." Max heard some whispering around the room at that. He had made an impression. Good. He was just getting started. "And pack your duffel. At 0600 tomorrow, you are to report to the midshipmen trainer for reassignment to middy quarters and to begin to repeat the units in 'Officer's Duties with

Regard to Training and Leadership of Enlisted Men,' plus the 'Intensive Hands-On Practicum in Ship's Cleaning, Maintenance, and Sanitation.' I hope you enjoy the sewage reclamation plant because you're going to be seeing a lot of it. I will not tolerate abuse of enlisted men by officers on my ship. Dis*missed.*"

Military justice in action. Quoth the Mikado: "Let the punishment fit the crime."

Goldman did an about face and stomped out of the room, dripping with insubordinate attitude. Max suppressed the urge to call him back and dress him down further. No. A repeat of the mids' course in the right way to teach and lead the lower ranks, plus a month relearning ship's cleaning, maintenance, and sanitation, should readjust that man's outlook. If it worked, Max would make him an officer again in four or five months. If it didn't, Goldman would see what the galaxy looked like from the perspective of an ordinary spacer third class.

Max then turned his attention to the cringer. He didn't look a day over eighteen. "Spacer, what's your name?"

"Onizuka, sir."

"Onizuka, how long have you been in Sensors?"

"Three days sir."

"Before that?"

"I was in Environmental Control on the *Hai Lung*. Then I got twenty-four days of training in Sensors at Llellewellyn Station and then they shipped me here."

"And was today the first time you had ever been asked to do a spectrographic identification protocol on a real contact?"

"Yes, sir. It was."

"Well, Onizuka, when I was a greenie, the first time I did a specident, I told the SSR commander that a Forthian customs probe was a Krag Limpet torpedo. The whole ship went to general quarters, and we came within a micron of firing on the damn thing. Forthia hadn't joined the Union at that point, so I could have started a war. Fortunately, the sensors officer in CIC insisted that we follow the dual phenomenology rule and not fire until we got another reading from another kind of sensor that gave us the same answer."

"What did they do to you, sir?" asked the young Spacer, wide-eyed.

"Do? To me? Not a thing except rag me about it. Endlessly. For the better part of a year, every time we encountered some sort of innocent target like a navigation buoy or a comm relay or a postage-and-parcel drone, someone or other would ask me if I thought it was hostile and whether we should fire on it. When we'd go to a bar on shore leave and the bartender would pass us some bar nuts or pretzels, someone would say, 'Hey Robichaux, you sure that's not a *hostile target?*'"

That got him a few chuckles.

"Now, who in here has spent some time on this console?" One man, an able spacer first, stood up. "And you are?"

"Smith, sir."

"And Spacer Smith, if my luck's holding, there will be more than one Smith aboard this ship. Right?"

"Yes, sir. There are three."

"Your first name, then?"

"James, sir. But that won't help sir. Every one of us is named James. Sir."

"So, you go by your middle names, then?"

"No, sir. I don't have a middle name and the two other Smiths are both named James Edwin."

"Merciful God. What genius decided to put you three on the same ship? I must have an enemy in BuPers. What are we supposed to use as names for you three so that no one gets confused?"

"Chief Bond decided we should go by our homeworld name. I'm from Greenlee four, so I'm 'Greenlee.'"

"Chief Bond has a lot of sense. Thank God none of you is from Zubin Eschamali IX. Or even worse, Fuhkher II." That one got a few laughs. The mood in the room was starting to lighten a bit. *Maybe these people can start to function now.*

"Okay, then, Greenlee. I want you to sit down right here and spend the next hour teaching Onizuka everything you can about specidents. Since he's had the course, he must know most of what he needs, so give him the practical tips you learned on the job that weren't in the training, and then run a few exercises. I've got some you haven't seen. Access the menu under 'Captain's Training Files.'"

Just then, Harbaugh came in, out of breath, pillow creases on the right side of his face, eyes bleary. The man obviously needed coffee. Max looked around for the pot. He couldn't spot it. A cola would do. Then he noticed that there were no coffee cups or mugs, nor any beverages of any kind anywhere in the compartment. Max looked at the CPO first with all the stripes. If anyone here knew what the hell was going on, it would be this man. "Chief, what's your name?"

"Kleszczynska, sir." When he got a blank stare from the captain, he spelled it.

Max looked imploringly at the ceiling for a second. "And what do the people who have not practiced Polish tongue twisters from birth call you, Chief?"

"Klesh, sir," he answered, smiling.

"Chief Klesh, where is the coffee pot for this compartment? And the drinks chiller?"

In a voice that did not entirely conceal his disapproval, the chief responded, "Both removed at Captain Oscar's orders, sir."

That figures. Men who stand rotating four hour watches around the clock are expected to stare at sensor readouts, in a darkened room, for two hundred and forty minutes, and not fall asleep at their stations without coffee or drinks to sustain them? Riiiiiiight.

Max went to the nearest comm panel. He stabbed the button savagely. "Quartermaster."

"Quartermaster's office, Chief Jinnah here."

"Chief, this is the skipper. Does this ship have the standard issue of coffee pots and drink chillers for a vessel of this class?"

"Absolutely, sir."

"Mugs and cups too?"

"The regulation number, sir."

"And Chief Jinnah, if I wanted coffee pots to be used to actually make coffee and chillers to be used to chill drinks, and some cups and mugs to be available to hold beverages rather than collecting dust somewhere, how would I go about finding them?"

"They are all in the spares bay. I can get you the grid numbers if you want them."

"All there at Captain Oscar's order, I suppose."

A resigned sigh came over the comm. "Affirmative, sir."

"Chief Jinnah. Make this your priority. I want those coffee pots and those chillers issued and stocked by fourteen hundred hours. Issue the cups and mugs too."

"Yes, *sir!*" Something told Max that the chief liked his coffee.

Max punched another key.

"Enlisted mess, Chief Lao here."

"Chief, this is the skipper. I need coffee and beverage service in the Sensor SSR ASAP. Are you the man who can make that happen?"

"Affirmative, sir. Just have the men key in what they want on the Tray Request menu, and the senior man in there key in an authorization, and I'll have it in there in under ten minutes." Most of the senior NCOs on this ship seemed to be on the ball, at any rate.

Greenlee explained to Max that Captain Oscar had prohibited beverages at stations because he thought they didn't "look shipshape" and because of fears of spillage (absurd because all the consoles were hermetically sealed). Accordingly, some of the men in Sensors had to be shown how to pull up the Tray Request menu from their consoles.

While all this was going on, Chief Klesh had brought Ensign Harbaugh up to speed, and Harbaugh had been to every console to see what each man was doing and to get a look at what each sensor was reading. Max put him on getting crash training to the five men who were new to the department, with the rest of the people there either helping those five or running training exercises until the next jump.

"And after the jump, when you've determined everything is clear, everyone but two of you go back to running exercises while two watch the consoles. All the senior people rotate through keeping an eye out.

"Harbaugh, Klesh, put your heads together and see if there's anyone off duty who would be helpful in increasing these men's proficiency in a big burning hurry. If so, get them in here. You have my leave to wake anyone in this department from both of the off-duty watches. Harbaugh, when the next watch comes on, put them to work doing the same thing this group is doing, and have them do the same for the next group."

"Yes sir." Harbaugh seemed eager, anyway.

"And Harbaugh, effective immediately, you're the new sensor SSR commander. I need green lights across the board from this room and I need 'em yesterday. Anything you need to make that happen, you come straight to me. Understood?"

"Understood, sir."

"Carry on, then."

"How in the hell did you get your hands on *that?*" Chief Tung pointed at the object on the table in front of him. It looked like a slightly oversize, bright yellow pancake with a few buttons and lights set in the center.

"The lock on Ordinance Locker Number Three has had an electronic fault since we were commissioned. You can open it by entering zero-one-two-three. I never reported the problem, in case I ever needed to liberate something." Chief Kapstein was proud of himself.

"Why didn't you 'liberate' something that would do us more good than one dinky little thermoflasher?" snarled Chief Larch-Thau. Resting at the center of the tiny table in the Goat Locker, the stolen device looked more like an hors d'oeuvre than ordnance.

"Because, dumbass," answered Kapstein, "there's a sniffer in there that reads the chemicals in the air. You take out too high a volume of ordnance, the trace compound concentration in the air goes down and the computer triggers an alarm. You can slip out one or two of these little jewels, but anything more or anything bigger and you're nabbed."

"But what," Tung asked, "can we do with a thermoflasher? All the drives, deflectors, reactors, and every other high-energy component is high temperature tolerant. A thermoflasher will just burn off the paint or melt the dials. Brown can just pop on new panels or a new control interface, and it'll be good as new."

"Come on," Kapstein chided. "You mean to tell me you can't think of a single *low-energy* system that's also mission critical?"

"You mean...?" Larch-Thau smiled, pointing at the ceiling.

"Absolutely," Kapstein answered.

Having skillfully removed the ceiling panel and an air return duct access panel, all three men were crawling along the air conduit, which was approximately one meter square. Tung had already entered a command from his percom, directing the computer to reduce the airflow through this duct so that there wouldn't be a pressure buildup to alert the computer that there was an obstruction consisting of three chief petty officers. After five minutes of stealthy creeping, they reached a branching duct that led toward the lower decks. Fortunately, there were rungs bolted to one of the sides.

Not saying a word, they moved more slowly as they went down. After descending almost two decks, they came to another horizontal duct, which they followed for just under twenty meters. By this time, all three men were sweating, not just from the warm air in the air return ducts and the exertion, but from fear of being caught. If apprehended, the very least they would likely face would be a court martial, and at worst, in theory the skipper could toss them out the airlock.

After a few minutes, they reached a grille that blocked their way. On the other side of the heavy metal grating they could barely discern a complex array of pipes, ducts, and electronics. Attached to the grille's corner were three small signs. The first read: "MAIN ATMOSPHERE PROCESSOR MANIFOLD." The second: "WARNING: ENTRY WHILE PROCESSOR IS IN OPERATION WILL KILL YOU IN LESS THAN ONE MINUTE. CONFIRM PROCESSOR IS OFFLINE AND UNIT POWER LOCKED OUT BEFORE ENTRY." The third: "ENTRY WHILE PROCESSOR IS IN OPERATION PROHIBITED BY 60 CNR 29623 AND WILL RESULT IN SEVERE DISCIPLINARY CONSEQUENCES."

Larch-Thau laughed. "I wonder what's worse: dying in less than one minute or the 'severe disciplinary consequences.'"

"Once you're dead, I'm thinking that the discipline isn't too bad," said Kapstein. "Okay, let's do this."

Tung pointed at the sign. "But..."

"We're not going inside, dipstick," said Kaptstein. "We'll just make a little deposit." He rotated four release catches on the grille from "LOCK" to "OPEN" and punched a few buttons on the thermoflasher; then he checked the display against his percom and firmly thumbed the largest button on the unit. It was red. He shifted one side of the grill far enough back for him to stick in his arm and toss the disk a meter and a half or so into the unit, after which he reset the grille, relocked the release catches, and turned to his companions.

"All right, boys, back to the Goat Locker."

The crawl back seemed much faster than going the other way, perhaps because three chiefs in an air duct could always be explained, but three chiefs in an air duct with one of those chiefs carrying a piece of thermoexplosive ordinance might prove a bit harder to pass off.

Once back at their starting point with the duct and ceiling panel returned to their original condition, Kapstein reached into a chiller and removed three soda bottles whose labels were an ever so slightly darker shade of green than the norm, and passed them out. Each man opened his bottle and quickly downed an "off the books" contraband beer, which—like all alcoholic beverages—was banned unless consumed in the wardroom or the enlisted mess and officially logged to the drinker.

"Here's the drill, boys," Kapstein said with a grateful belch. "Our little deposit is set to do its business in the middle of the next watch. If you're on watch, be sure to be doing something that's in view of other people, preferably a senior chief or an officer or two. If not, be sure to be in the mess or someplace where there's lots of people to say you were there. That way, you've got a triple-shielded alibi and Bob's your uncle." They laughed together and, as one, dropped into the chairs that surrounded the table.

Just as the laughter started to die down, they heard a faint noise in the corridor. Before they could begin to stand, the hatch lock cycled, and two gigantic Marines burst into the room, pulse rifles slung, but sidearms in their hands. They were followed a second later by Major Kraft, his sidearm pointed at the center of Kapstein's chest.

"Hands on the table and freeze!" he demanded in a voice that threatened to crack the bulkheads. "We've got the last forty minutes of your lives on video," he added. "And Bob is no longer your uncle. Your mother's sister just divorced him. Zamora, Ulmer, put cuffs on these... individuals. Let's see if they like the brig as much as they like the Goat Locker."

Max left Sensors just as the coffee and drinks arrived—he had not ordered anything for himself—and started for the wardroom. He still craved that coffee and chicken-salad sandwich. He was just bellying up to the pot of dark roast—at least that idiot Captain Oscar hadn't banished coffee from the wardroom—when his percom beeped. He looked at the screen. "NDED IN BRG." Needed in Brig.

Great.

One of the benefits of serving on a small vessel was that everything was close to everything else. Climb down one level to C Deck, walk forward about eleven meters along the one corridor that ran along the center of the inhabited portion of that deck, and turn right into the second to last hatch.

There he met Major Kraft, the Marine commander. As always, Kraft seemed to be enjoying his job. "Captain, that little hook we put in the water a few hours ago has already caught us some fish. We got Tung, Kapstein, and Larch-Thau on visual surveillance, trying to plant a thermoflasher in the atmosphere processor primary manifold. They're in there." He jerked his thumb over his shoulder at the closed security door.

The Primary Manifold was a ton-and-a-half, fifty-eight-cubic-meter, bewilderingly complex apparatus that ducted all of the air recirculated from the ship after it came in through the primary air return duct, scrubbed out the carbon dioxide, analyzed its composition, and adjusted it. If the air were too dry, the manifold added water vapor. If it were oxygen depleted, it added O_2. If there were too much argon, krypton, or radon, the air was routed across a catalyst bed that removed it, and so on. The unit was triple and, as to some functions, quadruple fault redundant, and the ship carried ample spares for any component of the unit that could wear out or break.

For that reason, and because it was so large and heavy that carrying a spare was impractical, the huge unit itself was one of the few pieces of critical equipment on the ship for which there was no backup and no replacement. In the unlikely event that a manifold were destroyed—usually by enemy action—the ship would go on emergency atmosphere scrubbers. If it didn't get back to base or have its crew offloaded to a rescue ship, the air quality would get bad enough to start doing damage to the men in two or three days. It was the perfect sabotage target, which is why Max had put it under surveillance. If the thermoflasher had detonated, it would have instantly melted the entire unit to worthless, unreparable, unsalvageable slag.

"What do you want to do with them, Captain?"

"What I *want* is to throw them out an airlock."

Kraft smiled as though the idea appealed to him. "Well, sir, as we *are* in a combat zone and as planting the thermoflasher was 'an overt act tending to give aid and comfort to the enemy in time of war,' it *is* within your authority." On a destroyer, the Marine detachment commander was also chief of security, which made him the resident expert on the laws and regulations pertaining to crime and punishment on board ship. Kraft had, in fact, served in the Marines' JAG Corps, retired, and was serving as a an assistant planetary prosecutor on Houstonia when it fell to the Krag while he was attending a continuing legal education seminar in a nearby system. He promptly re-enlisted and requested a combat assignment.

"I could gin up the paperwork for you and the XO to sign in no time at all. Hell, I bet we could have these three bastards sucking vacuum before dinnertime. It won't be any trouble. Happy to do it. Sir."

"Major, as appealing a prospect as that may be, I don't think that executing three senior chiefs on my first day in command would be the best of ideas. For now, make sure they are in separate cells and that they can't communicate with each other or anyone else. Feed them normal rations, and let them have full terminal access; just disable the ability to send anything. I don't want to talk to the bastards—traitors give me an itchy trigger finger, but I want you to do a full interrogation. Bring in Dr. Sahin if you think there are psychological issues worth worrying about. I need to know if anyone else was working with them. Other than that, they'll keep for a while."

"Yes, sir. But if you change your mind and want them outside, dancing with the stars, you just let me know."

"You'll be the first, Major."

Max went back into the corridor and rolled his wrist to look at the time display on his percom. Still forty-five minutes away from the jump point. He'd have time for that coffee and sandwich after all. And maybe some pie. He wondered if the pecan pie on this ship was any good. The way things were going, he doubted it.

CHAPTER 6

14:29Z Hours, 22 January 2315

Much to Max's surprise, the pecan pie was top notch. After all, the Navy was never short of nuts. The ship's progress through space was also more than satisfactory. *Cumberland* had made ten jumps in just over eighteen hours, wearing two of the three watches to a frazzle. Crews were used to making one or two jumps a day at most, not one jump every hour or two. So when Max asked Engineer Brown if he needed to take the jump drive down for maintenance, he took the hint. The Engineer gamely replied that because it had never been put through so many jumps in so short a time, he would be more comfortable if he could tear it down for inspection, which was at least a twelve-hour process. Max concurred that it was better to be safe than sorry, and so kept the *Cumberland* to .52 c as it crossed from the Alpha to the Bravo jump point in the Van Berg Minor system.

Max decided that his plan to cross each of these systems in just a few hours was too optimistic. This crew was not prepared for the pace of all those jumps so quickly. But he still wanted to get to the Free Corridor before he was expected. So, he arrived upon a compromise. The ship would travel at 10 c on compression drive about halfway across each system and at roughly 0.5 c for the remainder, allowing the crossings to be made in anywhere between nine and ten and a half hours. It was clear that this crew needed the extra time in transit for training. Lots of training.

All of the jumps so far had been uneventful, and Max had noted that the Sensor section was performing more briskly and accurately with each jump. It was still not up to the standard he had been accustomed to on the *Emeka Moro* and other ships on which he had served, but had already risen to adequate and was rapidly approaching fair. Intense drills and training were taking place all over the ship, from reloading missile tubes in the bow to targeting the "Stinger" aft-firing pulse cannon.

Max had visited those parts of the ship where her key functions were performed, all the while encouraging, exhorting, teaching, and occasionally ordering changes to procedures and practices that weren't working. This was how he had spent the entirety of the middle watch: a little touch of Maxie in the night.

Things were improving. But for reasons he could not put his finger on, Max could see that they were not improving as rapidly as they should, given this crew's undoubted ability. Perhaps it was some mental barrier left over from Captain Oscar.

Max even managed to find the time to eat a hot meal, the main course of which was something called "Navy noodle casserole," a moderately savory offering that consisted mostly of noodles and cheese, but also contained visible quantities, very finely chopped, of various frozen vegetables. The official description of the dish mentioned meat as one of the ingredients, but if meat were present, it was in quantities below the threshold detectable by modern scientific means. It didn't taste bad, and at least someone in the galley had enough sense to make sure to pack some zing into it in the form of onions (frozen, reconstituted), garlic (same), and various other spices, including cayenne pepper.

After that, he managed a shower and a five-hour nap before returning to CIC in time for the next jump, this time from Van Berg Minor to Tesseck A. This crew was getting good at jumps, and this one went even smoother than the one before, the CIC crew benefitting from some rest. The men were managing to restore the systems more quickly and smoothly with each jump. The jump completed, Max again craved food and drink, this time boiled crawfish and beer. Good luck finding *that* on the *Cumberland*. As Max was trying to figure what food and drink might satisfy his *envie* and could be found on board, he noticed Kasparov suddenly tilt his head, reflexively touch his earpiece to listen to someone in his back room, and then quickly punch a few buttons on his console, all in less than a second and a half. Max knew exactly what came next.

"Contact," Kasparov nearly shouted, "designating as Uniform one, probable ship, approximate bearing zero-one-five mark zero-niner-zero, working on ID and range."

Oh, shit. No way was this a Union ship. "General quarters. Ship versus ship." Max gave the order that sent the entire ship to battle stations.

Klaxons immediately erupted, loud enough to grab one's attention, but not so loud as to be distracting. In the background, Max heard the ship-wide address system broadcast the voice of the able spacer who manned the Alerts Station: "General quarters, general quarters. Set Condition One throughout the ship. Close all airtight hatches, and secure all pressure bulkheads. All hands to action stations: ship versus ship."

The overhead lights dimmed slightly, and red lights went on in various places, providing a visible reminder that the ship was on alert. The crew quickly prepared themselves and their vessel for a possible battle with another warship: racing to the stations assigned to them for that kind of combat, closing hatches that divided the ship into seventy-eight separate airtight compartments, each of which could sustain life if the others lost atmosphere, arming weapons systems, and securing items that could become dislodged in a battle.

That was all fine and dandy, but what Max really needed right now was for his sensor people to give him a precise location and an accurate identification of that contact. Rapidly. Until he knew who it was and what they were up to, he needed to do something. Mainly, that something involved not dying.

"Maneuvering, let's clear the datum. Give me twenty seconds at flank on the sublight and hard delta-v in X and Y and a thirteen-hundred-meters-per-second kick from the maneuvering thrusters minus Z; then reduce the main sublight to one-quarter, engage Stealth, and from whatever course that puts us on give me minus fifty degrees in X, plus thirty degrees in Y, and give me an additional seven hundred MPS push from the thrusters minus Z."

He wanted to impart some speed to the ship quickly while making rapid changes in course in all three dimensions, to throw off any firing solution the other ship might be working up; then basically drop off their sensors while making another series of course changes, again in all three dimensions, so the *Cumberland* could not be targeted or found simply by extrapolating from her prior course. In space combat, two-thirds of the battle was crossing the staggering distances that separated everything just to get to where the enemy was, and 90 percent of the rest was finding him when you got there. Max planned to use his ship's excellent stealth capabilities to make the *Cumberland* difficult to find.

Max heard the engines going to peak output, saw the men at the Maneuvering Stations pushing the ship through the course changes, and felt it twisting and turning through space.

"Weapons, give me a firing solution on the contact ASAP, but do not arm warheads, do not open missile doors, and do not engage any targeting scanners. On the off chance they can read what we are doing, I don't want to escalate this until we know who is out there and what they want."

"Roger, Skipper."

Kasparov was busy, talking and listening over his headset as he started to get useful information from his improved but still not proficient back room. Max bet that demoting Lieutenant Goldman and getting coffee in there boosted performance 15 percent.

"Bearing on Uniform One is firming up. Now three-five-one mark one-zero-three, range approximately two-five-zero-triple-zero kills. Change of aspect on target—target is changing course to intercept our former track before we engaged Stealth. He may not see us now. We are certainly not seeing him: between his low-albedo hull coating and how far away we are from this system's star, he's totally dark—no visual detection at all. We are reading him on mass, graviton flux, and very faint EM only."

Short pause, as he listened to his back room. "Starting to get some size parameters from occultations, though." Every now and then the other ship would come between the *Cumberland*'s visual scanners and a star or other light source, causing it to wink out, known as a stellar occultation. Complex calculations of the relative movements of the two ships, their ranges, and the exact apparent location of each occulted object, plus which objects were not occulted, allowed the computer to make some inferences about the other ship's size and shape. The *Cumberland*, however, was so small that she created very few occultations and was very hard to spot in that manner, or in any manner for that matter.

"And?"

"Just coming up now, sir." Ten seconds went by. Finally, Kasparov said, "Bogie is very long and very narrow, somewhere between one-eight-zero-zero and two-three-zero-zero meters in length with a fifty-two to seventy-five-meter beam. He's got reactionless drive, so we don't have a drive spectrum to work with on identification. On the other hand, there aren't many races with that technology, so that narrows down the possibilities."

Reactionless drive was an exotic technology that gave its possessor sublight propulsion without having to shoot hot gases out the back end of the ship. Because a hot sublight drive emitting brilliant plasma flying out a thruster nozzle at an appreciable fraction of the speed of light tended to stand out against the dark, cold background of interstellar space, everyone wanted reactionless drive, but only a handful of the most advanced civilizations had it.

There were only three known races with ships that combined large size, long and narrow shapes, and reactionless drive: the Lakirr, who would randomly decide either to ignore you or vaporize you in a heartbeat with their obscenely advanced weaponry—no one could ever predict which; the Sarthan, who were not dangerous at all unless you let them try to sell you something; and the Vaaach, a very powerful but highly insular species who did not get involved in anyone else's business but who dealt swiftly and severely with anyone who got involved in theirs.

In any event, Max was not going to let pass an opportunity to gather intelligence and train his crew at the same time. Precious little was known about all three of these races, and anything learned from close observation of their vessels would be valuable to Naval Intelligence. Plus, his people needed practice tracking, identifying, and closing on ships unobserved. That was the best way to kill the enemy: sneak up on him and stab him in the back before he even knows you're there. Besides, his crew needed confidence pronto, and the only way for them to get it was to do something difficult and live to tell about it. This was the chance to do just that.

"People, we are going to work up this target. Let's see how close we can get and how much we can observe without being observed ourselves. Maneuvering, reduce drive to 10 percent, and allow the target to get ahead of us, and then let's slip in on his six o'clock. Maintain range of at least eighteen thousand kills until I tell you to close." Max pulled up the sensors' best estimate of the contact's course plot, increased the scale to maximum, and squinted at it for a moment.

"Aye, sir. Reduce drive to 10 percent, slip in on his six, keep range in excess of one-eight-triple-zero kills until ordered otherwise."

"Skipper?" said Garcia softly, his voice carrying no farther than the edge of the command island occupied by only him and the captain.

"Yes, XO?" Max matched his volume.

"Ballsy move, sir. Risky too. What if they take offense at being tailed?"

"This crew needs to practice these skills under conditions of risk, and they need to succeed at something. Anything. If we're spotted, we apologize, or we evade and escape, depending on who it turns out to be."

"They might not give us that chance, sir. If it's the Lakirr, and they woke up on the wrong side of the mossy rock this morning, they could hit us with their antiproton beam, and we'd evaporate in about three-eighths of a second."

"Between you and me, XO, it's not the Lakirr."

"How do you know, sir? We've got no drive spectrum, no comm traffic, no markings, and no read on configuration except that the ship is something of an alien phallic symbol."

"I can tell from their ship handling. If you watch the plot of their trajectory at large scale, you can see they're not moving in a smooth path." He pointed to a screen on his display, showing an almost imperceptible serpentine motion in three dimensions. "They slew their bow around ever so slightly to change the angle of their sensor beams relative to any target in their path. It reminds me of an animal following a scent by moving its nose back and forth. It's the Vaaach. I've seen them do that before."

"It's not in the recognition protocols."

"I sent it up the line, but Intel never included it in any of the official protocols, saying that 'the purported observation was not supported by sufficiently variegated phenomenologies to be regarded as an authoritative indicium of vessel origin,' which I think is IntelSpeak for 'We didn't think of it, so we're not going to sign off on it.'"

Garcia chuckled. "Been there. Done that. Bought the memory wipe."

"Anyway, trust me on this one. It's the Vaaach. I want to see how long it takes the children to figure it out and how they do it. And no prompting from the studio audience."

"My lips are sealed." Whatever a studio audience was.

Chief Petty Officer First Class Claude LeBlanc directed the activities of the three spacers at the Maneuvering Stations, giving drive and course change orders. The tactical display showed that the bogie was slowly pulling ahead and the *Cumberland* was tiptoeing around to get behind it. After a few minutes, the bogie was dead ahead.

"Captain, I think we have an ID on the bogie," said Kasparov. "But it's not by the book. We have only a single phenomenology, and the one we've got isn't even an accepted recognition protocol but, well, I think it's pretty solid, sir."

"Mr. Kasparov, when I was in Sensors, I made an identification or two that wasn't in the ARPs, so tell me what you've got."

"Now that we're nearly on her six, we're getting some good images of a few viewports the contact is showing aft. God only knows why they aren't shuttered, but there they are. Maybe they think that no one would ever be back here, or maybe it's an oversight."

"And maybe they want us to see them so that we can do whatever it is you just did," Max suggested. "I hear there are some species out there that are very much into the sport of tracking and being tracked."

"Anyway, the guys in the back room brainstormed that if we aggregated the light from all of those viewports, we might have enough photons to do a reasonably good spectral analysis."

This was pretty damn smart. Max and Garcia smiled with approval as they worked through the concept. "So, you're thinking that the people who design lights for a ship are going to give the crew light that closely approximates the spectral balance of their sun as seen from the surface of their homeworld, right?"

"Exactly, sir, because that's what we do on our ships."

"And did you get a match?"

"Yes, sir. The spectral curve from those viewports is a nearly perfect fit with what you would see at local noon on a partly cloudy day on the surface of Grrlrrmgkruhgror."

It sounded like he had something caught in his throat. "Growl...what?"

"It's the name of the Vaaach homeworld, sir. Sigint finally decrypted it from a civilian traffic routing message a few days ago."

"Good job. Never seen that one before. Write it up and I'll kick it up the line. Maybe in a month or two folks around the fleet will be taking spectra on viewports to do a 'Kasparov ID.'"

Kasparov beamed. Max knew he could be counted on to pass that information on to his back room and that the confidence problem in that department might well be solved for good.

"And Kasparov?"

"Sir?"

"Unless I'm missing something, you just identified this target, so…"

"Oh. Sorry, sir." He changed to his CIC announcement voice. "Target tentatively identified as originating from a neutral power, the Vaaach sovereignty. Redesignating Uniform One as Nebula One."

"Intel, now that we know we're dealing with the Vaaach, what does that tell us?"

The ensign at the Intel console, whom Max knew to be on his first war cruise after being promoted out of the twenty-seven-man Intel back room on a battlecruiser, could only manage to stare like a Volem Woodsgrazer caught in the vehicle guidebeams.

Once again, the wisdom of Commodore Middleton came to Max's mind: "A warship captain is a lot like a teacher, with a life-and-death grading scale." School was in session today, and CIC was the classroom.

"Mr. Bhattacharyya, you're one of the most intelligent people on this ship, not including myself and the XO, of course. I'm sure you could stand there and talk to me for fifteen minutes, summarizing everything known to Naval Intelligence about the Vaaach. That doesn't help me. You explaining to me about what their lawmaking process is like or whether their poetry rhymes doesn't help me do my job today."

Max stepped off the command island, crossed over to the Intel console, put his hand on the young man's shoulder, and looked him straight in the eye. "What I need you to do, and what a capable intelligence officer does, is take all that wonderful information you have in your head about the Vaaach, and *apply it to our current situation*, distilling from that vast body of data in your skull the few sentences of facts, conclusions, and informed conjecture that will assist me in making the decisions I'm going to make over the next few minutes. The ability to do that is what distinguishes a mere database from an intelligence officer. Now, Ensign, what do you have to tell me that I can use?"

Max could see the wheels turning in the young man's head. According to his records, he really was quite brilliant. "Well, sir, first, the Vaaach are an arboreal species, and the trees on their homeworld are more than a kilometer tall, with the Vaaach living in multiple levels in the forest canopy. Accordingly, one would expect them to be skilled at three-dimensional thinking. Their tactics would probably not be subject to the two-dimensional bias that humans and others descended from surface-dwelling species have to struggle with. Second, previous interactions with humans show them to be very deliberate. Our experience is that they tend to act slowly, after careful consideration, but are very sure and resolute about decisions once they are made and change their minds very rarely.

"Third, it is known that they have an elaborate code of honor and that, unlike some species who are honorable only in their internal dealings, the Vaaach conduct their dealings with other races under their code. You can expect them to be very honorable, for their word will be their bond, and that they will not lie to you or manipulate the truth to obtain advantage." He stopped, considering how he needed to qualify the previous statement. "On the other hand, they are tough negotiators and skilled bargainers, in part because they are very patient and are not afraid to walk away from a deal and come back days or even years later when the situation has turned to their advantage.

"Fourth, in combat they are tenacious, skillful, and extremely courageous. As best we can tell from secondary sources, they have never lost a war. If they are fighting, I would very much want to be on their side, and I would very much not want to be their enemy.

"Fifth, although we have had little contact with them, what little information we have suggests their technology to be significantly more advanced than ours, a fact suggested by their possession of reactionless drive technology." He stopped, apparently searching his mind for other relevant data. "Does that help, sir?"

"Very much. Thank you, Ensign." Max walked slowly over to the chief at Maneuvering. "Chief LeBlanc, you wouldn't happen to be a Coonass, would you?"

Max used the slang term for a Cajun, one that, though it sounded insulting, was generally used in a friendly fashion, especially from one Cajun to another. The older man smiled, revealing a mouth full of large, only slightly crooked teeth. "Only if there is gumbo to be eaten, crawfish to be boiled, two steps to be danced, or beer to be drunk. Um, sir."

"Sounds good to me. You from Nouvelle Acadiana?" The chief nodded. "*Moi, aussi.* Maybe we'll both see it again, someday." Max did, after all, still have some cousins there he got along with pretty well, and his grandfather was still alive. "When we win this war and get back home, let's round up a yard of friends and family and boil us up a big pot of crawfish, with corn and potatoes, and a cooler full of beer on the side."

"And pecan pie for dessert," added the chief.

"You got it." Max got back down to business. "Chief, you ever crawl a duck pond?"

"*Mais*, yeah."

"That's what we're going to do today. Let's see if we can start closing that range up a little, Chief, *lentement*, like we're crawling a duck pond to jump us some Pintails. Increase our speed relative to the target by one hundred meters a second until the range is sixteen thousand kills. Then match the target and stay on his tail."

"Aye, sir, crawlin' dem ducks. Increasing relative speed one hundred feet per second, then matching speed with target when range is one-six-triple-zero kills."

Max had keyed his display so that the range to the target was constantly displayed on one of his screens. He watched warily as the number slowly dropped. A quick look around CIC showed that the same set of numbers was on a lot of displays beside his. As the numbers got smaller, the tension got higher.

"Kasparov, any sign the target has spotted us?"

"Negative, sir. He is sweeping his path with his sensors, but because of our angle, any returns he might get from our hull are far below any possible detection threshold. There have been some aft scans, but between me and Chief LeBlanc, we've been able to dodge them so far." Apparently, Kasparov had been getting readings on where the aft scans were going and was feeding them directly to the chief who was making minor "discretionary" course changes—slipping the ship a few hundred meters in one direction or another—to avoid them, changes deemed too small to require orders from the captain. Standard procedure, but a little bit more than Max thought Kasparov was capable of.

"Watch for an aspect change," said Max. "He may alter course suddenly, and we need to stay on his tail no matter what he does."

Most ships, even those with reactionless drives, had a major blind spot immediately astern. When a space vessel reaches an appreciable fraction of the speed of light, typically at 10 percent, it needs to clear the space in front of it of all matter, even the rarefied hydrogen and helium that fill interstellar space, because at those speeds the atoms pierce the ship's hull like bullets and shoot through the crew like particles of high-energy radiation. Accordingly, starships use a kind of interstellar "cow catcher" called a deflector, an integrated electromagnetic-graviton system that moves the interstellar medium aside to make a path for the ship.

In doing so, the ship leaves a "wake" of disturbed, ionized gas and particles behind it that confuse and block sensor readings in an approximate ten-degree arc behind the ship. There were ways to counter this problem, including high-power active sensor scans directed dead aft, towed sensor arrays, autonomous probes, and launching a smaller ship into the wake, all of which presented various disadvantages. Mostly, warship captains dealt with the problem by making radical and unexpected course changes, suddenly bringing their sensors to bear on the area and causing the following ship to overshoot the wake and travel into clear space, where it could be scanned.

"Kasparov, do you know how to tell whether a reactionless drive ship is about to change course? I mean, before you can see an aspect change."

"No sir. I didn't think anyone had ever followed one before."

"Let's just say it's been done once or twice."

Max got up and walked over to Kasparov's station. "Reactionless drive propels the ship by polarizing and amplifying gravity. Pull up a gravimetric flux profile. No, larger scale. Still larger. There. That's it. Now, see this slight notch in the outer isograv right in front of his bow? That notch is always aligned with the direction of thrust from his drive system. It's sort of like being able to see the rudder of an ocean vessel you are trying to follow through the water—the rudder turns before the ship changes direction. When this notch shifts, the ship is going to turn in the direction the notch moved. Put a marker dot in the notch, and have the computer tie the dot to the notch.

"Now go to a rear view so that the dot is in the center and project degree markings around it on the screen. Get the computer to project a bright green circle around that red dot—just one pixel more in diameter than the dot. There. Now, any motion of that dot will be clearly visible, and you can see exactly what the direction of the turn is going to be. When you see that dot shift, you sing out the direction in degrees as fast as you can. You have to be fast. Only about a second—maybe two—elapses between the shift in his drive field and the ship starting to turn.

"Chief LeBlanc," Max said, walking over to Maneuvering, "put an aspect outline of the Vaaach ship on your display." The chief complied.

"Good. When Kasparov tells you which way the ship is going to turn, you have to be ready to follow it. Go ahead and start your turn as soon as he sings out. Do not, repeat, do *not* wait for an order from me—and then adjust your rate of turn based on your observation of the aspect change on the target. Don't watch where the target goes. Watch for the ship's change in orientation, and let that tell you how hard he is turning. We have to stay in his wake or he'll spot us and the game is over."

"Aye, sir. Understood."

Max went back to his own station, sat down, and pulled up a few status readouts. Everything looked good. He heard LeBlanc order the man on drives to reduce thrust just as the range reached sixteen thousand kilometers. *Cumberland* was on the Vaaach's tail, right in his wake. Max hit the comm button on his console, to let him talk to the Sensor back room.

"People, this is the captain. Kasparov has his attention fully occupied right now, so that's why I'm on this loop. We want to take this opportunity to learn as much about the ship ahead of us as we can. Do anything you can think of to learn more about the contact, except using active scanning. Use every instrument; apply every kind of analysis. Tie up as much bandwidth as your hearts desire. Just get the data. Captain out."

Half an hour went by, crawling like an arthritic snail on a cold day. "Maneuvering, inch us closer. Same closure rate. Bring us to fifteen thousand." For just over six minutes the *Cumberland* slowly closed on the Vaaach ship.

"Captain." It was Nelson at Stealth. "The heat sink is nearing capacity. Should we radiate aft?"

One of the hardest things to conceal about a warship, or any working machine in space, is its heat. Stealth requires that the ship's heat signature match that of space itself; otherwise, it stands out on infrared detectors like a beacon against the near absolute zero background of interstellar space. One of the functions of the stealth systems is, therefore, to prevent heat from radiating from the ship into space. Doing so requires that the ship's hull be chilled to within a fraction of a degree of absolute zero (a process that paradoxically generates considerable heat), and demands that the heat from the fusion reactor, the electronics and machinery, the crew's bodies, and the heat removed from the ship's air by its cooling system must all be stored in a heat sink, essentially a large tank equipped with heat exchangers and filled with an exotic heat-storing granulated metal/liquid polymer slurry, to be radiated into space later.

That heat sink was now reaching its capacity, becoming so hot that the liquid metal slurry it used to store the ship's heat was on the verge of boiling. If that happened, the ship would radiate large amounts of heat in all directions, making it immediately detectable. The solution, when the location of one's adversary is known, is to radiate heat away from him so that the body of your ship blocks his view of your thermal radiators, which is why stealth-equipped ships have retractable thermal radiator fins all around the vessel, pointing in every conceivable direction, so that they can radiate heat in the direction or directions they choose.

"Affirmative. Radiate aft. Be ready to retract if the Vaaach get behind us."

Nelson keyed in a command that extended four radiator fins from the rear of the ship, fins that would soon be glowing red hot once they shed the ship's heat into space.

"Radiating aft," said Nelson. About a minute later, "Heat sink temperature starting to drop."

"Let me know when the heat sink gets down to 50 percent. I may want to retract the fins then."

Nelson acknowledged the order and went back to watching his systems.

"Turn warning, angle three-one-five degrees," Kasparov snapped out.

LeBlanc quickly gave orders that got the ship yawing to port and pitching up at about half of its maximum turn rate. After about two seconds of squinting hard at his screen, LeBlanc told the pitch and yaw man, "Hard over, all the way to the stops; she's turning sharp." A few seconds later, "Ease off fifteen degrees in yaw and ten degrees in pitch." Forty-three seconds later, "All controls amidships."

Apparently, the other ship was finished turning. The chief made slight adjustments to match the destroyer's course exactly to that of the Vaaach ship and stay in her wake. LeBlanc squinted some more. "Two degrees to starboard. Prepare to come amidships. Straighten her out...now. Pitch one degree down for about five seconds....There you go...amidships...now." He practically put his nose onto the display and then nodded. "Skipper, turn complete. We're right in the groove and I can guarantee"—he pronounced it "gare-on-TEE"—"that we didn't stick so much as a toe out of her wake."

"*Ça c'est bon*, Chief."

"*C'est pas rien, mon Capitain*."

"Captain," Garcia spoke up.

"Yes, XO?"

"Analysis of the turn, sir. The Vaaach vessel yawed to port one hundred and twelve degrees and pitched up ninety-three. Duration of the maneuver was seventy-three seconds. Pretty sharp turn for a vehicle travelling at 42 percent of lightspeed. She must have twenty times our mass, maybe fifty, but she almost out-turned us."

"I know. Pretty damn impressive. And," he announced to the CIC in general, "we should not assume she can't turn any harder than that. We do not know the capabilities of this race's technology, and the fastest way to get into trouble is to assume that an advanced alien civilization works under the same limitations we do."

Max returned to Garcia. "If we could get them into the war with us against the Krag, that would turn the tide in a hurry."

"Sure," Garcia said, just as confidentially. "And if my uncle were made out of yellow corn, he'd be a taco." A few seconds' pause. "I think he knows we're on his tail, though. Expect another turn soon."

"That makes sense. Give the order."

"People," said the XO more loudly, "be sharp. She might try another turn soon. Her skipper probably feels us as an itch between his shoulder blades. If Vaaach have shoulder blades."

"Sensors, are we getting anything good out of this?" Max asked.

"Affirmative, sir." Kasparov was actually starting to sound enthusiastic instead of terrified. "They've been blasting everything in sight with every kind of active scan we know of and three or four no one has ever seen until now. We're not in the beams ourselves, or we would have been detected, but we're picking up reflections from bodies in the system and from the interplanetary medium, so we're getting recordings of frequencies, phase alignments, pulse length, waveform polarization—basically, their whole sensor profile.

"Plus they have sent two messages. Not a hope in hell of decrypting them, but we got a lot of dope on their transmitter characteristics, what frequencies they use, their data bandwidth—things like that. We also have nearly enough data points for our computer algorithms to spit out a good estimate of their ship's mass, density, location of its center of gravity, and maybe even a few good guesses about its hull composition. We have nearly doubled what we know about them, sir."

"Well, at least Intel is getting something beneficial in exchange for my additional gray hairs." Max considered for a moment. "Maneuvering, resume closure maneuver, same rate. Bring our range to one three triple zero."

"Aye, sir, resuming closure maneuver, same rate, closing to one three triple zero." Thirteen thousand kilometers. Roughly the diameter of the Earth and, for most purposes, not that close, but for two warships from non-allied and potentially hostile races in a neutral star system, Max was practically crawling into the Vaaach's back pocket.

More minutes crept by. That's what being in the Navy in wartime was all about: weeks of unbearable tedium interrupted by hours of unbearable tension punctuated by seconds of unbearable terror. Max ordered sandwiches delivered to CIC. Everyone had already been getting good use out of the recently reinstalled coffee pot and chiller. Humans dealt better with tension if they could eat and drink a little. Or at least Max did, and what went for him went for other personnel under his command.

"Course change warning," announced Kasparov. "Turning one zero seven."

LeBlanc went with his instinct, betting that this turn would be as sharp as the last. "Yaw hard to starboard, all the way to the stop. Pitch down ten degrees. Drives, back off 10 percent." He watched his display for a few seconds. "Pitch, push her to the stop. She's out-turning us. We've got to slow to stay in his wake. Drives, null the main sublight. Engage braking drive and bring it to 50 percent."

The ship's main sublight drive ceased to push the ship, but with virtually no friction in the vacuum of space, the ship would not slow appreciably unless a counteracting force were applied, so the braking drive, forward-aimed thrusters mounted on four projections that ringed the hull, fired at half power.

The chief watched both ships' trajectories and velocities with an expert eye. He'd been handling the ship since the day it came out of the yard, and he was damn good at it. He had the help of a brilliant fly-by-wire computer that adjusted the relative thrust of the braking drive thrusters so that the ship would continue to answer the turn being commanded by the maneuvering controls even as the ship slowed.

"Kill the braking drive. Engage main sublight at 28 percent." After a few seconds, "Drives, make it 30 percent. Pitch and yaw, steering amidships on my mark...NOW. Yaw, two degrees to port...and amidships...now. Captain, we're through the turn. That one was close. If she turns any tighter, we're not going to be able to stay with her."

"Understood, Chief. I don't want to press our luck. Back us off to thirty thousand kills. Let's see if we can sneak away from this guy and go on about our business."

Max pretended not to notice the obvious wave of relief that washed through CIC. He had to admit, though, that as the range to target reading on his own display showed a steadily growing number, he was breathing more easily as well.

An hour and fourteen minutes went by, and the range to the Vaaach ship was now 28,890 kilometers. Max hoped to sneak his ship out of the Vaaach's wake and slip away with his new haul of priceless intelligence. Max was polishing off a sandwich that the galley had earnestly insisted was made from roast beef, but which Max strongly suspected came from an animal of a distinctly different heritage, when he heard Kasparov gasp.

"Captain," the sensor officer's voice was far too loud and far too high-pitched for Max's comfort, "the Vaaach grav curves are doing something I don't understand. The whole pattern is twisting into something like an 'S' shape."

Max knew what that meant. That "S" stood for "shit." Very deep shit.

Automatically, Max came to his feet. "Maneuvering, pitch up hard, give me a delta Y of one-three-zero degrees, Main sublight to Emergency." He wanted to veer off from the present course and also slightly away from the Vaaach ship in order to get out of its path and open up the range at the same time.

"Target has turned *in its own length* and is accelerating back down its previous course. They are already at point two five," said Kasparov.

Sweet Jesus. In its own length? How was that even possible? As if that weren't bad enough, the other ship had dumped .42 c of forward velocity and had put on .25 in the other direction—that's a total delta V of 67 percent of the speed of light in under a minute. God only knew how many Gs that entailed. If the *Cumberland* tried a velocity change even a tenth that violent, the ship would tear itself apart. The biggest piece anyone would find would fit easily into a shot glass.

Obviously, the Vaaach were more advanced than anyone had suspected. The ships that had so impressed the humans with whom the Vaaach had previously made contact were probably two-hundred-year-old sixth and seventh raters. Today, Max was up against a ship of the line.

"They're altering course to intercept. Closure is so rapid I can't measure it—I'm not sure they didn't go superluminal for a fraction of a second." There was a violent lurch. Station harnesses kept anyone from falling out of his seat or being thrown around the CIC, but Max was certain that one of his eyeballs was rolling around on the deck somewhere. "We're being held by a very powerful grappling field, sir."

"Power rating?"

"Over two million Hawkings, sir."

"We'll never break that. Maneuvering, null all drives, take maneuvering thrusters and inertial attitude control off line. Let's not burn out anything trying to fight a two-million-Hawk grapfield."

The *Cumberland* hung stationary in space, like a dragonfly on a collector's pin, with the now brightly lit and decidedly menacing Vaaach ship a scant sixteen hundred meters off the bow, stabbing it with nearly a dozen brilliant spotlights. In contrast to the familiar cylinder, ellipsoid, or elongated-box forms that dominated human, Krag, Pfelung, and most other species' design, the Vaaach vessel was a long, narrow, flattened wedge with a sharp bow and angled corners at the stern that bent back toward the central drive unit like a giant, barbed spear point aimed threateningly at the comparatively tiny Union destroyer.

"Sir," said Tactical. It had to be more bad news. "They've locked some sort of antimatter cannon on us. I'm pretty sure that one shot would, well…"

"I get the picture. We'll just have to convince them not to shoot, now, won't we?"

"Ready to transmit, visual, aural, or text," prompted Chin, a bit too eagerly.

"Negative. Not when we're dealing with the Vaaach. They've got us. It would be…impertinent to speak without being spoken to. Here's the way this plays out." He tried to make it sound like plot summary for a trid vid comedy program. "They're going to let us hang here for about a minute and a half so that there will be just enough time for it to sink in how helpless we are and how we are entirely at their mercy, but not enough time for us to detect any weakness they might have and start to formulate a plan to get away. Then they'll hail us on visual. They don't care if the standard protocol for interspecies communication is text. They're carnivores who hunt by sight, so they like to lay eyes on who they are talking to. Or who they might be having for dinner. They like to use channel 7. The forest victor, or grove guardian, or tree tamer, or whatever his title is will engage us in witty blood-and-guts warrior banter, after which they'll either let us go with their blessing or blast us to dust with that antimatter cannon."

Bhattacharyya at Intel snorted softly. It was clear that the captain had asked for that briefing on the Vaaach to educate Bhattacharyya, not Robichaux. "Captain?" he interjected quietly.

"Yes, Bhattacharyya?"

"So, you've encountered the Vaaach before?"

"Let's just say for now that we've met and I'm still alive to give evasive answers about the experience," Max answered, evasively.

Ninety-four seconds elapsed on the chrono before Chin said, "Captain, we are being hailed. Visual. Channel 7."

"Let's see it."

Several screens in CIC cut to an image of a large, brownish-gray, furry face with a small black nose and white fluffy tufts where the ears would go on an Earth mammal. The Vaaach looked like an overgrown Koala bear, except for the penetrating intelligence in its yellow-green eyes, the forty-five-centimeter-wide mouth from which protruded six 20-centimeter fangs, and the 10-centimeter claws with which it was grooming the fur on its forearm. A forearm that Max knew to be twice the diameter of his own neck.

The average Vaaach was just over four-and-a-half-meters tall, weighed roughly three-quarters of a ton, and armed with nothing but claws, teeth, and attitude could easily take down a fully grown grizzly bear. The grooming gesture gave Max hope. It usually represented mild condescension with a hint of rebuke, as to a wayward but promising cub.

A series of roaring sounds, interspersed with growls and snarls, thundered from the audio outputs around the room. This lasted for about fifteen seconds. Then the computer produced a translation text on a screen beside the image of the Vaaach, complete with supposedly helpful explanations, set off by brackets, of terms and cultural references. The Vaaach sat, regarding the camera placidly while it allowed the humans to read the translation.

"I am Forest Victor [a rank believed to be equivalent to a senior captain or a commodore] Chrrrlgrf of the Vaaach sovereignty, son of the perilous Rawlrrhfr Forest, slayer with these claws of the strangling Targruf [a forty-meter-long anaconda-like snake, strong enough to crush a ground car, that lives deep in the Rawlrrhfr Forest and is believed to kill several hundred adult Vaaach per year], and victorious commander at the Battle of Hrlrgr [a fleet engagement against Species 9, fought on 8 August 2313, involving more than seventy-five capital ships and resulting in a decisive victory for the Vaaach]. I greet you, tiny, pink, clawless, fangless, furless human, child of the ridiculous gibbering monkeys that so amuse us in our zoos. Identify yourself and state your purpose in straying so far from the trees out of which your ancestors so foolishly descended."

This had to be done exactly right. Max made a subtle hand gesture that the computer would recognize as a command to include his whole body in the imager shot. He stood, drew his boarding cutlass, and held it across his chest in a kind of salute.

"I am Lieutenant Commander Maxime Tindall Robichaux, Union Space Navy, fierce son of planet Nouvelle Acadiana, a dangerous world completely infested with carnivorous reptilian alligators and swarming with venomous snakes." A minor exaggeration: the snakes and alligators generally avoid the polar regions.

"A frigate under my personal command has vanquished a Krag battlecruiser of superior force and I have personally slain seventeen Krag with the steel you see before you, two before the sap of manhood had risen in my limbs. My people are at war with the Krag. We go to attack their ships in neutral space. We intend no harm to any Vaaach, nor shall we venture anywhere near your dread sovereignty."

The Vaaach replied with more pissed-off lion and bear sounds, this time consisting of more deep bass rumbling and low snarls. Somehow, Max got the impression that the tension level had just dropped a notch. The translation appeared.

"The Vaaach have nothing to fear from your feeble little vessel, so do not waste our time convincing us that you are not a threat to us. We can see that at a glance. You state that you travel to meet the Krag in battle. Good. They are skilled opponents, but not worthy ones. They begin wars without declaring them. They kill the innocent for no purpose. They take what they do not need. If your purpose is to kill them, we would not hinder that. The more of them you kill, the more pleased we shall be. Why, though, did you follow our vessel, like a blood-drinking pest riding a predator's tail? This act does not appear to show the respect that one hunter gives another."

"Dread Forest Victor, many of my crew have never seen the face of the enemy and have neither drawn his blood nor had theirs drawn. Stalking skills must be practiced against a wily target or, when the trail of the true prey is found, it will elude the stalker and vanish into the trees."

Max watched as the eyes of the huge alien warrior read the translation of his words. The black nose wrinkled twice, which Max thought was the equivalent of a nod. The claws stopped grooming the arm fur. The Vaaach held his claws with the points aimed at his own face and seemed to inspect their sharpness. A few rumbles ensued, followed by several low, almost relaxed roars.

"So, you seek to sharpen your claws on us before you sink them into the entrails of your enemy. It is very likely that your claws are longer than your fangs, but your goal is worthy. Your stalking was not proficient, but neither was it entirely unskillful. We will not kill you. At least, not on this hunt. Now, go forth to kill Krag. We may even amuse ourselves by leaving some of its fur behind so that you may take the scent. But do not stalk us again, lest we kill you for your monkey impertinence. This transmission ends now."

The screen went blank, the grappling field disengaged, and the huge warship drew away from the *Cumberland* at astonishing speed.

Still alive.

"Maneuvering, resume course to the jump point, point four five c. Comms, check all EM records for the last few seconds of that transmission for something buried in that message. If there's nothing there, have the computer folks run a file survey and see if there's any new data that we didn't put there. I think the mighty forest victor just sent us a present."

"Aye, sir," answered both Maneuvering and Comms.

"Let me know when you find it. I'll be in my quarters. XO, you have CIC."

"Aye, sir. I have CIC."

Max needed to change uniforms. It would not do for the rest of the men in CIC to get a whiff of his sour, cold sweat.

CHAPTER 7

19:12Z Hours, 22 January 2315

Two more jumps, no more surprises. One of the systems had contained a few civilian freighters making their slow way between jump points at 0.08 c. That was in a system popularly known as Merrick's Crossing because a disoriented navigator named Austin Merrick had accidently discovered that the system had six instead of the expected three jump points. None of them went anywhere particularly important, but one of the lesser routes between some marginal asteroid mines and some equally marginal foundry planets did traverse the system, which is why the freighters were there.

The steadily improving Sensors section speedily and accurately identified the freighters; Comms extracted the registry and flight plan information from their transponders; and Weapons practiced generating firing solutions on them and simulated their destruction with simulated weapons, resulting in not-so-simulated jubilation from the personnel involved.

Max alternated between studying the service records of the three chiefs who tried to sabotage his ship and the bizarre service history of the ship itself, when his comm buzzed. He hit the button. "Skipper here."

"Sir, this is Rochefort in Crypto. Compu section found that Easter egg you were looking for. Somehow the Vaaach managed to write it into our database of space traffic control system approach protocols, but we've run every decrypt routine we have on it, and we can't even tell what type of file it is, much less read it."

"Rochefort, what do you know about Vaaach maps?

"Nothing, sir."

"They aren't your run of the mill maps. They show two projections. One is the one we are all used to seeing, of a static display of the position of objects, and the other is a changing perspective following the point of view of the traveler as he moves along various routes. Try decrypting the file as something like that instead of a standard text or numerical message."

"Aye, sir. Rochefort out."

The perspective changes as you go, Max said to himself. He took a sip of his coffee, gone cold hours ago. Somehow, probably when he had first poured it, Max had sloshed a bit of the coffee on the outside of the mug, where it had run down the side and formed a ring around the base. Max had seen thousands of such rings over the years, yet this one held his gaze. Though consisting of the tiniest amount of coffee, somehow the mysterious physics of surface tension and capillary action had managed to distribute the spill into an even circle that went all around the base of where the mug had been, with no part of the ring holding more coffee than any other. It was very close to geometric perfection, and yet, had a man taken that same amount of coffee and tried to draw a perfect circle on the desk with the coffee spread evenly all the way around, Max was certain that the man with all his intelligence would fail where unthinking physics succeeded brilliantly.

Max wiped up the coffee with his napkin, pulled his keyboard toward him, and typed a short order.

Less than five minutes later, the XO, Dr. Sahin, Lieutenant Brown, and Major Kraft were sitting in Max's day cabin, sipping coffee. It was the first time he had brought together these four men, whose posts traditionally made them a sort of "kitchen cabinet" or "brain trust" for a ship's captain. Some skippers met extensively with these officers or a subset of them, whereas others tended to make decisions on their own. Max had no idea what his natural command style was. All he knew was that at this hour, on this day, he wanted the benefit of their opinions.

"Gentlemen, I have brought you together so that we can discuss an item of great concern to me. Because this is the first time we have met, I want to make clear what my rules are for these gatherings. You are absolutely free to say whatever is on your mind, without any regard for rank. Everything we say here is unofficial, off the record, and is never to be repeated to anyone under any circumstances. You will never be questioned or be made to explain or answer for anything that happens in this room. And I, personally, will never hold against you any opinion that you state here. You are, therefore, expected to give me the benefit of your entirely candid, unguarded, and forthright views. Further, I expect everyone here to abide by these same rules. Do I have your agreement?

"XO?"

"Damn straight."

"Doctor?"

"Indeed."

"Major?"

"*Jawohl.*"

"Wernher?"

"Quite right."

"Very well, then. As you know, we recently apprehended three senior chiefs trying to sabotage the atmosphere processor manifold so that we would have to abort the mission. The major has interrogated these men and is convinced that they're not working for any foreign power, but that their actions indicate a concern that the crew and this ship's new commander are not equal to the mission we have been assigned. Simply put, they were convinced that the mission would end in certain death, and they sought to save their own lives and the lives of their shipmates. I would like to talk about what to do with these men." Kraft opened his mouth as if to speak. Max halted him with his upraised hand.

"Before anyone voices their opinion on this subject, I think a few facts need to be put before you. All of us are new to this ship, so none of us know firsthand how this ship got to be the way it is. I've been through the files, and Admiral Hornmeyer made some records available to me that I would not otherwise be able to see. Together they tell an interesting story. It is a story you should hear.

"You all know about the chaotic first years of the war and how they led to the appointment of the inspector generals, including Captain Borman." It was familiar but uncomfortable lore: how the beginning of the war was marked by defeat after defeat, fleets withdrawing in disarray, ships rushed into battle from the yards unfinished, virtually untrained men being led straight to their deaths, poor discipline, chaotic logistics, ships in space for years at a time with spacers denied leave and living in horrible conditions, irregular pay, inedible food, and borderline mutinous morale. Just as it seemed these problems might destroy the Navy before the Krag could do the job, the chief of naval operations appointed five inspectors general with almost complete power to clean up the mess. One of those inspectors was the famous or, perhaps more accurately, infamous

Captain Frederick Joseph Borman, reputed to be the toughest man in the Navy. Certainly the most feared.

"Now, here's the part you don't know. In order to conduct his famous surprise inspections and snap evaluations, not only did Borman have to be able to get around the entire theater of operations, he had to be able to get around quickly and secretly. The only way to do that was to give him his own ship. It had to be fast enough that he could cover a lot of ground and it had to be reasonably powerful so that it could fight its way out of trouble if the Krag penetrated the battle planes and ambushed it, which is the sort of thing that happened all the time back then.

"So they gave him one of the best designs to come out of that period, a *Rubicon* class destroyer, the USS *Seine*, whose skipper was—you guessed it—a young lieutenant commander named Allen K. Oscar. As you can imagine, with an IG on board, the *Seine* wasn't a fighting ship. She was more of an admiral's yacht. Oscar and his crew learned, probably under Borman's direction, to make their ship an example of perfect cleanliness, polish, and obsessive physical perfection. And because Oscar probably suffered from some minor form of mental disorder, these tendencies became more exaggerated every year. And why not? The *Seine* never saw combat and was too busy playing taxi to Captain Borman to participate in exercises, so her deficiencies were well concealed. No one knew that her missiles gleamed but couldn't hit a target.

"Then, when Borman retired and the now obsolete *Seine* was converted into a training vessel, Oscar and his crew—who had gotten stratospherically high fitness reports from Borman—were reassigned en masse to a new destroyer, the *Cumberland*.

"Obviously, if BuPers had possessed the merest whiff of a glimmer of a hint of a clue as to how FUBAR this ship was, Oscar would have been given a desk job or been sent to one of those hospitals with lots of grass and trees and birds, where they don't let the patients have any sharp objects. They would have broken up the crew, retrained the men, and scattered them all over the fleet. But no, that's not what happened because, based on the sacred and holy fitness reports done by Inspector General Borman himself, this was an exemplary crew who should be kept together in a new command to preserve their fighting efficiency.

"As if that wasn't enough of a prescription for disaster, I will also tell you that Captain Oscar and his XO Pang were both exceptionally abusive. Both had a habit of berating the men *for as long as an hour and a half*, singly and in groups, in the most insulting terms. When you add to that Oscar's habit of throwing men in the brig for arbitrary reasons, you have a crew that has been greatly traumatized and has been put under enormous stress. It is so bad that, even though this vessel has not seen action in eight months, the men all have scores on the Reed-Brannon Psycho-Physiological Stress Test that make it look like they've been in continuous combat for months. Now, bearing *that* in mind, what should we do with them?"

There was a long silence, lasting the better part of a minute, as the officers pondered what they had just heard. Garcia spoke first.

"I sympathize with them. I've seen a lot of what you're talking about. The rot on this ship runs deep, and this crew should have been broken up and reassigned. But I don't trust these three. Not for a minute. So what if they've got squirrels in their attic? It just means that they're more likely to do some other crazy thing some other time, like when we're even farther from home or just as we enter combat. Given our destination and our mission, it's just too dangerous to give them the run of the ship.

"Our objective comes first, the safety of this crew and this ship second, and what we feel for these men—men who, I admit, have had a very difficult time—comes a very, very poor third.

My loyalty is with the men who did their duty, not with the ones who—whatever their intentions—were giving aid and comfort to the Krag. Remember that we have aboard 212 men who have been through everything these three men have been through, but who did not betray their shipmates by trying to sabotage the life support systems in their own vessel.

"I say leave them in the brig for the duration, and then present them for court martial when we get back to the task force. They can be Admiral Hornmeyer's problem, or the judge advocate's, or the fleet headshrinker's. This is one time we should pass the buck—somebody else made the problem, so let somebody else solve it. We have enough problems of our own."

"I'm sorry, but I don't feel for them at all," Major Kraft said. "The enemy is supposed to be out there," he jabbed his finger at the stars showing through the viewport, "not in here. Traitors are traitors. Reasons don't matter. Let them be an example—you can't betray your ship and your shipmates, no matter what the reason, no matter what was done to you. You always have a choice. Loyalty to the Union. Loyalty to your shipmates. Or treason. In the final analysis, it really *is* that simple. We should carry out the law and execute them. Today. Before another hour passes. Swift and certain execution will leave no doubt for others about what choices *they* should make."

Sahin shook his head. "Yes, they committed treason. Of that there is no doubt. But did they have a choice? Did they *truly* have a choice? Or did Captain Oscar and the inspector general twist these men's minds and souls into such knots that they couldn't think for themselves any more? Maybe they were so traumatized and mentally beaten and threatened and manipulated that, in certain situations, they were deprived of their power to choose what to do and could act only under the constraint of internal compulsion.

"We must remember, gentlemen, that this is a ship that fled the enemy twice and that when it fought simulated battles against other ships, it lost and was ruled to be destroyed. Every time. These men were operating under the certainty that if this ship with this crew faced the enemy, they would all certainly die. Under those circumstances, were they capable of doing anything other than what they did? If not, then they did not *choose* to be traitors and we cannot in good conscience punish them.

"Punishment should follow as a consequence for a wrongful choice—for a malicious and evil exercise of the will. If you take away a man's choice and deprive him of his will, then punishment is unjust, and executing him would be a travesty of justice. These men were not fully responsible for their actions. We cannot simply toss them out an airlock or shoot them."

"All of you are forgetting something," Brown said. "These men all stand the same station. They are the number one missile fire control technicians for the Blue, Gold, and White watches. They are each other's reliefs and replacements. The only way they were all able to be away from that station at the same time was that Larch-Thau had a utility man standing in for him. Now, every man with a Comet is certified as being able to operate missile fire control systems, but these men are the experts on the nuts and bolts, the subassemblies and the workarounds. They are best qualified to maintain, calibrate, troubleshoot, and repair those systems if damaged.

"If we take a hit to that part of the ship and have to rebuild fire control from spares, those are the men I would assign to do it. There are others who could probably work it out from the schematics in the database, but it would take them ten times as long as our traitors. My department cannot spare—this *ship* cannot spare—these men.

"Captain, you should know that if you execute all three, it will be my duty under naval regulations to request formally that we return to the Task Force and obtain replacement personnel, because loss of them will impair our combat readiness. And I will do the same if you leave them locked in the brig for the duration. I need them on duty."

"But, Lieutenant," Major Kraft said, "this becomes an issue only if fire control takes severe damage. When was the last time you were on a ship that had to rebuild fire control from spares? I've never heard of anyone doing it. I can't see twisting the arms of justice to preserve our ability to deal with a very remote contingency. If you're worried about it, take a few of your best men from the most similar system—pulse cannon fire control, for example—and give them a crash training course in what these fellows did. That will replace much of what you will be losing. Enough, at least, to cover this remote eventuality."

The captain raised a silencing hand. "Gentlemen, I thank you for your views. They have clarified my thinking on this issue. My strong personal inclination is in line with Major Kraft. I cannot abide treason and feel that the wages of treason are death. But my personal wishes can't be decisive here. These men are valuable to this ship, and they're valuable to the Navy. I believe that there's a lot to what the Doctor said here as well—that these men have been damaged in such a way that their choices weren't their own in many ways." He turned to Dr. Sahin meaningfully, "Not in *all* ways, mind you. But I don't want to be the final judge of that.

"The needs of the ship come first. I aim to return them to duty." Kraft started to say something. Max stopped him with a warning index finger. "I aim to return them to duty *under strict guard*. They are confined to quarters when off duty. When on duty, they will remain under observation by an armed Marine, and they will be kept away from any systems other than the one to which they are assigned. We will turn them over to the authorities when we return to the fleet. Admiral Hornmeyer and the Judge

Advocate will decide these men's ultimate fate. Until then, I want you to examine them, Doctor, and to give me a sense of the state of their mental health. I also want to meet with them and impress upon them the seriousness of their position, that if they go astray again, they will be shown the airlock, but that they also are being given a chance for forgiveness and redemption.

"Men, many of our ancestors believed that lost souls could be reclaimed and find redemption through the power of mercy, love, and understanding. That's one of the central teachings of my faith, as well. I'm a warrior, and my areas of expertise are conflict and death. But I'm willing to try my hand at something different for the sake of these men. They are our shipmates. They deserve the best we can give them. I will not cast them into the darkness unless I have no other choice. Dismissed."

Dr. Sahin remained seated as the rest of the men filed out of the compartment. "Captain, may I have a word with you?"

"Sure, Doctor, what's on your mind?"

"You issued a set of separate written orders to each senior officer, including me."

"Yes. I wrote them before I assumed command. Is there a problem with any of those orders?"

"Not at all. I find them very sensible indeed. They were things that I would have done in any case, but your order makes it easier to get them done—they are now captain's orders. It makes them a priority."

"What of my orders, Doctor?"

"As you recall, one of the things I was ordered to do was to review the medical records of the ship's complement to determine whether anyone had any special medical needs that were not being adequately addressed. I am constrained to point out to you that there is one such person on board who has a severe and unmet medical need that may adversely affect his ability to carry out his duties. I believe that he requires treatment immediately or his performance is likely to begin to deteriorate rapidly to such a degree that within a very short time he may become unfit for duty."

"Can the treatment he needs be provided on the *Cumberland*?"

"Yes. He can receive all the treatment he needs on board."

"Then he must begin to receive the proper treatment at once."

"I suspect that he may be resistant to this course of action."

"Then he must be ordered to submit to treatment. As I said just a minute ago, the needs of the ship come first. Who is this person?"

"His name is Robichaux. Maxime Tindall Robichaux."

"Doctor," Max sputtered. "There must be some kind of error. I was slightly—*very* slightly—wounded during my last deployment and received treatment from one of your colleagues on board the *Halsey*. I was thoroughly examined and found to be in perfect health back in mid-November and again just a few days ago. There's absolutely nothing wrong with me."

"Really? Are you sure about that? Captain, as you may recall, I saw your reaction when a comm panel alert signal interrupted you. I recognized that response immediately and did some extensive research into your medical records, service records, and other pieces of the digital puzzle we all leave behind as we live our lives in the service. I have also watched you very carefully since then. The pattern is undeniable. If you are to sit there and tell me that there is absolutely nothing wrong with you, then you must be telling me that you are not experiencing nightmares, disturbed sleep, exaggerated startle responses, emotional volatility, pain in the extremities, an irrational need to avoid sitting with your back to any room with people in it, difficulty trusting others, and profound feelings of worthlessness and inadequacy. Do I understand that to be your contention?"

Max felt an internal lurch, followed by a sense of vertigo, as though he were riding in an elevator that suddenly dropped three stories. He could literally feel the blood draining from his face. He said softly, "I've never reported any of those symptoms, Doctor."

"But you are *experiencing* them nonetheless, aren't you?" Realizing that he had sounded as though he were cross-examining the captain, he adopted a more sympathetic tone. "Please, sir, I am not asking for the benefit of any report, but because as a physician I have sworn an oath to alleviate human suffering, and I have every reason to believe that you are suffering. Further, as you said yourself, the needs of the ship come first. In the coming days, this ship and this crew are going to need a commanding officer who is not coping with the additional burdens imposed by serious emotional impairment. Captain… Max, you have done me more than one kindness in these past few days. Let me do you a kindness. I know what you are experiencing. I am an extremely acute observer. I miss very little."

Max sat silently, of two minds. He had survived and functioned all these years by keeping these problems sealed off behind a heavy pressure bulkhead. But as a perceptive leader, Max knew enough about how the human mind worked to know that under the added stresses of command, that bulkhead might be starting to crack. Perhaps this brilliant physician was already starting to see the signs. This wasn't just about him any more. Max realized that his mind, his intellect, his judgment, were the most critical systems on board.

"Doctor, I will not lie to you. The things you describe are a part of my life. But I've lived with them ever since I can remember. They're a part of me. I don't know what they are or how they might be connected, and I don't know what you or anyone else can do about them."

"Captain, these things are not disconnected from one another. Together, they are all symptoms of post-traumatic stress disorder.

I believe they stem from two events in your childhood that I know of, and perhaps other events of which I do not know."

"Absurd. You can't mean to tell me that I'm today, at age twenty-eight, having trouble sleeping and jump at sudden noises because of something that happened when I was thirteen or fourteen."

"No, I do not mean to tell you that. I do mean to tell you that you are today having trouble sleeping and are jumping at sudden noises because of events that transpired when you were eight, and when you were ten."

The emotional elevator dropped another three floors. "Oh, you mean…"

"Exactly, Captain. I have pieced it together from hints in your jacket, peculiar turns of phrase you have used in your After Action Statements, reports, orders, and memoranda, from things I have seen you do or heard you say, and from news items. It is all very subtle, but the conclusions are plain for anyone with eyes to see them.

"At age eight, you were not merely orphaned by the Gynophage. You were horrifically, searingly scarred by it." Sahin did not relish what he was about to say, but he knew that this man's defenses would shrug off anything less than a brutally vivid explanation. "If I am not mistaken, on the first day of the attack, you were at home with your mother and your sisters when the weapon struck. You, an eight-year-old boy who had never seen physical disease or severe pain in your life, helpless, unable to summon assistance over the jammed communication systems, *watched* as your mother died in screaming, writhing agony before your very eyes. Unless I miss my guess, she pleaded with you to help her, and all you were able to do was to stand by and watch her die. Am I right?"

"Yes." A whisper.

"Then, before you could find another adult to help you and before your father got home—was it only an hour or two later?—you watched the same thing happen to your twin sisters, infants less than a year old. You were just as helpless, equally alone. Your father came home *six hours later* and found you with only corpses for company. From what I can tell, he was shattered emotionally. So he sent you into space a scant two weeks later. The chief medical officer of the *San Jacinto* noted in his log that you were dehydrated and malnourished from having hardly eaten or drunk for what he guessed to be about two weeks. Captain Lo noted that you hardly spoke a word to anyone for nearly a month after you came on board.

"Then, sixteen months later, your world came apart around you again when your new home, the cruiser *San Jacinto,* was boarded and your new family, its crew, killed by the Krag. All but a few of its crew of more than four hundred perished. According to the citation that Commodore Middleton wrote when he awarded you the Navy and Marine Achievement Medal, you hid in the air ducts and access crawlways and eluded them for twenty-six days, stealing food from the cargo holds and drinking from the water reclamation units.

"I suspect very strongly that you watched with your own eyes—through the vent gratings perhaps?—as the Krag tortured your shipmates for information or merely tortured and killed them because we all know that is what the Krag do. And they hunted you, day and night, did they not? Relentlessly. Day after day; exhausting, sleepless night after night. Is it any wonder that you continually wake in the middle of the night, screaming, drenched in sweat, dreaming of being pursued?

"Finally, by a miracle, the ship was retaken by Union forces, and you were found. According to what you said during your lengthy debriefing, when you heard human voices in the corridor, you sprang out of an air duct and hacked off the arms of two Krag from behind with a boarding cutlass you grabbed from an arms locker when the Krag boarded the ship. You carry that same boarding cutlass to this day. My guess is that you sleep with it near your bed, and you like to have it within reach whenever you are under stress. I ask you, sir, with every kindness, am I incorrect as to any material fact?"

Long pause. "No. You're not." He shook his head, stunned by the accuracy of the doctor's deductions. "Even if you're right, though, what can be done? I have a ship to command. I've no time to engage in extensive self-examination and navel gazing. I don't have endless hours to spend lying on a couch in your office, talking about my dreams and telling you what I see in ink blots."

"There is no couch in my office. Perhaps I should requisition one. But no, I do not propose any of those things you see in those overdone trid vids. After all, as you can see, I have no beard, no Viennese accent, and no cigar. We would start by just talking. We would work around your schedule—perhaps we would talk over dinner now and then, much as friends would. Let me be your confidante. I can listen to you. You have not even admitted much of what you are experiencing to yourself, much less expressed it to another human being. By speaking to me about it, you will be teaching yourself about your feelings as well. Unburden yourself to me from time to time. My guess is that you have never had a true, confidential friend. You need one. Let me fill that role."

The two men sat together in silence for several seconds.

The comm buzzed.

Max stabbed the button. "Skipper."

"Captain, this is Rochefort in Crypto. You were right. The data is a cartographic file, not text. And you've *got* to see this."

"On my way." Max smiled. "Later, Doctor." Pause. "Ibrahim."

"It's Bram. My friends call me Bram.'"

CHAPTER 8

23:07Z Hours, 22 January 2315

"Hey, Starry, it just happened again." Recruit Spacer First Class Siersma made that announcement in the standard naval issue area broadcast voice—a voice seemingly possessed by all military personnel of all services going back at least to the time of Pharaoh Thutmose III, not much louder than ordinary speech and not nearly as loud as a shout, but one that is clearly audible across even the largest room even though filled with humming, buzzing, whirring equipment.

"What happened again, Peapod?" Petty Officer Third Class Starcevik responded in the same kind of voice. "Peapod" was a reference to the hue of the SCUs and working uniforms issued to recruit spacers, a thoroughly repulsive shade between that of bread mold and the algae that grows on the surface of cesspools. "You managed to find the enlisted head without wandering into the galley?"

"Now, Starry, you know that happened only that one time the day I was transferred on board. Anyway, most exalted petty officer, sir, this is important. I just picked up another decoherence event

TO HONOR YOU CALL US

in one of the compression phase regulator feedback streams. It's the number four again."

All business now, Starcevik stepped quickly across the ten meters that separated his station from Siersma's. "Play it back."

Siersma instructed the console to locate and replay the performance visualization for regulator stream coherence during the time period in question. "What speed?"

"Let's have it at one one-thousandth," he responded after a judicious pause.

"You got it." Siersma entered a few commands. Within a few seconds, one of the displays on his console showed an animated graphic representing the phase, frequency, and polarization coherence of the feedback stream. Initially, it showed a tightly packed bunch of sine waves of precisely the same bland yellow color, stacked neatly one atop the other, with their peaks and valleys lining up with near perfection. Then the pattern suddenly broke down into a jumble of waveforms of different sizes, their sinuous curves out of step with one another, and the lines representing them on the display shining out in an array of different colors. This chaos lasted for a few seconds of playback time, after which the wave forms settled back into their orderly march across the screen.

"Yep, that's a triple decoherence, all right. How many does that make?"

"Four in the last three hours," Siersma answered. "This is the longest. Duration of 3.7 milliseconds. And—"

"And four milliseconds is the longest the unit can handle without possibly triggering a compression phase anomaly," Starcevik finished. "Well, it sounds like the regulator buffer is starting to go. Damn thing is supposed to have a service life of fifteen hundred hours, and it's got fewer than two hundred. I guess we've got ourselves a defective unit. Shit. We've got to swap it out, but we're not going to be dropping to sublight for hours, and we can't wait that long. If we lose the compression phase modulator while we're on the compression drive…"

Siersma nodded soberly and started to narrate in a voice copied from hundreds of educational trid vids: "In a brilliant flash of light, the *Cumberland* Gap is suddenly and beautifully transformed into the small but astronomically interesting Cumberland Nebula—only a few hundred kilometers across, but packed with a higher than normal concentration of aluminum and titanium from the ship, not to mention lots of carbon and nitrogen from you and me."

"Right. Very funny. So that means a hot swap. Rhim's the man who's had the practice performing that lovely operation. He's off checking a power conduit somewhere. I'll get him in here to take care of it."

Starcevik walked back to his three-meter-long console, slid his seat down the retaining rail past two and a half meters of compression drive controls and status displays until it was in front of the I/O terminal, and typed in a command to the computer to send Spacer Rhim a message on his percom summoning him to that compartment. He then opened a voice channel to the Master Engineering Control Center (MECC, pronounced "meck"), notified Chief Engineer Brown of the situation, and received from him the pro forma "order" to do what he was already preparing to get done.

Just over nineteen minutes later, Rhim strolled into the compartment. "You sure took your sweet time getting here," Starcevik snapped. "I was less than a minute from calling the COB and having him send a Marine to find you and frog march your sorry ass in here. It's a small ship. You should have been here in five minutes, tops. What the *hell* too you so long?"

It took a full five seconds before Rhim answered. "Sorry, Petty Officer, I was tracing a fault along one of the conduits and was

TO HONOR YOU CALL US

near the access for one of the main fusion reactor cooling pumps. It's a little noisy in there and I didn't hear the percom beep."

That's why it vibrates as well as beeps, dumbass. But the petty officer said nothing. Starcevik was more interested in getting the buffer swapped out than he was in addressing Rhim's increasingly sluggish attention to his duties. He explained what he needed and the three men made everything ready for the hot swap.

As the junior man present, Siersma went to Spares, obtained the regulator buffer, and input its serial number so that the ship's computer would "know" that the part had been replaced and could factor its unique performance, ever so slightly different from the part it replaced, into its management of the ship. He unboxed the part and set it on top of a table/cart near the compression drive phase regulator. Starcevik and Rhim removed the main access cover from the compression drive phase regulator, after which the two men took off the smaller cover for the number four feedback stream conduit.

This action revealed a two-and-a-quarter-meter-long conduit, like a tube cut in half lengthwise. From one end to the other ran a bluish purple strand of high energy coherently modulated tachyogravitons. Inside the stream was a gleaming metallic rod just like the one resting on the cart—the regulator buffer. Rhim picked up the replacement unit in one hand and picked up a wrench in the other. He squinted at the numbers engraved on the tool.

"Yep, Rhim, I checked it," said Siersma. "It's a twenty-four-centimeter wrench, and the part's wrench fitting is sized at twenty-four centimeters."

Rhim nodded.

Starcevik looked at him gravely. "Now remember, Rhim, when we shut down the stream, you've got eight seconds. At the end of eight seconds, the unit will automatically restart the stream. There's nothing we can do to stop it, other than shutting down the unit and dropping the ship to sublight. But you've done this a dozen times before with no trouble. This time will be a cinch. So, you ready?

Again after a few seconds' delay, Rhim answered, "Affirmative. I'm ready."

"All right." He strode briskly over to his console and, remaining standing, pulled up the touch panel that controlled the feedback modulator. He looked up at Rhim over the waist high console.

"I know you're an old hat at this procedure, but I'm going to go over how we're going to do this to make sure we're all tied into the same data channel. I'm going to give you a countdown from five to zero, shutting down the stream at 'zero.' Then, I'm going to give you a count up to eight. You've got to have your hand out of there at 'eight' because those dang tach-gravs do some nasty shit to human tissue, all right?"

Rhim just stared at him blankly.

"Hey, Rhim, get your head back in the game. We're not playing spacers and rat-faces here. Do you understand the procedure?"

"Uh, sure, Petty Officer. Like you said, I've done it a dozen times."

"All right," Starcevik said doubtfully. "Siersma, you get over there and stand by to help him if he needs it." Starcevik doubted that Siersma or anyone else could provide any meaningful assistance during the eight seconds that the task would take, but he felt better having the bright, young greenie there. Siersma moved over so that he was standing on Rhim's right, half a meter from where he was going to perform the swap.

"You sure you're ready?" Starcevik asked.

Rhim nodded and said, "Ready, Petty Officer."

"All right, I'm about to start the countdown." He keyed the clock he had programmed at his console to display, counting down from five and up to eight. "Five. Four. Three. Two. One. Zero. Stream is off."

Nothing. At "zero" Starcevik expected instantaneous action from Rhim. Instead, he stood there frozen. Starcevik forced his eyes back to the clock. The digit changed. "One." Finally Rhim started to move, reaching into the conduit. "Two." It looked as though Rhim was struggling to get the wrench seated on the buffer. "Three." He had it seated and was rotating it to the "remove" position, which was three quarters of a turn from the "operate" position in which Rhim had found it. "Four." Rhim removed his hands from the conduit, carrying the buffer and the wrench.

"Five." Siersma took the old buffer from Rhim and handed him the replacement part. "Six," Starcevik said with a note of urgency. Rhim reached back inside the conduit, seated the buffer and put the wrench on it. "Seven." He rotated the buffer from "remove" to "operate." When he tried to lift the wrench from the buffer, it wouldn't move. The wrench fitting on this unit was ever so slightly larger that on the other unit. Rhim pulled with all his strength. The wrench came loose and Rhim began to pull his hands out of the conduit. His left hand cleared the unit but his right was slightly behind. "Eight."

At "eight" the stream started to power up, sending a trickle of tachyo-gravitons down the conduit. Rhim's hand was caught in the edge of the stream's fifty-centimeter-wide path. The pain was excruciating and, reflexively, he dropped the wrench, staggering back from the unit just as the unit's stream containment field came up to full power. Rhim was free of the unit and apparently uninjured. The problem was that the unit was not designed to operate with a 1.37 kilogram drop forged vanadium steel wrench in the particle stream. Siersma and Starcevik realized at the same moment that the wrench was in the particle stream. While Siersma, who knew something bad was about to happen but had not yet figured out what, frantically searched his memory for everything he knew about tachyo-gravitons, the petty officer reached for his console as fast as he could to initiate an emergency shut-down of the compression drive in order to avert disaster.

Disaster was faster.

Although the tachyo-gravitons flowed freely through the carbon-carborundum composite nanofiber lined conduit, they had an affinity for ferrous metals. As a result, the wrench began to capture the particles that continued to zoom around inside the molecular recesses of the alloy from which the wrench was made, careening through the spaces between the electron shells without losing their inherent faster than light velocities. Before long, the wrench had acquired a tach-grav polarity matching that of the particles in the stream.

As with magnetic and electrical charges, the stream and the wrench repelled each other, causing the wrench to be pressed against the edge of the containment field with ever-increasing force. Unfortunately for all concerned, the forces generated by tachyo-graviton repulsion, as one might expect from the knowledge that these are the particles that allow the compression of space-time to propel tens of thousands of metric tons of warship through space at well over a thousand times the speed of light, were extraordinarily powerful.

Siersma figured out what was going to come next and, not trusting to Rhim's glacial reflexes, simply tackled the man right above the knees, knocking him to the deck; he landed with a surprised "Ooof."

Inside the conduit, after 2.42 seconds the repulsive force overcame the containment field and the wrench shot out of the conduit like a howitzer shell, passing through the space occupied a split second before by Rhim's chest. Making a distinct, ear-splitting *CRACK* as it broke the sound barrier and ripped through the air at Mach 8.9, it created a powerful shock wave that knocked all three men in the compartment to the deck, leaving them stunned. The wrench then rocketed its way through two engineering consoles, passed through the compartment's bulkhead like a rifle bullet through cheap plywood, transited the corridor, which thankfully was empty, and punched its way into Engineering Maintenance Equipment Storage Compartment #2. There the errant wrench, travelling with a slight down angle, passed down the main aisle between the storage racks and struck the destroyer's outer hull near the intersection between the hull and the compartment's lower bulkhead, or floor.

As the hull was designed to withstand anything short of a direct hit from a thermonuclear warhead, there was no chance that the wrench would penetrate it, particularly since the earlier collisions had slowed the wrench to the comparatively sedate velocity of Mach 7.2, and atmospheric compression heating had begun to soften the metal. Rather, when the wrench struck the hull, its kinetic energy was instantly converted into thermal energy, much as with a meteor strike, vaporizing the wrench in an explosion with a force equal to several hand grenades, filling the room with a fog of molten steel droplets and incandescent vaporized iron. Every piece of combustible material in the compartment caught fire in less than a second.

For Ensign Bhattacharyya in CIC, taking only his second turn as Officer of the Deck, what had been an exceptionally dull watch suddenly became very exciting. Being a bit of a nonconformist, he was drinking jasmine-scented green tea from his own personal mug when the deck took a sickening lurch, sending his tea nearly to the ceiling before it rained all over the now thankfully unoccupied XO's station. Bhattacharrya reflexively spun his chair 120 degrees to the right to face the row of systems consoles.

"I have a commanded emergency compression drive shutdown," Chief Supangat announced from the Engineering console. "Source is the compression drive equipment-room primary control console. It appears to be an authorized command. No reason known at this time. I will now attempt to ascertain the reason by voice channel."

"Very well," said Bhattacharyya reflexively, knowing this to be the correct procedure and wondering what the hell was going on.

Then, from the row of Emergency Control Stations another forty-five-degree turn of the CO's chair to the right came an announcement from Chief Moranski, manning Damage Control Station Number One, "Multiple internal bulkhead breaches, A Deck, Frame Seven, in the vicinity of the compression drive equipment room."

Then, from another station in the same row, "Fire! Explosion and fire in Engineering Maintenance Equipment Storage Compartment #2; suppression equipment now responding." Petty Officer Second Class Murray at the Fire Control Station had never dealt with an actual fire on ship, and his voice had a frightened edge to it.

"Murray," said Bhattacharyya soothingly, "Forget that it's a real fire. Work it just like it's an exercise."

"Aye, sir. It appears that all of the suppression equipment in that room is functioning normally. Temperature is already dropping, and gas analysis shows the rate of combustion is also decreasing rapidly." The nozzles for the fire suppression gas in that compartment, as in all compartments, were shielded from explosion by insulated panels designed to retract three seconds *after* any explosion in the area so that they would survive to fight the fire.

"Sir," Supangat threw into the mix, "I am getting no answer from the compression drive equipment room, but the status log for that compartment shows that a regulator buffer swap was being performed at that exact moment."

Regulator buffer? That didn't make any sense, but with multiple bulkhead breaches and a fire, the manual was clear as to what he should do. "General Quarters, unknown internal hazard, set Condition Two throughout the ship, firefighting team and damage control party to A Deck, Frame Seven."

Gustavson at Alerts punched up MC1: "General Quarters, General Quarters, set Condition Two throughout the ship. All hands man your stations for unspecified internal hazard. Marine detachment, secure the ship."

As he was repeating that announcement, Max and Garcia cycled through the hatch. Max had been on the toilet and Garcia in the shower, which is why it took both of them nearly two minutes after the ship precipitously dropped into normal space for them to make their appearance.

Max barely had his nose inside the compartment before he called out, "Bhattacharyya, status."

"Sir, we have an apparent commanded and authorized emergency compression drive shutdown, reason unknown. No answer from that compartment, but their status shows that they were swapping out a regulator buffer at the time. Fire and explosion in Engineering Maintenance Equipment Storage #2, which, by the way, is directly across the corridor from the compression drive equipment room. Fire suppression is active in that compartment and appears to be working. Fire crew on its way; no report from them at this time. Damage control party dispatched; no report. Marine detachment activated; no report." He then read from the status display on his console, "Ship is subluminal, heading two-two-one mark zero-one-five, speed zero-point-three-five c, main sublight is nulled, attitude control is active in all modes, all other systems and stations report nominal status."

"Very well, Mr. Bhattacharyya, and well done. I have CIC."

When the change of minute-by-minute control of the ship was acknowledged and logged, Max replaced Bhattacharyya at the Commander's Station. He noticed Ensign Gilbertson mopping up some sort of unidentified fluid at the XO's Station. It smelled strange. *Definitely not coffee.* Max was reaching for his comm panel when it beeped for attention. He knew who it was before he even looked at the source ID. He opened the circuit.

"Wernher, what happened?" With the chance of there being some sort of serious casualty down there, no way was Max going to engage Brown in the usual levity.

"Bloody balls up, that's what. I'm at ground zero as it were, and I've got three unconscious men. My compression drive is shut down, with the feedback regulator access covers sitting on the deck, two smashed consoles, and a bulkhead with a hole blasted in it." The sound of a cycling hatch came over the circuit. Max could hear Dr. Sahin's voice in the background, telling the pharmacist's mate to look at one of the men and Nurse Church to look at the other, while he looked at the third, presumably the one who appeared to be the most seriously injured. "As I'm sure you heard, the medical team just arrived. I can hear the fire people across the way going about their business. The lads got here quite briskly. In any event, it's pretty clear what happened here."

"Wrench in the stream?" said Max.

"Give that man a kewpie doll. That would be my working theory as well." The hatch cycled again. Max could hear Brown speaking to whomever came in. "Gonzalez, Teng, isolate those damaged consoles, and do a type two inspection of that unit and this console. Let me know the moment you are done. Get three more lads in here to help you. I want it done in fifteen minutes."

Then, to Max: "Of course, I'll review the logs and surveillance, talk to the three men when they're able to talk, and go over the physical evidence, but it looks pretty clear-cut to me. What I don't understand is how the wrench got dropped in there. I'm sure Rhim was the man performing the swap, and he's experienced on that operation. As I recall, he's performed that procedure ten times at least—maybe a dozen—all with at least two seconds to spare."

"Very well, Wernher. As this is an Engineering casualty, you are in charge of the investigation. Be sure, though, to have Dr. Sahin take a close look at these men, especially the one who was performing the swap. I want to rule out any medical or psychiatric causation."

"My thinking exactly, sir." The comm picked up some unintelligible discussion in the background. "It's looking more and more like the feedback unit was not damaged and that none of the consoles essential to operating the compression drive were damaged either. I've got two consoles that are now junk, but one is an auxiliary console for the ship's emergency power, and the other is a training/simulator console. Unless we discover something unexpected, compression drive will be available in less than fifteen minutes."

"That's good news, Wernher. CIC out." He closed the circuit.

CHAPTER 9

07:47Z Hours, 23 January 2315

All three of the injured men had regained consciousness, and Dr. Sahin was intent on giving all three a thorough exam of the kind one cannot perform on an unconscious patient. Having learned who had been standing closest to the path of the hypersonic wrench and who had most likely caused the accident, Sahin had the man sitting on the examining table in his underwear, having asked him to strip off his SCU, while the doctor sat on the little stool with wheels that physicians had been putting in their examining rooms for nearly half a millennium. "What's your name, Spacer?" The doctor knew to whom he was speaking, of course, but he liked to observe how men answered all kinds of questions, even obvious ones.

"Rhim, sir," the man answered slowly.

The doctor touched his padcomp a few times to pull up the man's records. "Ordinary spacer second class, right?"

"Right." That answer seemed sluggish as well, which struck Dr. Sahin as odd. Spacers were not slow. They had to score in the eighty-fifth percentile in general intelligence just to be accepted for space duty, and the ones who were not quick witted never made it to recruit spacer. And what was it about this man's eyes that seemed odd?

"Been on the *Cumberland* for thirteen months, correct?"

It took the man a few moments to count the months. "Yea, that's right."

"Born on Jeffries IV, right?"

"Right. No. Jefferson IV." He blinked for the first time since the doctor had been speaking with him. That is what was odd about his eyes. The man was hardly blinking.

"All right, I have your medical history right here. Nothing unusual that I need to be worried about. Are you experiencing any new symptoms since the incident?"

"My hand, doctor." He held up his right hand. "I've got this feeling—a tingling—but it's almost painful, and it's been getting worse the last few hours."

"I think a colloquial expression for that, Spacer Rhim, is 'pins and needles.' Is that it?"

"Yeah, exactly. That's what it feels like."

"Let me see it." The man extended his hand and the doctor took it, carefully checking the texture and rigidity of the skin, the color, its size relative to the other hand, its temperature, how damp it was, and several other qualities.

Sahin trusted his senses first, before having recourse to instruments and laboratory tests. He had noticed earlier that the hand was slightly inflamed, being redder, larger, and damper than the other. It was almost as if the hand had suffered a mild sunburn or been very lightly scalded in hot water. Sahin had observed these signs earlier, but had explained them with the preliminary hypothesis that the man had raised his hand to shield his face from the event and that the hand had therefore received more than its share of heat and shock from the wrench's hypersonic travels. But when one added the pins-and-needles sensation, another hypothesis suggested itself. During this conversation, the doctor was shining his penlight into Rhim's eyes to check his pupil response, looking in his ears, feeling his pulse, checking his cervical glands for adenopathy, and so on.

"And did this hand happen to come in contact with one of the compression phase regulator feedback streams recently?"

"Yes, it did."

"I thought there were safety procedures to be sure that the stream never touched human tissue."

"There are. But—well, Doc, it's like this. Every now and then, we need to swap out one of the regulator buffers that the stream flows around. It's just this little cadmium-praseodymium-ytterbium rod with a liquid boron core that plugs into a socket in the stream conduit. You open the conduit, pull the old rod, and insert the new one. We don't shut down the drive when we do that.

"Since there are ten streams, we run the other nine at a hundred and eleven point two percent and shut down the one we need to do the buffer swap out on. It's okay, since the system lets us shut the stream down for up to eight seconds at a time and the book says they can be run at up to a hundred and thirty percent for up to a minute. So, we get past all the access covers, shut it down, pull the old rod, stick the new one in, close the door, and restart the stream. Simple."

"But you were a little slow pulling your arm out as the stream restarted, and it caught your hand as it was just beginning to power up."

"Hey, you got it pegged, Doc. That's exactly what happened."

"And who ordered you to perform this procedure?"

Answering this question seemed to require considerable reflection. "Petty Officer Third Starcevik. He's the senior man in that compartment for that watch."

"Did Petty Officer Starcevik speak with you before he had you perform this procedure? I mean, did he have a chance to see how alert you were, whether you were up to executing an operation requiring speed, dexterity, and precision?"

Another delay. "I suppose. He asked me what took me so long to get there and I answered him." Pause. "And we talked about the job and how many times I did it before, so, yea. That would be a yes."

"I see." The doctor walked away from the man to the corner of the examining room, as though in thought, while slipping his penlight out of his pocket. Without warning, he turned and tossed the light to Spacer Rhim. "Here, catch."

The light hit the spacer squarely in the center of his chest and fell to the examining table before the man so much as flinched.

"Spacer, look me in the eyes and tell me how long you've been a tranker."

Rhim gazed back at him in apparent shock and horror at the accusation. "Doc, I don't use that stuff. You know it's against regulations to even have it on the ship."

Sahin actually smiled. "Now, Rhim, that line may work on some worn-out, second-rate, gone-to-space-because-he-can't-make-it-in-a-modern-clinic doctor, but it doesn't fill the water-skins with me. I can spot it a mile away. Your movements are slow; your answers to questions were slow; your reflexes are slow; and you hardly ever blink your eyes. Most spacers are nervous in the presence of the chief medical officer, but you haven't even so much as fidgeted or twitched. Your pupils are dilated and unreactive; your facial capillaries are dilated; and there is a characteristic pigmentation change in the oral and nasal mucosa. To trained eyes, you might as well have painted a sign on your forehead.

"Now, I know that most of the drugs used by men on a warship do not show up very well in ordinary blood tests. But they can be tested for very easily from a sample of cerebrospinal fluid. Spacer, are you going to tell me what you are taking, or do I need to perform a spinal tap?"

"Spinal tap?"

"More properly called a lumbar puncture. Very simple, really. I take a one-hundred-and-twenty-five-millimeter needle and insert it directly into your spinal column right between your L3 and L4 vertebrae," Dr. Sahin jabbed him with his index finger roughly in the middle of his back, "and slowly push through the tissue until I feel a slight 'give'"—he gave the finger a slight shove—"which tells me that the needle has penetrated the *ligmentum flavium*. Then I continue to push the needle deeper into your spine until it 'gives' once more"—another shove—"telling me that I am through the *dura mater* and—I see signs of alarm on your face, Rhim.

"Truly, the needle is not all *that* long, only as long as your hand is wide. There are many larger ones that we commonly use, so put that concern aside. Once the *one-hundred-and twenty-five-millimeter needle* is inside your spinal column, very near your spinal cord, I carefully withdraw some cerebrospinal fluid for testing. Of course, if I penetrate too deeply, the needle could puncture your spinal cord and paralyze you for life, but there is only a very slight risk of permanent paralysis resulting from the procedure. Don't worry. I am quite the old hand at jabbing long needles into people's spinal columns. I'll be right back with a nurse and a spinal tray." He started for the door.

"No, Doc. Wait," the spacer pleaded. "You don't need to do that lumbar-tapping spinal-puncture thing. I admit it. I've been tranking. But only when I'm off duty."

"Thank you. And what exactly are you using?"

"The Chill."

Of course. It *had* to be the Chill. The Chill was the street name for Atanipine, a prescription medication used to treat cases of extreme anxiety disorder. When a patient was so severely anxious that he could not even speak about his problem to a therapist, this drug was a godsend, virtually eliminating the anxiety so that the patient could talk about his issues without suffering an anxiety attack. It was generally administered only a few hours before a therapy session, and even then only for a period of a few months because, as the treatment went on, the drug was known to slow reflexes and mental responses long after its anti-anxiety effects wore off. It could be synthesized by most MediMax units if the authorization protocols were disabled.

"Rhim, just sit right there for a moment. I'll be right back."

"You're not going to get…"

"No, I'm not going to get the spinal kit. I'm going to get a piece of diagnostic equipment."

In less than three minutes, the doctor returned with a device that looked like a black gauntlet with mitten fingers and two thumbs (one on each side), with a small numerical readout on the forearm.

"This is a neural transmission analyzer. It stimulates the fingertips and then measures the timing and the intensity of the neural response as it travels up the nerves through the upper forearm. It tells how efficiently and rapidly the nerves are transmitting their impulses.

"We have a more sophisticated test that involves putting a measuring device on your head and stimulating several different parts of your body, but this is accurate enough for our purposes today. Just put your arm in here—no, the other one. I don't want to use the hand that you injured. There. Now, you won't feel anything except a bit of a tickle, then a vibration, then a gentle poke or two, all on your fingertips. Nothing terribly unpleasant."

Rhim inserted his right hand, and the doctor activated the device. It was just as promised. First he felt a light brush across his fingertips, almost like a feather; then a slight vibration of each finger in turn; and then pokes by a sharp, but not penetrating object, much like a somewhat blunted pencil point, on the tips of each finger. The stimulation then stopped, and a green light came on at one corner of the readout unit. The doctor removed the device and pressed a button. Two numbers appeared: 7.1 and 6.5.

"Doctor, what do those numbers mean?"

"The first number is the speed of your neural transmission. It is an index calibrated for each patient's gender, age, and other factors—I input the calibration data before I stepped in. Ten is normal. The second is a similar index for the sensitivity, accuracy, and precision with which your nerves respond to the impulses. Again, ten is the calibrated norm. Your responses, I am sorry to say, are significantly below normal in on both indices. How long have you been using this substance? Please be honest with me. I already have a good idea from the degree of neural impairment."

"More than a year. Thirteen and a half months, I think."

"That is not surprising. How much do you take?

"Usually a pointer when I get off duty. When I have a day off, I take a deuce."

"A pointer is one and a deuce is two milligrams?"

"Yea, that's right."

"At least you're not a heavy user, although the drug has still taken a substantial toll on you. Now, young man, again I need you to give me a perfectly and completely honest answer to my next question. It is my job to treat this problem and see you returned to full health, and in order to do that, I must have accurate information. My job is to cure, not judge."

The spacer nodded his understanding.

"If you do not use for a day or two, do you experience any symptoms, such as nervousness, anxiety, loss of appetite, inability to sleep, or muscle twitches, particularly around the eyes and corners of the mouth?"

"Uh-huh. All of those. I get real edgy-like. Can't sit still. Ants in my pants."

"How about feelings of persecution, the sense that people are out to get you, or that everyone is against you or doesn't like you?"

"Nah, none of that stuff. What's that mean, anyway?"

"What that means is that you are addicted to this pernicious substance, but not severely so. Once you stop using, you will go through an uncomfortable period of withdrawal where you will experience the symptoms we just talked about, and perhaps some moderate nausea, all for a few days, and then you will be fine."

"You said 'Once you stop using.' Does that mean—?"

"Oh, yes. It most assuredly means that you are going to stop using, young man. There is *no* doubt about that. You and everyone else aboard this ship. No one is going to deaden their dendrites and blunt their brains on the USS *Cumberland*. Not while I am her chief medical officer."

The doctor realized that his voice had gotten inappropriately loud for the small room. He continued more softly. "But I almost forgot. With all the discussion of this other issue, I have let your original injury slip my mind. I'll be right back."

He shortly returned with a loaded pressure syringe and administered its contents. Navy doctors don't ask first, especially with enlisted men. Any prescription or treatment is essentially an order from a superior officer, so they administer the shot or lance the boil or otherwise go ahead with what they need to do. Explanations, if offered at all, come later.

"The energy stream in the compression drive triggered a degenerative process in the nerves in your hand. Left untreated, the nerves would essentially have died, rendering the hand useless. This medication, known as Synaptoflex, will reverse the process and allow the damage to heal. And incidentally, it will also speed the rate at which your nerves recover from the Chill you have been taking. Starting tomorrow morning, I am going to begin working with you to address why you have been taking this terrible drug and how you can prevent yourself from taking it again. I will do everything within my power to see that you and this dangerous chemical are not mated for the rest of your life. Until then, however, I have an unpleasant duty to perform."

"What's that?"

"I am required by regulations to relieve you until further notice. You are simply too impaired to function properly. As this and the incident in Engineering demonstrate," he pointed to Rhim's injured right hand, "you are a hazard in your present condition, both to yourself and others. You will receive appropriate bureaucratic paperwork shortly, explaining that you retain your current rate of pay unless it is modified or stopped due to a separate disciplinary action by proper authority, as well as your right to an appeal hearing before a panel of enlisted men or to have your case reviewed at a Captain's Mast, *et cetera, et cetera, ad nauseum, ad infinitum*, within a day or two."

There was a knock on the examination room door. The doctor opened it to admit two rifle-carrying Marines and Major Kraft. The doctor said sadly, "I'm afraid I called them a moment ago, when I was out of the room. The regulations are quite specific on that point."

Major Kraft announced, "Spacer Rhim, you are under arrest for consumption of a prohibited substance. After I read the doctor's report, there will likely be other charges too, but that one will do for now. I need you to come with us."

Turning to one of the Marines, "Carlsson, go to the quartermaster and draw a plain jane for him. We can't have this man sitting in the brig in his underwear."

The Marines led him from the room. Common sense, not to mention a specific naval regulation, said that one did not put a man in the brig in an SCU, with its oxygen generator full of volatile chemicals and various metal hooks, straps, fittings, and other hardware just asking to be used for mischief by a prisoner. So Rhim was issued a plain jane, a standard ship's Working Uniform, but without any insignia, patches, or other markers of naval rank, occupation, and service history. A Navy man in a plain jane was clothed but visually stripped of his identity.

Sahin picked up Rhim's SCU and deposited it in a bin for patient clothing. Then he strode to his workstation and wrote a hurried message for the commanding officer. "Need to see you as soon as possible regarding matter of great urgency."

Less than five minutes later, the doctor was in Max's day cabin. When a senior officer said "matter of great urgency," Max took him at his word and acted accordingly. When Max found out what the problem was, he buzzed Garcia, Kraft, and "Wernher" Brown, telling them to meet him and Dr. Sahin in the wardroom. Seventeen minutes had elapsed since the CMO sent the text message, when a steward, having brought coffee to everyone except the doctor, who was "in the mood for tea today," bowed out of the wardroom and closed the hatch. The meeting came to order.

The doctor briefly explained what he knew and the effects of the Chill.

"That explains a lot," said Max.

"Explains what?" asked Brown.

"This crew's performance," Garcia finished Max's thought. "Lots of things are just plain slow, slower than they should be, even given all the other problems on this ship. The performance against the enemy when Captain Oscar was in command, the performance in the fleet exercises, the performance in the training exercises I've been running since the change of command. I was wondering just a few minutes ago if something like a third of the crew—excepting the officers and the NCOs—was ill or had some sort of mental disorder. Now, I'm betting we've got a significant fraction—not most, but a significant minority—on this drug. And at least a few of the NCOs and maybe an officer or two, unless I miss my guess."

"A third would be about right," Kraft said. "I was about twelve hours away from coming forward with a program of random neural testing or quarters searches or something. There's not a doubt in my mind that a lot of these men are on something. A blind man could see it. I watch the Discrepancy Reports from every department, and there are just too many minor errors being made all over the ship, even for a ship in a low state of training. Plus, I can see it in the crew's eyes and their movements. What I don't get is why so many? In training for this post, I learned that most ships have some kind of issue with drugs, but usually it's only a small percentage of the crew. A manageable number. I've never heard of anything so widespread."

"I have," Max said. "You get it on an unhappy ship. If things are going well, you never have more than 2 or 3 percent using, if that many. But if you have a bastard skipper and the ship isn't performing well and men don't have pride in her, if she's picked up an insulting nickname like 'The Pitiful *Pittman*' or 'The *Cumberland* Gap,' you can get as many as half of the men taking something to get them through it. Having a happy ship, a ship where the men know their duty, a ship that performs well and has a creditable record against the enemy—those things are the long-term cure for this."

Accustomed to being dismissed by his seniors, the doctor was openly surprised that his observations were immediately being taken so seriously by the other officers. "Thank you all for being so ready to act to resolve this problem. I can identify who is using with comprehensive neural testing. The neural performance—"

Major Kraft's percom beeped, halting the doctor in mid-sentence.

"Major," Max said, annoyed. "Decorum dictates that an officer mute his percom when meeting with other senior officers, particularly when one of them is the CO."

"I understand that very well, sir, but begging the Captain's pardon, I assigned this sender a tag that would let the call come through. I believe it to be urgently relevant." He flipped the cover open to reveal the main screen. He read for less than a minute and then nodded.

"When arresting a man for any drug offense, SOP is to conduct a thorough search of his quarters and all other areas under his control. The search of Rhim's quarters turned up seventeen very small blue tablets that were not in a standard Navy prescription container as required by regulations. We brought them to be analyzed by Pharmacist's Mate Nguyen. The results are on data channel 208, classified for access only by the people in this room. The tablets are clearly Atanipine. I'm betting Dr. Sahin here can tell us more than that from the analysis."

Sahin had already gotten up from the small meeting table and helped himself to the captain's workstation. He studied the screen for a few minutes, scrolling up and down, occasionally nodding to himself or quietly saying "ahh" and "hmmm." Then he turned to the others.

"This sample was synthesized in a MediMax Mark XIV. All MediMax machines insert a microscopic marker chip, called an Auster dot, in every pill or capsule. The Auster dot is stamped with the make, model, and serial number of the machine; the name of the medication; the dosage; and the date the drug was made. And don't worry—it is quite harmless. It passes through the alimentary tract and is eliminated in the feces. Very useful, by the way, as a simple fecal sample tells us what medication the patient is taking. So unless the marker routines have been tampered with—and this is very, very difficult—the time stamp shows that the tablets were made only yesterday. As we have been in deep space all that time, it is clear that someone has a MediMax on board and has gone into the recreational pharmaceuticals business."

"And we have no reason to believe that the bloody thing is being used only to make the Chill, either," said Brown. "Whoever has this beastly device could be making God-knows-what other pills for the men to pop and is selling them all over the ship."

"Say, Doctor," he continued, "what exactly are those Auster dots made of? Is the material anything that would break down in shipboard waste processing?"

"The material is some polymer that is impervious to digestive fluids. It is biologically inactive, so I never had any reason to learn the composition in more detail than that. I think it is very likely to be impervious to breakdown by saprophytic bacteria as well as by the kinds of enzymes used in waste processing."

Brown seemed to have grasped the thread of an idea in his hand. "And what is their size, exactly?"

"One thousand microns."

"That big? That's a tenth of a millimeter! I'll be able to tell you exactly what we're dealing with here. Captain, if I may use your workstation, I need to get my people on this."

"Help yourself, Wernher."

Sahin relinquished the workstation to Brown, who pulled up the text message utility before typing furiously for two or three minutes. He hit SEND with a certain relish and leaned back in the chair. "There. That should do it."

"Care to let us in on your brilliant plan, Wernher, or are you going to keep it to yourself until you have results to announce? We know doing it that way is good for increasing the dramatic tension." Max's light tone took the sting out of the words.

Brown nodded. "Gentlemen, as you know, the waste that goes down the head in your quarters and all the drains around the ship is rather heavily processed, particularly to extract the water for reuse. Virtually all of the mass is taken out, either by water extraction or by enzymatic and bacterial breakdown of the solids, but there is always a residue. We irradiate the residue to kill any remaining microorganisms and then compress it into rectangular shapes that we call 'black bricks' because they are very dark, hard, and dry. And rather than tossing them into space, we generally store them until we get back to a base because *some* captains," he said, throwing a significant glance in Max's direction, "are paranoid about an enemy being able to track our vessel or glean some intelligence about us if the bricks were found in deep space and their contents analyzed. We completely cleaned our treatment plant at Jellicoe Station, and we've produced several kilograms of black bricks since then.

"I just ordered that representative samples be pulled and pulverized finely, before being run through a particulate screen set to trap every particle between 950 and 1050 microns in size. My people will deliver the resulting particles to the Casualty Station, which has equipment for scanning objects of that size in detail, and we'll know what our people have been taking."

"Outstanding," said Max.

"Let me call my people and give them instructions on how to get the results we need," said Sahin. "They'll need to exclude from the results the Auster dots from the pharmaceutical synthesizer in the Casualty Station, the ones from Jellicoe Station and the Casualty Stations from ships in the Task Force, and those from the five or so drug companies from whom the Navy buys pharmaceuticals."

"Why not just look for dots from this one MediMax?" asked Brown.

"Because we aren't certain that there is only one MediMax," Kraft said. "We might have two or more capsule capitalists on board ship."

The doctor went to a corner of the room to have a lengthy conversation with his percom.

"Let's assume, for now, that we just have one," Max said. "How do we catch him?"

"That is a standard law enforcement problem," said Kraft. "Generally, this is accomplished by having an undercover operative or a confidential informant put out the word that he is in the market for a purchase, after which he's contacted by the seller, a controlled buy is made, and the seller apprehended."

"That's fine when you're on a large station or planetside, or even a large ship like a battlewagon or a carrier, but it doesn't work on a small ship like this one," Max said. "The seller knows his buyers all too well. Except for some officers and a few senior NCOs, this crew has been together for well over a year, most of them for several years. Our man is not going to sell to someone he doesn't know, and we can't turn one of his customers into our undercover buyer because the jungle telegraph on this ship is way too efficient. This seller will know almost right away if we pick up one of his users."

"Why not just search the ship for the machine then?" Kraft asked.

Max shook his head. "Ships are thoroughly searched for contraband every time they put into a station or receive any repair or refit. It this man has a MediMax on board, he's found a brilliant hiding place for it, or it would have been turned up in one of those searches. If the refit crews didn't find it, we're not going to."

"Until now, I've always been on stations or planetside, Captain, so I don't know this. How *do* you get these people on board ship?" Kraft held up his palms in a gesture of inquiry and ignorance. Max was impressed that Kraft was so ready to admit his own lack of knowledge and to learn from someone with greater experience. This trait was anything but universal, particularly, for some reason, at the level of seniority occupied by Max and Kraft.

"You catch them by being observant and patient. It's a standard command problem. Over time they always make mistakes," Max explained. "The crew goes on shore leave and there are rumors about some able spacer second being flush with cash, buying drinks for all his buddies, eating at the high-end restaurants, patronizing glamorous call girls, picking up expensive souvenirs and luxury items—that sort of thing. Or some crewman turns up in the Casualty Station obviously beaten by two or three other crewmen who are overheard yelling at him about cheating them or not giving them the stuff they paid for or going up on the price or cutting off their credit. Maybe you have a crewman who is a complete slacker, but seemingly, as if by magic, he has a superior who never puts him on report and two or three other crewmen who are all too willing to do his work for him.

"You see, one way or another, a man selling drugs on a ship is an anomaly, a deviation from the pattern. He has too much contact with too many people, spends too much money, receives too much deference, garners too much attention, and exercises too much power. Over a period of weeks or months, he stands out."

"I'd rather not wait that long," said Kraft.

"Neither would I," said Max, "but I don't know if we have an alternative."

Brown smiled. "What if we don't approach it as a law enforcement problem or as a command problem?"

"What kind of problem would it be then," asked the major.

"An engineering problem."

An hour and a half later, Major Kraft, Lieutenant Brown, the doctor, and Garcia were in the captain's day cabin, ostensibly to share with their skipper a mid-morning cup of coffee. There *was* coffee, and there were even some reasonably appetizing breakfast rolls, but a morning pick-me-up was not the purpose of this little get-together. The men were present to implement the engineer's idea without alerting the ship's ever-churning rumor mill that something was afoot.

With a nod from the captain, Kraft kicked things off. "The doctor has gotten the results of the Auster dot screening. There's lots of Chill being taken; we estimate somewhere between thirty and sixty users, depending on how many are purely recreational and how many are heavy addicts. There's also a smattering of other recreational drugs: mainly an assortment of the current generation of stims, a couple of the more popular pain meds, one or two of the muscle relaxants that people like to take with alcohol, and it looks like we've got one or maybe two men on 'lucies.'"

They needed to find that last person or persons right away. A crew member on hallucinogens was a serious hazard. "Every one of the dots came out of the same machine, so we're looking for one guy. We ran the serial number and it's a naval machine, last in official service on a Corvette, the CMD-1815. She made a forced landing on an asteroid in 2311 in some out-of-the-way system, and the crew died of hypoxia before they could be rescued. The ship was salvaged last year, and the salvage crew logged the Corvette's MediMax as having been destroyed. So, somehow, the MediMax from the CMD-1815 got from that asteroid onto this ship, where it is poisoning our crew."

"Then we need to catch the bastard. Well, Wernher, we *are* going to catch him, right?" Max asked.

"I am loathe to make promises, but it is very likely we shall. The doctor gave me access to his database on the MediMax Mark XIV, which contained a complete set of specifications and schematics. Unfortunately, it did not contain the data that I needed about its electrical characteristics when in operation, so we built one."

"What?" Max interrupted. "You *built* a working MediMax! In an hour and a half? That thing must have over a thousand separate parts."

"It's not as though I worked some sort of miracle, you know. I had five men working on it in addition to myself, and some of those men are truly promising engineers. We got it done in just over an hour. In point of fact, it has only 193 parts. We used all eleven of our FabriFaxes to churn them out. The main problem was the operating software, but we were able to copy the operating system from the ship's unit, which is compatible with the smaller machine. We got it built, calibrated, and tested. It is working exactly according to the manufacturer's specifications."

Max looked at the doctor, who confirmed Brown's statement. "Indeed. I manufactured several samples of some of the more difficult pharmaceuticals, and the device produced them in a manner identical to the factory unit. As far as I can tell, it is indistinguishable from the real thing except for the manufacturer's markings and the color."

"The *color?*" Max was curious.

"Yes, sir, the color," Brown answered. "The real thing is mostly green and yellow, the colors of which the Krag are so fond. Ours is in a proper naval color scheme: Blue and gold."

"*Ça c'est bon,*" Max nodded his approval.

"We tried to see if it gave off any special EM that we could pick up or had any other characteristics that would let us find it, but we couldn't turn up anything. Then two of my brighter electrical and environmental systems guys, Aaron and Liebergot, thought to measure the current this thing pulls when it's producing medications. It turns out that when the MediMax is in the chemical synthesis phase of production, it draws different amounts of power, depending on what it's making, but at one point in the process, it runs a nucleon spectrographic analysis on the product, and when it does that, the machine pulls a current load of exactly eighteen-point-two-seven amps for three-point-two seconds, which is a lot for a device that's not hardwired directly into the ship's power grid. So, I've set the computer to monitor electrical usage in every compartment throughout the ship, and when we see a spike of eighteen-point-two-seven amps, we have our man."

"Outstanding." Max was impressed.

"And the computer is set to notify Major Kraft, or whoever the senior Marine is on duty, about which outlet in which compartment is drawing the current," said the XO. "The Marines swoop down on the guy, nab him and his infernal machine, and our drug problem is solved."

"You mean our drug *supply* problem is solved," cautioned the doctor.

"If you eliminate the supply, you eliminate the problem, don't you?" Brown asked.

For all his technical competence, Brown could be surprisingly obtuse when it came to the human side of the equation. "Not that simple," Max explained. "There is an existing supply in the hands of the people who have bought these damn pills. This Rhim guy had seventeen tablets in his quarters. What's that—enough for a week, plus or minus?"

The doctor nodded.

"If all we do is stop the supply," Max continued, "people are still going to have the drugs on their hands. Some of them are going to have enough for ten days, maybe even two weeks, which means they are going to be under the influence for that long and will be feeling the withdrawal effects for weeks after that. I won't have a crew that's back to normal for more than a month."

"Okay. We need to take away the source, and we need to take away whatever the men have on hand. I understand that," Garcia said. "But how do we do that? At last count there were exactly three-point-seven-four bazillion places on a destroyer to hide something as small as a few pills. Regs say we can search everyone's quarters and effects any time we want, and that works fine when you're looking for bottles of whisky or big bags of Havala weed, but pills? Some of them not much bigger than a millimeter across? No way would we ever find them all. Maybe I'm the pessimist here, but I don't think we'd find even a tenth of them."

"Oh, I think you're not being pessimistic at all, XO. But I have an idea about how to handle that," Max said, smiling. "I just need to get my hands on the seller."

"I'm afraid all of you have overlooked the largest ramification here," Sahin insisted. "We've got dozens of addicts on this ship. When we cut off their supply, these people are going to go through withdrawal symptoms. The slang term for withdrawal from the Chill is 'defrosting.' When people 'defrost,' they experience nausea, anxiety, irritability, sleeplessness, headaches, muscle twitches, cramps, and a host of other side effects. Many of these people are not going to be fit for duty, some of them for days."

"Perhaps, then, we should let well enough alone," said Brown. "Certainly, the crew are slow and don't learn very well, but at least they're not throwing up on the deck, doubled over with cramps, or losing their temper with their shipmates because they're 'defrosting.'"

Sahin had started shaking his head as soon as Brown began speaking. "Totally unacceptable. Totally. That is not a course of action that I can even reasonably consider. These people are doing physiological damage to their bodies and their brains. Some of that damage may be irreversible. It is my duty as their physician and our duty as their officers to protect them. Every man and boy on this ship is my patient, and I owe to each a duty to do no harm, even by inaction. Gentlemen, we have a responsibility, all of us. The collective, of which we are the leaders, must protect the welfare of its constituent individuals, or the collective will perish."

"But they are adults, Doctor, and trained spacers to boot, not children who need to be told to put on a Mac when it's raining and to eat their Brussels sprouts before they can have their pudding," Brown said, rather loudly. "As officers we have a *military* duty to protect their lives, which means that we don't risk killing them in action against the enemy imprudently, that we operate the ship in a safe and responsible manner, and that we provide them with oxygen and food and water and clean clothes and medical care. It does not mean that we have a personal duty to intervene in their personal choices. If we had such a duty, where would it end? Do we follow them around on shore leave to keep them out of the bars and the brothels? Do we stand over them off duty and take away their cigarettes and their cigars and their alcohol ration?"

Max cut off the discussion before things got too heated. "Thank you. What you said here helps me a great deal, not only because you stated your points of view so clearly but also because you showed respect toward each other's opinions, which can be difficult sometimes. I've been in dozens of meetings like this, and I've learned that nothing tends to destroy productive discussion any faster than folks assuming that differences of opinion are the result of the other guy being stupid or misinformed or ill-intentioned, rather than being a consequence of differences in philosophy or values. Can you think of a better way to alienate someone you are trying to persuade than treating him like an idiot? Maybe you can, but none comes to my mind. Anyway, you all have my thanks.

"As interesting as those points are, I have to base my decision not on political theory, but on principles of command and military effectiveness. This ship is a weapon, and the crew is one of its components. My job as the master and commander is to make that weapon as effective as I possibly can and then bring it to bear against the enemy to inflict the maximum damage possible. That is the compass by which I steer. And that principle dictates my decision.

"These men must be made ready to fight. All of them. That means we cut off their supply of this drug as soon as humanly possible; we help them through the withdrawal; and then we get them as healthy as we are able, so they can wage war against the Krag. I appreciate the arguments, gentlemen. In another place and in another time, I could be a man of philosophy considering the eternal question of individual versus collective responsibility. Or I could be a man of God and selflessly minister to and care for my fellow men. But today, here, on this ship, I am a man of war. As a warrior, I must do whatever I can do to make these men ready to kill.

CHAPTER 10

13:22Z Hours, 23 January 2315

With his XO handling the system crossings and the jumps so well, Max felt comfortable leaving CIC to make the rounds of the ship. He was thorough, going to all three decks and inspecting every compartment in which there were men stationed or likely to be working. On three separate occasions, he stopped men from engaging in cleaning and polishing to the insane level established by Captain Oscar, insisting instead on merely the fanatical standard that was the norm in the Navy. All three men followed his orders, but with obvious reluctance. Max made a mental note of their names so that he could check on them later, as he expected that they would return to their old habits if given half a chance.

As on all Union warships, the decks were assigned letters of the alphabet, starting from the ventral level, or "top," with "A" and going down. Max was on C Deck when he opened a compartment almost all of the way aft toward the Engineering spaces. Max's knowledge of some parts of the ship was still a bit fuzzy, so he didn't know what was behind that particular hatch. Most compartments on warships were not labeled with anything more specific than a number, so as not to aid enemy boarders. It was not known whether any Krag outside of their Intel sections read Standard, but no one was going to take any chances.

Opening the hatch, he found the Small Arms and Edged Weapons Training Room, occupied by an older NCO and seven squeakers. In fact, they looked to be the squeakiest of the squeakers, the youngest of the midshipmen on board.

The NCO appeared to be almost sixty and might have acquired just a tiny bit of roundness around the middle, but he had muscular arms, broad shoulders, and a warrior's bearing. His iron-gray crew cut accentuated a craggy face that had the lines to support either a warrior's grimace or a beloved grandfather's smile. His service stripes showed that he had probably been in the same training class as Gus Grissom. Max received a quick once-over from intense gray eyes that clearly missed very little.

These boys had joined the ship at Jellicoe Station just a few days ago. This was their first ship. Today, they were getting their first taste of basic combat instruction from Chief Petty Officer First Class Amborsky, the lead midshipman trainer and the second most senior noncom on the ship. If a man who held this job was well liked on board, he was generally called "Mother Goose."

As soon as Amborsky saw Max, he barked, "Captain on deck!"

All of the little boys, between ages eight and ten Standard years, came immediately to a fairly good version of attention. But not good enough for Amborsky.

"My dear little lambs," he growled ferociously, his words almost a comic contrast with his tone, "when you hear 'Captain on deck,' that means you come to AH-TEN-*SHUN*. Feet together! Arms at your sides! Stomach in! Shoulders back! Chest out! Head high! Eyes straight ahead! Like you are *proud* to be in the Navy, even though the Navy has yet to have any cause to be proud of *you*. That's better." As he was talking, he moved around the room, nudging one boy's chin a little higher, adjusting another's shoulders a bit farther back, pushing another's feet closer together, his touches firm, but not rough or unkind.

Once the chief was satisfied that his charges had come properly to attention for their commanding officer, he pivoted and saluted the captain. "Captain, Chief Petty Officer Amborsky, reporting seven newborn squeakers participating in Unit One, Module Two of Basic Combat Instruction. They have just been introduced to identifying the enemy and learned his basic characteristics, sir." It was apparent that, somehow, the Fates had seen to it that this FUBAR ship had wound up with a solid-gold Mother Goose.

Max returned the salute, and the chief snapped his hand back to his side. He looked at the earnest faces arrayed in front of him. Max put on his stern warrior face. "Identifying the enemy—sounds pretty easy to me, Chief. If it's as tall as a man, with a rat face and tiny pink ears, it's a Krag and it needs to die."

"Captain, we were just about to begin the basic instruction with the dirk. Would the captain like to watch, or would the captain like to conduct the instruction himself?" Aha, the old veteran has decided to administer a test to his new captain.

"Thank you, Chief. I believe I will conduct the instruction, at least for a while." The chief nodded, a slight glimmer of provisional approval in his eyes. Score one for Max. Max reached into a slot in the leg of his SCU and withdrew an edged weapon, holding it up before his audience. The old chief let slip the merest hint of a smile when he saw that the skipper still carried a dirk in addition to his sidearm and cutlass.

Max gripped the weapon's hilt between two fingers so that his hand did not obstruct their view. "This, gentlemen, is the general issue, Union Naval Dirk, Model M-28-2. It is not, I repeat *not*, a 'baby sword' as you may hear some people call it. The dirk is a real weapon used by real spacers to kill real enemies. This particular dirk is the same one I was issued when I was your age. It has drawn enemy blood. I used it to stick a Krag in the gut, and then a Marine took off his head. This blade saved my life.

"Some of you may be wondering why we are issuing edged weapons in the twenty-fourth century. Here we are, on an FTL-capable starship propelled by nuclear fusion, handing out a weapon almost identical to that which the British Royal Navy issued to its midshipmen five hundred years ago on wooden vessels propelled by the wind. As you remember from the tour you got of this vessel when you came aboard at Jellicoe, the *Cumberland* is a pressurized metal tube surrounded by the vacuum of space, crammed full of pressure vessels, pipes full of toxic liquids and gases, radioactive nuclear detonators, and other things that will kill you and lots of other people if they get holes poked in them with bullets. So spacers need a weapon that will kill but that doesn't send little bits of metal flying through the air at three hundred meters per second. Second, edged weapons can be used by small people with very little training—you do not need to be taught how to load, aim, fire, field strip, and clean them. Edged weapons do not jam; they do not go off accidentally; and they do not run out of ammunition.

"According to official naval records, in the course of this war over two hundred Krag have been killed or seriously wounded by midshipmen wielding dirks. This simple weapon has saved hundreds of midshipmen's lives. It is not a toy. It is the first weapon issued to you in your naval career. It is going to be issued to you today, as soon as you complete this training. From that moment until the day you retire and are mustered off your last ship, naval regulations require that you keep it, or some other deadly weapon, at hand at all times. When you receive your weapon, you are no longer a boy; you are a member of the Union Space Navy, carrying arms and trained to use those arms to kill the enemy. From that moment, you are a warrior.

"The M-28 is approximately 483 millimeters long overall, weighs 510 grams, and does its work with a 330-millimeter-long, double-edged, high-carbon steel blade. It is issued with the edges razor sharp, and you are expected to keep them that way, making it an extremely effective slashing and cutting weapon; but that is not how we normally use it."

He slid his own dirk back into its pocket and picked up one of the blunt practice dirks on the table. "We are not going to send you into the fray against the Krag until you are a little bit older, but it is always possible that the Krag will come to you, and if that happens, your dirk is your weapon of last resort. The best way to use it is just like I did when I was fourteen."

He walked over to the chief. "You hold it underhand like this, and you stick it in at the top of the Krag's belly, right here"—he pressed the practice blade against the chief's abdomen about halfway between his navel and his solar plexus—"not where the belly ends on a man, because Krag have rib cages that come down farther than ours, but right here in the middle of its upper body. You shove as hard as you can, and you keep pushing until it won't go in any farther—all the way to the hilt if you can. Then, you pull it out so that if you cut open any blood vessels you leave a hole for it to bleed out through.

"If the Krag does not go down, do it again and again and again until he does. So, that's the drill: stab, withdraw; stab, withdraw; stab, withdraw. Keep it up until the Krag is at your feet in a puddle of its own blood. Now, we'll pair you off, except for . . . you," he pointed to the smallest of the lot. "You will be my partner."

Training classes such as this always had an odd number of students for precisely that reason: so that the instructor could pick the student most in need of closer instruction, greater encouragement, or more attention, as his partner. "What's your name, son?"

"Park, sir," he managed to choke out, obviously intimidated by the presence of his exalted commanding officer. "But everyone calls me 'Will Robinson.'" The boy couldn't have been much more than a hundred centimeters tall. He looked far too small to be hundreds of light years away from his mommy.

"A respected and time-honored naval nickname—I carried it myself for sixteen weeks."

"You did, sir?"

"Absolutely. I was the Will Robinson of the Cruiser USS *San Jacinto*, old number CRM 1228, back in 2295. That's back when starships had steam engines and we punished disobedience by keelhauling." The little boy smiled at that. "Where are you from, Mr. Park?"

"A small town in Korea. On Earth, sir."

"All right, Mr. Park. Just do what I show you and you'll do fine."

He then proceeded to have one member of each pair pick up the practice dirk and hold it as if to stab a Krag in the belly. Max went around the room, correcting their grips. Once the grips were right, he showed them the stance that would deliver the most power, weak-side foot slightly forward, strong-side foot slightly back, leaning forward just a few degrees, and then thrusting with the strong-side arm while bracing the body by pushing forward with the legs. Finally he came back to his partner. He made sure that the boy had the correct grip and the correct stance.

Once everyone had the stance and the grip right, Max made sure each boy knew how to put them into motion, practicing stabbing and withdrawing over and over again, with Max and the chief correcting the boys' form. Those who were initially handed the dirks then traded with their partners, Max and the chief again going around the room, gently correcting grip, foot placement, and body posture.

"Now," Max announced when that was accomplished, "some of you may have noticed that Mr. Park had some difficulty reaching the right point on my belly. You will not always be able to get to the Krag's abdomen. You may be out of position. The Krag may be standing on a higher level than you are. You may be too short. But that doesn't mean your dirk is useless. In a fight, stab or cut whatever you can reach. Even if you don't kill the Krag, you may help your shipmates by wounding it enough to put it out of the fight, or even by hampering and distracting it enough so that other naval personnel can attack it successfully. When I was sticking that Krag in the gut with my dirk at age fourteen, I had his undivided attention, and that allowed Marine Lance Corporal Halvorsen to come up behind it and take its head off with a battle ax."

Max stood on a six-inch-tall wooden box, about half a meter square, apparently constructed for precisely that purpose. "Now, Mr. Park, suppose that I am a Krag warrior and I am drawing my sidearm to shoot you right in the head. There is nowhere to hide, so if you run away, all that will accomplish is getting you shot in the back of the head rather than the front." Max pointed his finger at the boy with his thumb stuck in the air, the universal pantomime for a handgun. "I'm drawing this pistol and I'm about to shoot you. What do you do?"

"Well, sir, I guess…"

"No, son. Don't tell me. Show me. Use your weapon. Do it. Now." The boy didn't move, but just stood there, looking at him timidly, as though afraid to attack the bulky, not to mention high-ranking, fully grown man in front of him. He seemed frozen in place.

"Son, listen to me. I'm a Krag, just like the one who killed most of the women in your family. I'm the reason you never got to meet your grandmother and your great-grandmother. I'm the reason all the old men in your hometown live out their lives in loneliness and sadness. Me and my rat-faced kinfolk have killed or enslaved billions of human beings. What's more, I'm going to shoot you right between the eyes in about two seconds. And after that, I'm going to go over there and I'm going to shoot Chief Amborsky too. And once I'm done with him, I'm going to shoot all your bunkmates here, one by one, in the belly and watch them die. Slowly. You and your dirk are the only thing between your friends and certain death. *Are you just going to stand there?*"

Max's harangue finally jarred the boy from immobility. He gritted his teeth and letting go an inarticulate shriek of rage, ran at Max full tilt and stabbed him in the groin with the mock blade, the thick SCU preventing any injury. After that blow, the boy kept on stabbing: first at the inside of Max's thigh right over the femoral artery, then at the back of Max's knee, then the other thigh, then the other knee, and finally he made repeated hacking motions at Max's hamstrings. Abruptly, the boy stopped, stood up straight, and smiled. "Like that?"

"Poo yai, son," Max said. "I think you've got the makings of an admiral."

After having most of his lower body perforated in simulated fashion by the diminutive Midshipman Park, Max turned the combat training back over to Chief Amborsky and started to make his way forward. He was tired. Brutally tired. He had barely slept since taking command, but there was still so much to do in order to get this poor, warped, and misused excuse for a ship ready to do battle with the Krag. And that was leaving aside everything that would have to be done when Lieutenant Brown managed to find the miniature drug factory on board. Dr. Sahin was already making surreptitious preparations to detoxify up to fifty crew members, but Max doubted that it was possible to be truly ready for something of that magnitude.

He came to an airtight hatch in the corridor, one of dozens throughout the ship present to provide airtight compartmentalization in the event of a hull breach or toxic gas leak. It was an oval steel door just wide enough for a large man to pass through, set in a metal frame that ran around it and filled the roughly square shape of the corridor. Max did what tired men often do when stepping over the raised edge of the hatch, known as the hatch coaming—he didn't raise his foot high enough and he tripped, falling on his face right onto the deck. Thankfully, no one was there to see it. Lying face down on the deck, Max discovered that his eyes were scant centimeters from a deck gun socket—a deck gun socket that had been worn into brilliant but useless smoothness by pathologically assiduous polishing.

Deck gun sockets allow the crew to deploy and securely mount various heavy antipersonnel weapons directly to the deck without having to lug around a large, cumbersome tripod in the confined quarters of a starship. These weapons, including various machine guns, high-capacity fully automatic shotguns, and light cannon for penetrating Krag armored fighting suits, were fitted to swivel mounts, each set on top of a roughly one-meter-tall pole with a base consisting of a probe-and-latch mechanism that fit into sockets set flush into the deck.

These sockets were found every few meters along every corridor and in every large interior space on board, such as the cargo holds and the hangar bay. The probe slipped into the socket and was rigidly locked into place by the latch, with the socket, in turn, firmly secured under the deck to the supporting members of the ship's frame, forming a rock-solid mount to support a heavy weapon, a mount that could stand up to the recoil of even a heavy machine gun. There were more than a hundred deck gun sockets all over the ship, each a prospective site for a heavy defensive weapons position to stiffen the ship's defense against boarders.

And this one had been shined within a millimeter of its life. Or maybe past that. It had been polished so much, in fact, with so abrasive a polishing agent, that the array of metal lips and ridges engaged by the latch mechanism to hold the weapons mount in place was worn nearly smooth. Max would bet his last credit that the latch would not engage or that, if it did, the socket would not hold the base securely enough to withstand the weapon's recoil.

He got up from the deck, no bones broken, but sore in several places. At least he still bounced well. A few steps brought him to the next socket. Same thing. And the next. And the next. After eight sockets he stopped looking and went straight to his day cabin damning Commander Allen Kent Oscar, USN, every step of the way.

He dropped into the chair of the day cabin workstation and logged in. He was about to ask the computer to tell him exactly how many deck gun sockets were on the ship, so he could start writing a memo to order that they be swapped out, when he saw a text message received from the XO about fifteen minutes earlier and marked "URGENT." Anything from the XO with an "urgent" stamp took precedence. It was in the format used for written naval communications of this type at least since the time of Admiral Chester Nimitz, if not the time of Admiral Horatio Nelson. None of those men, however, wrote memos the way Roger Garcia did.

To:	Robichaux, M.T., LCDR USN, Commanding USS *Cumberland*
From:	Garcia, R.T., LT USN, XO USS *Cumberland*
cc:	MAJ G. A. Kraft, Marine Detachment Commander LT V. J. Brown, Chief Engineer
Date:	23 January 2315
Priority:	URGENT
Re:	Heavy Weapons Proficiency and Deck Mounts

Pursuant to your order of 21 January 2315, I have reviewed this crew's training history in detail and identified several areas of deficiency. Of the three million and two areas requiring immediate and intensive training, the worst, by far, is repelling boarders with heavy weapons. Review of the training logs reveals that this skill had not been drilled for so much as a minute since the ship was put into service. When I attempted to conduct a training exercise involving the mounting of an M-22 HASG, we discovered that the mount would not secure to the deck socket. The latch lever goes down and appears to engage and lock, but when you let go of the weapon, its weight just pulls the mechanism out of the socket, and the whole assembly falls over and hits the deck. Examination of the deck socket showed that it had been polished repeatedly to the point where it was too worn for the locking mechanism to engage it.

Some experienced chief *must* have told Captain Oscar that he was going to wear out the sockets. It won't be hard to figure out who it was because I am sure he was still in the brig when you took command.

A spot check of the sockets around the ship indicates that all or virtually all are in the same condition—brilliantly polished but absolutely useless. Immediate fabrication and replacement of every bracket on the ship is recommended. It is further recommended that we begin by replacing every fifth socket so that there are working sockets in every part of the ship ASAP. In that way, if we are boarded six hours after we start work, we won't have all of the sockets replaced on A Deck Frames 1–4, but no sockets anywhere else. That would be very bad.

Smart man, that XO, thought Max. It was a relief to Max to see that the problem would have been spotted and addressed even if he had not tripped going through that hatch. Max hit the comm switch.

"Engineering, Brown here."

"Wernher, this is the skipper."

"Ah, yes, Captain. I've been awaiting your call with bated breath ever since I received this sparkling prose missive from the XO scant moments ago."

"I need this done ASAP."

"Of course you do. If you were to request a task that did not have to be completed for a fortnight, I am quite certain that I should expire on the spot. In any event, I anticipated your order and have already started fabricating the parts. I loaded the specifications into a FabriFax as soon as I got the memo, and the first socket came out of the machine three or four minutes ago. We are testing it right now to be sure it actually works—sometimes 'built to spec' doesn't mean 'built to work,' you know. If it is satisfactory, we'll start turning them out and installing them.

"We should have all 117 of them replaced in about twenty hours, depending on how long it takes to cut the old ones out. No one in living memory has ever had to replace one of these things without having to replace the deck plate as well, so we don't really know how long it takes."

"Wernher, you're the best."

"Perhaps not, but I am the best *you'll* ever get."

"You do know, Wernher, that sometimes you border on insubordination."

"Only border, sir? That calls for greater effort."

"I look forward to it. Speaking of borders, what if we are boarded between now and then?"

"Doing my best to ignore the leaden rapier of your purported witticism, I respectfully suggest, sir, that you endeavor to avoid that eventuality."

"Wernher, one of your great virtues as an officer is that you're always ready with an idea I could never have come up with myself."

"We do *so* aim to please, sir. And by the by, we've not had a peep on that other matter."

"Thanks, Wernher. Please keep me apprised regarding both these items. Skipper out." Between Garcia and Brown, Max didn't know who was the best officer on the ship. But they were both damn good.

At 16:00 hours, the Afternoon Watch gave way to the First Dog Watch, one of the two short (two- rather than four-hour) watches slipped into the rotation, to throw the schedule "out of step" so that it repeated only every third day rather than being

TO HONOR YOU CALL US

the same one day to the next. Long ago, some wit remarked that these were called "dog" watches because they are "cur tailed." The joke remained fresh for each new generation of midshipmen and would likely continue to be repeated so long as there were ships to be manned and watches to be stood.

As this was the third day of the cycle, the Blue Watch came off duty and would not be going back on for four hours, at 20:00. This four-hour gap was both too short and at the wrong time of day for most men to be able to sleep, so the majority of this watch was in the enlisted mess, taking their evening meal, which many of them washed down with a fair amount of beer, wine, or stout.

The Navy allowed enlisted men to drink alcoholic beverages on a daily basis, so long as all drinking took place in the mess, with careful records of each man's consumption so that it could be regulated if necessary, and so long as an excessive amount was not consumed too close to going on watch. Men risking their lives and spending months or even years in space, away from not only their families and sweethearts but also from sunlight and fresh air and the feel of sky over their heads and grass under their feet, were owed the opportunity to seek a little liquid comfort in reasonable quantities from time to time.

At a table in the corner, four men who had seen more than their share of black sky out the viewport were partaking of liquid comfort in its amber, frothy variety. They were: Amborsky; two other chief petty officers, each with more than fifteen years service; and Heinz Wendt, the Chief of the Boat, the most senior enlisted man on board. Wendt, more commonly known by his job title as COB (pronounced "Cobb"), was doing far more listening than talking, as was his habit.

One of other CPOs was a man from planet Highlandia, named Voss, who was holding forth on the subject of the ship's new CO. Many of that world's natives, known as Highlanders, sounded more Scottish than their kin in Aberdeen and Edinburgh on Earth.

"I dinna ken what to make of this laddie. On one hand, you can look around and see that the man has some sense, not like that craicte bastard, Oscar. Och, what a doo-lally he was!" Then, when he turned to practical matters, the chief's accent faded almost into nonexistence, something that always amused his shipmates.

"Putting back the coffee pots, putting back the weapons lockers, replacing the deck gun mounts. At least the men are going to be awake when they stand watch, and if we're boarded, we'll be ready to give yon wee squeakie the welcome he deserves. I mean, you've got to be pure gud for that, right?" The other men nodded sagely.

"But the rest? Playin' Stare Me Down with the Vaaach? The Queen's bloomers, boys! They've got to be five hundred years ahead of us technologically, not to mention bein' foul tempered and blood thirsty to boot. I know destroyer captains are supposed to be aggressive, but there's a difference between courtin' danger and tyin' it to your bedposts and havin' your way with it." He finished with his burr in full bloom again.

Another chief petty officer was shaking his head. He was a small man, but seemed to be made of tougher material than most, as though he had been put together from bone, sinew, and gristle rather than the mere flesh from which most men were assembled. He brought nineteen years of service to the table. His name was Tanaka. He began in a very good approximation of Voss's accent.

"The bagpipes are loud, laddie, but ya' don't know the tune." He then switched to his normal, extremely precise Standard. "You weren't in CIC then, Vossie; I was. The skipper did all right in my book. The last two times that Captain Oscar faced anything that smelled like a threat, he ran. This time, not only did we not run, but the skipper also deliberately subjected the ship to a calculated risk; we handled the situation, and we're alive to tell the tale.

"Vossie, most of these men aren't like you and me and Mother Goose and the COB here. They've never seen the elephant. You get men ready to face danger by facing danger. He's toughening them up for the real thing. He handled that Vaaach skipper all right. Stood up; told him how he'd killed seventeen Krag with a blade up close, nose to whiskers; and got treated with respect like a hunter instead of being laughed off like a little banana-eating monkey."

The COB leaned back, took a long pull of his brew, and then fixed his knowing gaze on Mother Goose. "I heard one of the squeakers say a little while ago that the skipper gave them instruction in edged weapons. So, Goose, you got a good look at the cut of his jib today. What's the brief on this guy? After Captain Oscar, this crew is due for a good skipper."

Mother Goose drained his mug and returned it to the table with a loud thump. He looked up and met the COB's eyes. "The skipper? I think he'll do, COB. I think he'll do."

CHAPTER 11

07:08Z Hours, 24 January 2315

Max was having breakfast this morning with the four officers whom he had begun to think of as his "brain trust." Seeing that every man had finished eating and was sipping his coffee, Max opened the meeting. "I asked all of you here to breakfast because I thought it was a convenient way for all of us to get caught up on what's going on without having to put a senior officer's meeting on the schedule. First, Lieutenant Brown, any sign of our little drug factory being put to use?"

"None so far, Skipper, but the doctor has done some complicated statistical and epidemiological analysis and has concluded that some person with an existing stockpile is going to need to make another purchase within the next twenty-four hours."

"Twenty-one hours," corrected Sahin.

"So, we need to be ready to put the bag on this bastard sometime in the next day," Max said. "Doc, are you ready for the fallout?"

"As ready as can be reasonably expected. I've been making extensive use of the ship's pharmaceutical synthesizer—the official one—to create a significant stockpile of the various medications I will need to help control the withdrawal symptoms associated with these specific drugs. I've also quietly prepared to sling hammocks for the junior midshipmen in the senior midshipmen's quarters to open up the former's space to use as additional in-patient beds for the worst withdrawal cases, and have drawn the necessary equipment from stores so that patients in that room can be monitored from the Casualty Station. My staff has reviewed the treatment protocols for treating these people, and I've refreshed my recollection of how to counsel them."

"Very good." Max continued to be puzzled by the doctor. The man was so clueless in some ways and so brilliant and accomplished in others that Max could never figure out from one moment to the next whether the next thing he did or said would reveal shocking ignorance or astonishing adeptness. "Can anyone think of any other preparations we should be making at this point?" They all shook their heads.

"Next subject. Major Kraft, what's going on with our three would-be saboteurs?"

"They have each stood at least one watch since we returned them to duty, and one of them has stood two. A Marine has been standing by each one of them, with no problems so far. Each of them has had his meeting with the doctor. They return to their quarters at the end of watch with no protest, take their meals in their quarters, and have been going along with the program. My sense is that they all understand that you could have easily put them out an airlock to go dancing with the stars and that you can still do so, which is certainly a meaningful incentive for cooperation."

"I thought it might be. Thank you, Major. Wernher, how're they doing in terms of job performance?"

"They were all reasonably proficient at their jobs before this happened, and they continue to be reasonably proficient. They all had a lot of room for improvement before, and they all still do. In other words, I'm not seeing any change. By the by, having a rifle-toting Marine standing around in Fire Control around the clock is something that I thought might put people off their game, but I have seen no sign of it thus far."

"Doctor, they've each had a meeting with you. Have you learned anything?"

"Well, Captain, the physical and psychological condition of these men leaves a great deal to be desired. They all show symptoms of having been subjected to severe and long-term stress. Two of them have clinically elevated blood pressure and I have put them on medication for that condition. The other one reports substantial and prolonged sleep disturbance, digestive difficulties, and a pruritis on his arms and back that I believe to be caused by stress. I am treating all three conditions. In addition, all three of the men show at least some level of anxiety disorder, which I am treating with anti-anxiety medications.

"Although it is not strictly relevant to this subject, I think it important to tell you that virtually every man who has come through the Casualty Station since we parted company from the Task Force has manifested some level of stress-related symptoms or anxiety disorder. I am prescribing medication only to the most severe cases. This is not to say that the same is true of virtually every man in the ship. I suspect that the men most vulnerable to stress are the ones developing symptoms and that it is these men who are coming to see me. Nevertheless it is troubling, and it indicates that these men have had a difficult time of it. I am hoping that as this vessel becomes a 'happy ship,' these problems will ameliorate themselves.

"Further, the men—not just these three but also the patients I have been seeing in general—have been very forthright in discussing with me the shortcomings of their previous commander. There are two issues that come up most frequently. The first was the totally capricious nature of the senior officers' leadership. At 0900, a given discipline lapse might result only in a gentle suggestion to do the thing differently in the future, whereas at 1330 the same lapse under the same circumstances would provoke paroxysms of shrieking anger and result in the malefactor serving forty days in the brig. So, if I may offer a medical suggestion regarding how to command these men, it would be to show them consistency. A steady hand. Predictability and stability."

"Doctor," Max said, nodding his acceptance, "that's been at the top of my list since the first minute. You said there are two main problems. What's the second?"

"Incompetence. Every man wants to be good at his job, to succeed in his calling. The men on this ship feel that they are not good at their jobs and that they are failures at their calling. No man with an inkling of self-respect can abide for a moment the feeling that he is a failure. It is extremely destructive of self-esteem and, as we all know, self-esteem is the foundation of mental health."

"And the cornerstone of good morale," Max said, completing the old naval maxim. "But they've got to know that the failings were those of their leadership and not themselves."

"No, sir, they do not. At least, they do not in the way that matters. Oh, most of them know that they had an incompetent, even mentally ill, captain and understand that their vessel has performed poorly because they were inadequately trained and poorly led, but even those who recognize this fact on an intellectual level may not have completely internalized it emotionally. Irrespective of the cause, they characterize themselves as failures. 'Failure' is part of their definition of themselves as men.

"They have met the enemy twice and run away both times. They have been virtually killed many times over in fleet exercises. Their vessel is known and reviled throughout the fleet as the '*Cumberland* Gap.' And perhaps most important, they believe that if they are forced to do battle with the Krag, they will prove unequal to the challenge and will die as a result. This state of affairs is inherently stressful, intolerably so, and is highly destructive of morale."

"I see a lot of the same things," said Brown, "but there's one thing, in particular, that's missing."

"What would that be?" asked Dr. Sahin.

"What do you see sewn on the right sleeve, right below the shoulder, of every SCU and Working Uniform of every man on this ship?"

"Lieutenant, I am extremely observant and I can tell you with near absolute certainty that I have seen nothing sewn in that location on any uniform."

"Exactly, Doctor. On most ships, early in the first commission, someone on the crew designs what we call the 'ship's emblem.' It's much like a family's coat of arms—a kind of crest or seal for the ship, generally with its name, registry number, some kind of artwork symbolizing the ship, and usually a motto on it. The emblem gets turned into a patch that gets fabricated on board and that the men sew onto their uniforms. A ship's patch is specifically provided for and allowed in the uniform regulations. So, the uniform of every man not only shows that they are Navy, their rank, their specialization, their years in service, what certifications they have, and their battle honors, but it also proclaims to everyone who sees them what ship they are a part of."

Max took up the theme. "No one on the *Cumberland* cared enough about her to design an emblem. No one on the *Cumberland* has enough pride in her to want people to see that they serve on her. It's almost like having a baby and not loving it enough to give it a name. The bottom line is that the men serve this ship, but they do not love her.

"And I don't see how to turn that around overnight," Max continued. "In the long run, though, we're going to have to do two things. First, make these men competent in their jobs. That's going to be hard enough."

"What would the second be?" asked Dr. Sahin.

"We're going to have to kick some Krag ass."

CHAPTER 12

10:42Z Hours, 24 January 2315

Breakfast was still sitting heavily in Max's stomach when he made his way to the first of the ship's classrooms (counting from the bow), all of which were located on A Deck, amidships, on the port side. This was where the older mids, mostly between fifteen and seventeen Standard years, took their instruction. By the time they got to this age, midshipmen were not little boys any more, instead forming into young men, spacers and officers in the making. They had all been in space for several years, and most of them had been on board a ship that had been in some kind of engagement with the enemy. A few of these boys had an even closer acquaintance with the enemy, having been involved in boarding actions. One boy by the name of Shepard had shot a Krag with a shotgun. Eight times. When asked by an officer why he had shot the enemy warrior eight times, his response was: "Sir, that's all the shells I had in the weapon."

That's the spirit.

When Max stepped into the classroom, the instructor, Lieutenant JG Alexei Siluanov, was covering a unit in tactics. If

Max had come at a different time, it might have been spherical geometry, calculus, astronomy, navigation, physics, history, government, or one of the other subjects covered in the midshipmen's curriculum.

At this moment, however, the class was discussing defense against boarders. From the illustrations on the graphics projector, Max could tell they were talking about Mobile Defense in Depth, which had been at the center of Union boarder defense doctrine since the third year of the war. Siluanov's back was to the door and he was so engrossed in talking about the crux of the concept, creating killing zones and enticing the enemy to enter them, that he did not see Max enter. One of the mids did, however, and snapped out a fairly spacer-like "Captain on deck."

All seven of the midshipmen in the room came immediately to attention while Siluanov gave Max a textbook salute. "Lieutenant JG Siluanov, reporting seven senior midshipmen receiving instruction in Advanced Tactics for Midshipmen, Unit Nineteen, Module Twenty-Nine."

Max returned the salute just as briskly. "As you were, gentlemen. Please carry on, Lieutenant. Don't mind me. I am merely observing."

The boys all sat down. Max knew that the "don't mind me" was a complete waste of oxygen, as neither a lieutenant JG nor a room full of mids were capable of ignoring the borderline divine presence of their commanding officer.

"Actually, Captain, one of these gentlemen raised a question a few minutes that I imagine you might be better able to answer than I." It seemed that the lieutenant, as well, wanted to take the measure of his new CO.

"Go ahead."

The lieutenant gestured to one of the mids, who came to rigid attention, facing Max. He seemed to be scared stiff. Captain Oscar must have been some piece of work to have inspired this kind of fear. Based on what Max had seen so far, he certainly terrorized the midshipmen as much as he had the officers and men. *Sorry bastard.*

"What's your name, son?"

"Shepard, sir." *Aha, it's Mr. Shoot-the-Krag-Eight-Times-with-a-Shotgun-to-Make-Damn-Sure-He's-Dead Shepard. And now he's the one with a question that the instructor wants the captain to answer. Even though he is paralyzed with terror right now, this kid might bear watching.*

"Wait just a minute. There's seven of you, you're in space, and the one named Shepard went first." He chuckled and, pointing in turn to each of the other six, Max said, "Then I suppose you're Grissom, you're Glenn, you're Carpenter, you're Schirra, you're Cooper, and you're Slayton. Don't worry about being last, Slayton, you get to boss the other guys around for years." Only the teacher smiled. "Never mind. A little humor. Anyway, ask your question, son."

"Captain, sir, uh, I was, uh, just, like, you know —"

"All right, Shepard, I'm going to stop you right there. Stand at ease." The boy changed his stance to parade rest, again done with perfect correctness.

"And relax a little. I've never sent anyone to the brig for asking a question." That seemed to blunt the sharp edge of fear somewhat.

"Now, son, you're in training not just to be a recruit spacer in a year or two, but as the years go by after that, to be a leader on a warship in combat. It may be as a commissioned officer and it may be as an NCO, but in either case, your objective is one day to be a man to whom others look for leadership and guidance, as an example. That means you have to communicate with them. And in the service, a big part of communicating is just talking—giving orders and asking questions. No one's going to follow you or believe you know polecats from pulsars unless you sound like you know what you're talking about.

"That means you compose your thoughts, put them in complete sentences, and organize those sentences into a complete sequence of ideas in your own mind before you open your mouth. So, Shepard, I want you to take a moment and form your question in your mind, word for word, organize the words into a sentence, and then ask the question, without saying 'um' or 'you know' or 'like' or anything of that sort. Can you do that?"

"Yes, sir." He almost had Max convinced.

"All right, then. You may fire when ready."

Shepard stood silent for about five seconds, his face a mask of concentration. Then, his face relaxed, and he spoke. "Sir, I was wondering why the Navy puts so much emphasis on defending against boarders to keep the Krag from taking our ships but does not take the obvious step of installing self-destruct mechanisms so that none of our ships could ever fall into Krag hands."

The boy didn't do half bad. But Max felt as though he had just been dropped through a trap door. His stomach took a sickening lurch, and his bowels contorted themselves uncomfortably. He hoped that the color wasn't leaving his face or that, if it was, none of these boys would notice. Still, there was nothing to do but put a brave face on it and go forward.

Max smiled broadly, resolved to give the boy the praise he deserved no matter how bad the question made him feel. "Shepard, not only is that a truly excellent and intelligent question, but you presented it well. Union warships, and the warships of our predecessor navies going back almost to the beginnings of space forces, have had destruct mechanisms to prevent them from falling into enemy hands. So, at the outset of this war all of our ships were equipped both with a stand-alone nuclear self-destruct mechanism, known as the Self-Destruct Mechanism

(Fusion), and also with a command sequence built into the main reactor control software that could be used to blow the reactor if the SDMF failed. All of that changed after the Battle of Han VII. Does anyone here know the brief on that engagement?" Shepard shook his head.

Another boy raised his hand, a painfully skinny young man with reddish hair and an almost comically prominent Adam's apple. Max pointed to him and he came to attention, prompting Shepard, quite correctly, to sit. The students in this class appeared to be very proficient in naval courtesy, at least.

"At ease, son." The boy changed his stance to parade rest. "Your name?"

"McConnell, sir."

"Go ahead, Mr. McConnell."

"Sir, the Battle of Han VII was a major fleet action that took place on 18 October 2298, between Union Task Force Bravo Victor, under the command of Rear Admiral Ian McConnell and Krag Task Force Iota Sigma, believed to be under the command of Admiral Grouper."

Union Task Forces were designated by letters of the Union Forces Voicecom Alphabet, so they had names like Delta Sierra or Echo X-Ray. Navy Intelligence designated Krag task forces by letters of the Greek alphabet, so they always sounded like evil college fraternities like Sigma Tau or Omega Lambda; Krag flag officers, when Intel thought it had identified them from their tactics or other clues, were designated by code names specifically selected to sound nonintimidating. At the time of the Battle of Han VII, Intel was naming them after fish.

"Was Admiral McConnell a relative of yours?"

"He was my grandfather's youngest brother, sir." Max nodded solemnly. So many losses. No family was untouched by this hideous, bloody war.

"Continue, Mr. McConnell."

"Han VII was a strategic target because of the large deuterium separation complex on one of its moons, designated as Han VII D, which has an ice-covered ocean similar to that on Europa, critical to fleet operations in that sector. Intel believed that the Krag were planning to destroy the complex by means of a direct attack across open space by a force consisting of corvettes, destroyers, and frigates. This force was to be met by Task Force Bravo Victor, consisting of four cruisers and several frigates and destroyers."

"Taking into account the firepower of the battlecruiser and four cruisers alone, the force was thought more than sufficient to repel however many ships the Krag were capable of sending. Admiral McConnell detected the attackers at a range of about a hundred AU and deployed his force in a properly structured Zhou Matrix in precisely the right location and correctly oriented to the threat axis.

"But then—and here's what I don't understand, sir; somehow, the curriculum database is silent on this point—all but one frigate and two destroyers of Task Force Bravo Victor were destroyed, and the three surviving ships had to withdraw, leaving the complex and the system to the Krag."

"Be seated, Mr. McConnell. Good recitation. Gentlemen, as you rise through the ranks, you will be learning many things along the way that someone has decided should not be widely known. What happened to Task Force Bravo Victor is one of those things." He paused and took a deep breath. "Task Force Bravo Victor blew itself up."

Seven young faces regarded Max in stunned silence for several seconds. They just couldn't wrap their brains around it. Max felt an echo of their shock within himself. He didn't like talking about Han VII. He didn't like *thinking* about Han VII. He preferred to keep Han VII locked in a lead-lined, triple-reinforced vault, just as the Admiralty did. But it was time that these young men learned this particular truth, and it was best that they learned it from him.

"That is not to say," Max continued, "that they self-destructed voluntarily. Our best evidence is that the Krag figured out some way to remote trigger the SDMFs in the ships. Fortunately, whatever they used to do it, they could use it on only one ship at a time. So, when they saw the other ships in the Task Force exploding one after the other without being hit by weapons fire, three ships out of the whole Task Force managed to guess what was happening fast enough and jettison their SDMFs. Being outnumbered and outgunned about fifteen to one, they made a hasty exit from the system, leaving everything behind. And everyone."

He paused for a moment, putting his stomach back where it belonged by sheer force of will. "They had no choice but to run. At least one of them had to survive to warn the fleet that their SDMFs were vulnerable. Otherwise, the Krag could pull the same stunt again at another battle. The Admiralty proved that it is capable of moving quickly every now and then, and wasted no time pulling all the destruct mechanisms and software from every ship in the Navy. Then, just to make sure that the Krag couldn't exploit some weakness in our reactor systems, they redesigned the reactor control software and the hardware itself to make it virtually impossible to induce the main reactor to explode, except by weapons fire.

"Despite our best efforts, we still don't know how the Krag did it. The best theory is that the Krag found a way to alter the relative strength of the nuclear force and the Coulomb force over a small area, causing the deuterium and tritium fuel in the warheads to fuse without having to detonate the fission trigger. God knows how. So, to this day we have no destructs on our ships. And the Krag don't put them on their ships, presumably because they're afraid we'll discover whatever it is they used and turn it against them.

"Therefore, it is possible for each of us to board and take the ships of the other, as both have done many times in this war. As near as we can tell, the Krag have nearly a hundred of our vessels in their navy and we have fifty-six of theirs. And *that's* why the tactics of boarding and repelling boarders are critical—not only to save you and your shipmates from being defeated by the enemy in face-to-face combat but also to keep them from getting their furry little paws on our warships and using them to kill our people. And now, if you will excuse me, gentlemen, I have a ship to run. Carry on."

He left the compartment and went straight back to his cabin. Every step of the way, he thought about the survivors in life pods and the hundreds of men at the deuterium complex on Han VII D. He thought about how those men begged the cruiser *Adrianople* and the destroyers *Capetown* and *Colombo* not to leave them to the mercy of the Krag, and how those ships ran like scalded dogs, fleeing the system as fast as their compression drives could propel them.

He thought about how those men sounded to the midshipman assigned to the Comms back room on the *Capetown*, who dutifully logged each of those incoming desperate signals by frequency, source, duration, and content, and about how that young man did his duty with a stern warrior face, without shedding a tear, while his heart turned to ashes in his chest. He thought about how that young man had nightmares to this very day in which he heard those men's pleading voices. Most of all, he wondered if that young man, a man named Robichaux, would ever stop hearing them.

Probably not.

■

After spending a few hours in his bunk, taking two of the pills that the doctor on the *Halsey* had given him for nausea, and eating some soup and crackers, Max was back at work, making some changes to the duty roster, when his comm buzzed. "Skipper here."

"Captain, this is Major Kraft. I have a present for you in the brig."

"On my way."

Max had determined that he could get from any point in the *Cumberland* to any other in two minutes, forty-nine seconds or less. From his quarters to the brig took just over a minute and a half, and would probably take less if he were willing to slide down the access ladders, as most of the younger crewmen did, rather than take them rung by rung. But Commodore Middleton had told him a long time ago that once one became a commissioned officer, people expected one to act with a certain degree of dignity, and that included not sliding down access ladders like a mid-third playing Marines and rat-faces.

Max entered Major Kraft's domain and was greeted by the major and Lieutenant Brown, triumphant smiles on both their faces.

"We've got him, sir," Kraft announced. "We nabbed our drug dealer red-handed, synthesizing a batch of the Chill. We broke in on him just as the drugs were coming out of the machine."

"How did you get there so fast?" asked Max. "The doctor tells me that the interval from the power draw to producing the drugs is less than a minute."

"Chalk one up to good old detective work, Captain. It's not that I didn't trust the engineering solution, but this is so important that I wanted to pursue a parallel line of inquiry.

"You remember that we traced the machine to the salvaged corvette. I pulled up the records on that salvage and discovered that a member of that salvage crew also happens to be a member of our crew: a man named Green, an able spacer third. Well, Skipper, I don't believe in coincidences." *Damn straight. No officer worth the brass in his uniform buttons believes in coincidences.*

"So I zeroed in on him. I also remembered what you said about him needing a fantastic hiding place for the thing; obviously not his quarters, so I started to work out the places Green would normally go in the course of his duties, looking for one where a MediMax could be hidden and where he could use it without being observed.

"Green is a high-energy systems technician, and he regularly services the main deflector emitters. There are some large storage lockers in the emitter control room, with hundreds of factory-sealed spare parts cases. He could keep his machine in one of those cases and dummy up a seal so that anyone conducting a search would take one look at it and pass it by. Chances are, he wouldn't be disturbed—you know how superstitious spacers are about picking up some stray tachyo-graviton output in there.

"I put the man under surveillance and, when he went to the control room, we had men nearby, ready to go as soon as we got the word. But don't discount the Engineering contribution. Being cued by that power signature let us burst into the room at just the right moment and catch him red-handed, pulling the tablets out of the machine. Teamwork triumphs."

"Outstanding." Max was impressed again, not only by Kraft's excellent detective work but also by his readiness to share credit with Brown, something that many officers were reluctant to do. The young captain was starting to recognize and appreciate how well the admiral had taken care of him in terms of giving him a set of highly able officers to offset the ship's other problems. Garcia, Brown, Kraft, and Sahin were all brilliant in their own way, and all had the prospect of marvelous careers ahead of them. "Has anyone questioned him?"

"No, sir. We just advised him of his rights and locked him up," Kraft said.

"Rights?" Max looked at the major quizzically. "This man's a spacer caught red-handed committing a felony on a Union naval vessel in time of war in a combat zone. What rights?"

A satisfied smile slowly spread across the major's face. "*Genau.*" Exactly. Yes, the man definitely loved his work.

Something clicked in Max's mind. "Spacer *Green*, is it?"

"Yes, sir."

"I believe I need to refresh my memory about Spacer *Green*. Let me sit at your workstation for a minute; then let's have a chat with our pharmaceuticals salesman."

A few moments later, the major took Max to the ship's small, Spartan interrogation room, where they found Spacer Green sitting in one of the room's three chairs at a small metal table. Green was just above average height, with a slender build, dark hair, close-set hazel eyes, and the kind of pasty complexion that comes with being of Anglo-Saxon descent, spending as long as a year without seeing any natural sunlight, and not bothering to avail himself of the UV safe tanning lamps the Navy provided so that men did not have to see a Dracula-like pallor every time they looked at themselves in the mirror.

Unlike many men under arrest while under the Navy's authority, Green did not look even remotely frightened. His face wore an expression of annoyed arrogance, as though he were a grand admiral's son put on report by an ensign for a minor uniform violation and had just told his father to bust the ensign to midshipman. Which was not too far from how he saw the universe.

Max put the ball into play. "Spacer Green, we caught you with the machine. We caught you with the drugs. We have conclusive physical evidence that drugs from this device have been sold to a large number of people on board this ship. With what we've got, I have enough for a conviction by order that will guarantee that you spend the rest of your life on a penal asteroid. Fortunately for you, I have sufficient discretion that I can convict you of a lesser offense, say trafficking rather than manufacturing, and see that you serve a sentence of a few years in a gentler environment. All I need is the names of your customers."

Green laughed, a grating, nasal sound. "It doesn't matter what you do to me on this ship, Captain. I know the law. You can't airlock me or shoot me for a drug offense. So, I'll be alive when we get back. And when we do get back to the Task Force or to a station, I have enough traction that whatever you sentence me to, I'll get off with probation or, at worst, get sent to a VIP detention farm for a year or two. I don't have any reason to talk to you clowns. A lieutenant commander and a major? You're wasting my time. Just lock me up and leave me alone."

Kraft leaned into Green's face. "What makes you think you've got that much influence, *Schweinhund?*"

He smiled again, even more smugly. "You don't know this, *Dummkopf,* but this isn't my first orbit around the planet. Every time, my father has gotten me out of it and had the records expunged. I only had to agree to continue to serve on active duty on a naval warship, so he could tell everyone that his son wears the Blue. La-di-dah. I hope you have fun detaining me, because I'll be free within two days once we get back."

So, the little twit likes to show off that he speaks a bit of German. "You're an arrogant little *Schwanzlutscher*, aren't you?" Max did not actually learn to speak German when he served under Captain Heimbach on the *Luzon*, but he did learn how to call someone a cocksucker. "When a record is expunged, it doesn't go away. The Navy erases nothing. Ever. The record simply gets *labeled* as 'expunged' and gets buried behind a higher-level access code. I've got access, so I know all about your previous three convictions for trafficking and manufacturing. And I know that your father is Schuyler Rudolph Green, one of the high commissioners of the Admiralty. And I know about the dirty deals done to get you off those other times. So does the admiral. Things have changed, Green. There are no more deals to pull your ass out of the fire."

"You're lying."

"Really?" It was Max's turn to smile, now. "Didn't you ever wonder why, with a high commissioner as a father, you were assigned to a cramped little destroyer on a high-risk deployment rather than a big, comfy battlecruiser protecting some high-value facility in a rear area?" The expression on the man's face showed that the question had, in fact, occurred to him.

"Or why, when you were restored to duty, it was as an able spacer third, with fewer privileges and lower pay compared to your previous rank of petty officer third? Or why you got saddled working in High-Energy Systems, one of the noisiest, most dangerous specialties on the ship, rather than in something quieter, safer, and easier, like Sensors maintenance or Fire Control?"

Again, Green's poker face slipped to show that he had considered these questions, probably at some length.

"Your father is smarter than you think. He found out about your little scam—the one where you sold interests in a nonexistent helium three mining consortium that he was supposedly heading up. High Commissioner Schuyler Green didn't take too kindly to his good name being lent to a fraudulent securities offering. He shut that deal down cold and paid the investors back out of his own, very deep, pockets. Then, he called his lawyers to write you out of his will and cut you off from your trust accounts.

"And when he was done with that, he saw to it that you got the orders assigning you to Admiral Hornmeyer's Task Force and to a destroyer being sent out to do some of the Navy's real work. Oh, and here's the bow on that package: dear old dad gave the admiral a personal, father–son message that was to be passed on to you if you found yourself in the condition you are in today. It's easy to remember. Nine words: 'I'm done with you, son. You're on your own.'"

Spacer Green had inherited most of his father's intelligence, if not his judgment. Accordingly, less than five minutes later he was writing down the names of the crew members to whom he had sold drugs, and the quantities. His excellent memory in this regard was aided by a computer file that appeared to be his personal exercise log but was really a rather cleverly enciphered list of customer names, sales dates, quantities of drugs, and monies received. That record, plus a comprehensive counting of all the Auster dots in all the black bricks in the *Cumberland*'s hold, allowed the doctor to compute with a fairly high degree of accuracy how many tablets or capsules, and of what kind, were in the possession of which crew members.

The next order of business was to extract the drugs voluntarily from the possessors and to provide to each the medical assistance he would need over the coming days. There were thirty-one customers, ranging from former Lieutenant JG, now Midshipman, Goldman, all the way down to a few greenies just promoted from mid. Each would be summoned to the Casualty Station for an appointment with the chief medical officer, made to look as though it involved some question about the user's medical history. It would start with Goldman.

Goldman, who was, at this moment, sitting in a chair in Dr. Sahin's small but functional office. Goldman sat on the edge of the seat with his knees and feet together and his back rigidly straight, as appropriate when asked to sit by a superior officer.

"Sit at ease, Midshipman," said Sahin. The midshipman allowed his back to touch the back of the chair. Barely.

"Goldman, I have a difficult subject to discuss with you. That discussion will proceed much more efficiently if you will be so good as not to insult my intelligence by telling me lies."

"So this isn't to clear up an ambiguity in my medical history."

"No, Goldman, it is not."

"I see." Short pause. "Oh, I *see*. Green was hauled off to the brig early this afternoon. Rhim was just involved in an accident in Engineering that half the crew thinks happened because he was tranking. So, this must be about the stims."

Sahin was impressed by the deduction, and it must have shown on his face. "Doctor, just because I went off on a crewman and got busted to mid doesn't mean I'm stupid, you know. You don't get assigned to Sensors unless you score very high in logical analysis in general and inductive reasoning in particular. For all the good it has done me." He sighed dejectedly.

"Stims. I knew the damn things would catch up with me eventually. In fact, it already happened. They give me a temper, a bad one. No way would I have reamed out that spacer if I hadn't been on the fucking things. So, what are you going to do to me—bust me all the way to mid-third? Bring me up on charges? Go ahead. I don't care. My career's blown out the airlock now. After the other day, I'm sure the skipper's already got a flamer in my jacket that, all by itself, will sink any chance I have of ever making lieutenant. Now with a drug charge on my CDR, the best I can hope for is to wind up at some rear-area station checking fluid levels in the fecal sediment digestion tanks. I've gone and fucked myself really good. Just like I always do. Story of my life."

"Mister Goldman, I don't think you understand this situation very well. In fact, I think you do not understand the situation at all. First, in preparation for this meeting, I reviewed your complete personnel records, including your Comprehensive Disciplinary Record, and I found no 'flamer' from the captain or from anyone else. There is simply a Record of Disciplinary Action from Captain Robichaux stating that your handling of an error by an enlisted man was less than optimal and that he had *temporarily* reduced you in rank to give you an opportunity to learn better how to correct deficient performance by subordinates. There are specific instructions in your jacket to restore your commission upon successful completion of the instructional units assigned to you and a certification from the XO that your attitude is satisfactory.

"As for the drug issue, we are taking a somewhat unusual approach to dealing with that."

Goldman was still stuck on the previous issue. "You mean the skipper didn't burn off three layers of my hull?"

"Not even one layer. Goldman, you have not fully come to grips with the full implications of the change in command on this vessel. Captain Robichaux is nothing like Captain Oscar. Captain Robichaux and the current senior officers on this vessel understand that you have suffered from incompetent leadership and cannot be held accountable for the consequences, at least not for all of them, at least not completely.

"You must bear some responsibility of course, which is why he rebuked you verbally, why you were demoted, and why you are now performing some less than desirable duties. But you have been and will be afforded the opportunity to learn from the experience, to redeem yourself, and to regain, through hard work and sincere reformation, what you have lost.

"It is the same with these stims. You have committed some serious errors. And you have harmed your career. You have set yourself back, but not irreparably, not permanently. You are going through a period of hardship. But you have an opportunity to overcome that hardship and, given time, to leave it behind and go forward almost as though it did not happen. You can start making amends right now by favoring me with an explanation of why you started taking stimulants."

"Why do you think? Why does anyone take stims? It's sure as hell not to feel good, like taking the Chill or floaters or something like that. Stims make you feel like shit *all the time*, all nervous and jittery when you're on them, sluggish and depressed when they wear off. I take them the same reason everyone takes them," he said with increasing anger.

Pausing, and then reconsidering his tone, he continued more reasonably. "Have you ever stood a watch schedule?"

The doctor shook his head.

"No, I don't suppose you have. You're on for four hours. And then you're off, maybe for four, maybe for eight, maybe for twelve; then you are on again for four, and then you are off again. And four, or eight, or twelve hours later, you're back on. On and off. On and off. In three-day cycles. And that's not counting the dog watches—where you stand for two and then go off again. There's one day of the cycle where you will stand three watches: First Watch, from 20:00 to 00:00, Forenoon from 08:00 to 12:00, and Second Dog from 18:00 to 20:00. That's ten hours out of twenty-four. One schedule for day one, one schedule for day two, one schedule for day three, and then it repeats. Forever. You are up working at all hours around the clock and have to try to sleep at all hours around the clock, and it is never the same two days in a row. Try staying alert when your body never—and I mean *never*—gets to settle into a regular schedule.

"It's not just the watches either. I wasn't just in command of the Sensor SSR for the Blue Watch, but of the entire unit—all three watches—so I had to set up the training schedule, supervise the work of all three watches, do quarterly evaluations on sixty men, write daily sensor contact reports, daily sensor array utilization reports, daily computer core access and utilization reports, daily reports on the performance of the equipment my men use and maintenance schedules, daily calibration reports and schedules, discipline reports, and every month Captain Oscar added a new kind of report or wanted an old report done more frequently because reading reports was how he kept track of what was going on around the ship, and you can't work on those when you are standing watch—*oh no!*—because you are keeping an eye on twenty different stations all at once, so you've got to do it when you're off duty, and that cuts into your time for sleeping and eating and taking a crap and everything else in a big way. Sometimes coffee wasn't enough, you know, so I started taking stims every now and then to get me over the hump. At least, that's how it started."

"And you are under their influence at this moment, are you not?" As if there were any question. If the man were to write down what he was saying, it would have all come out as one, long, run-on sentence.

"Yes. I just came off watch. I still stand watches as a mid, plus attending class and doing homework."

"Goldman, we want to help you, but we need something from you. From what Green has told us, we estimate that you have between thirteen and seventeen Afterburner tablets—that's what you call this kind of stim, isn't it? Afterburners?"

Goldman nodded.

"We want you to turn them over to us. All of them. And wear a biomonitor for thirty days so that we know you are staying clean. In exchange, we will treat your withdrawal medically, give you support and counseling, and not impose any discipline on you for any drug-related conduct between when you joined the ship until the moment you turn the pills over to me."

"What if I don't go along? You mean I don't get treatment when I run out of pills?"

"I'm going to pretend that I didn't hear that," Sahin said stiffly. "I have taken a sacred oath as a physician. I would never withhold treatment from anyone who needed it. Ever. You will receive the appropriate treatment at the appropriate time irrespective of whether you cooperate with us. But I am given to understand that the captain would discipline you for possession of dangerous drugs, consumption of dangerous drugs, and reporting for duty while impaired or under the influence of dangerous drugs. I am also given to understand that he would bring a separate count for possession of each tablet, for each time you took a tablet, and for each watch for which you reported while under the influence. My estimate is that we would be contemplating at least three hundred counts, and more likely something like a thousand. I shudder to think of how long your sentence would be upon conviction on all those charges."

Goldman pondered that for a minute. "Ohhhh, I see. I get it now. This isn't about establishing discipline and proving to us that we can't take drugs in defiance of the captain's wishes. You have to understand, that's what it would have been about with Captain Oscar. What *your* guy is trying to do is to restore combat effectiveness in the shortest possible time. Right. That's got to be it. You need everyone to turn in their pills now, so you can get everyone through withdrawal or recovered from that slowing down thing you get with people on the Chill, and get everyone back on duty ASAP. Am I interpreting my readings correctly?"

"I'm not going to tell you that you are wrong." Dr. Sahin could not help but smile. Even with his mind disordered by the stimulants, Goldman had analyzed the fragmentary evidence at his disposal and rapidly arrived upon the correct conclusion. If he could break the shackles of drug dependency and his self-defeating attitudes, this man could become an exceptional officer.

"I sank a lot of money into those pills. I'd be throwing away several hundred credits."

"There are more important things than credits. Do not think of this as a matter of throwing the money away. Rather, I invite you to characterize it as, shall we say, tuition, the money one pays to receive a valuable education."

"There may be something to that, Doctor." He paused, considering. The doctor didn't rush him, as he knew that this man was weighing the alternatives, using the best rational analysis he could bring to bear. Sahin sat in silence. He had seen this man's mind at work and was confident of the outcome.

"Okay. Deal. Oh, Doctor, as one person who evaluates data to another, kind of a professional courtesy, I want you to know that your estimate is off."

"What do you mean?"

"In calculating the number of pills I have left, you made an erroneous assumption. You assumed that I am taking the pills only to prop myself up near the end of a watch. I'm also taking them to get myself going after a short sleep period too."

Sahin made a note to revise his calculations with regard to other stim users.

"I have ten tablets left, exactly. Where do you want me to bring them?" Sahin had no doubt that Goldman was telling him the truth.

"To me. Personally. Put them in my hand. I will expect you back here in less than five minutes. And if you take any of them before you come, I will know."

"Five minutes." He paused and turned back to meet the doctor's eyes. Was that fear? "Bones, I tried to stop taking them before. It was pretty bad."

Yes, it *was* fear. While the doctor was reading Goldman's eyes, Goldman was reading his. For the first time he could remember, Goldman looked into the eyes of a superior officer and saw sympathy, understanding, and—of all things—kindness.

"Goldman, the entire staff of the Casualty Center will be here to help you through it. I am here to help you as well. We will give you medication to ease your symptoms. If they become severe, we will put you in the Casualty Center where someone will be watching over you every moment. Remember, young man, you are in the Navy, and in the Navy you are never, ever alone."

CHAPTER 13

"**V**erify destination." The XO could not hide the excitement in his voice.

"Destination is Alfa jump point in unnamed system, catalog designation Uniform Sierra Nebula Galaxy Sierra 4-1195-1486-5912-4109. Coordinates as displayed." Even Stevenson's reading of unexciting star catalog designations seemed to carry with it a hefty dollop of adrenalin.

"Very well," said the XO.

"One minute to jump," Stevenson called out.

"Jump Officer, safe all systems for jump," said Garcia.

"Safing." Around the CIC, console after console went dark or to static or flat gray.

"I want the ship stealthed as soon as possible after we come out of the jump," Max interjected into the routine. The order was promptly acknowledged.

Everyone watched the jump clock. Then the jump officer began the countdown. "Ten seconds. Nine. Eight. Seven. Six. Five. Four. Three. Two. One. Jumping."

This time, no one retched. That was always a bonus. One man at point defense systems looked a little green, but he looked almost that green before the jump. He was on the closely held list of men who were going through withdrawal. Five men, so far, had been taken off active duty: three were in their quarters and two were in the Casualty Station. The rest were standing their watches and doing their duty, with the help of a meticulous, individually designed medication regimen put together by Dr. Sahin, whose skills as a physician Max was beginning to suspect were nothing short of the genius level.

"Jump complete, restoring systems," Stevenson announced. The now-familiar routine progressed as one system after another stirred from enforced slumber; sensor information started coming in; drives were restored; and the ship inched into tentative motion to clear the datum. But this time the routine was not routine at all.

The Vaaach map had shown the expected routes and schedules of four Krag freighters as they moved through the Free Corridor. As best could be told from analysis of the file, the original source of the data was the computer of a Krag vessel. Apparently, the Vaaach had met the Krag vessel somewhere in deep space, hacked the computer, and downloaded the file. This wasn't surprising given that they had sufficient skill to penetrate the *Cumberland*'s intricate system of serially redundant firewalls and lockouts to place a file in her systems without anyone being the wiser. Perhaps they hacked the computers of every ship they met, in which case the Vaaach must have accumulated an amazing body of intelligence.

Two of the Krag ships were positioned so that the *Cumberland* could not reach them before they crossed into the Romanovan Imperium, a neutral power whose space Max was ordered not to violate. However, two ships appeared as though they could be intercepted, and Max was going to try.

As always, Max needed to hear from Kasparov. Fortunately, the man and his back room had progressed by leaps and bounds in only a few days. Minutes elapsed with no ship contacts other than a few freighters crawling across the system at 0.05 c. Sensors typed and classified them anyway, and Comms pulled up their transponder information in less than ten seconds. They turned out to be a heavy ore carrier operated by Shoulder Freight Lines, ridiculously named *Shoulder's Boulder Holder*, and an eighty-five-year-old, bare-bones, barely able to pass inspection microfreighter bearing the improbable name *Queen Mary*, its tiny hold full of small but high-value items: gourmet coffee, something known as Beluga caviar, precision machine tools, and surgical instruments.

By the end of this cruise, this crew might turn out to be moderately proficient.

Max saw Kasparov's shoulder muscles tense and his hands fly to the controls for his console. He must have heard something from his back room.

"Distant contact. Designating as Uniform seven. Bearing two-seven-five mark zero-five-three. Reading a bearing change from right to left and from bottom to top. Range is still uncertain, but the weakness of the mass detection indicates it is in excess of two-five AU. Bearing change is rapid for such a distant contact, and I'm getting a hint of a high Doppler as well, so I'm classifying contact as fast—probably a warship. Request course change to zero-niner-five mark zero-five-three to get a cross bearing on contact."

"Maneuvering, make it so. Make your speed zero point two five," Max ordered. The ship came about to a heading perpendicular to the contact's bearing. If the line of the first bearing to the target was the "b" side of a right triangle, the idea was for the ship to now travel along "a" side, or the base, and then take a cross bearing down the "c" side, or hypotenuse, allowing it to calculate the range. Of course, with active sensors Max could have the range measured to the meter in a few minutes, targeting the enemy with a sensor beam. But like submarines in the oceans of Earth centuries before, stalking warships, rarely gave away their positions by using active sensors, preferring to detect their prey by the target's own emissions, while they remained hidden until the last second. The deadliest attack was the one you did not see coming.

Minutes passed, then the better part of an hour. Working a target takes patience and nerves of steel. With all the coffee Max had been drinking these past few hours, it also took a bladder the size of a beach ball. Max had needed to take a leak for the last twenty minutes but hated to leave his station for more than ten seconds. If he didn't go now, though, he'd be forced to leave to change his uniform. "XO, I'm headed for the head. You have CIC."

"Understood, I have CIC."

He was back in less than ninety seconds.

"XO, status." Tradition demanded that he ask, as if there were anything that could have changed meaningfully in a minute and a half that would not also be immediately obvious from the main status display and the condition monitors.

"No change, sir," Garcia responded.

Max would have been willing to kill or to die himself to get more and better information from Kasparov, but the man couldn't tell what he didn't know. He was talking furiously to his back room, so they must be learning something. Max itched to know. He was used to being in the trenches, not back at the chateau drinking champagne, talking on the field telephone, and moving markers around on a map. If he chose, Max could listen to their voice loop, or any other of the circuits between any of his CIC officers and their back rooms. For that matter, if he had the patience to navigate his way through all the levels of all the menus, he could pull up any display from any console in the ship. But no captain with any sense did that (Max noted, though, that Captain Oscar had configured his console with easy navigation shortcuts to do exactly that—monitor loops, scroll through every display of every CIC console, and all sorts of other ludicrous micromanagement). Max relied mostly on what his CIC people told him, plus what he could tell from a few of the normal "CO Displays" that were on the standard main menu for the commander's console.

"Captain," Kasparov said, "cross bearing indicates range to target is twenty-six point seventy-four AU. Target motion analysis indicates target is bound for this system's Bravo jump point at speed of approximately zero point five two c. Naturally, as we accumulate more data, we will be able to refine that estimate.

"And sir, this is a very dusty system. Both we and the target are in the plane of this system, so our line of sight right now is right through the bulk of the dust, and it's obscuring visual imaging. At first, we thought that the target was enormous, but as we start to get a better angle, the target image appears, under extreme magnification and enhancement, to be resolving into three ships in a line abeam formation. Configurations are not visible at this time, but from the amount of light reflected from each, our best guess right now is that we are looking at the fast military ore carrier we were expecting and two escorts of some kind. Probably destroyers, but they might be large corvettes or small frigates at this point. So, the largest ship retains the designation Uniform seven and we are designating the apparent escorts as Uniform eight and nine."

"Thank you, Mr. Kasparov." *Oh, yes, thank you so bloody much, Mr. Kasparov. Two—count-em, two—probable Krag destroyers. We wouldn't want to make things too easy, would we?*

"Maneuvering, plot a course at a forty-five-degree angle to the plane of this system with an azimuth that will put us on the six o'clock of that little Krag convoy while keeping us more than half a million kills away from them at all times. We'll slide into their six and sneak up behind them from that far back." Max wouldn't normally give such a complex order to Maneuvering; instead, he would break the order down into a series of simpler steps and give each as the previous one was completed. But LeBlanc had impressed him so far. This man could handle what was just thrown at him, plus some.

LeBlanc acknowledged the order, spent a minute or so working with his console, and then projected a proposed course in the tactical display. Max saw that it was exactly what he wanted and nodded to his fellow Cajun. The old chief began giving orders to his people, and the *Cumberland* started once again to crawl the duck pond.

"Sensors, you *will* let me know when you get a better ID on the Krag vessels, won't you?"

"Affirmative, sir. It's going to be a while. They are still very distant, their drives are masked from us so we can't get a specident on them, and we are still too far for optical scanners to resolve a configuration." Max had served his time in Kasparov's position, so he knew all that. It didn't make it any less frustrating.

Patience. Max was tempted to run the main sublight up to full and go charging into battle, guns blazing. It would be better than taking all these hours to creep into position and make a sneak attack. No, it wouldn't. Chances were, in a fair fight those two Krag escorts would mop the floor with him. Max remembered the words of Commodore Middleton: "A fair fight comes from poor planning. Your goal is an unfair fight. You want to use every trick, artifice, and deceit possible to make every fight an outrageously unfair contest tilted completely in your favor, every time. If you are above using surprise, guile, stealth, and misdirection in battle, you are too noble to be in the Navy. Consider a career in education."

An hour and a half of creeping. "Skipper," Kasparov said, "we've finally got an angle that lets us do a specident on the targets' drives—all Krag signatures. So all three targets are now posident as hostile. Redesignating the probable ore carrier as Hotel One, and the two probable escorts as Hotels Two and Three. We should have the IDs narrowed down to class before long."

Whatever their precise designation, the three targets had been keeping a ruler-straight course across this star system since they were first detected, and were making no effort to make themselves hard to detect. Whether it was because of Max's strategy of getting into his patrol area several days early, or sheer luck, these ships appeared to have no idea that there was any chance of a hostile ship in the neighborhood.

Or maybe, just maybe, they wanted it to look *as though they weren't expecting trouble.*

"Mr. Kasparov, I want you to put two men in your back room on optical scanners. Watch the area like hawks, from twenty thousand to five hundred thousand kills behind our little convoy. Look for any occultations, reflections, glints, glimmers, tiny flashes from attitude control thrusters, flicking cigarette lighters, toddler's nightlights, or any artificial light source of any kind. Tie the computer detectors into those circuits too—sometimes they will spot something that eyeballs miss. Then, I want you to take two more men and align the main mass detector on that azimuth, and ignore everything else."

The main mass detector usually scanned in all directions, allowing it to detect approaching vessels but greatly decreasing its sensitivity. By training it in one direction only, Max was increasing the chance of detecting even a distant target that was taking active measures to conceal its mass signature.

"Crank up the gain way above the background noise threshold, and then have those men watch the noise. Look for any repeat detections more than one standard deviation above random. If there is something hiding in that space, you are going to slowly build up a pattern of higher than average detections along the other ship's line of bearing."

"Aye, sir. What about EM detection? We can orient the high-gain array that we use to monitor low-power eavesdropping devices from long range."

Designed with the idea that she might someday be used to penetrate enemy space and collect intelligence, *Cumberland* was equipped with an exquisitely sensitive broadband EM sensor capability that allowed her to receive signals from covertly planted "bugs" at extreme range. The same equipment might pick up faint electromagnetic signals escaping from the hidden enemy vessel.

"Good idea. Do that. Maybe they have some signal leakage they don't know about." Kasparov started giving orders to his back room.

"Maneuvering, let's crawl that duck pond from the west instead of the north."

"You want to come up behind this hypothetical trailing ship?" LeBlanc was instantly on the same page.

"You got it. Assume the trailer is less than half a million kills behind the ore carrier. Let's give him a wide berth and put ourselves on his six. Hopefully, he's going to be watching the backs of the ships he's protecting, rather than his own."

"Aye, sir."

"Captain, if I may?"

"Yes, XO?"

"What makes you think anything's back there?"

"Call it a hunch. Well, it's more than that, actually. This little mini-convoy just smells fishy to me. You see, it's very hard to use a single ship, no matter how powerful it is, to protect a gigantic target like an ore carrier that has no point defense systems. If we want to attack that formation, we just use our superior stealth to sneak in to missile range, fire, and then use the combination of high speed and an exit vector screened by the exploding target to get away before we can be fired on. But if they put *two* escorts in there along with the ore carrier, then it's a different ball game."

"I get it." The XO caught on quickly. "With two escorts, the old 'crawl, maul, and haul' tactic won't work because at least one escort will have the right firing geometry to cover our exit vector. We would need to get a guaranteed kill on both escorts at the same time, and the Krag know that our standard tactical doctrine for doing *that* is to sneak up on their six o'clock and hit them simultaneously at close range with a missile, one from each tube. That way, they don't even know they are under attack until the missiles are too close for them to evade."

"Exactly, so if they have a third very stealthy ship…," Max prompted.

"He can sit back there, behind our firing position, silhouette us against the drive emissions of the ore carrier, and blow us to hell just as we are setting up our shot. Those sneaky rat bastards! Putting two escorts right where we can see them *dictates our tactics*. He knows exactly what we are going to do and exactly where we are going to go—and we generously oblige him by putting ourselves right in his cross hairs."

"Bingo, XO. And when you add in that these guys aren't zig-zagging to throw off our firing solution, and they don't seem to be making any effort to hide their drive emissions or their EM signature, they start to look more and more like bait."

"I see it now. And Skipper, how much you want to bet that when we type those escorts they turn out to be very old destroyers ready for the boneyard?"

"Or even corvettes, just powerful enough to be credible escorts for an ore carrier but not so powerful as to deter us from thinking we can attack successfully. No, XO, I wouldn't dream of taking that bet.

"So, here's a command training exercise for you. Assume that there is a ship where we think and that the Krag really, really want us dead. They're serious about it: it's a cruiser. Make it a *Crustacean* class. With their good performance under compression drive, they've been slipping through open space into rear areas and ambushing people right and left. And the two escorts we see are corvettes: *Cormorants* or *Cottonmouths*. What's our attack profile?"

"Tough exercise, Skipper." He thought for about twenty seconds. "Okay. Here's what we do. We load a Raven in tube one and a Talon in two, with an Egg Scrambler in tube three."

The Raven was a heavy antiship missile with a large warhead capable of destroying ships up to cruiser size with just one hit. They were precious—the *Cumberland* carried only five. The Talon was the standard antiship missile with a smaller, variable yield warhead—the *Cumberland* carried twenty of those. And the Egg Scrambler was a device fired from a missile tube that, when exploded, scrambled the interface between normal space and metaspace such that for nearly an hour it was impossible for a ship to operate its compression drive; more important to the present situation, the ship wouldn't be able to transmit any comm signal faster than light, to alert anyone about the attack or call for help.

"We come up behind the cruiser and fire all three tubes at about fifteen thousand kills—time on target firing with the Raven targeted on the cruiser and the Talon at one of the corvettes. Assuming that we kill both, we bore in on the second corvette at flank and open up with the pulse cannon as soon as we're in range, while we reload all three tubes with Talons. We fight it out with the second corvette until we destroy it, then use the cannon on the ore carrier."

"Good plan. Give the orders."

Garcia gave the order to Weapons to change the missile load out. Normally, "three-tube" destroyers carried Talons in all three tubes, which meant that this attack would require the unloading and reloading of one of the forward tubes as well as the rear tubes. Max looked at the tactical display—he hadn't glanced at it for a good forty-five or fifty seconds—and saw that his ship was slowly curving around behind the still theoretical location of the hidden enemy ship. As of yet, the three visible ships had held to their previous course and speed, plowing on straight and stupid, looking more and more like the bait Max suspected them to be.

Every now and then, Max would look at Kasparov, who would shake his head to say that he had no news. An hour passed. Then two. Max had finger food delivered to CIC and the chiller restocked. The coffee pot was getting a workout too. Every now and then, someone would leave his station for a few moments to relieve himself, his position being taken over for that interval by a petty officer reasonably proficient on all stations, known as the "Shortstop," standing watch in CIC for that purpose. Now the tactical display showed that the *Cumberland* was nearly at the six o'clock position relative to the convoy.

Kasparov tilted his head as though hearing something in his headset. He said a few words to his back room and listened again for a few seconds. Somebody saw something.

"Skipper, we're getting a very faint mass detection in the zone, about sixty-five thousand kills behind the ore carrier, right on his six. The mass profile is definite but very flat, as though they're running a highly efficient graviton capture field to suppress their signature. No way to guess their mass, sir."

"Very good, Kasparov. Keep your eyes peeled.

"Maneuvering, now that we have an idea where they are, adjust your approach to bring us in closer. For now, keep us fifty thousand kills behind Kasparov's best guess on a position for the trailer."

"Aye, sir, fifty thousand behind." LeBlanc entered some commands into his console to pull up the data channel from the mass detector so he could put the ship just in the right spot.

"And when we get situated in the slot, talk to Kasparov and get his best guesses on an exact position relative to the other ships; then make some minor course adjustments to try to get lined up to see if we can image the trailing ship against the glow from the ore carrier's sublight drive. Wiggle us around a bit and see if we can spot him."

"Aye, sir."

"Sir," Kasparov said, "our EM array is starting to pick up some leakage from the trailer. Internal comms, wireless devices, and so on. The Krag usually shield these things very well, but I've seen reports that they sometimes leak EM dead astern in some of their larger classes—something about ionized gases from their waste gas ports creating tiny gaps in the shielding. Anyway, I've got their location pinpointed within about a hundred meters now. Revising the plot to incorporate the new data."

The tactical plot of the trailing ship shifted almost imperceptibly forward and to the left. "Thank you, Kasparov," Max said. "Talk to LeBlanc and see if the two of you can use this better position to give us a look at these guys."

The two men talked over their headsets. LeBlanc started giving minute course adjustment orders to his man who controlled pitch and yaw. Max could feel the ship being "wiggled around" to try to find the point in space where the *Cumberland*'s optical scanners were perfectly aligned with the hidden ship and the roughly one-hundred-meter-square drive exhaust array of the ore carrier.

"Skipper," Kasparov spoke up. "We're close enough now to get a posident on Hotels One through Three from their drive signatures. One is a fast ore carrier, *Oriole* class. Two and three are both corvettes, *Corpuscle* class."

"Very well." This was looking better and better. *Corpuscles* were an older class dating back to before the beginning of the war. Two such vessels were hardly a match for the state-of-the-art, practically fresh-out-of-the-yards *Cumberland*. Hell, four or five wouldn't be much trouble. This might prove to be an easy kill.

Several minutes passed, with LeBlanc continuing to "wiggle" the ship based on suggestions from Kasparov.

"Captain, we just got a clear silhouette shot of the trailing ship, now designated as Hotel Four," Kasparov said, finally. There was a definite "oh, shit" tone to his voice. Well, maybe it wouldn't prove to be an easy kill after all. "It's a battlecruiser, heavy. *Barrister* class."

Max and Garcia looked at each other.

"I think we need a new plan," said the XO.

"I think you're right." Long pause. Then, in a studiously calm voice, "Maneuvering, steady as she goes. Cease closure maneuver—maintain current distance to the battlecruiser."

LeBlanc acknowledged the order.

Now, even calmer, in an almost soothing tone, Max ordered, "Stealth, I want a thorough check on all your systems, recheck all emission monitors, verify status of anything on board ship that radiates or could possibly radiate if it were to malfunction. Let's be absolutely positive that we aren't leaking any signal or particles or radiating anything that can cause us to be detected.

"Have the midshipmen visually confirm that all shutters are closed, all docking, hatch, and running lights are off, all thermal radiator fins fully retracted with the doors closed, and all waste vents deactivated and sealed. And by 'visually' I mean *visually*. I mean I want them to use the inspection optics and their eyeballs, not the tell tales, the indicator lights, and the status monitors. And if there's anything else you or your back room thinks we should check, check that too. Twice."

Nelson at the Stealth Station acknowledged the order, and started typing commands on his keyboard and talking into his headset. He had a small back room, and they were going to be very busy for the next few minutes. A few minutes later, an older mid rushed into CIC, talked to Nelson face to face, and dashed out again.

"Bartoli, talk to me about the *Barrister* class," Max prompted. "Refresh our memories as to what we are dealing with."

"Sir, the *Barrister* class is the newest and one of the largest Krag battlecruiser classes, designed both for very heavy firepower and extreme stealth, or as much stealth as you can have in something that big. Displacement estimated at between fifty-five and sixty-two thousand metric tons, length just under three hundred meters, beam roughly thirty meters.

"The only time one has been seen before is at the Battle of Sylvan B, and it didn't fire any weapons, so we don't have a clear idea of what she's packing, but based on prior designs and her size, we would expect at least sixteen missile tubes: something like six forward, two each port and starboard, two dorsal, two ventral, and two rear. She almost certainly has their newest generation of pulse cannon, which is a turret-mounted, two-hundred-gigawatt unit, usually arrayed in batteries of three. She will probably have somewhere between twelve and eighteen of those, most likely fifteen. Plus the standard array of point defense weapons, countermeasures, grappling fields, projectile guns, and so on. Intelligence estimates that she's got four-meter composite armor all around."

Max could almost hear every asshole in the room puckering in fear. "Okay, Bartoli, I'm sure you have the manual of arms for the *Khyber* class of destroyers practically committed to memory.

So, what is the official line on what a *Khyber* is supposed to do when it encounters a *Barrister*?"

"ELEVES, sir, the standard tactic for a detached destroyer encountering an enemy of superior force." ELEVES was pronounced "elves." It stood for ELude, EVade, and EScape. *No shit.*

"Or more plainly, run away. Well, I don't plan to run away," Max declared. "Not today, at any rate."

"But sir," Bartoli countered, almost pleadingly, "given that ship's size, and with what we know about Krag shielding, structural integrity fields, and active blast dampers, we would have to hit it with four Ravens, and the safest bet would be to hit it with four Ravens *simultaneously*."

"Then we'll just have to hit it with four Ravens simultaneously."

Bartoli looked at his captain as though he had proposed attacking the battlecruiser with a thong slingshot and a water pistol. "But we've got only *two* forward missile tubes. And you can't launch two missiles cold and have them just sitting there in space while we reload two more and then fire all four. The drives on the first two missiles won't get them going fast enough to penetrate the Krag point defense batteries. If they aren't launched with the starting velocity imparted by the accelerator coils in the launch tubes, the Krag will just shoot them down."

"Then, that's not what we're going to do." He hit the comm switch. "Engineering."

"Engineering. Brown here."

"Wernher, this is the skipper. Do you happen to know how many regulations there are about proper use of the hardware issued to this vessel?"

"Not precisely. I should think that there would something on the order of two or three hundred."

"Well, get up here then. I need your help breaking about fifty of them."

CHAPTER 14

12:10 Z Hours, 26 January 2315

The *Cumberland* had very slowly and very carefully closed within twelve hundred kilometers of the immense battlecruiser, which continued to lumber on, seemingly oblivious to the comparatively tiny destroyer in her wake. Max supposed that she was straining to spot a destroyer slipping in where it was expected, so intent on looking forward that she hadn't a thought that she was, herself, being stalked from behind.

Twenty minutes before, the destroyer's hangar deck had opened and her cutter, a small, nimble, multipurpose auxiliary vessel, capable of carrying ten men plus a flight crew of two, slid out on maneuvering thrusters only, then slowly eased in its sublight drive, taking up station thirty-five hundred kilometers behind its mother ship. Ensign Mori, the best small-craft pilot on the ship, settled the tiny vessel into its designated place, experiencing unaccustomed difficulty handling the cutter because of the awkwardly placed additional mass.

Max counted down the seconds to the first step of the minutely calculated timetable that he, Bartoli, Garcia, and Brown had quickly put together. "Maneuvering, *EXECUTE*."

LeBlanc brought his hand down on the right shoulder of his drives man, Able Spacer First Fleishman. Two sharp pats. "Go. All ahead Emergency."

Fleishman pushed his main drive controller all the way forward to the stop, bringing the main sublight drive to 125 percent of its rated power. Like an eager cavalry mount spurred by its rider, the *Cumberland* leaped forward. The range to the battlecruiser fell rapidly as the ship accelerated: 11,000 ... 10,500 ... 10,000 ... 9,500 ... 9,000. At that rate of acceleration, stealth went out the window, so at 8,800 kilometers, apparently having gotten a general detection of the destroyer, the Krag vessel began to sweep the area with her powerful active sensors, instantly pinpointing the ship on her tail.

"Battlecruiser has increased her sublight drive to Emergency," said Bartoli. The larger ship's top speed was slower than the destroyer's, and she accelerated more slowly; still, the increased acceleration substantially slowed the closure rate between the two ships. "Battlecruiser is sweeping us with targeting scanners ... she's initiating a lock sequence."

"Fire the Egg Scrambler" Max ordered. The communications jammer shot from tube three and immediately detonated, making interstellar communications impossible. Unless their enemy survived the battle, any news the Krag passed on about this attack could travel no faster than the speed of light. It would be years before anyone heard it.

"Evasive India Three. Countermeasures." Immediately LeBlanc started giving a series of intricate orders to his men, jinking the highly maneuverable destroyer erratically to slow the ability of the enemy to get a targeting lock while still continuing to close the range to the battlecruiser. Meanwhile, one Countermeasures officer in CIC and seven of his back room colleagues activated and managed various scrambling pulses, confusing echoes, jamming signals, infrared drones, chaff dispensing missiles, and other kinds of subterfuge designed to confuse, deceive, distract, divert, or otherwise discombobulate the Krag targeting systems so that the battlecruiser's deadly pulse cannon could not get a killing shot.

Max stabbed the comm switch. "CIC to Mori."

"Mori here."

"You ready?"

"I've got my eye on the sun and my paddle in the water." Mori was born on a tiny island in the Micronesia chain on Earth. His people, in an almost inconceivable feat of seamanship and navigation, had paddled dugout canoes across thousands of miles of the open Pacific without chart or compass to make precise landfall on tiny islands smaller than the average farm in the American Midwest. Mori himself had spent much of his childhood in such craft before deciding at age nine to venture into an infinitely vaster ocean.

"Go at the designated mark."

"Affirmative. Three. Two. One. Now." Mori engaged the powerful sublight drive on the cutter, which, even with the extra weight, quickly began to overtake the destroyer. The accelerating battlecruiser had not spotted him yet, having a more immediate threat to deal with.

The *Cumberland*'s evasive maneuvers combined with an excellent countermeasures deployment helped confuse the Krag targeting systems, for now. Determining that they could not get a positive lock, the Krag decided to fire by bearing rather than firing by lock, meaning that they pointed their cannon along the measured bearing of the destroyer rather than having a coaxial lock between the targeting scanner and the weapon bore.

Brilliant pulse cannon bolts streaked past the *Cumberland*, some passing within meters of her hull. Space was big, but it wasn't *that* big. It was only a matter of time before the Krag got a hit by this method, or before the decreasing range allowed the targeting scanners to get a lock.

The *Cumberland* began firing its own, somewhat less powerful pulse cannon, on the off chance of doing some damage or at least helping confuse the enemy targeting systems. It was impossible to miss a nonevading target of that size at that range, so every shot scored a hit on the battlecruiser, but her deflectors and immensely thick, armored hull prevented any major damage. The fifth shot did, however, actually manage to destroy one of the battlecruiser's two aft targeting scanners. With only one targeting scanner operating, the chances of getting a lock decreased significantly.

Concealed by the *Cumberland*'s attack, the accelerating cutter came up behind her mother ship, matching its speed at .60 c. The two ships exchanged quick digital signals verifying that each was prepared for the next step, starting a five-second countdown clock on each vessel. When his clock reached zero, Mori nudged his drive controller forward and pulled around the *Cumberland* on its port side. Just as the cutter drew even with the *Cumberland*'s missile tubes and reached a speed of .61c, the *Cumberland* fired a Raven heavy antiship missile from each of its two forward missile tubes.

At that same moment, four explosive bolts on the port side of the cutter and four on the starboard detonated, each set releasing a hastily fashioned bracket that had held a Raven to the hull of the Cutter. Following their recently altered flight software, these two Ravens yawed away from the cutter for two seconds at low power before their drives went to full stage and rapidly accelerated the missiles to attack speed, matching that of their two brethren just fired from the *Cumberland.*

"Maneuvering, break away," Max nearly shouted. "Missile rooms, reload with Talons."

LeBlanc gave the preplanned orders to his men, veering the destroyer ninety degrees away from its previous course while continuing to accelerate at Emergency so that the Krag gunners would have to try to follow the fastest possible change in bearing. As the range opened up and the *Cumberland* continued to accelerate, the pulse cannon bolts trailed hopelessly behind.

The four Raven missiles streaked toward their target. Communicating with one another in microsecond-long coded bursts, their sophisticated onboard computers coordinated their attack second by second, working together like a pack of wolves to confuse and destroy their prey.

After flying together in a rough box formation for a few seconds, the missiles separated from one another, each approaching the huge vessel from amidships as though each were approaching from a different cardinal point of the compass. Within its designated target zone, each missile scanned its quarry, selecting a particularly vulnerable point—a hatch, a junction between two hull plates, a cluster of waste gas vents. Three missiles slowed slightly and one speeded up so that they would impact and detonate at exactly the same microsecond, placing the maximum stress on the structure, shielding, integrity fields, and blast suppression systems of the Krag vessel. Finally, at 99.28 percent of the speed of light, all four streaked past the Krag defenses and detonated as one.

Four 1.5-megaton fusion warheads exploded—four suns born around the Krag's hull, growing and merging into a gigantic four-lobed fireball consuming the battlecruiser in less than a second. The orb of destruction assimilated metal and plastic, bone and flesh alike, taking atoms forged by nucleosynthesis billions of years ago in the cores of now long-dead supernovae and hurling them back into the void.

Max watched the expanding globe of light as it filled his screen. He had never seen four of the big warheads used on a target all at once, and he was awed by the enormous destruction that could be unleashed at his order. And by how powerful the bombs were in comparison to the puny men who made them.

The fireball faded. There was still work to do. "Tactical, what are our remaining friends doing?

"The ore carrier's course and speed are unchanged—he's still headed for the jump point, ETA six hours, thirty-seven minutes. A reasonable hypothesis is that the vessel is automated. And the corvettes are running for it—drives are redlined. Heading is two-two-five mark zero-one-five. That's a course for the nearest edge of the zone messed up by the Egg Scrambler"

"Can we get within pulse cannon range before they get there?"

Someone in Tactical's back room who was paying close enough attention, either watching the overall situation or listening to the conversation in CIC or both, decided that just such a calculation would be needed and had put it up on one of Tactical's screens. "Affirmative, sir. With the main sublight at 'Full,' we can still catch them with about six minutes to spare. And even if they get there, sir, *Corpuscles* have a top speed on compression of only about twelve hundred c. We could overtake them pretty quickly."

"That's good to know, Tactical, but I prefer not to engage a superluminal target if I can help it. Maneuvering, reduce to full and shape course to intercept the corvettes."

"Ahead full, course to intercept corvettes, aye." LeBlanc implemented the drive setting change, spent a few moments with his console, calculating the new course, and then gave the course change orders.

The *Cumberland* overtook the two smaller ships, rapidly drawing within pulse cannon range of the fleeing vessels.

"Weapons, bring pulse cannon one and pulse cannon three to Prefire. Target cannon one on Hotel Two and cannon three on Hotel Three. Hold pulse cannon two on Standby."

"Aye, sir, pulse one and three to Prefire, two remaining on Standby." Weapons acknowledged. Eleven seconds passed as the systems that diverted plasma from the ship's main reactor and routed it through shielded conduits into the cannons' firing chambers were energized, their cooling systems powered up and engaged, and the cannon aiming systems enabled. Two green lights on the Weapons console came on.

"Pulse one and pulse three at Prefire. Targeting now." The huge magnetic coils that guided the pulse blasts came to life, drew aiming data from the targeting computer, and synched with the targeting scanner, which had already locked onto the targets. Two more green lights came on. Each cannon's target appeared on one of Tactical's screens, along with the target's ID, course, speed, and range.

"Pulse one locked on Hotel Two. Pulse three locked on Hotel Three."

"Pulse one and pulse three to ready."

Weapons stabbed two orange buttons, one for each cannon to be fired, which caused plasma to flow from the reactor into the firing chambers, building up sufficient quantity to fire the weapons. This took four seconds, after which two more green lights at Tactical winked on. "Pulse one and pulse three ready."

"Set for maximum power, synchronized firing."

"Max power, synch firing, aye."

"Range to targets?"

"We are 9,355 kills to Hotel Two, 9,357 kills to Hotel Three." Maximum effective range was 10,500 kilometers.

"Confirm targets."

"Pulse one is targeted on Krag corvette designated Hotel Two off our bow, range 9,355 kills. Pulse two is targeted on Krag corvette designated Hotel Three off our bow, range 9,357 kills."

"Captain, I think we are missing something important here," Garcia interjected.

"Like what?" Max was not entirely successful in concealing his irritation at being interrupted just as he was about to kill these two targets.

"Why aren't they evading? Corvettes are very maneuverable. I mean, as soon as we got in range these guys should have started jinking all over the place, right?"

Good question. Why the hell not? What could they possibly have to gain by not zigzagging? Max could think of only one thing: if the corvettes maintained a constant course, then the *Cumberland* was more likely to maintain a constant course as well. Therefore, the Krag must want his ship to stay in a constant position relative to theirs. Why would they want that? *Oh. Crap.*

"Forward deflectors to maximum—tune for metallic object about two meters in diameter with extremely low relative velocity. Point defense batteries, zone firing. Blanket thirty-degree cone forward. Spaceframe reinforcement to maximum. All hands brace for impact."

CIC held its breath for two and a half seconds, at which point the console screens showing output from the forward optical scanners flared white and then went dark, their receptors burned out. A split second later, the ship trembled mildly as the shock wave from the explosion, almost vanishingly tenuous in the vacuum of outer space, struck the hull.

"All right, now that we've got that settled, let's fry the bastards. Weapons, fire pulse one and two."

Weapons pressed both fire controls and two glowing balls of compressed plasma about two meters in diameter streaked through space, each striking its target dead center and exploding as its containment field—generated by a tiny liquid helium–cooled emitter inserted in the plasma pulse as it left the gun tube—shattered with the explosive force of about half a kiloton.

It wasn't much compared to a missile, but the blast equivalent of five hundred tons of TNT, not to mention the thermal and structural stress of being struck at an appreciable fraction of lightspeed by a ball of compressed, ionized gas as hot as the interior of the sun, was enough to spell the end of two superannuated corvettes. Both ships tore themselves apart in twin orgies of glaring explosions and shredding metal.

A few moments later, as normalcy returned to CIC and the destroyer shaped course to intercept the now defenseless ore carrier, the XO turned to his skipper.

"Sir, do you mind telling me what the *hell* just happened."

"Oh, that." Max managed to sound almost nonchalant. "New weapon. One of our spy ships witnessed a test of it inside Krag space a few months ago, but we didn't know that it was deployed yet: code name 'Remora' or something like that. Nasty little fucker. It's a stealthed, remote-controlled fusion bomb designed to kill an overtaking ship. The bastards launch it cold, and it comes at you slowly and undetectably just as you think you are boring in at them on their six. The stealth is so good that the point defense grid doesn't pick it up, and the speed relative to the chasing ship is so low that the deflectors don't even budge it. They just let it crawl back until they've got it snuggled right up against the hull and then BLAM. You never see it coming."

He turned toward Tactical. "That looked like—what?—a one-fifty or one-sixty kiloton burst?"

"Our reading is one-five-two kilo tango, Skipper," Bartoli answered.

"Okay, a hundred-and-fifty-two kt thermonuclear burst. *Inside* the deflectors. Right up against the hull. That's a 100 percent kill for anything from a medium cruiser on down. Who knows how many times they've used it without us being the wiser? No warning. No survivors. Just another ship 'missing, presumed lost.' If it hadn't been for your question, XO, they would have gotten us too."

Max shook his head ruefully. Already he could think of five lost Union ships that had left debris patterns perfectly explained by what he had observed about this weapon.

"Anyway, tuning the deflector for an object of the right size and relative velocity pushed it away from the ship where the point defense batteries were able to get a lock once the deflectors had it. The computer on board the weapon determined that it was going to be destroyed, so it detonated before we could hit it. We lived. They died." *This time.* "That's the name of the game."

"Chin, raise the cutter." Chin clicked a few keys.

"Cutter, Mori here."

"Mori, this is the skipper. Didn't want you to think you'd slipped our minds. What's your status?"

"The cutter lost some external antennae when that second Raven lit off, but other than that, no damage. I'll be at the rendezvous point in thirteen minutes."

"Excellent. See you there. Keep on piloting like that and I might just let you take the cutter out again some time. Skipper out."

The ore carrier, which was the real target all along, continued to plow toward the jump point with dogged, robotic determination. Because Krag remote navigation software is almost totally immune to tampering and because robot vessels are usually heavily booby-trapped, there was little chance that the ore carrier could be diverted or boarded. There was only one thing to do with it, then—blow it to flaming atoms.

The vessel's destruction was anticlimactic—a straightforward approach from the starboard beam, two shots from pulse cannon number two, and the half-million-ton freighter and its bulky but strategically valuable cargo became a cloud of debris. None of that ore would ever be refined into metal to make Krag guns, Krag swords, and Krag ships. A small but measurable blow to enemy war production had been struck by the USS *Cumberland*.

For the first time since its commissioning, the *Cumberland* had met the enemy in battle and had defeated him. Victory. It really *did* taste sweet.

CHAPTER 15

14:38Z Hours, 26 January 2315

Max had been writing his After Action Report detailing the destruction of the Krag battlecruiser, two corvettes, and ore carrier for a little over an hour, trying to find the right balance between bland, bureaucratic description and tooting his own horn and that of his crew in vigorous prose. Such things were best done when the engagement was fresh in one's mind. After two hours doing single combat with the Standard language, Navy style, Max completed the report and hit the key that made it a part of the ship's log before marking it for transmission to the Task Force and to the Admiralty as soon as the ship came off EMCON.

Because he was at his workstation, he decided to check his messages. The screen helpfully informed him, "Your in box contains 247 new items." *That's a lot.* Particularly as he had cleared out the box less than eighteen hours ago. He selected the command to "Rank Items According to Priority." The computer algorithm balanced the priority assigned by the sender to the message; the identity of the sender; and its assessment, based on content, of how important the message would be to the recipient.

The result of that analysis was that a communication from Dr. Sahin landed at the top of the heap. It said that the doctor had found out from Goldman that one of the sources of stress on the officers and senior NCOs was that they had to prepare too many reports to comply with a thicket of inane standing orders imposed by Captain Oscar. He recommended that Max review the reports required by the ship's standing orders and eliminate the unnecessary ones.

Max scrolled through the list of other incoming emails and could not help but concur. A *daily* Sensor Contact Report from Harbaugh. Three separate reports from Chief Jinnah: one indicating that he had issued the coffee pots, one indicating he had issued the beverage chillers, and one indicating he had issued the cups and glasses. A report from the galley indicating how many kilograms of various foodstuffs and how many liters of various beverages were consumed by the men. Yesterday. Another report from the galley listing total consumption of liquor, beer, stout, and wine. Yesterday. One set of numbers for officers and one set for enlisted. And the other 242 were of the same ilk.

Dreading what he expected to find, Max pulled up the file that contained all of the ship's standing orders. "There are 1,232 standing orders on file." *Damn, damn, damn.* Max was kicking himself, hard. Why had he not checked the SSO file sooner? Stupid mistake. Correction: *another* stupid mistake. He knew he couldn't afford many more of those.

"Display in list form, summary form, or as full text in order issued?" Max chose "list" and spent about a minute scrolling down looking at the reference lines: "Organization of Cookware and Utensils in Galley According to Principles of Time and Motion Science; Eating in Quarters Prohibited Save for Personnel

Confined Thereto; Use of the Phrase 'The Fact That' in Any Correspondence Addressed to the Captain or Being Sent to Higher Authority Prohibited..."

Sweet baby Jesus! He had never seen such a load of crap. He kicked himself again. He *really* should have checked the standing orders. This crew didn't need to take drugs to addle its brains—they were already dizzy from chasing their own tails.

The doctor had suggested that he go through the standing orders and eliminate those that imposed an undue burden on the crew—careful use of the scalpel. This problem didn't need a scalpel. It needed a bone saw. No—a battle-ax.

He pulled up the computer form for a standing order and checked the list of previous orders for the correct number (only eleven so far this year, as Captain Oscar had been relieved on January 4th). He began to type:

USS *Cumberland* DPA-0004: Ship's Standing Order #15–12

Effective immediately:

1. All previous ship's standing orders (SSOs) are revoked. "All" means all.

2. Until further notice, this vessel will be governed by the Union Space Navy Model Standing Orders for vessels of this type.

He hit ENTER. *There. That should put a stop to some of that insanity.* He shook his head—what else had he missed? When and how would it rear up and bite him in the ass?

Max gulped down the last of the cold coffee at the bottom of his mug and looked at his bunk. God, he was tired. Maybe a short nap. Just an hour or two. He had just about talked himself into it when his comm buzzed. "Skipper."

"Captain, this is the chief medical officer. I am in C-24," Sahin announced formally. "I regret to report that we have a fatality."

"On my way."

Max's quarters were on B Deck just forward of amidships, whereas C-24 was one deck below, and aft. Still, Max was there in less than two minutes, making a point not to look as though he were in any particular hurry or that anything was wrong. When he emerged from the corridor alcove containing the access ladder he had used to change decks into the main corridor on C Deck, he saw that he need not have bothered. There were at least twenty people in the corridor, milling about and talking, blocking his way to Compartment C-24.

When he was about ten meters away from the crowd he stopped and, using his best parade-ground voice (one of the loudest in the fleet, truth be told), barked, "AH-TENNN-*HUT!*"

Instantly, the milling, babbling mass of humanity froze in rigid, silent, attention. "I want this corridor cleared. If you are on duty, get to your station. If you are off duty, get to your quarters or the mess or somewhere, just so long as it is not here. Now, *MOVE.*" In eight seconds, the corridor was empty, save for Max and the two Marines that someone had sensibly posted outside the hatch to C-24.

The Marines, having gone back to parade rest when Max ordered everyone to leave, snapped to present arms as Max reached the door. When posted as a guard with shoulder arms, present arms was the Marine equivalent of a salute. Max saluted back; the men went back to parade rest, and one of them triggered the door.

Max entered, encountering what appeared to be a blizzard. Tiny white particles were swirling around in the air like snowflakes in the winter wind. The computer had put the air circulation system in the compartment on maximum, triggered by the presence of seven people in the compartment and that of unusually high levels of combustion products and particulates. Max scanned the room. What had happened here was clear to him in about a second and a half. He had seen it before. More than once.

Priorities. First, stop the snowstorm so people could work and think. "Computer, activate voice interface." Few people used the computer Voice Command Interface, but the workstation was definitely something he did not want to touch right now, and it would take too long to peck out the series of commands on his percom.

"Voice Command Interface active," said the purring contralto that someone back in Norfolk thought was a good way for a computer to sound. Rumor had it that the voice was patterned on that of a centuries-dead wife of a television producer. If so, that would be immortality in one of its most peculiar forms.

"Initiate voice recognition protocol."

"Voice recognition protocol activated. Please state your name and rank."

"Robichaux, Maxwell T., Lieutenant Commander."

"Robichaux, Maxwell T., recognition successful. Please input command."

"Input two commands. Command one: Stop air circulation in this compartment. Command two: Activate AICLSS in this compartment. End input."

AICLSS was pronounced "ay-kliss." The computer voice confirmed the orders. Now, the air would be kept breathable by the auxiliary independent compartment life support system, which would extract the CO_2 with a miniature scrubber and infuse oxygen from a reserve supply; oxygen would be replenished periodically from the ship's main reservoir rather than by the brute force method of circulating high volumes of air blown in from the ship's ventilation system. The white particles in the air immediately began to settle out, leaving Max alone in the compartment with Kraft, Sahin, a nurse, and four corpsmen. And one nearly decapitated corpse.

As the man was clearly dead, the nurse was not necessary to assist Dr. Sahin, and the corpsmen would not be needed to carry the patient to the Casualty Station, so Max dismissed them. He then walked over to the workstation, careful not to disturb anything. In front of it sat a man, in his service-issued "long-john" single-piece undergarment; he was missing most of the top of his head. An M-62 pistol was on the floor near his limp right hand, and the remains of a pillow were messily comingled with his skull contents. Apparently, the man had used the pillow to muffle the sound of the pistol, exploding it and filling the room with disintegrated bits of the foam with which it had been stuffed. After dying, the man had fallen over onto his workstation, bleeding profusely onto the keyboard and touch interface pad. Bits of blood, bone, and brain decorated every surface in a murderer's parody of abstract painting.

"Who was he?"

Kraft answered, "Ranatunga. First name, Dayani. Positive ID from his Q-chip. These are his quarters. Age twenty-eight."

Max's age. No doubt about the identification as Kraft had scanned the ID chip embedded deep in the left thigh muscle of every man in the Navy. It was called a "Q-chip" because it was embedded in the quadriceps muscle.

"Chief petty officer second class. Assigned to the Tactical section; he did Intentions and Capabilities in the Tactical SSR. Good record. Three battle clusters before being assigned to this ship. Outstanding FitReps. He was in line to be some ship's COB in five to ten years or to do a rotation at one of the NCO tactical schools.

One of our best. I'll do the forensics, but a greenie could put this one together. The man sat down at this terminal, typed a suicide note, took his service weapon, muffled the report with the pillow, and blew his brains out. No sign of forced entry or an intruder of any kind. Computer records indicate no one else in the room. Environmental monitoring shows a sharp increase in particulates and carbon dioxide, carbon monoxide, sulfur dioxide, nitrogen oxide, and the other gases you expect from a weapons discharge. This took place at 15:26 and twelve seconds. And yes, there is generally an alarm for such things. But I think you can guess how this sentence ends...."

"Captain Oscar ordered that it be deactivated."

"*Genau.* Apparently, there were a few false alarms that interrupted him during his interminable senior officer meetings. Finally, at 15:42 and six seconds, the computer determined that no oxygen was being consumed in here, even though it logged one person as being present, so it sent an automatic alert to the Security Station. I tried to reach Chief Ranatunga on the comm and on his percom. When he didn't answer, at 15:42 and thirty-nine seconds, I used my override to turn on the visual input on the workstation.

"I saw a slumped man and blood on the lens, so at 15:42 and fifty seconds I summoned the doctor and came directly here with two Marines. Computer records show the doctor using his CMO override to enter the compartment at 15:44 and eleven seconds. The computer logged that he entered along with five other people—the nurse and the four corpsmen.

"I entered at 15:44 and twenty-eight seconds and posted the Marines at the door. When I came in, the first thing I did was secure the compartment, and it has been secure at all times since that moment. Nothing has been removed or touched yet. You, me, the doctor, and his people have been the only personnel in this room. I would regard this as a near-pristine crime scene."

Max turned to Dr. Sahin, who looked absolutely shattered. "Doctor, was he…"

"Yes, yes, yes, yes. Oh, yes. He was. Absolutely." He shook his head slowly, mournfully. "I killed him."

"No, Doctor, you're wrong. This man had been dead for more than seventeen minutes when you arrived," blurted Kraft.

"Oh, yes, Major, you may be certain that I was sitting in my comfortable chair in the Casualty Station, feeling very satisfied and capable, wallowing in the delusion that I was in control of the situation, watching some of my patients on a monitor, when this good man picked up a pistol and violently ended his life," said Sahin, his voice dripping with sarcasm and trembling with anger, "but I killed him just as surely as if I had held the weapon to his head and pulled the trigger. His blood is on my hands, to be sure, and the smell of it will never fade. 'All the perfumes of Arabia shall not sweeten this little hand.'"

Max needed data, not self-recrimination, and certainly not Shakespeare quotes. "Lieutenant Sahin, I require a cogent report from my chief medical officer, and I need it now. Are you capable of delivering that to me?" He would have added, "If not, I will summon your relief," but there was no relief for Ibrahim Sahin. He was the only physician on the ship. After him, there were a few nurses, a pharmacist's mate, and some corpsmen. If Max needed a physician, he would have to figure out a way to get useful information from this man or do without.

Dr. Sahin nodded slowly and sat on the man's bunk. The blood trajectory had not made it that far. "Captain," he said, "this man was one of the crewmen I was treating for drug addiction and withdrawal. He was a very heavy Chill user, and his withdrawal symptoms were initially very severe. I prescribed

Exemitrol to control the nausea, Anodynamil for the rebound anxiety, Niltremulin for the shakes, and Synaptoflex to speed his nervous system's recovery.

"I kept him under close observation for eighteen hours and returned him to duty with instructions to check in with the Casualty Station every eight hours, to make sure he was not having any additional symptoms. He seemed to be doing well, and I had every hope that he would make a full recovery without any additional discomfort. My plan was to start weaning him from the medication in about thirty-six hours."

"If he was doing so well, why…"—Max made a clumsy gesture encompassing the room—"why this?" he asked.

"Because, my good Captain, a small number of people who take Anodynamil and Synaptoflex and who have residual amounts of Chill in their central nervous systems can suddenly and inexplicably experience sudden depression and kill themselves. It has happened before. It is right there in the literature for all the galaxy to see, and I took no special precautions to prevent it. I should have kept him under strict observation until he was weaned from the medication. I should have had him in the Casualty Station right under my thumb where I could have kept him safe from harm. I was trying to help him reclaim his life, and instead I killed him. I have never seen so much blood. 'Who would have thought the young man to have had so much blood in him?'"

Great. Another Macbeth *quote. An unlucky play. This is not going well.* "How often? I mean, in what percentage of the people in this situation does this occur? Ten percent, 20 percent?"

"One."

"Only 1 percent?"

"No. One other case."

"Out of how many?

"With this combination of drugs?"

"Yes. That's the only way it is known to happen, isn't it?"

"Yes. One out of two or three million, I suppose."

"Doctor, *Doctor*, one case? Out of two or three million? My God, man, one out of two or three million could have been caused by anything! Maybe he was exposed to cosmic rays that scrambled his brain proteins. Maybe his lover jilted him. Maybe his goldfish died. Maybe the drugs triggered a genetic predisposition to suicide.

"You're the scientist, Doctor—not me. You know better than I do that when you're dealing with an event this rare, it is statistically impossible to identify causation. Even if you could, you don't take precautions against a one-in-a-million event. When I make plans, I don't prepare contingencies for outcomes that are that remote. If you did that, you wouldn't have the time or the energy to do anything else."

"But I knew it could happen and did nothing."

"No, Doctor, you evaluated the risk and determined that it was not sufficiently likely to justify precautions against it. Big difference. Every drug you administer has side effects that can affect a small number of patients, right?"

"Of course. That is a given."

"How many patients do you have, right now, receiving some kind of medication on this ship?"

"With all of this business going on, slightly more than half. Under ordinary circumstances, just under a third would be taking some kind of meds, generally for minor concerns such as allergies, blood pressure, and sleep disturbance."

"Now, think of all the remotest side effects of all those different medications reported in all the medical literature ever published. Is there any way you could watch for and take precautions against all of them, or would doing so take up such an enormous amount of time and effort that you could not properly care for the patients who are right in front of you, with immediate medical needs that you can see and verify? You don't need to answer that. Even a scientifically illiterate destroyer skipper knows the answer. No. Of course not. Trust me on this. Doctor—*Bram*—you did not do this."

Dr. Sahin pondered that. After a few moments, some, but by no means all, of the weight he seemed to be carrying appeared to lift from his shoulders. "I will consider what you have said, Captain, and I will go on with my work."

"Good. Very good. In the final analysis, you didn't kill this man. The Krag did. If they hadn't invaded, this man would be sitting at home going about his civilian life, eating dinner with his wife and children. Now, I think there's no need for you to stay here. You should go back to the Casualty Station. We'll let you know if we need you."

He left. Max walked over to Kraft. "You mentioned something about a suicide note."

"Yes. I have located it but have not yet read it." He opened up his percom to reveal the larger inside touch screen and entered some commands. Some text appeared on one wall of the compartment, a roughly one-by-two-meter area of which doubled as a secondary computer display or entertainment viewing screen. Both men stood together and read it.

"Same old," said Max. "Who would have imagined that with all the varieties of human experience, with men in the Navy coming from every kind of economic circumstance and religion and culture on hundreds of worlds, almost every suicide note would say almost exactly the same thing. Are civilian suicide notes like this?"

"No, they are not," Kraft answered. "This is the eighth suicide I've investigated. I got curious about them one time and did some research. The civilians all seem to talk about how much pain they're in, how no one understands them or cares about them, and how they can't bear to live any longer. The military ones seem to be about how they have failed their shipmates and the Union and the Navy, how they're consumed with guilt for their failures, and how they do not *deserve* to live any longer. This one clearly follows the military pattern."

Max looked at the remains of Dayani Ranatunga. "Damn it, man, you were not a failure. We could have used a man like you. *I* could have used a man like you."

Then, to Kraft, "I suppose that wraps it up, then. Man blows his brains out in a locked room and leaves a suicide note. Mark it a suicide and go on."

"I just have a few things to finish in here for my report. I need to find the slug, if anything is left of it; locate the shell casing—it must have rolled under some furniture or be sitting in a flower pot or a coffee cup somewhere because it has not turned up yet; take a few measurements—that sort of thing. I will be in here another hour or two. Then I'll notify the Casualty Station to remove the body, and we can get maintenance in here to clean things up. I'll send you my report when complete."

They stood together in silence for a few seconds, their eyes running over Chief Ranatunga's last words still displayed on the wall. Kraft blanked the wall with a touch to his percom. "The doctor is taking it pretty hard."

"Yes, he is," answered Max. "But I don't think a man like him could take this sort of thing any other way. He just hasn't seen the things we've seen."

"Right. I've investigated about one of these a year since I became an officer."

"And there have been dozens on the ships I've served on over the years," said Max. "I hate it. I hate it more than anything."

Max walked over to the viewport. It was just smaller than a meter square, but it still gave a good view of the stars. He fixed his gaze on one star that drew his attention because of its distinct reddish hue. It reminded him of Antares, once pointed out to him by a lovely young woman on an Earth beach years ago.

"Rival of Ares," is what the star's name meant, because its red hue reminded the Greeks of the red planet named for their God of War, whom the Romans called Mars. Antares too was supposed to be associated with war, perhaps because it was always high overhead in the night sky during the late spring and summer, the season of war, when ancient armies took to the field to spill each other's blood with bronze, iron, and steel. Bronze-clad Spartan Hoplites and Persian Immortals alike must have gazed at it, a red beacon in the darkness, as they sat around their campfires, anticipating the killing that would come at dawn.

When humans attached their myths to the planets and the stars in the night sky so long ago, they had no idea that their distant grandchildren would venture among those stars, only to find there a deadly enemy who would force them to fight for mankind's very survival. In 2315, the descendants of the Spartans and the Persians and the Romans and the Chinese and all the rest no longer ventured into this region of space for peaceful exploration, scientific inquiry, or to open up new avenues of commerce. Instead, they came only for one reason. To wage war. *Rival of Ares?* Max thought bitterly. *Out here, Ares has no rival. Men serve no god but him.*

"It's this goddamn war, Kraft," he said. "These men kill themselves because they have lost hope." A long, silent minute passed, the two men together, yet alone with their thoughts. "Sometimes I think that there will never be an end. Do you ever feel that way?" Max asked.

"*Natürlich.* On the days when the clouds hang low over my head. But most days, when the clouds are elsewhere, I believe and hope that there is an end, and I even pray and hold out hope that I may live to see it. Hope keeps me going—keeps *us* going."

"That, and one more thing."

"*Ja?*"

"The will to survive."

"*Sieg über alles,* then."

"*Jawohl,* my friend, victory above all. Victory at all costs."

They both looked at Chief Ranatunga for a long moment; then Max turned and took a few steps toward the door, but stopped and looked back at Kraft. "At all costs. It's easy to say, isn't it?" He pointed to the dead man. "But when we pay, that's the currency we use. How much more, Kraft? How much more will we have to pay?"

CHAPTER 16

05:44Z Hours, 28 January 2315

"This plan of yours strikes me as being excessively complex and prone to failure at several discrete junctures," Dr. Sahin said to Max, his voice pitched so as to be inaudible beyond the command island in CIC.

Garcia nodded his agreement. "Sir, I have to agree." He was just as quiet as the doctor. "There is a lot to be said for just charging in, blowing that little freighter to flaming atoms, and getting out before anyone even knows we've been there."

"Gentlemen," Max said amiably, "I'm just as fond of getting in and getting out as the next man, but there are other factors you're failing to consider. Although the cartographic data we received from the Vaaach *says* that this is a Krag ship with a Krag cargo, she's broadcasting a Ghiftee transponder ID. That means that there is a strong possibility that she has a legitimate Ghiftee registry and is therefore officially classified under interstellar law as a neutral vessel.

"And gentlemen, I can't just go gallivanting around the galaxy blowing neutral vessels to hell and gone, because," he counted off the points on his fingers, "one: they'll court martial my happy ass and throw me in the brig until I'm about a hundred and twenty-seven years old. Two: I will be held liable in damages by an Admiralty court for the value of the ship and its cargo, which is more money than any of us will ever see in our lifetimes. And three: the Union Foreign Ministry is doing everything in its power to get the Ghiftee—not to mention the Romanovans, the Rashidians, Pfelung, the Texians, and just about every other human and nonhuman neutral power in this end of the swamp—to come into the war with us against the Krag.

"Now don't you think that it is just possible that a Union warship launching an unprovoked attack on an innocent neutral freighter merrily navigating through unclaimed space, not to mention the deaths of its innocent, neutral crew, just *might* undermine those efforts? Does the name *Lusitania* mean anything to you?"

Both men silently conceded the point. "But," the doctor pressed on, "if the Ghiftee are neutral, how can we interfere with their ship at all, much less do what you're planning?"

"It's the law. By their repeated unprovoked attacks against neutral shipping, the Krag forfeited their right under customary interstellar law to have themselves and their goods carried in neutral shipping. There is occasionally some fairness in law, you know. It's a natural consequence of their actions: because they did not respect neutral rights, they do not get to avail themselves of neutral rights. So the Krag, both their rat-faced selves and their cargo, are legally contraband and can be seized wherever they are found. But we have to have evidence that the contraband is on the ship, so to do that, we have to board her."

"Then why not just board her without all the elaborate, and apparently gratuitous, play acting and deception that your plan entails?" the doctor asked.

"Because the instant this little freighter suspects us as a Union warship, she'll run."

"What if she does?" the doctor asked. "If she runs, we know she is guilty, so then we catch her. My understanding is that our vessel is a very speedy one."

"It is, but *this* freighter is faster. This particular design is built for and marketed to smugglers and blockade runners. Her top speed is a hair faster than ours, and since she's lighter, she accelerates like a rabbit. We need to convince her to heave to and permit us to lock on a grappling field, or we'll never get on board."

"But won't she flee the moment she sees us?"

"There, Doctor, is where you're showing yourself to still have dirt on your feet."

"Dirt?" He looked at his boots.

"It's an old spacer expression. To have dirt on your feet means that you think like a planet dweller rather than someone who lives and works in space. You've been on ship for so short a time that you still have planetary soil on your footwear. Your question shows that you approach vessel identification like someone who has seen it on trid vid dramas but never done it in real life."

Max continued, warming to his subject. "Telling friend from foe out here is no easy matter. From a million kills away, even if a ship were painted bright white and lit up like the *Galactic Princess* on New Year's Eve, a high-resolution optical scanner would pick it up as just a bright speck, so we mostly rely on transponder ID signals and IFF codes exchanged electronically. Those can be faked, so at closer range we try to verify visually what the electronics tell us, but most of the time you still can't see a damn thing unless you light the other ship up with half a dozen of your own high-power collision lights, which is a good way to get shot at because lots of folks interpret that as a distinctly unfriendly act.

"Even at close range, most of the time you can actually see very little. We're in deep space, nearly forty AU from this system's sun. It's dark out here. Really dark. And no one—and I do mean *no one*— paints warships anything but black. Not just black but with layers of coatings that absorb visible light and lots of other forms of energy. Generally, all you can see is an area where you can't see any stars, sporadically filled in with an occasional running light, collision light, or viewport, but little or nothing of the shape of the hull itself."

"So," the doctor said, "that is why you have taken, I hear, every crew member not strictly needed to operate the ship and put him to work installing false running lights, self-illuminating panels that look like viewports, and making various dummy antenna and fixtures to attach to the hull."

"Exactly, Doctor, we're going to be a Romanovan revenue and inspection cutter, a vessel that's very roughly the same size and shape as we are—not surprising since the Romanovans habitually copy Union designs, at least generally. In the dark, it will be close enough. People see what they expect to see. And that's where you and your linguistic talents come in."

Max's comm panel buzzed. He hit the button. "Skipper here."

"Brown here, Captain. We may need a postponement."

He suppressed a sigh of exasperation. "I don't think we can do that, Wernher. What's the problem?"

"Sir, in order to mimic the profile of the Romanovan ship, I'm having to make a very large number of fittings, fairings, dummy antennae, and other attachments to the hull. I've got all three metal shops working full tilt, but they're falling behind."

"What about putting additional men to work with hand tools?"

"We've got the extra tools, but all the people skilled in metal working are already at work in the existing shops. There just aren't that many people on board who have the necessary skill. I know: I've already determined that I need to train more men in metal-working skills, but that won't solve my problem in the next few hours."

Max thought for a minute; then it hit him. The engineer's thinking was stuck in a box. A metal box. "What about all that damage control *wood* we keep on board to shore up bulkheads and build temporary compartments and fixtures?"

"What about it?"

"Can't we use that? I know we've got eight or ten men with reasonably good carpentry skills."

The comm line was silent, but for the engineer's inarticulate sputtering. After about ten seconds, he was able to form words. Barely.

"Surely. Sir. You aren't…you can't be…suggesting that I place…*wood* on the *hull?*" His tone sounded as though Max were suggesting that he replace one of the gleaming white Verrakian marble pillars at the Temple of Universal Justice with rude columns made from mud bricks mortared with musk ox shit.

"Wernher, think about it. These things are nothing but props. They don't have to carry any structural loads. They don't have to withstand weapon fire or atmospheric friction. They just have to sit on the hull and look like what they are supposed to look like for about thirty minutes. They could be made of papier-mâché or PlayKlay for all the difference that it would make. If it makes you feel any better, we will remove them at the earliest convenient moment."

"Well, sir, it still feels improper, somehow…."

"Great. I knew you were too good an engineer not to follow the data, Wernher. Now fire up the wood shops, and let's get these frauds fashioned and fitted. CIC out." He closed the connection.

"And now, Doctor, speaking of frauds, let's get you to the quarter-master for a fitting."

"Approaching jump point Alfa," announced LeBlanc. "Coming to full stop. Thirty seconds or so passed. "There. Skipper, we are at full stop, right on top of this system's Alfa."

"Very well. Okay, people. Operation McGruder One: Execute."

The first step belonged to the stealth officer. "Emitting a burst of Cherenkov-Heaviside radiation. Switching from Stealth Mode to Emulation Mode—electronic and drive signatures now mimic a Romanovan revenue and inspection cutter, *Flavius* class."

One of the missions for which the *Khyber* class destroyers were built was penetrating into enemy space and destroying his shipping to cripple his war production, much as United States submarines had penetrated Japan's Pacific defense perimeter to destroy her Merchant Marine during Earth's Second World War. To enable them to perform that mission, in addition to a highly effective stealth suite to hide the ship's own emissions, each also had a sophisticated "emulation" suite consisting of emitters designed to mimic the electronic signatures radiated by the drives, weapons, sensors, and other systems of a variety of other ships. She could not change her color or her shape, but in terms of her electronic, graviton, and other emissions, the *Cumberland* was the space-faring equivalent of a chameleon.

"Ahead at zero-point-zero-five c, steering the first leg of standard Romanovan search grid. Prepared to increase speed according to Romanovan jump-recovery procedures," said LeBlanc.

"Broadcasting transponder ID code copied by Naval Intelligence from the RRIC *Caracalia*," announced Comms.

"Visual inspection confirms that all our shutters are closed, all dummy viewport panels are illuminated, and all false running lights are activated and operating," said midshipman Kurtz in a steady, if still treble, voice. Max had put the midshipmen in charge of much of the visual deception scheme, and as the midshipman in CIC, Kurtz was their liaison with Command.

"Beginning active sensor sweeps. All sensor types, frequencies, polarization schemes, modulations, and phase variances calibrated to mimic Romanovan sensor protocols," said Kasparov.

As a result of these deceptions, Max was hoping that the sensors on board the Ghiftee freighter (freighter sensors were usually pretty rudimentary) would show what appeared to be a ship coming through the jump point that led to Romanovan space, identifying itself electronically as a Romanovan cutter, emitting the same sensor beams as a Romanovan cutter, recovering from jump at the same rate as a Romanovan cutter, and carrying out the same search patterns as a Romanovan cutter. The purported Ghiftee should conclude, therefore, that the *Cumberland was* a Romanovan cutter. If it walks like a duck, swims like a duck, and flies like a duck, it must be a duck.

"Speed is now at point two eight," said LeBlanc, forty-six minutes later, "which is what the Romanovans like to cruise at in this class. Executing second leg of search pattern."

"Active sensor contact," announced Kasparov. "Bearing, range, course, and speed congruent with previous passive contact identified as November two. Getting a good, strong return. Sir, that would be a solid detection for a Romanovan ship."

"Very well. Now we act like we just spotted them. Maneuvering, increase to what would be flank for the Romanovans and shape course to intercept."

"Romanovan flank, intercept course, aye."

In a few minutes, the *Cumberland* had accelerated to 0.55 c, just as a Romanovan cutter would under the circumstances. An hour and a half later, the destroyer had matched course and speed with the freighter and was holding station eight hundred meters off her starboard beam.

Just then, Dr. Sahin walked onto the bridge, resplendent in the crimson and gold uniform of a Romanovan cutter captain, glittering with enough multicolored braid, oddly shaped insignia, and jewel-encrusted medallions to decorate a dozen admirals and the bellmen from every five-star hotel in the quadrant, and made only slightly more ridiculous by the matching riding breeches tucked into gleaming cavalry boots, complete with loudly jingling, jeweled spurs. An absurdly long sword in an elaborately bejeweled scabbard hung at his side. Several men broke out laughing.

"Dr. Sahin," the skipper exclaimed, "you look as though you outrank God!"

"I beg you, sir, to say nothing further along those lines. It is a most impious remark," said Sahin, genuinely horrified.

"I beg your pardon, Doctor. It was an improper thing to say. But that uniform!"

"You have my pardon, certainly. Indeed, it is a bit excessive. But the Romanovans do have an exaggerated sense of grandeur, as one would suspect for a colony of upstart Italians with pretentions of being successors of the Roman Empire. They even speak Latin, of all things."

"Now, Doctor, let's not have any illiberal remarks about Italians."

"Certainly not. Admirable people. Can there be any a nobler tribe than the race that sired Vivaldi and Verdi, Da Vinci and Michelangelo, Dante and Cima? No. I refer to the Romanovans as a distinct species sprung from the Italian *genus*. One need only look at this comic-opera costume of a uniform, much less listen to their interminable bombastic symphonies or view their grotesque, grandiose architecture to know that, as a people, they have a deep-seated sense of inferiority and an overwhelming need for external validation."

"That, Doctor, is beyond me. Now, you are certain that you can pass for one of them—to convince someone who has heard their speech many times that you are a native?"

"Certainly. I have studied Latin since the cradle and spent a great deal of time in Romanovan space with my father, selling machine tools and purchasing gourmet olive oil. Their language is merely classical Latin with a Tuscan accent and with some rather idiosyncratic grammatical errors."

"Outstanding. Then have a seat right here." Max got up from his station and gestured for the doctor to take his place. The doctor's sword collided with the skipper's console, causing the tip to swing around and hit Garcia in the knee. The XO grasped the sword and guided it so that it would follow the doctor into the seat.

"Careful, Doctor," said the XO, "you'll put someone's eye out with that."

"Indeed," Sahin said with an embarrassed smile. "I mustn't make more work for myself." Then, sheepishly, as if to explain the accident, "It *is* an unusually long sword."

The XO smiled. "They must be compensating for something."

"Indeed," said Sahin.

Temporarily evicted from his accustomed place, Max sat down at the Commodore's Station, a comfortable seat with a compact console on the command island, usually unoccupied, placed there for use by visiting senior officers, largely to keep them out of the way.

Now it was time to talk like a duck. "Comms, send the first message," Max ordered.

"Aye, sir."

The Romanovans, like the Romans before them, were enamored of all things traditional, and invariably hailed and communicated with foreign vessels using the old Interstellar Text Transmission Protocol, the same protocol that, with the interposition of a translation matrix, was used to communicate with alien species. The *Cumberland*, therefore, had prepared a series of communications in that clunky, hundred-year-old code, which did not allow the sending of lowercase letters, punctuation, or special characters. The first message read: "GHIFTEE FREIGHTER THIS IS THE ROMANOVAN CUTTER CARACALIA STOP PREPARE TO BE BOARDED FOR SAFETY AND CARGO INSPECTION STOP NULL ALL DRIVES AND DISABLE ANTIGRAPPLING FIELD STOP MESSAGE ENDS."

The freighter, like most ships, had an antigrappling field. Such fields could be overcome either through brute force by a hugely powerful grapfield, such as the one generated by the Vaaach ship they'd encountered, or through finesse by jamming. The *Cumberland*, however, lacked the power to overcome an antigrap and could not jam such a field in less time than it would take for the freighter to escape. Max needed to convince the freighter to null its field.

About a minute passed. "Response message, sir," said Comms.

The text appeared on Max's console, and on several others: "WE ARE IN UNCLAIMED SPACE STOP OUR COURSE DOES NOT TAKE US INTO OR THROUGH YOUR JURISDICTION STOP STATE AUTHORITY BY WHICH YOU CLAIM RIGHT TO BOARD THIS VESSEL STOP MESSAGE ENDS."

"Exactly what we thought they'd say," said Max. "Wait thirty seconds and then send the second message." In response to Chin's puzzled look, Max explained, "We don't want it to look like we had the message already written, do we?"

Chin nodded. "Aye sir. Wait thirty and then send message number two."

At the appropriate moment, Chin hit the key for the second transmission. It read: "THIS SYSTEM HAS A JUMP POINT WITH COUNTERPART IN ROMANOVAN SPACE STOP THEREFORE UNDER ARTICLE XXIX SECTION 8 PARAGRAPH 12 OF THE SECOND INTERSTELLAR CONVENTION ON NAVIGATION CUSTOMS COMMERCE AND TERRITORIAL CLAIMS THIS SYSTEM LIES WITHIN OUR SYSTEM DEFENSE AND IDENTIFICATION ZONE STOP AS SUCH WE ARE ENTITLED TO BOARD YOUR SHIP TO INSPECT IT FOR COMPLIANCE WITH INTERSTELLAR SAFETY PROTOCOLS AND TO DETERMINE WHETHER YOUR VESSEL OR CARGO POSE ANY THREAT TO THE SECURITY OF OUR IMPERIUM STOP MESSAGE ENDS."

This message had the dual attributes of not only copying exactly a message sent under similar circumstances by a genuine Romanovan cutter but also of being a scrupulously accurate statement of the applicable interstellar law. The Romanovans might be pompous asses, but they were punctilious about interstellar treaties.

"Sir," said Comms, "they are requesting visual. Receiving a carrier on channel 5."

"Doctor, that looks like your cue. Everything ready, Chin?"

Comms checked to be sure that the camera was set for a tight shot of the doctor, just his head and shoulders, with so little of the background included that no one could tell from the image that he was on a Union destroyer instead of the Romanovan cutter. "Aye sir, all set."

"Now, Doctor, remember you are playing a part. Imagine yourself as Admiral Sir Joseph Porter, K.C.B."

The doctor sat up straighter, donned a Romanovan-style headset, adopted the stern aspect of aloof, haughty condescension that went with the Ruler of the Queen's Navy from Gilbert and Sullivan's *H.M.S. Pinafore*, and nodded imperiously to Max.

Max gestured to Comms who said, "Opening channel 5."

The several screens punched into channel 5 briefly showed the standard interstellar visual comm test pattern, a black circle transected by two wide bars at right angles to each other, the bars each divided into several blocks containing different shades of gray. Because color perception varied so greatly from species to species, standard transmissions were in a monochrome mode inaccurately referred to as "black and white." Color communications generally took place only between ships of the same flag.

The test pattern was soon replaced by the face of a human male with light hair, light eyes, a long, thin nose, and a small, pointy chin. He appeared to have an unadjusted age of about sixty, which meant he could be anywhere between 50 and 150. To the doctor's trained eye, and to Max's practically experienced one, the man appeared to be extremely nervous.

"This is Fergus McKelvie, Master of the Ghiftee freighter *Loch Linnhe*. We request further verification of your identity before we consent to boarding."

"Captain McKelvie," the doctor replied in an unaccustomed accent, presumably Romanovan, and with equally unaccustomed steel in his voice, "you *will* be boarded, whether you consent or not. This cutter is armed, and in these dangerous times my orders are to treat as hostile and to fire upon any vessel that does not heave to for inspection. I suspect that your owners would not appreciate having to tow your vessel to the nearest yard to replace the drive unit that I am prepared to vaporize five seconds from now." Romanovan cutter captains did not ask nicely. They started with bluster and threats, then worked their way on up.

"Cutter captain, you know that we can outrun you."

"Granted. But you cannot outrun my pulse cannon, sir. I will have your main sublight drive burned off before you can even get it run up to 'flank,'" said the doctor as prompted by Max via headset.

He turned his head to the right, where he had been told the Romanovans put the weapons console on their cutters and barked: *"Armis dominum, para incendere."* As previously arranged, the stealth officer created the semblance of what would happen if a real cutter captain ordered his weapons officer to "prepare to fire." He activated emulation emitters, giving off a power signature similar to that given off by a cutter's pulse cannon being placed in Prefire Mode.

There was no doubt that the deception fooled the freighter captain, as reflected in his expression of abject horror. In fact, he looked as though he were about to become physically ill.

"No, no, no, no, *NOOOO*," he nearly shrieked. "Don't fire. That won't be necessary. Not necessary *at all*."

He turned to his right. Still speaking Standard, he ordered in a panicked voice, "Null the drive, kill the field, prepare for boarding and inspection."

Back to the camera, he said, quaveringly, "Captain, we await your boarding party."

"Wise decision, Captain." To his imaginary weapons officer, *"Armis dominum, qui inrita ordinem."* And then to the camera, "Very well. Prepare to be boarded. *Finum nuntiante.*" In response to those orders, stealth killed the false pulse cannon emissions and Comms closed the channel.

The instant the channel was closed, Max turned to Weapons. "Engage grappling field and put the freighter in docking position. Maneuvering, as soon as we get a firm lock, null the drive."

He hit the comm switch, "Major Kraft, you and your boarding party ready?"

"Chomping at the bit, sir." Max preferred not to think too carefully about what that would look like.

"Mister Kurtz, escort the doctor. Make sure he gets to boarding hatch Charlie by the most direct route." Max had no high opinion of Dr. Sahin's ability to find quickly any part of the ship other than the Casualty Station, the wardroom, and his own quarters. Kurtz, who knew every corridor and access ladder like the back of his hand, led the garishly costumed doctor *cum* cutter captain out.

"Major Kraft, the doctor is on his way. CIC out."

In less than three minutes, Sahin was standing in the boarding airlock, a compartment about seven meters square, near the boarding hatch with Major Kraft and eight Marines. Kraft and his men were all clad in crimson and gold uniforms similar to the doctor's, but less ornate, and all carried the stainless steel, polymer-stocked, sawed-off shotguns, Sig-Sauer pattern sidearms, and short swords carried by boarding parties in the Romanovan Revenue and Inspection Service. The Marines seemed perfectly familiar with the weapons. As one Marine manipulated the controls, the boarding tube extended from the destroyer's airlock to that of the freighter, a green light indicating that the tube was fully extended and pressurized. The party went into the tube, closing the hatch behind them.

Reaching the other end after only about seven meters, the same Marine hit another switch. A red light indicating that there was an excessive pressure difference between the freighter and the boarding tube switched to amber, indicating that the pressure was being equalized, in this case by opening a valve admitting air into the tube from a tank of high-pressure reserve air installed in the tube's extension hardware for that purpose. A countdown clock appeared on the control console, initially showing 0:45, meaning that the equalization process would take 45 seconds.

The doctor whispered something to Kraft. The major's eyes hardened.

One Marine, a private, elbowed a lance corporal, who presumably knew marginally more than he, and said, "Sven, why do we got to keep up the play acting? We've got them grapped. They're not going anywheres."

"'Cause, they might really *be* Ghiftee neutrals, that's why. If they are, we don't want them to know they were boarded by a Union ship, as it might create an interstellar *in-sye-dent*, that's why. If they are, we can just say they passed inspection, cast off, and send them on their merry way, none's the wiser, *that's* why."

Kraft turned to his men. "Remember, men. Don't say a word unless you have to. Keep your eyes open and be ready for anything, but don't shoot unless we are attacked first or you hear me give the order. But don't be surprised if there are Krag on that ship. All right. Just a few seconds."

The counter reached zero, and the hatch on the freighter opened with a slight hiss, admitting the boarding party to an airlock. The hatch closed behind them; the airlock mechanism verified that there was adequate pressure in the chamber; and the inner hatch opened. Five Marines stormed through the opening, shotguns held high and fanned out in a rough semicircle in what looked to be a corridor, rather narrower than those on the destroyer. Seeing nothing any more threatening than Captain McKelvie standing in the corridor and sweating nervously, one of them sang out, *"Securos."*

Kraft, the doctor, and the rest of the Marines entered the corridor, with Kraft, who was apparently uniformed as some sort of officer, and the doctor coming to the fore. The doctor stood before the captain, who bowed to him formally. The doctor returned the bow, just a hair less deeply, and said, "Captain, kindly take us to the bridge."

He then turned to a group of five Marines who were standing
a little apart from the others and said, "*Quaere navis.*" Search the
ship. The remaining four Marines, Kraft, and the doctor followed
Captain McKelvie forward. As soon as the captain was out of sight,
one of the five Marines in the first group produced a handheld
scanner from his equipment belt, pushed a few buttons, glared
narrowly at the display, pressed a few more buttons, glowered at
the device's tiny screen, pulled his percom out of a pocket in his
uniform, and pressed a few keys on it in a preestablished sequence.

Tiny ear buds placed deep in the ear canals of the doctor and
Major Kraft softly beeped. The two men shared a glance just as
they stepped onto the freighter's bridge where, in addition to the
captain, there were three men at various stations.

"Captain, your documentation, please," Sahin asked.

The captain pulled a blue cube, measuring about one centime-
ter on each side, out of a tiny compartment in the Commander's
Station and handed it to the doctor, who inserted it in what was
dummied up to look like a standard Romanovan ID Cube reader.
The reader told him that the Romanovan device that this reader
purported to be would have shown the cube to contain the genuine
Ghiftee Ship's Registry, Space Frame Inspection Certificate, Engine
Inspection Certificate, Environmental Systems Sufficiency and
Operability Certificate, Safety Equipment Inspection Certificate,
Galley Health Inspection Certificate, flight plan, cargo manifest,
and personnel manifest for Ghiftee Cargo Vessel *Loch Linnhe.* It
also told him, because the circuitry was from a state-of-the-art
Union Naval ID Cube Reader, that the cube was a sophisticated
forgery, probably of Krag manufacture. He ejected the cube from
his reader and put it in a small pocket on his tunic, just the right
size for holding a few ID cubes.

"And your personal ID, if you please." The captain reached
into his tunic and produced a green cube, the same size as the

blue one. The doctor's scanner showed this cube to be forged as well. Even the man's name was probably made up. "It says here, Captain, that you are a native of Ghifta Prima."

"Yes. Born and raised."

Ghifta Prima was only the fifth extra solar planet settled by humans. The colonization expedition was put together by an idealistic dreamer named Solomon Ghift who drew colonists from, quite literally, every nation on Earth. And because Standard had not yet become standard and they spoke hundreds of languages, he made every one of them learn Esperanto, a language still spoken as a cradle tongue by all that world's natives.

"So, then you would speak the Esperanto."

"Yes, of course. Do you?"

"No. Not really." The captain was relieved at this news, although he tried not to show it. "I do, however, know enough to share this little joke with you. *Via patro estas malpura kovarda.*" At that, the doctor laughed loudly and slapped the man on the shoulder. The captain laughed with equal gusto, proving what the doctor suspected based on the faked ID cube, that this man was not a Ghiftee. If he were, after all, he would not have laughed when the doctor told him, "Your father is a dirty coward."

The doctor ejected the captain's ID cube and handed the reader to one of the Marines, abruptly ceasing his laughter. He then elaborately dropped the cube on the deck, affected an exaggerated shrug of apology, and suddenly stomped it with the heel of his right boot, shattering the cube into ten thousand tiny, glittering shards. Before the captain could even gasp his shock, Sahin had shattered the second cube in the same manner. "You are no more a Ghiftee than I am Solomon Ghift. Marines, arrest them."

"Marines? You're Union!" the captain exclaimed, reaching into an equipment bin, grabbing something, and pulling the object free. Suddenly Sahin's sword flashed out and he brought it down, edge first, on the captain's arm, slicing neatly through the man's uniform sleeve, but not breaking the skin.

"This sword, as you can see, my dear sir, has a keen edge." As did Dr. Sahin's voice. "And if you do not want me to perform a nonsurgical amputation of that arm, you will drop whatever is in your hand and put both hands, slowly, where I can see them."

"You'd best do it, mate," said one of the Marines. "If he's even a hair slow on the sword, this shotgun will do you just fine." The other Marines covered the remaining bridge crew with their shotguns, carefully positioning themselves so that no one was in anyone else's line of fire.

"Truss 'em, men," said Kraft. Covering each other in series, the Marines produced wrist ties and cinched the crewmen's wrists behind their backs. When this task was accomplished, Kraft pulled out his percom, strapped it to his wrist, and pushed the call button. "Aft party, status."

"We've got two men in Engineering and one Krag that was holed up in a cargo bin," said a Marine from the other group. "It used its sword to express its objections to being taken captive, so I had to blow its arm off with a shotgun. Tell the doctor that I put the stump in a tourniquet and I've saved the loose arm. It's still flopping something fierce—don't know whether he'll want to try to reattach it, hang it on his wall, or give it to his girlfriend to wear as a stole, but I've got it wrapped up.

"The two humans are uninjured—they're trussed up nice and neat. Two interesting discoveries, though. First, there was a helluva bomb bolted to the main reactor—set to blow if tampered with or if the ship was hit by weapons fire. Dokate disarmed it, and we jettisoned the explosive. Second, we found their cargo. You'll never believe it, sir. It's gold. Tons and tons of it."

CHAPTER 17

10:44Z Hours, 29 January 2315

Max and Dr. Sahin were sharing a relaxing, if not perfectly flavorful, dinner in Max's day cabin. The evening's menu included a spicy vegetable soup, undoubtedly
made with frozen vegetables, followed by an even spicier meat
and vegetable goulash (the fewer questions asked about the
meat, the better), freshly baked bread (flour, baking powder,
powdered eggs, and so on, were compact and easily stored for
long periods, so there was always fresh bread on a well-ordered
warship), mashed potatoes (dried, reconstituted), green beans
(canned), and lemon pound cake for dessert (what goes for
bread also goes for cake). All washed down, in Max's case, with
the better than fair, but not quite good, ship's beer (every ship
brewed its own beer unless the CO_2 scrubbers were malfunc-
tioning) and capped by the ubiquitous naval fuel, Navy coffee—
hot, strong, and black. Dr. Sahin drank fruit juice (reconstituted
from freeze-dried powder) with his dinner but shared coffee
with Max.

Having finished the meal, the men moved to the day cabin's sitting area, where both men sipped their coffee and enjoyed a second slice of the really quite creditable pound cake.

Dr. Sahin had eaten only about half as much as Max, but he had just emitted a long, loud belch and seemed utterly satisfied with the fare. "The victuals on board this vessel are certainly better than they were on Travis Station."

"Really? I'd have thought that the food on a station would be better than on ship. Stations get more frequent resupply, from more sources. The variety should be better, at any rate."

"I haven't been on board ship long enough to develop an opinion regarding variety, but the food here is more flavorful than on the station. Station food was abundant but unspeakably bland."

"That won't be a problem here. I've got some genuine Cajuns back in the galley. Even when the dishes aren't traditionally Cajun, they're going to have more flavor than you're used to getting from naval cooking. My experience in the Navy is that the cuisine is influenced primarily by that of the Midwest of North America and the Southeast of Great Britain."

"Vast, desolate culinary wastelands," said Dr. Sahin, shaking his head.

"Meat and potatoes and overcooked vegetables."

"I'm going to enjoy this posting. I have not eaten this well in years. My only concern on board ship is encountering swine flesh without knowing it."

"Not a problem. Nearly a quarter of the Navy is Muslim, so pork is not a part of the naval diet, with the exception of bacon and ham, which are always served separately and with alternative dishes available." Then he put two and two together. "Doctor? I didn't know you were Muslim."

"I have made no secret of it."

Max made a dismissive gesture. "No matter. You know the old saying, 'We were birthed by a hundred faiths, but the Navy is father to us all.' Speaking of secrets, I was wondering how you knew there were Krag on that freighter. Major Kraft told me that you whispered in his ear, before any sensor readings were taken, that you were almost certain that there were Krag aboard."

"That? That was a perfectly elementary deduction. When the boarding tube mated to the freighter boarding hatch, it took forty-five seconds for the pressure to equalize, and I felt in my eardrums that air was being pumped into the tube rather than being allowed to escape. That meant that the air pressure on the freighter was about 30 percent higher than the pressure used on this ship, which is the naval standard—mean sea level pressure on Earth, which is just over one hundred kilopascals. Ghiftee ships are normally equalized for sea level pressure on Ghifta Prima, which is ninety-eight kilopascals. So, if that freighter were a Ghiftee ship, we should have bled a little pressure, not packed in nearly a third more. Further, I know that the Krag insist that all ships that have even one of their kind on board run at their standard pressure, which is 135 kilopascals, just over a third more than what we use. So, I suspected Krag."

"I am impressed, Doctor. I am also impressed that you had the ship's armorer sharpen that ceremonial sword the metal shop made for you."

"Not precisely correct. The armorer, at my request, made it from the same alloy as the ship's boarding cutlasses and put a fine edge on it from the outset. Accordingly, whereas the sword is in the *form* of a ceremonial blade it is, in reality, a true weapon. A wolf in sheep's clothing, as it were. My people have used swords for two thousand years and never abandoned the tradition. I am very comfortable with them. I would not carry one if it were not a real weapon."

"Very wise, Doctor. Now, how's your Krag patient?"

"He will do very well, Allah willing." Max cringed inwardly at the doctor's use of the pronoun "he" for the Krag, but did not correct him. The official naval protocol was to refer to all Krag, regardless of gender, by the impersonal pronoun "it" rather than "he" or "she." Max supposed it was to dehumanize them. Based on his personal experiences with the species, Max didn't need a pronoun to do that.

"They are a remarkably resilient species. I stem cell–cultured the necessary soft tissue and bone and used them to reattach the severed limb. It now has circulation, sensation, and movement, and should recover about 95 percent of its former usefulness. I'm keeping him unconscious for now, as the nerve regeneration is still taking place and it's a very painful process. He should be ready to be reawakened in a day or so, and then he can converse with our friend from the UMID." He pronounced the customary acronym for the Union Military Intelligence Directorate so that it rhymed with "humid."

"Ah, him. I've never liked those guys. They always keep to themselves, sitting in their quarters spying on you by using their high-level access to surf through every database and sensor feed on the ship, until you get a prisoner. Then they come out of their hole and monopolize the interrogation process with it and never tell you what they learn."

"This is my first experience with one. I see him every twelve hours, regular as a pulsar, inquiring whether the patient has regained consciousness. He's very polite to me, not demanding or imperious in the least."

"That, Doctor, is because the prisoner is not yet awake. When he has someone to interrogate, I suspect that he'll change his stripes. In any event, I'm pleased the Krag is doing well. Perhaps we can get something useful out of it. Maybe it knows about other Krag cargoes in the area."

"That would be very useful. Perhaps it is this possibility that has so cheered the crew. Or perhaps it is their recent capture of the freighter. The whole lot of them seem astonishingly happy right now. In fact, they appear far happier than when we destroyed the Krag warships, which perplexes me, as the earlier victory seems the greater of the two."

"Perhaps in a strategic and tactical sense, but taking this freighter is much more important to them personally."

"How is that—because it required more skill?"

"No, Doctor. You mean...I can't believe it. You really don't know?"

"Know what? You must not practice upon my credulous simplicity."

"My friend, haven't you ever heard of *prize money*?" He said the words in the way a hungry carnivore might say "grilled steak."

"Certainly, I've heard of it. If a crew captures a warship intact, it can be of some monetary benefit to them. I do not really know the specifics."

Max shook his head. "There're articles in the database, Doctor, well-written articles adapted to the most planet-bound reader, about Navy life and regulations and customs. A man of your obvious brilliance could read and assimilate them quite easily, you know."

"But my time is so short, and I have so much to learn of more pressing application."

"It's been a long war and the Navy needed something to make protracted service more attractive. The Chief of Naval Operations, something of a saltwater naval historian, suggested the idea of prize money to the Admiralty; he knew about it from his studies of the British Navy in the Age of Sail. It seemed a good idea, so we borrowed loosely from the British, just as we have borrowed so many other things.

"In our system, which differs somewhat from the British one, when an enemy vessel or cargo is captured, one-fifth, or 20 percent, of the value goes to the complement of the capturing vessel as prize money. One half of that amount, 10 percent, goes to me as captain. One half of the remainder, or 5 percent, is divided equally among the other commissioned officers, and that includes the chief medical officer, while the men divide the other 5 percent among themselves, by heads."

"I can see why the men might be experiencing unusual cheer."

"You don't know the half of it. Prize money includes the cargo of the captured vessel, which can come to quite a nice little sum. In this case, that smallish freighter was carrying forty-two metric tons of gold."

"Really? That much? All I saw was two chests, and not very large ones at that."

"You forget how dense gold is. A single cubic meter of gold weighs more than nineteen tons. Each of those chests contained just over one cubic meter of pure gold, in twenty-kilogram bricks. The value of that gold at the current market price is just over a hundred and thirty million credits. Each man aboard ship has earned more money than most of them have ever had at one time in their lives, and her captain is now quite a wealthy man.

"And that doesn't count that sweet little freighter. I've sent it back to Lovell Station with a four-man prize crew. She will be sold privately or used by the Navy, which is always in need of cargo vessels of various sorts. In either event, we will share in either her appraised value if the Navy takes her or in her sale price if sold. She's fast, has reasonably comfortable accommodations, and boasts a superb sensor suite for a civvy. She'll fetch at least ten or eleven million if she fetches a dime."

"With fourteen million credits or so, you could retire from the Navy."

"Perish the thought, Doctor. The Navy is my family, my career, my life. I know no other. Besides, with this war going the way it is going, the Navy cannot spare any competent officer, particularly one with my combat experience. I'm in this until I'm killed, crippled, too old to fight, or the war ends. My hope is to see this war through to a victory for the Union, and my goal is to be instrumental in that victory. I am ambitious enough to see myself hoisting my flag and leading a Task Force in the decisive battle that wins the war for us. Absurd, I know."

"I think not. Seriously, my friend, though you have your foibles and human weaknesses, you clearly and obviously have a gift for leadership and inspiration. Men follow you. And although I am not equipped to judge this aspect of your performance, I am told by people who are so equipped that you display a certain gift for tactics."

"Who told you that?"

"I'd rather not say. It is, however, the general opinion of certain knowledgeable people aboard. Such consensuses of informed crew members are invariably correct, or so I have heard. They regard you highly, as a commander and as a man."

"I'm not so sure about that. I almost got every man and boy of us killed the other day."

"You mean the incident with that new Krag weapon?"

"Exactly. I was so intent on what I was going to do to the enemy, I forgot to consider what he could be doing to me. It is so fundamental a mistake that I think even Ulysses S. Grant warned against it."

"You would not be the first to make that mistake, surely. General Grant must have seen it many times."

"No, I'm not the first, but the next time I make that mistake, it might be my last. In that case, everyone aboard would die with me. It was an unforgivable error."

"Nonsense. Ridiculous!" the doctor said with unexpected vehemence.

"No, Doctor, you weren't there. It was a clear error in judgment."

"I'm not disputing that it was an error. In fact, for the sake of argument, I am willing to grant you that it was a profound error, of incalculable enormity. What I am disputing is that the error was unforgivable. There is no such thing as an unforgivable error."

He grew grave. "I mean this most sincerely. That is one of the most important things that you, and I mean you most personally and particularly, must learn as a commander and as a man. There are almost always chances of ameliorating the consequences of the wrong, and there is always the prospect of forgiveness. Always. We are all the children of a merciful God. We are all imperfect, flawed, weak, limited, and prone to temptation and error. If we are contrite, strive to right our wrongs and to abjure that transgression in the future, and if we earnestly and humbly beg his forgiveness, Allah will bestow it upon us. And if you are forgiving of faults and errors in others, you will find that men will forgive your errors as well."

"'Forgive us our trespasses, as we forgive those who trespass against us.'"

"What's that? It sounds familiar."

"A line from the most famous prayer in my faith. I'm not sure I ever understood, *really understood*, what that meant. Until now."

"Perhaps. Or perhaps there is more for you to learn. In any event, the crew certainly knows all about the incident with the Krag weapon and, almost to a man, they hold you blameless. You are very well liked by all but a few on board."

"Well, maybe I won't be so popular after I do what I have to do with these human prisoners off the freighter."

"You've decided?"

"There isn't much to decide. Their IDs were all forged, so we ran their DNA through the system. It turns out that they are all in the database. They're citizens of the Union, every one. So, they're not enemy combatants, to be treated as prisoners of war. They're not neutrals, to be sent to a labor camp for five years or so and then repatriated. They're traitors, plain and simple. *Fils de putain*."

"Why would anyone do such a thing?"

"Thirty pieces of silver. The same old low treachery repeated down through the ages. A man takes his noblest loyalty and sells it to the highest bidder for a greasy bag of dirty coins. They didn't do a very good job of covering their tracks in the ship's computer. On delivery to a Krag cruiser just inside their space, the freighter captain was going to get 3 percent of the gold and the rest of the crew, 1 percent."

"What were the Krag going to buy with the gold anyway? Don't they typically use their pharmaceuticals and high-speed computer cores for foreign exchange?"

"They're not going to buy a thing. They have plenty of purchasing power. What the Krag don't have plenty of is gold. I mean the actual metal—it's an accident of geology that most of their planets are poor in heavy metals: gold, mercury, and so forth. They need gold for industrial purposes, mainly for electrical contacts in precision equipment on their warships. Intelligence says they have a real shortage, even to the extent that it is becoming a bottleneck in their industrial production. And a little goes a long way. Forty-two metric tons is at least a year's needs for their whole military industrial complex. Taking this cargo will put a real dent in their plans."

"But if gold is so precious, why would the Krag pay the freighter crew with it rather than something else that is less valuable to them, like Romanovan Sestertii, notes from a neutral bank, or pharmaceuticals that are readily sellable on the black market?"

"My guess is that the freighter rats wouldn't have been paid at all. Once that freighter got into Krag space under the guns of their cruiser, the Krag would just kill the crew and keep the gold. The ship too."

"I cannot say that they would not deserve it. So, what's to happen to the freighter crew?"

"I will be consulting with Major Kraft and completing some documents in a few moments, but it's all just a formality."

"You mean that you...that they..."

"Yes, Doctor. They die. Firing squad. Right before breakfast."

"Sudden death tends to ruin my appetite."

"It never did mine much good either."

CHAPTER 18

05:59Z Hours, 30 January 2315

Like all but the smallest naval vessels, the *Cumberland* had a shooting range, so the crew could acquire and maintain proficiency with firearms in the only way possible: shooting real weapons with live ammunition. The range was not very large, and the maximum distance between shooter and target was only fifteen meters, but most shooting by naval personnel takes place in close-order combat, often at arm's length or even less, so this limitation was not considered much of a problem. When not being used for firearms, the room doubled as a small gymnasium.

This morning, however, the armed men arrayed on the firing line were not going to be shooting at targets. They were going to be shooting at their fellow men. Men with mothers and fathers and wives and children. Men who, like them, were citizens of the Terran Union but who, for reasons that the men holding the M-88 pulse rifles could not fathom, had decided to betray the human race to an inhuman enemy bent on the annihilation of mankind.

For that, they would die. Today. Minutes from now.

The five condemned men stood in a line against the armored back wall of the range, looking mostly dead already. Pale, drawn, unshaven, bleary from lack of sleep, eyes vacant. Two appeared to be in a near stupor, perhaps from the injections they had received from the doctor because they were shaking so hard they could not stand or walk. These were not military men, hardened to danger and long accustomed to the idea that death might claim them on any given day. They were freighter rats, and not particularly successful ones at that, whose slippery sense of honor and loyalty allowed them to sell out the human race for a few credits. But this payoff was more than they'd bargained for.

Go to bed with the devil, you wake up in hell.

The prisoners stared at the line of armed men in unconcealed horror. The Navy did not believe in blindfolds or hoods; more than thirty years of brutal war had taken away whatever squeamishness the service may once have had about death. The shooters looked into the faces of the men they were killing, and the condemned men saw death coming to meet them.

The only sounds were the faint hum of the air handlers, weaving an almost subliminal, bass-clef harmony with the distant thrum of the engines. All present stood in grim silence: five condemned, fifteen shooters, the commanding officer, the executive officer, the chief medical officer, the Marine detachment commander, the nonentity assigned to the ship as chaplain, and—for their education and instruction—the three chiefs who had tried to sabotage the atmosphere manifold.

The shooters had been selected at random by computer from the 116 men on board who had qualified as "Marksman" or higher with the M-88 pulse rifle. Eleven spacers and four Marines. The rifles were not loaded with the standard expanding/tumbling rounds used for Krag, but with old-fashioned full metal jacket ammunition. The wounds would be neat. No unnecessary blood would be spilled.

At precisely the stroke of 06:00, Kraft hit a comm switch already configured to pipe sound to every comm unit in the ship and video to whoever wanted it. Max produced two pages from his tunic and began to read.

On 28 January 2315, as evidenced by the affidavits of a commissioned officer of the Union Space Navy and a commissioned officer of the Union Space Marine Corps, which affidavits are attached hereto and made a part hereof for all purposes, the five men present here today: George M. Tremonte, Hikaru Akazaki, Alexander Wong, Mohammed Bahir, and Seamus O'Leary did give aid and comfort to the enemy by knowingly transporting cargo useful as matériel of war for the purpose of selling, bartering, or otherwise transferring said matériel to the enemy, the accused being citizens of the Terran Union and the Union being in a state of war at the time.

Under the Fourth Revised and Supplemental Articles of War of 9 September 2312, by the authority vested in me as an officer of command rank in actual command of a Rated Warship on Detached Service in a war zone, I hereby sentence the five men named above to death by firing squad, said sentence to be carried out immediately on this day, the 30th day of January in the year two thousand three hundred and fifteen. May God have mercy on their souls. Signed, Maxime Tindall Robichaux, Lieutenant Commander, Union Space Navy, commanding the USS *Cumberland*.

"Chaplain, have the prisoners been given opportunity for the religious observances associated with impending death in accordance with their respective faiths?"

"They have," responded the chaplain. None had wanted so much as a prayer.

"Chief Medical Officer, are the prisoners of sound mind and competent to stand for execution?"

"They are," responded the doctor. Not much competence was required. So long as a man understood that he was about to be shot and why, he was fit to die.

"Advocate Officer, have these men been given the protections and legal process that they are due under the circumstances?"

"They have," responded Major Kraft, the vessel's legal expert. For traitors caught in the act these days, under the rules of "due process," very little process was due.

"Executive Officer, have all procedures required for the execution of these men under the Articles of War and Naval Regulations been fully and completely carried out to the best of your knowledge, information, and belief formed after reasonable investigation?"

"They have," responded the XO, whose job it was to ensure that if men were to be shot, they would be shot according to the book.

"Does any officer present know of any reason why these men may not be executed by firing squad here, on this day, at this time?" Everyone stood silent for the prescribed count of five.

"Hearing none, we now proceed." Max took a deep breath. He had never done this before. He had seen this done before only once: when he was twelve and a midshipman on the old *Agincourt*. He had thrown up on the deck.

"Detail, ready your weapons." The shooters raised their rifles to their shoulders and worked the charging handles, each mechanism stripping a 7.62×51 mm round from the rifle's box magazine and pushing it into the chamber.

"Aim."

Fifteen index fingers moved from ready positions alongside the trigger guards, pushed the safety mechanisms forward into the fire position, and came to rest lightly on the triggers. Fifteen men aimed, three shooters for each condemned man, each framing the tiny bead at the top of his weapon's front sight in the round aperture of the rear and then aligning both with the center of a condemned man's chest.

Unbidden, a line from a centuries-old film—he could not remember the name—came to Max's mind—a line shouted by a condemned man to his own firing squad: "Shoot straight you bastards! Don't make a mess of it!" Don't make a mess of it, indeed. He took a shuddering breath.

"Fire."

Max clearly heard fifteen separate weapons discharges, despite his hearing protection filters. The echo seemed to hang in the air for an eternal instant, after which all five men, with five separate thumps, fell to the deck like puppets with their strings cut.

"Safe your arms and shoulder." The men returned their weapons to safe and shouldered them, making the range "cold" once more and allowing Dr. Sahin to step into the target area and check the prisoners.

It took less than a minute for him to examine all five men. He stood and formally addressed Max, his voice sounding hollow and distant to ears still stunned by the firing of fifteen rifles at the same time in a confined space. "Captain, I have examined the prisoners and certify to you that they are all dead."

"Very well. Let the record reflect and let all those assembled witness that sentence was carried out and that the condemned were pronounced dead at"—he looked at the time display on his percom—"06:04 hours, on 30 January 2315. Ten HUT."

All came to attention.

"Dismissed."

From start to finish, it had taken four minutes. The living filed out of the room, leaving the dead where they fell, sightless eyes still open, three tiny and nearly bloodless holes clustered within a hand's breadth on each chest, the smell of powder mingling with the sour scent of two men's evacuated bowels.

In a few minutes, corpsmen from the Casualty Station would come to take the bodies away to cold storage in the ship's morgue, eventual cremation at a station or on board a hospital ship, and—if someone wished to claim the remains—a long, slow trip for their ashes on a low-priority transport back to their homeworlds. Until then, though, they lay silent and alone, the bodies now empty of whatever had driven them to live and love and eat and breathe and strive and struggle and, in the end, to betray their own people and suffer death as a result.

Later, sensing that there had been no movement and no living occupant in the compartment for more than four minutes, the computer turned off the lights, plunging the room into total darkness.

CHAPTER 19

02:27Z Hours (11:18 Local Time), 2 February 2315

Dr. Sahin shaded his eyes from the unaccustomed glare of the sun—well, of *a* sun at any rate—as he stepped out of "his" microfreighter onto the landing pad. He took a deep breath, his first of unprocessed air in more than two years, expecting to scent the exotic aroma of a strange, new world. Instead, all he could smell was the burned rock aroma of thermal concrete scorched by landings from the big passenger shuttles that were the bulk of the spaceport's traffic. The exotic strange new world scent would come later, he supposed.

In less than two minutes, a ground vehicle came across the spaceport's vast distances to the pad. A bored, dirty driver scanned the doctor's credit chip, debited his account, lowered a tow coupling, inserted it into the socket on the freighter's front landing gear assembly, and gestured for Sahin and his pilot, Able Spacer Fahad, to climb aboard. He put the vehicle into drive and headed toward a hangar, towing the freighter slowly behind, clearing the pad for the next ship.

After a short drive with the silent, sullen driver at the wheel, the microfreighter was situated in the hangar with about a dozen ships of roughly similar size. A spaceport official then appeared and handed Sahin a padcomp presenting him with several forms for his electronic signature, certifying that the ship did not have hazardous cargo, had been inspected within the past year, that he would pay all hangar charges promptly, that he understood that he should remove any valuable property from the freighter and deposit it in the spaceport's vault or in one of the high-security cargo hangars provided at a reasonable charge, that the Spaceport Authority disclaimed responsibility for all thefts, and that he would not attempt to taxi the freighter out of the hangar himself.

Finally, Sahin and Fahad, each carrying a nondescript over-night bag, got into one of a pair of smaller ground vehicles parked near the door to the hangar and closed the door.

There was no steering wheel. Instead, there were twenty buttons on the dashboard, labeled Incoming Travelers, Departing Travelers, Freight Terminal, Customs, Ground Transport to City, Air Passenger Terminal, and Hangar 1 through Hangar 14. Max hit the button for Incoming Travelers.

Following an electronic track in the pavement, the vehicle quickly took them to a building marked in several languages "Incoming Travelers." Entering the large building, they got into a fast-moving line and came to a desk behind which sat a pleas-ant man wearing the tan and medium-brown robes that most of the natives, plus the doctor and Fahad, were wearing. He was of apparently Arabic descent, as were most of the inhabitants of this world, in his middle fifties, with a short, neatly trimmed beard and sharp, piercing brown eyes. Eyes that the doctor could easily see belonged to a very perceptive man.

He turned to the doctor and said in Standard: "ID cube, please."

Sahin produced his cube and handed it to the man, who placed it in his reader. The cube was, of course, an excellent forgery manufactured by the crack Intelligence Section on Admiral Hornmeyer's flagship. As the Navy had access to the same equipment that the Union Identification Service used to make the real cubes, naval forgeries were indistinguishable from the real thing. Following the standard intelligence procedure of making the lies as close to the truth as possible, most of the information contained on the cube was correct, save that there was no evidence that Sahin was a naval officer.

"Ibrahim Sahin. Occupation: physician and independent trader. Born: Tubek. My sympathies to you, sir. Citizenship: Terran Union. Large number of entry visas for various worlds in the Free Corridor and elsewhere, short visits, perfectly ordinary for a trader. *Provisional* master's license, small craft only. You might want to work on those piloting scores, Doctor; they are too low to allow you to fly anything solo in our space. Trader's licenses and interstellar commerce permits from several jurisdictions. Comprehensive Medical License from the Interspecies Coalition for the Licensure of Health Care Providers. A *very* difficult credential to obtain. Most impressive. Additional credentials in natural science, interest in reptiles. What is the purpose of your visit, Doctor?"

"Business. Purchasing victuals for various freighters owned by a concern related to my family enterprises. Purchases to be transported on my *Shetland* microfreighter now in Hangar 3."

"Length of stay?"

"Short. Anywhere from a day or two to two weeks at most."

The immigration official, a lieutenant colonel according to the discrete insignia worn as a broach on his robe, gave the doctor a hard look. He was an experienced and senior officer in his world's immigration and customs service, and also had unacknowledged connections with its intelligence establishment, all of which meant that he was a man of unusual perceptiveness. Every formal indication and every rule said this doctor was what he said he was and that he should be admitted, but something was telling the colonel otherwise. He had a great deal of discretion, but not enough to detain or to refuse a visa to a man with Dr. Sahin's credentials, when he did not have a shred of any specific and identifiable justification for suspecting him.

"Everything seems to be in order. Welcome, Dr. Sahin. Enjoy your stay on Rashid IV." The doctor stepped aside for Fahad to complete the same process.

After he was finished with Fahad and both men had moved on, the lieutenant colonel entered a series of apparently random characters into his workstation, resulting in his screen displaying a menu that was nowhere on any official site map. He filled in some of the blanks, copied the ID information from the doctor's and Fahad's ID cubes, and advised his superiors that both men should be watched. Carefully.

Still in the Incoming Travelers building, Sahin and Fahad went to an open area labeled Device Compatibility. There they found about two dozen booths, each with a table containing a compact array of electronic equipment, a computer display, and a credit chip reader. Both men took out their flipcoms, distant descendants of the smartphone, used by virtually all humans on all but the most resolutely nontechnological worlds, and set them on top of an analyzer pad, of which there were four at each table. After a few moments, the computer screen split itself into two columns, one column for each flipcom, containing identical text:

Welcome to the Galactic Telephone and Telecommunications (GT&T) Device and Communication Service Compatibility Analyzer, a service of GT&T Interspecies Enterprises, a

GalactiComm Corporation. Copyright 2314. All Rights Reserved.

Device: Nokia/Sprint Uhura 1966 Ultra

Universal Band, No Metaspacial Capability

This device is compatible with local network.

Note: Your voice/data plans do not include communications on this planet.

The display went on to list the various voice and data plans available and their cost in various currencies. Dr. Sahin selected the unlimited plan for a cost of 212.14 Union credits, and paid with his credit chip.

"There, Fahad, our phones are enabled on this planet now," he leaned and whispered into the pilot's ear, "but assume that every word you say is being recorded."

"*Der Feind hört mit.*" The enemy is listening—a maxim famously imprinted on every field radio issued by the German army in the Second World War.

"Indeed. Now, one more stop and we will be ready to leave."

"Good, this bag is getting heavy," replied Fahad.

The two men went around a corner and came to a rather ornate and impressively decorated area of the building, at the entrance of which hung a large sign reading: Currency Exchanges and Banking. Inside the area were several booths labeled with the names of numerous banks, both local and interstellar. Sahin and Fahad walked up to one of the largest: The Royal Standard Chartered Bank of Rashid IV. There was no line. The two sat down at a desk in front of a handsome young man with dark skin, black hair, an aquiline nose, and dark eyes.

"Welcome to Royal Standard Chartered Bank," he said, pleasantly. "My name is Abdul Hamani. How may I be of service today?"

"I need to purchase some currency," answered Sahin.

"What kind of currency will you be purchasing?"

"I will be needing Rashid dinars—1000 dinar notes."

"Very good. And what will be the purchase medium?"

"This." The doctor gestured to Fahad, who unzipped his overnight bag and produced one of the twenty-kilogram gold bricks taken from the *Loch Linnhe*. The man's eyes widened ever so minutely before he resumed his mask of bland amiability.

He opened a drawer and pulled out a small, gray box with an even smaller gray screen, placed it on top of the gold brick and pressed a button. He read from the screen and typed some numbers into his computer terminal. "Gold, twenty kilograms. Point nine-nine-nine fine. At the current rate of exchange, we will purchase at 808,325 dinars."

The doctor smiled. "That, young man, is *yesterday's* rate." He pulled out his flipcom, opened it with a flip of his wrist, and touched a few keys.

"At the current rate on the Rashid Central Commodities Exchange, and allowing your establishment the standard 2.5 percent discount/handling fee, the buy price would be 816,052 dinars. But given that this is an unusually large amount of gold to be used in a straightforward currency exchange transaction, and given that the market is unusually volatile due to the present war, I would be willing to accept a price of 815,000 on the understanding that I may have need to exchange gold for currency at some point in the future, at which time I will expect to receive the full current rate of exchange, minus, of course, the bank's 2.5 percent handling fee."

The banker considered briefly. "Agreed, provided that our understanding is not of unlimited duration. It shall apply only to transactions taking place within the next year. Is that acceptable?"

The doctor nodded his acceptance. Hamani keyed a complex set of instructions into his terminal, turned to the doctor, and smiled.

"Our understanding has been entered into the records of this bank and accepted by management. May I have your ID cube so that we may know with whom we have dealt in this matter?"

The doctor handed over the cube, and the young man put it into a reader, ejected it a moment later, and handed it back. "It has been a pleasure transacting business with you, Dr. Sahin. A porter will arrive momentarily to deliver your currency and collect our gold."

Two hours later, the doctor, Fahad, and a third man were sitting in the shady courtyard of a sprawling house about a dozen kilometers from the spaceport, drinking Earl Grey tea with sugar and lemon and listening to the voices of three blue-tiled fountains murmuring in the background.

Sahin was enjoying the interesting sensation of carrying on his person what he regarded as a huge sum of money, enclosed in a money belt strapped to his belly under several layers of robes, defended by an M-1911 pistol and a curved sword of moderate length, in the fashion carried by honorable merchants on this world. Under local laws both weapons were perfectly legal for him to carry, and under local custom, perfectly accepted and normal.

The currency amounted, in fact, to the equivalent in local bank notes of nearly three-quarters of a million Union credits. He could, of course, have deposited the proceeds of the gold sale in an account that the amiable young man at the bank would have been pleased to set up for him, but credit chip transactions always left a data trail, whereas cash did not.

"Here, cousin, is a list of the items I require. They need to be loaded on standard cargo palettes and packaged for long-term storage on board ship," said Sahin. "I will pay the current market rates, in cash, in Rashid dinars, plus a fee of 5.125 percent for your trouble, as has always been our family custom."

"That is very generous," said the other man evenly. He took a sip of his tea, and then set it down gently. "However, business conditions are not what they were when you left the family concern. The handling fee is now 10 percent."

The doctor took a sip of his own tea, stirred it with the exquisitely engraved sterling silver spoon in his cup, took another sip, set it in its saucer, and regarded the dark liquid. He briefly mused upon the curiosity of two Turks sitting in a Moorish courtyard on a mostly Arab planet, drinking a British blend of a Chinese beverage flavored with a fruit domesticated in India, sweetened with the sap of a plant from Southeast Asia, crystallized by a process invented in Louisiana by a man born in Illinois and educated in France. Truly, he thought, the civilization being spread by humans through the galaxy was the product of the whole Earth and all her children.

All men are brothers, but business is business.

"Cousin Yassir, I believe in generosity and fairness in all dealings with members of my family, but that does not mean I intend to treat you with outright charity. I am very familiar with business conditions in this sector, and they are not as treacherous as you make them out to be. Given that the merchandise I am purchasing is entirely ordinary and is sitting in your warehouse right at this moment, and given that some of what I wish has been collecting cobwebs in that same warehouse for more than sixty days and you are already looking for secondary buyers to take it off your hands at a discount, and even further given that you will be paid in Standard Chartered Bank notes rather than in electronic credits or currencies that you will have to exchange at highly volatile rates, I think that a handling fee of 6 percent is entirely fair."

"I would be interested in knowing how you became aware of my inventory situation."

The doctor had gotten his information because the communications section on his ship had intercepted Yassir's communications with prospective buyers and had needed only about nine and a half seconds to break his commercial level encryption. Yassir had no idea that his communications were so vulnerable.

"You want information. Like any other commodity, information has a price. I assure you that you will find *this* information very valuable."

"Eight and a quarter percent, and you tell me how you found this out."

"Six and one half percent. The price of the information to be separately negotiated."

"Seven and three quarters, including the information."

"Seven. And we *trade* information. I tell you precisely how I know about your inventory, and you tell me what you know about certain transactions going on in this sector, without giving away any proprietary information about your own business."

An appreciative grin slowly spread across Yassir's face. "We have an agreement. You bargain like your father."

"And you bargain like yours. We should have been brothers."

"Many have died in both our families. Perhaps, now, we are." They embraced.

Eight hours later, the doctor and Fahad were walking through a bustling marketplace in Amman, the third largest city on Rashid IV, nearly a thousand miles from the spaceport. As in Sidon, the city on whose outskirts the spaceport was located, they blended in with the locals and moved through the sea of people as though they had been raised in the city, the doctor having spent many years of his life traversing marketplaces such as this, and Fahad because he had a pilot-athlete's natural gifts for moving in a comfortable, easy manner and for copying the movements of others. Neither of them noticed another man, just as unobtrusive, making his way through the same crowd at a discrete distance.

Yassir had given Sahin the names of five people who, according to rumor, had been operating as middlemen, purchasing various heavy metal ores, bulk foodstuffs, and machine tools for sale to yet another set of middlemen who were believed to be selling them to individuals who were striving greatly to remain anonymous. Whereas Sidon was the shiny, upright face that Rashid IV showed to the galaxy, Amman was the rough and gritty side known mainly to the natives and to those outworlders who needed to engage in certain kinds of transactions: the kinds of transactions that, although in most cases not strictly illegal, were best kept in the shadows.

The doctor had already spoken to four of the five middlemen and was on his way to see the fifth. As was typical, these men were far more perceptive and intelligent than the people with whom they did business credited. Although the off-world middlemen thought they had never tipped their hands, all four of the Rashidians knew that the goods were all going—very indirectly, of course—to Philistos, a prefecture of the Romanovan Imperium that was waging a low-intensity rebellion seeking its independence. As Rashid IV and the Romanovans had close trade relations and a strong mutual defense treaty, the parties had a strong interest in preventing the sales from becoming known to the Romanovan government.

These four men also knew that the fifth middleman, the man whom Sahin was about to see, was not dealing in goods bound for Philistos. Rather, they believed he was supplying another buyer whose need for secrecy was even more compelling—so compelling, in fact, that the fifth man's buyer had succeeded where the other buyer had failed. The fifth man did not know the ultimate purchaser's identity.

The Navy men walked into a shop, closing the heavy door behind them. The interior was dim and cool and, as their eyes adjusted from the sunlit glare of the marketplace, they could see that the shop was much larger than it looked from the outside, extending far back from the street and widening into what had probably once been the back spaces of the adjoining establishments. The merchandise appeared to consist of glassware. Exquisite glassware. Hand-blown, brilliantly tinted, intricately shaped glassware that even the rudest eye could see exemplified the highest order of artistry and could be purchased only by those whose resources allowed them to gratify the most discerning tastes.

The doctor's attention was held by one piece in particular: a vase, standing by itself on a simple Doric pedestal of the purest alabaster. Nearly a meter tall and ten or twelve centimeters wide, its living lines flowed with no trace of symmetry, yet with the seductive, sinuous shapeliness of cascading waters or a desirable woman. It called to the doctor's mind a succubus, an enticing female demon that insinuated itself into a man's dreams to tempt him to dark acts of sinful, sensuous abandon. He stared at it, thinking it the most beautiful creation ever made by the mind and hands of mortal beings. Just as Sahin thought he could not be more captivated, Rashid IV's slow rotation moved a sunbeam from a skylight high above into contact with the edge of one of the object's impossibly graceful curves. In an instant, the vase burst into heart-stopping glory as it bent the light to its will, making every perfect sweep radiant with swirling, glowing currents of luminescence painted from a palette such as God Himself would wield—cool ceruleans evoking the crisp sparkling afternoon skies of autumn, the infinite blues of the fathomless ocean depths, the shimmering turquoise of a shallow coral sea on Midsummer's Day, purples to make the richest emperor's robes look like rude rags, and violets to cast clear midwinter's star-birthing twilight as a poor, pale imitation.

Sahin had to remind himself to breathe. Some inner sense told him that the work of art in front of him was not merely expensive. It was priceless.

"I have never seen its like." A cultured voice, carrying just a trace of what would, centuries ago, have been called an Oxford accent, gently but irresistibly returned Dr. Sahin to the world of mundane light and ordinary colors.

"It is the work of a Pfelung Vitreusist named Farnim-Shee 121. He worked on it full-time, night and day, for nearly a year, to the near exclusion of sleep, nourishment, social contact. His wife was so desperate to regain his attention that she laid a clutch of eggs, which he refused to fertilize. He nearly died twice from lack of, shall we say, 'congress' with his mate. I could stand here contemplating it for hours on end. We have other works of his around the shop, of course, even some with the same color set, but nothing quite like this one. It is called *Birth of the Waters* and is considered the greatest work of its kind ever created in Known Space. It is, without exception, the most beautiful art object I have ever seen. And it can be yours. Good day to you. My name is Wortham-Biggs—Ellington Wortham-Biggs, at your service."

The man was dressed like a stereotype of a British art dealer whose clients came from the upper nobility: perfectly tailored dark wool suit, vest complete with pocket watch, and silk tie with matching handkerchief in the pocket of his suit coat. He even smelled of pipe tobacco. His skin and hair, though, were anything but British.

He seemed to be descended from blended Middle Eastern and East Indian stock, with skin nearly dark enough to be African,

black hair, nearly black eyes, and finely chiseled features dominated by an almost hawk-like nose. He appeared to be just on the
far side of middle age, but had not begun to gray or wrinkle or
add weight to his lean, athletic frame. He came to a sort of loose
attention, brought his heels together not quite briskly enough
to click, and bowed slightly, a salutation used widely on Avalon,
Woolcombe, Victoria Regina, and other British-influenced
worlds.

Sahin returned the bow in the same manner. "Ibrahim Sahin
at yours, good sir. May I introduce my associate, Muhara Fahad?"
The able spacer perfectly, and with no prior practice, copied the
bow he had just seen performed.

"Ah, yes, Dr. Sahin, I have been told to expect you by certain
mutual acquaintances." He reached into his vest pocket, apparently
activating some discrete device. Within five seconds, another man
dressed similarly to Wortham-Biggs appeared through a door,
which, if not hidden, was certainly not obvious.

"Giles, I will be taking tea with these gentlemen. If you
would…"

"Certainly, sir."

"Please come with me, if you would." He led them through
the shop, through a carved wooden door marked "Private" in
three languages, and into a room that resembled nothing more
than a gentleman's study from a nineteenth-century English
manor house, complete with leather-bound books, a large desk
of dark and deeply oiled wood, paintings in muted colors of various scenes drawn from English country life, and an enormous
apricot-colored mastiff sleeping (and snoring loudly) in front
of the currently fireless fireplace. The dog raised his head from
the floor, regarded the two newcomers placidly, quickly and
accurately assessed that they posed no threat to his master, and
promptly went back to his noisy sleep.

"I invited you for tea, to which you are certainly welcome, but I prefer coffee. What would you gentlemen prefer?"

It was coffee, of course, which was promptly and expertly served by a young lady, wearing a simple white silk blouse and a dark, knee-length skirt. She had dark skin and features that echoed those of their host, but with less severity. Her long, glossy black hair hung loose, just below her shoulder blades. A belt made of engraved gold and silver links glittered in the room's subdued light, accentuating her narrow waist and the womanly curves that flowed from it in both directions. Exquisite knees led to perfectly sculpted dancer's calves that narrowed sublimely to shapely ankles.

The woman smiled as she poured the coffee, parting her full lips to reveal teeth as white as piano keys. She was the most beautiful creature the doctor had ever seen. She looked up at him and he spent a breathless eternity, lasting for less than two seconds, gazing into the warm, liquid depths of her dark eyes before she blushed, blinked, and turned away.

When she finished pouring the coffee, she stood attentively facing the host, as if awaiting further orders. Wortham-Biggs said gently, "Thank you, Elisa. That will be all."

The doctor and Fahad exerted a laudable effort to keep from staring at Elisa as she floated out of the room with the unconscious grace of a virtuoso ballerina.

"My daughter, Elisa. If I may say so, a brilliant girl, splendid eye for art. She assists me."

All three men sipped their coffee appreciatively. It was a fine, rich, dark brew, full of complex aroma and robust flavor, but without any trace of bitterness. "Your coffee is excellent. I have never tasted better," said Sahin.

"Thank you. Coffee is one of the commodities in which I trade. What you are drinking is a blend that I compound myself for my own use and that of certain privileged others—personally selected beans, purchased without regard for expense from the finest coffee estates in four different worlds, carefully roasted at minutely controlled temperatures, freshly ground precisely to the correct grind for the roast, and brewed to perfection. It is—no doubt—far superior to that to which you are accustomed in the Union Space Navy."

When the doctor started to speak, he waved his hand dismissively. "No need to deny it, Doctor, my business, being somewhat more sensitive than that of the gentlemen with whom you have been drinking *tea* the last few days, requires that I be extremely well informed at all times. And I must admit, my connections are rather better. So, I would very much prefer that our relationship not be soiled with falsehoods, even the *pro forma* denials required by your patriotism and your duty as an officer." He smiled briefly, as if to signal that he took no offense.

"I know that you, Doctor, are Lieutenant Ibrahim Sahin, Union Space Navy, Chief Medical Officer of the USS *Cumberland*, and I believe or surmise that your vessel is at this moment deeply stealthed and quietly nestled up against one of the more run-of-the-mill icy bodies in this system's Kuiper belt, all the better to conceal its mass signature and waste heat. I further know that you have been making some not entirely indiscrete inquiries into some business dealings that the parties involved would prefer not to be widely known. You need neither confirm nor deny the accuracy of these statements as, aside from my speculation about the location of your ship, I am quite certain of their correctness. Again, my sources are excellent."

Something told the doctor that, in order to obtain the information he sought, he would have to be forthcoming himself, at least to some degree. "I will simply say that you are better informed that I expected."

"I thank you. Now, to the more interesting and ultimately, I believe, more important subject: What I do *not* know. At least, what I do not know for certain. First, I should like to turn to what I believe or have surmised but cannot confirm. The pattern of your inquiries is strongly suggestive that you wish to learn more about the activities of certain parties who are the ultimate purchasers in a series of transactions to which I have been a party. The pattern also indicates, not quite so strongly, that, unlike me, you do know the identity of these purchasers, Doctor."

"For the purposes of our discussion, you may assume that your analysis is correct."

"Very good. That moves things along quite nicely. Now, shall we turn to that which I do not know and which I am not prepared even to guess?"

The doctor nodded.

"So we shall. I do not know why you would seek this information or what precise use you would make of it, except that it is a matter of military intelligence. I further do not know the identities of my ultimate purchasers. I do strongly suspect, however, that if I were to know the answer to the second question, the answer to the first would be quite apparent. As you might expect, I am quite eager to learn the answers to both questions and would be willing to offer consideration of quite substantial value to obtain them."

Aha. The man is ready to deal. "If you can provide me with detailed information about the movement of the cargo you are selling, or provide me with access to the cargo so that I can place tracking devices in it, I would consider your actions more than adequate payment for my telling you what I know about your purchasers. I assure you, my knowledge is very precise, and you will find it quite valuable."

"I believe that a trade of the kind you propose would be equitable. I do, however, have one concern. We are both men of honor, and you will understand that honor is an important component of my business dealings. I must be satisfied, as I already suspect to be true, that you are not making these inquiries as part of some scheme to obtain greater profits or some business advantage over a competitor. The information I have, limited as it is, is considered commercial intelligence, and I could not in good conscience divulge it if it were to be put to commercial use. Given your naval connection, as I said, I am surmising that you are seeking this information as *military* intelligence, to gain some sort of strategic advantage for your people in their war against the Krag, in which—by the way—they have my entire sympathy and support."

"That is correct."

"Would you be willing to swear an oath to me to that effect?"

"Gladly."

Wortham-Biggs stood and removed a long, beautifully curved sword from a pair mounted above the mantelpiece. The doctor could see that it was not merely decorative: its handle was darkened with the oils it had absorbed in many hours of use, and his experienced eye caught the gleam of a keen edge. He stood and drew his own blade from beneath his robes.

The two men stood facing each other, about a meter and a half apart, and brought their swords together, flat to flat, touching about a third of the way from the tips.

"I, Ibrahim Sahin, swear before Allah the Merciful and the Just, Creator of all things, whose name stirred the blood of my fathers and who is the holy source of my honor as a man, that I seek the information for which I came today for no purpose of wealth or lucre and that I will use this information neither for personal gain nor to obtain advantage over any business competitor. Should this oath be broken, may He cause these blades to swiftly avenge my perfidy.... Is the oath satisfactory?"

"Perfectly."

"Admirable weapon, you have there, sir," said Sahin.

"Thank you. Yours appears to be quite deadly as well. Have you drawn blood with it?"

"Touched, but not drawn."

"So, a man of restraint. An admirable quality. But not unexpected. It can be very difficult to show your enemy your edge but not cut him with it," said Wortham-Biggs.

"Quite. Now, shall we return to your excellent coffee? I should like another cup before we conclude our business."

"Capital notion." Each man returned his sword to its former place, and Wortham-Biggs poured more coffee for all three men.

"Now, as the one who did not swear the oath, it is incumbent upon me to show my good faith by making the first offer of information."

He walked over to his desk with his coffee, sat down, and pressed an unobtrusive switch. A keyboard in a hidden tray slid out, and a wafer-thin screen rose from a concealed slot in the desktop. He typed rapidly for a few moments.

"There. Doctor, if you will instruct your flipcom to access data channel 113, and input the password 'mastiff,' you will have in your hands the complete cargo manifests and shipping schedules for all of my transactions with the party in whom you are interested, including the future shipment dates along with the names and transponder ID codes of the freighters on which the goods will be placed. Of course, the shipments are always transferred to other freighters in deep space, but the coordinates of those transfers are in the file I am sending you. From those freighters, the cargo is transferred again at least once, perhaps more times after that. I presume you have a set of tracking devices."

"Yes." The doctor nodded to Fahad, who produced from deep within his robes a small flat case, similar to the kind in which a gentleman carries his cigars.

"Here are six devices of the standard kind. Kindly hide one in each shipment. They are the standard metaspacial transponders, but coming from Union Naval Intelligence are more sophisticated than most. The tracking signals are impossible to distinguish from background noise unless you know the five-hundred-character encrypt sequence. Before you implant them, simply remove the tip to activate."

"Very well." He took the case.

Fahad had pulled out his flipcom, accessed the designated file, downloaded it, and looked quickly at his screen to see if it was data of the kind promised. He nodded to the doctor.

"And now," Dr. Sahin said, "we come to the answer to your questions. What if I were to tell you that your ultimate purchasers were the worst kind of infidel?"

"They are not People of the Book?" Meaning not Muslim, Jewish, or Christian.

"Indeed not. They are not even, strictly speaking, people at all."

"Biologically absurd. What aliens would have use for human foodstuffs and would be able to use equipment designed for eyes that see the same frequency range as ours?"

"Aliens whose distant ancestors are from Earth."

After a short pause, the shop owner's face hardened, his lips a thin line of fury. "You cannot mean," he said in a voice the temperature of liquid helium, "that I have been selling to the treacherous Demon-Rats." He used the local name for the Krag. "I would require evidence of such a startling conclusion."

"I can provide you with an intelligence report tracing palettes of frozen meat, machine tools with manufacturers' serial numbers, ore still in shipping containers, and even small arms still in the maker's crates, all captured from Krag ships in Krag space or from Krag industrial installations, and all traceable to your warehouses.

"In addition, the ion drive on a captured Krag surveillance drone was found to have mercury propellant with an isotope profile showing it as having been mined here on Rashid IV. It is a small mine and you are the only seller of its output in interstellar commerce. Of course, we hold you entirely innocent. The Krag went to great and highly sophisticated lengths to hide their identity from you, knowing you were too honorable to sell to them, no matter what the price."

"Have you personally reviewed these reports?"

The doctor knew what the man wanted. Or needed. "Yes. And on my honor, I regard their findings as conclusive."

Wortham-Biggs sighed with resignation. "Then that is the only proof that I need." Under Rashidian custom, if a man's honor were sufficient basis for a Sword Oath, it was sufficient for all purposes. "I presume that the items already purchased must be delivered to these...vermin."

"Yes. They must. But I promise you I will do everything within my power to see that not so much as one grain of corn or one gram of ore ever reaches the Krag. And afterward, you will never again suffer the dishonor of having any dealings with them. It is my sad duty to tell you, however, that the matériel thus far purchased from you have been of substantial aid to their war effort."

"I can understand how that would be so, and it grieves me greatly. Do not be misled by this London shopkeeper exterior—it is a necessity when one deals in the kind of art in which I specialize. Although my ancestry is mixed, my fathers were Bedouin. My heart is Bedouin. These dealings with the rat-faced infidels are a matter of grave dishonor to me and my family. The Krag have killed many of my people, laid waste to whole worlds, massacred innocents, desecrated holy places of many faiths. They are a stain upon Allah's holy creation. Having aided them is almost more than I can bear. It is a great dishonor. I fear I shall never be free of its disgrace." He was genuinely and profoundly upset, deep emotion cracking the veneer of British reserve.

"Their rich, warm blood will wash away your dishonor and your family's."

Both men turned suddenly to Fahad, who said the first words he had spoken since stepping into the shop.

"Sir, unless I miss my guess, my captain is going to take the information you gave us and follow those transponder signals to destroy the freighters that carry the goods to the Krag and to destroy the Krag ships that bring the goods home. He'll get them, sir. He'll blow them to flaming atoms. All of them. Since he took command, we have vaporized every Krag ship we have found, and we have shot every human traitor we could lay our hands on. We'll kill them for you. We'll kill the cocksuckers by the bushel fucking basket. Pardon my Frennish."

"Hear him. Let us be your agent, my brother." The doctor picked up the ball and ran with it. "We shall collect their payment for you. Payment in blood. Dishonor shall stain neither you nor your family."

Wortham-Biggs sighed. "Thank you. Thank you both. Had you not come to me, I might have continued to provide these unclean, unholy creatures with the means to kill my own kind for years to come. I owe you a great deal more than merely the information I have provided to you, as you have kept the additional blood of thousands, perhaps millions, of innocents from my hands. Nothing I could ever do would even come close to paying my debt to you. Please. Tell me what more can I do to express my thanks. "

The doctor waved his hand dismissively. "I am here in my capacity as a naval officer and not for the purpose of obtaining anything for myself. If you would, however, care to thank my shipmates by providing at the current market rates fitting food-stuffs to sustain them on their long voyages between the stars, I would consider any debt between us to be entirely satisfied."

"I will accept no payment. I know you have made some purchases already, so kindly let me know the remaining capacity of your microfreighter's hold, and I will see it filled with such stuff as will fill their bellies and gladden their hearts. I already know where you are hangared."

About an hour later, having left the shop with their precious cargo of information, the two men were making their way down a broad avenue with only a few pedestrians on the walkways. It was just after 19:00 local time, and most of the locals were eating their evening meal or watching a highly anticipated soccer match between the Crocodiles, Rashid IV's planetary team, and the Jackals, their cross-system rivals from the mining and foundry moon, Rashid V C. Casually, the doctor grasped Fahad by the arm and guided him to a shop window displaying an array of local spices and smoked meats, as if to show him an item there. "Do not look, Fahad, but I believe we are being followed."

"You mean the guy with the blue headband and the Fenkep-style beard about fifteen meters to my left?"

"Precisely. You have noticed him too?"

"Naturally. Do you think Captain Robichaux sent me to a nonaligned planet near a war zone on a covert intelligence-gathering mission along with one of his most valuable officers just because I'm a good drive and thruster man?"

"I suppose not."

"I spent three years in the Navy's Criminal Investigation Division in covert surveillance and countersurveillance, special-izing in tailing and slipping tails. I had to get out when I became too familiar to too many of the wrong kind of people."

"Then I defer to your professional expertise. What do you recommend?"

"Well, Bones, I was thinking about taking him."

After a short discussion of how that was to be accomplished, the two men walked on about half a block until they ducked inside a small sundries shop that Fahad had noticed earlier. Fahad pretended to shop for local souvenir knickknacks, consisting mainly of poorly made plastic camels, of all things, from a counter that allowed him to see out the window while Sahin made a quick purchase.

A few moments later, the doctor exited the shop, holding an aerosol can while fumbling with the nozzle and to all appearances not looking where he was going. He then walked right into the man who had been following them. "Oh, my pardon to you, sir."

"Think nothing of it," said the other while the doctor made a great show of straightening the man's robes, which had become somewhat disarrayed by the collision.

"My most sincere pardon, most sincere. Tell me, sir, you sound as though you are local. The way this can works is different from how they operate on my home, and I can't get it to spray. Perhaps you can assist me. See? Nothing happens when I press here."

The doctor then, apparently accidentally, sprayed the man in the face with a sunburn treatment product, temporarily blinding him, while, at the same moment, Fahad—who had slipped out of the shop through the delivery entrance—jabbed the man in the neck with a pressure syringe disguised as an ordinary pen. Before the man could say a word, Fahad said firmly into his ear.

"You will say nothing and will come with us." And then to the doctor, "I'll call us a cab while you call your new friend."

Eighteen hours later, Dr. Sahin stood beside Max while the quartermaster and several men under his command used four small, highly maneuverable electric forklifts to remove cargo palettes from the microfreighter on the hangar deck and drive them down a corridor leading to the *Cumberland*'s main cargo hold. Once the unloading operation was running smoothly, Max began scrolling through the microfreighter's cargo manifest.

"Doctor, you did us proud, no doubt about that." Max was even more than customarily enthusiastic. "We're going to be eating better than any crew in the Navy outside of the Core Systems. Two tons of fresh-frozen beef. *Real beef.* Three tons of fresh-frozen chicken. Plus frozen turkeys, sausage, ham, salami, fresh and frozen vegetables, fresh and frozen fruit, frozen fish, frozen shrimp, olives, dates, real butter, honey, cheese, fresh eggs, fresh milk, a quarter ton of frozen ultra-concentrated orange juice, Russet potatoes, red potatoes, sweet potatoes, beans, rice, Arabica coffee. Morale on board is going to go up 100 percent. And your other cargo is even better."

A predatory grin spread across his face. "Much, much better. Let's go to the Casualty Station and look in on our new passenger."

The two men walked to a closed examination room in the Casualty Station, meeting Intelligence Officer Grade 4 "Robert Jones," a moniker that only the most gullible on board believed to be his given name, along with the tail man from Rashid IV, who was strapped securely to an examination bed, and Nurse Church to monitor the tail man's vitals during interrogation.

"Well, Jones, what have we learned so far?"

"This man was given 85 ccs of Agent 11 eighteen hours and seventeen minutes ago," said Jones. "As such, he has been completely cooperative."

"I had never heard of Agent 11 until today. I'm not sure I am particularly happy that such a thing exists," said Dr. Sahin.

Agent 11, or Compliazine, was a drug first devised for the mental health industry as a treatment for highly oppositional and noncompliant patients. But as soon as some unusual side effects of the drug were discovered in clinical trials, it quickly vanished from sight. For a period of roughly twenty-four hours, it suppressed to the point of nonexistence the ability of the subject to exercise any independent will. He would obey without question virtually any command given to him, including a command to provide truthful answers to questions.

The drug came with certain disadvantages, though. First, in suppressing the will, Agent 11 also suppressed intelligence, such that a subject could tell you what he knew but could not make any use of that knowledge or draw any conclusions from it. Second, the drug did not so much wear off as break down in the body to component compounds, most of which were highly toxic. If the subject was not detoxified starting about twenty-four hours after administration, he would die.

Finally, any subject could be given Agent 11 only three times, four at most, without suffering permanent brain damage. Even with these limitations, though, the drug was extremely useful for interrogations and was proving especially useful now. Because of the obvious misuse to which such a drug could be put by unscrupulous individuals, not only was the drug itself strictly controlled, but its formula and even its existence were closely guarded secrets.

Jones continued his briefing. "Name: Ernilum Grek. Occupation: espionage, specializing in surveillance and assassination. Works for the Krag, planted to feed them information on whether the Union or the locals ever started to zero in on their source of supply on Rashid IV and to kill anyone who got too close to the truth. He was planning to kill the doctor and Fahad by attacking their air car on its way from Amman back to the spaceport, and then returning to kill Wortham-Biggs and his daughter.

"He has assassinated twelve others on five planets, some for the Krag, some for hire to various criminal organizations. Ten of those deaths are in our records as unsolved murders and the other two as accidents. We have his contacts, comm frequencies, check-in schedule, authentication codes, cipher and encryption keys, cut-out and dead-drop locations—everything.

"This lets us wrap up a nice package to give to the local authorities that will let them clean out the entire Krag intelligence network on their world and will let us get in one or two good pieces of disinformation to lead the Krag by the nose to exactly where we want them. Capturing this fellow has worked out very well for us.

"I have also gotten from him a wealth of information about how the Krag run their local intelligence operatives, what the procedures are, how they are paid, and what systems they use to protect each cell. And because this man had worked for them on several other worlds before this one, we can get a general idea of the logistics they use from planet to planet. And—"

Jones was cut off by the loud buzzing of the Casualty Station comm panel, the volume of which the doctor had set to an unusually high level to get his attention, as he had a tendency to become absorbed in what he was doing. He poked at the switch with his finger, missing it three or four times before hitting it. "Casualty, Sahin here."

"Doctor, this is Chief Xang in Cargo Handling. In unloading and stowing the contents of the microfreighter, we came upon a crate that is labeled 'Personal: For Ibrahim Sahin.' What do you want us to do with it?"

"I have no idea what it is. What might be the size of this mysterious crate?"

"About a meter and a half tall and about seventy-five centimeters in the other two dimensions. It's gotta weigh a couple of hundred kilos."

At this, Max stepped over to the panel. "Xang, this is the skipper. I want you to have two of your best men, and I mean your *best* men—in fact, make it yourself and your best *man*—take the crate to the doctor's quarters. By the time you get there, he will have set up a one-time-only entry keyed to your voice—that's *your* voice, Chief. Take it inside, open it, and whatever it is, set it up, lay it out, or whatever is appropriate. Understood?"

"Perfectly, sir. Don't worry; I'll take care of it personally."

"Very good. Let me know when you're finished."

"Aye, aye."

Jones got to finish his rapturous description of the "take" from the captured Krag spy. Sahin's own enthusiasm was dampened substantially when he learned that the man was a Union citizen, born and raised on Alphacen. That unpleasant revelation, of course, meant that sometime in the next day or so the doctor would get to start his day off with a bang.

Once this cheerful news was announced, the doctor had to detoxify the prisoner to make sure that he didn't die in an hour or two of the poisonous byproducts of his body's efforts to metabolize Agent 11, rather than dying in a day or two from having five 7.62-millimeter full metal jacket bullets pierce his heart at 843 meters per second. Dead is dead, but timing is everything.

When he finally got to his quarters and palmed the entry scanner, all the doctor could think about was taking a shower and getting into bed. To his surprise, stacked neatly in front of his desk were several dozen bright-red, rectangular packages, each about half the size of a loaf of bread. When he walked over and picked one up, he could see that the packages were vacuum-packed polyfoil labeled "Wortham-Biggs Coffee: Rashid IV Community Special Reserve, Four-Planet Blend. One Pound Net Weight."

Leave it to Wortham-Biggs to package his special coffee in that archaic quantity. There had to be fifty or sixty pounds. The doctor knew he could never drink that much coffee himself. He decided to give several pounds to the captain and to others to whom he wanted to show special appreciation or kindness, and to turn most of the rest over to the wardroom steward to serve to the ship's officers on special occasions.

Just as he was feeling good about that, savoring the memory of how good that coffee had tasted in the shop back on Rashid IV and mentally composing a note of thanks to send back to the giver of this unexpected gift, the doctor turned a corner into the main sitting area of his quarters.

And stopped, dumbstruck.

Chief Xang had been busy. He had brought in and set up one of the small but elegant pedestal tables kept in ship's stores to display trophies, plaques, and other honors awarded to the ship. He had installed several microspots, small but powerful and tightly focused lamps that cast a bright, precisely directional beam of light and that drew their power from hair-thin, almost invisible wires plugged into tiny pores every half-meter or so in the bulkheads. And he had placed on the table, turned to its most flattering angle, perfectly lit from above and four sides by microspots, filling the doctor's quarters with an ethereal radiance of shimmering blues and purples and violets, the exquisitely glowing *Birth of the Waters*.

CHAPTER 20

19:52Z Hours, 5 February 2315 (Navy Day)

The *Cumberland's* wardroom was full of singing. Not particularly tuneful singing, as those assembled were not chosen for their musical abilities. And not particularly articulate singing, as those assembled had been partaking rather liberally of the excellent beer and wine and ardent spirits taken aboard at Rashid IV. But what the singing lacked in musicality and precision, it made up for in volume and enthusiasm, for it was Navy Day, the Union holiday set aside to honor the men (and very, very few women) who defended humanity's very existence by service in deep space.

The men in the wardroom were singing a particularly naval song, one with its roots sunk deep in the traditions of the service, back to the days before man reached for the stars, before he even managed to coax his frail, little ships into sailing against the wind and tide by pushing them with smoky boilers, scalding steam, and whirling machinery. This song was a legacy from the days of oaken hulls and billowing sails, of "ships of wood and men of iron." For more than five hundred years, men had handed it down like a cherished family heirloom, until now it was given booming voice in the cold void between the stars, a thousand light years from home.

The words had evolved to fit the needs of a time harsher and more desperate than the age that gave rise to the original, but the tune was one that would have brought a smile to the face of Lord Nelson. He knew it as "Heart of Oak." Over the centuries, it had become "Hearts of Steel."

> To stations, my lads, 'tis to glory we steer,
> Oh, sons of the Union, we fight without fear;
> 'Tis to Honor you call us, for Honor we stand;
> We brothers in valor await fame's command.

And the chorus rang out with even more gusto, as the half-dozen or so senior midshipman who did not know the verses joined in. These boys, ages fifteen to seventeen, were even more thoroughly inebriated than the officers because, although naval regulations prohibited giving them alcohol, by immemorial naval tradition they were permitted beer, wine, ale, and stout on certain holidays, including Navy Day (February 5), Union Day (July 20), and the birthdays of Admiral Nelson (September 29), Admiral Halsey (October 30), and General Patton (November 11).

> Hearts of steel, that's our ships; hearts of steel, that's our men.
> We always are ready; steady, boys, steady!
> We'll fight, not surrender, again and again.

When the next verse began, the mids stopped singing and went back to drinking. The officers carried on, sounding very much as though they had the blood of Mars in their veins.

We'll take payment in blood for the debt Krag must pay,
And carve them with cutlass when they come to play;
Our courage defiant ennobles the stars,
Stalwart sons of Ares, strong offspring of Mars.

The mids joined in the chorus again, this time even more loudly, many arm in arm and swaying back and forth in unison while Max's booming bass and "Wernher" Brown's tuneful yet powerful baritone practically rattled the china with "steady, boys, steady," a phrase that had endured without change from the song's "hard tack and salt horse" roots.

The officers forged on into the concluding verse while the mids refilled their glasses.

We still make them bleed and we still make them die,
And we shout mighty cheers as they fall from the sky;
So cheer up me lads and let's sing with one heart,
We will win this war if we all do our part.

The song was topped off by another repetition of the chorus, sung even more loudly than the first two iterations and ending with a resounding thump as each man in the room honored tradition by pounding his fist on the table with the last "again." Tradition also required that, after any singing of "Hearts of Steel," glasses be drunk down and refilled—a tradition that never went unobserved.

A delightful meal, superb drink, manly singing, and naval companionship all combined to create a fine, warm mood in the wardroom, the kind of mood that made up for days and weeks of long, lonely service, short rations, protracted hardship, and extreme danger.

When glasses had been filled all around, the captain stood at the head of the wardroom table and began to speak, the talk in the room dying quickly.

"Gentlemen, I have two toasts. And only two." Cries of "Hear, hear!" made their way round the table, as many officers had endured endless litanies of Navy Day toasts from inebriated COs who had no inkling of when to shut up.

"First, to our greatly esteemed Dr. Ibrahim Sahin, who acquired for us this outstanding food and excellent drink. I shall never again wonder which of my officers is best suited to go planetside and act as this vessel's victualer." He drained his glass, containing about two fingers' worth of the warm, dark, fragrant liquid distilled only in an exotic corner of the galaxy known as Kentucky.

"Hear, hear! To the doctor!" the officers responded, and drained their glasses.

"Now, recharge your guns, gentlemen," he said. All refilled their glasses.

"Today is Navy Day. I'm just a plain-speaking fighting man, so I can't give you a stirring speech about what the Navy means to each of us. But I can say this. Every one of you is a volunteer, most from boyhood. Every one of you has had at least one chance—and most of you several—to leave the service at the end of a tour and has instead re-enlisted. You have decided to make the Navy your life not just once but many times. There is something about the Navy that has kept you here. Only you know, deep in your hearts, what that is. It is likely different for each of you.

"I want to take this time to tell you what it is for me. For many years, I had the honor of serving under one of the greatest men to ever wear the uniform, Commodore—now Fleet Admiral—Charles L. Middleton."

Several of those present rapped their knuckles on the table or raised their glasses in tribute. Admiral Middleton was almost universally loved and respected not just for his strategic brilliance but for his psychological insight, which was reputed to be better than that of any other man in the Navy.

"At a gathering like this, when I had just been commissioned as an ensign on board the old battlecruiser *Margaret Jackie*, someone asked him what it all meant. 'Commodore Middleton, what does it all mean? Life, the Navy, our purpose for being, the Universe, and everything else?' Now, as many of you know, old Uncle Middy can be a bit long winded"—a few men smiled at their own recollections of the admiral's infamous loquaciousness—"and we all expected quite a speech, but not this time. He just smiled and said one word: 'love.'

"I didn't get what he meant back then. I thought he was talking about romantic love or maybe the love that parents and children have for each other. But now I understand. He was talking about the kind of love that we have here, in the Navy. It may seem a strange thing to say about a service that has as its goal taking or killing the enemy, but at its very core the Navy is all about love. Because, gentlemen, *loyalty is love*—love for your ship and love for your shipmates. Patriotism is love—love for the Union and the things that it stands for and protects. And even courage is love—the love of all these things and added to it the love of duty and honor that is so powerful that for its sake you reach down to the very bottom of your deepest well of resolve and do what you have to do, no matter how difficult it is and no matter how afraid you may be.

"Understood in that light, the Navy is the greatest home and repository and source of love in the galaxy. She has no equal. So, gentlemen, raise your glasses and lift your hearts to that which moves us, to that which sustains us, to that which protects us, to that which gives us life, and to that which calls us to love, to duty, to honor, to glory.

"To the Navy. May she live forever."

As one man they stood and drained their glasses.

There was even more eating and drinking and singing one deck lower and sixteen meters aft in the enlisted mess, where food was generally served cafeteria style, and the men helped themselves to whatever drink suited them. The songs included "Hearts of Steel," just as in the wardroom; other patriotic songs; and some others of a bawdier variety. Indeed, one old able spacer managed to lead the company through seventeen of the twenty-nine verses to "The Dirty Old Whore from Alnitak, Rendezvous" before passing out, slumped against the soft-serve ice cream dispenser.

Even Clouseau, the ship's cat who joined the *Cumberland* when she was docked with the *Loch Linnhe* by running through the docking tube after springing out of the locker in which the Krag on board had insisted he be stuffed, was enjoying the festivities, circulating from one mid's lap to another, begging little scraps of meat with an endearing tilt of the head and an occasional quiet meow. Indeed, he was not above stealing some of the tastier-smelling morsels from the plates of men and boys whose vigilance was impaired by drink.

Clouseau was generally successful in obtaining whatever he wanted. In spacer lore, all cats were lucky, because of their "nine lives." Black cats, into which category Clouseau fit quite comfortably, were even luckier. And cats that "joined" the ship on their own by running across a boarding tube or up a docking ramp were luckier still. Clouseau, then, was thrice charmed, and much cherished—even spoiled—by boys and men alike.

Most of the squeakers, the youngest midshipmen who spent more of their day in the ship's school than in official duties, were present and were even allowed tiny amounts of the weakest beer and of wine diluted with ginger ale under the watchful eye of

Midshipman Trainer "Mother Goose" Amborsky, who on this day was celebrating his thirty-second Navy Day in uniform.

Old Mother Goose had taken a bit more than usual of the potato vodka he favored and was in a talkative frame of mind, almost a different man from the gruff and laconic, but inwardly gentle, man the squeakers were used to seeing. Sensing this difference in mood, the boys had drawn out the chief, getting him to reminisce about his younger days in the Navy and the changes in the service over the years. At the end of one such story, about how in the *Portugal* class battlecruisers all the midshipmen were crowded into one cabin and slept on hammocks suspended from the ceiling—hammocks that, along with their boyish burdens, tended to become hopelessly tangled if the ship's artificial gravity failed—the youngest midshipman, Park, the one stuck with the nickname "Will Robinson" until someone even younger came aboard, asked, "Chief, is it true you was in the Navy on the first day of the war?"

"Aye, lad, that I was." He paused to take a sip of his vodka. "Sometimes I want to forget that day, and sometimes I think it is my duty to remember every detail until the day I die. Mostly, I try to remember." Another long pause as he considered whether to stop there or to go on. Hell, these hatch hangers would have to hear the story sometime.

"I was a recruit spacer second class on the old battlecruiser *Repulse*. The War of the Fenestrian Succession had been over for fifteen months, and we were with what they used to call the Twenty-Second Fleet, jumping from system to system along the Fenestra Treaty Boundary as a deterrent. We were cruising along, fat, dumb, and happy, with no idea of what was about to happen. A few freighters had reported some compression trails in deep space near the border, but we gave them no mind. We thought it was space-happy sensor officers seeing star fairies from spending too many hours at their scopes. We sure as hell didn't suspect the Krag."

"Why not, Chief?" asked the eternally curious Will Robinson. "Why not suspect them?"

"Because no one had seen their beady little eyes for nearly a hundred years, that's why. Hell, when we encountered them in 2183, we thought we were going to be fast friends with them. They were sure smart enough. Seemed friendly. And curious they were too, right eager to learn everything they could about us and not afraid to tell about themselves. We traded whole libraries of history, literature, trid vid programming, art, music—everything.

"But things went all pear shaped when the biology information started flying back and forth. Anyone could see that life on the two planets was two pages from the same chapter of the same book. The same biology. Not similar—the same. Same basic anatomy, same biochemistry, same DNA. Life from the whole Krag planet could have almost been from some remote island on Earth that split off from a land mass long ago, kind of like Australia.

"They had sent us the complete genetic information for hundreds of life forms on their world, and when our DNA guys worked through it, they figured out what happened pretty quick. All the life on the Krag homeworld had clearly evolved from plants and animals that were alive on Earth eleven million years ago. In fact, from just 150 or so species if you don't include the insects and bacteria. Well, paints a pretty clear picture, doesn't it? Somebody terraformed the Krag homeworld, visited Earth eleven million years ago, picked up some specimens, and gave them a new home. No telling why.

"Maybe they wanted to study Earth life in a new setting. Maybe they wanted a bloody zoo. Who the hell knows? Unless we find those aliens—and if we do, I've got a helluva bone to pick with them, let me tell you—we'll never know. What we do know is that those animals included the ancestor of our Earth rats. But on this new world, the ugly little critters didn't evolve into rats. They evolved over eleven million years into the Krag.

"When we shared that theory with the Krag, they went totally batshit. Now, they're not stupid. They can read their fossils in their rocks just like we read the fossils in our rocks. They had the same facts, but just about the same time we were developing the Theory of Evolution, they came up with a totally different kind of theory. According to them, eleven million years ago their Creator-God found a hostile world, remade it into a hospitable paradise, and then created perfect life to place on that world with the plan that it would evolve into his holy children, the Krag, and into creatures and plants to be their servants and their food.

"What about us? Did that make us the Krag's sacred brothers and sisters under the skin, united by bonds of kinship and chemistry? Not a bloody chance. What it did was make us unholy blasphemers for saying that life on their world was merely a transplanted offshoot of life on ours. On top of that, it made us a living, eating, breathing biological insult to their Creator-God because we were demonic spirits that had chosen to defy him by cloaking ourselves in the shape and chemistry of his true handiwork. When we wouldn't agree to be ruled by genuine creations, meaning the Krag, they just got madder and madder, until in 2184 they cut off all contact. They refused to respond to or even acknowledge our messages, turned back all diplomatic ships, stopped all trade—everything.

"Just before they cut off contact, they sent one last message. It said: 'You and all the infesting vermin spawned by your world are an affront to the Creator-God and exist in defiance of His holy will. The stars will be cleansed of you.' And then, nothing. Not a squeak. That is, until June 26, 2281.

"Suddenly, they showed up in a dozen systems with more than a thousand ships. It looked like they had spent the whole time since 2184 busting their rat asses to build a fleet just to wipe us out. Twelve systems fell in the first ten hours. Fifty-four in the first week.

"The Twenty-Second Fleet was cut to pieces in a matter of hours. I was in Auxiliary Pulse Cannon Fire Control standing by to assist with DC in that compartment. I didn't have anything better to do than watching the tactical repeater as ship after ship just dropped off the display. The *Rhine, Formosa, New Zealand, Galapagos, Aegean, Volga, Lincoln, Bolivar*, and a dozen others."

He paused, experiencing a powerful echo of the horror he felt watching, mute, as ships crewed by thousands of spacers simply winked out of existence. Clouseau hopped in Amborsky's lap and rubbed his head against the old chief, who absently stroked his black fur.

"Still, their tactics showed that they expected to get the whole fleet with their first salvo. Didn't happen. Our defenses had improved more than they expected during the last war, but we lost two-thirds of the fleet in less than three hours. Then Commodore Fuchida on the battleship *Texas* pulled what was left back four jumps, taking the jump point marker buoys with us in each system, all the way back to the Theater Strategic Reserve Force in orbit around Milvian III.

"Because the Krag had to find the jump points by following the resonance lines and then had to compute from scratch the coordinates for their counterpoints, even with no defenses in place in any of those systems it took them nearly twelve hours before they managed to pop into the Milvian system. When they came, they did that thing they do where they jump a bunch of ships at a time instead of just one, which is the only way we can do it, and suddenly there were two battleships and six heavy battlecruisers right there.

"We were ready for them and opened up before they could recover from the jump. We got four right away, but the rest cleared the datum, and inside of ten minutes there were another eight right behind them. Everyone knew that if they did that one more time, we would be outnumbered again; the Krag would take the system, and that would open up the jump point to Syrtis Minor, leading right into the heart of the whole Washtenaw cluster: eighty-nine worlds full of farmers and fishermen and families with nothing to defend them.

"Fuchida ordered every ship but the *Texas* back to a defensive formation around the jump point leading to Syrtis and then steered his ship right into the jump point just as the next wave of Krag came through. Of course, his ship and every ship coming through the jump were instantly converted into pure energy. The explosion fried most of the Krag fleet in the system and so disrupted the fabric of space-time that the jump point was unusable for 78 days. This put a real monkey wrench in the Krag plans, kept them out of the Washtenaw cluster until we could get some ships in there to defend it, and probably kept them from winning the war in that year. It bought us time to get most of our fleet out of mothballs, manned, and put to space.

"Just before he hit the jump point, Fuchida sent a last message. It said: 'We will meet again in that place where warriors go to take their rest.' We've been fighting ever since. And though we've fallen back, no Union system, station, or vessel has ever, ever surrendered to the Krag. And none ever will."

He paused a moment, as if to attend briefly to some echo of the past, still petting Clouseau.

"So, now, if you ever hear anyone say that a man is as brave as Commodore Fuchida or that a ship has gone on to rendezvous with the *Texas*, you'll know what they are talking about."

"Chief?" Will Robinson had another question. Always another question.

"What is it?"

"How many men were on the *Texas*?"

"On the *Texas*? Let's see, *Hesse* class battleship...just under fourteen hundred. A drop in the bucket of those who fell that day."

"Did they die for nothing?"

"No, son, they didn't. You and I are going to make sure of that."

CHAPTER 21

10:49Z Hours, 6 February 2315

After the *Cumberland* had paid a call at the abandoned asteroid mining station in an uninhabited system that harbored the first of its hidden supply caches and had restocked its missile racks and fuel bunkers, Max was feeling a little better about the next phase of his mission. It was about time for him to meet the Krag prisoner taken when the *Loch Linnhe* was boarded.

The intelligence officer had been interrogating it extensively and Max had read Smith's report. Jones's report. Jones? Yes, Jones. Because their names were entirely fictitious, why couldn't they have names that were easier to remember? The last one Max had worked with was "Johnson," the one before that "Gray," and the one before that, who looked distinctly Germanic and had a slight Teutonic accent, was imaginatively named "Schmidt." Why not "Beddingfield" or "Kleinknecht"—something that a brain can hang on to?

Max entered the brig, which held seven wedge-shaped cells arranged like slices of pie with their ends cut off, all opening into a circular central guard area. The prisoners could be isolated from being able to see or hear one another by extending wall panels that telescoped out from the bulkhead between each cell to a clear partition that surrounded the guard. Since the human spy had been executed and Green was in the gym for his exercise period, the Krag was the only prisoner. The outer wall of the cell was a polymer barrier two centimeters thick with a door in it. The wall could be rendered transparent or opaque by polarization. At the moment, it was opaque—a flat black.

"Okay, Futrell, let me see Squeaky here."

Marine Lance Corporal Futrell turned a dial, and the wall went from black to transparent, revealing the Krag curled up on the cot. Literally curled, the way a mouse curls up when it sleeps. The cell brightened from the wall being made transparent, alerting the Krag that it was being observed. It sprang to its feet, looking for all the worlds like a man with hunched shoulders, spindly legs, short but powerful arms, a tail, and a rat's head. There was a wary intelligence in its eyes, and the top of its head was dome-shaped to enclose a brain capable of inventing star drives and formulating plans for the eradication of humans from the galaxy. Just looking at one made Max want to pull out his boarding cutlass and start hacking.

"Activate the translator."

No one actually *spoke* the Krag language, as human vocal apparatus could not duplicate many of the squeaks and chitters that made up about half of the sounds it used. And no human could understand Krag because many of the squeaks were above the range of human hearing, and many of the chitters were so fast and so similar to one another that most human ears could not distinguish them. Supposedly, Krag had similar difficulties understanding human speech.

At Max's command, the upper left-hand corner of the wall went from transparent back to opaque and displayed text in large amber letters: "Standard (spoken) to Krag (written) and Krag (spoken) to Standard (written) translation matrices activated. Begin when ready."

The Krag made some chittering and squeaking noises interspersed with a few sounds that vaguely resembled human speech. The translation matrix considered the Krag's statement for a few moments and displayed: "When I get back home, I must inform the zookeeper that he has left the monkey cage unlocked again. If you are looking for a banana, I'm afraid I have none with me."

The Krag homeworld had both monkeys and bananas. Only, unfortunately, it was the rodents instead of the primates that had developed big brains, harnessed fire, and mastered nuclear fusion.

What was it about so many alien races that compelled them to make fun of how humans were descended from primates? Every sentient species evolved from some wild creature. The Krag developed from scurrying rodents, the Vaaach from some sort of carnivorous tree sloth, the Pfelung from bottom-feeding, pond-dwelling lungfish. What made having apes as ancestors so worthy of ridicule? No one started off interrogating a Pfelung by asking if he knew his grandmother would taste good fried in cornmeal with hush puppies on the side.

"Make all the monkey jokes you want, Mickey, but I'm the zookeeper and you're the one in the cage. And don't you forget that I can do whatever I want with you. You give me information I can use, I might just keep you around and turn you over to the Prisoner of War Authority. They can put you in reasonably comfortable confinement until we kick your skinny little rat tails back to where you came from, and then send you back to your rat buddies to live out the rest of your miserable little rat life.

"If you don't, I'll just put you in an airlock, vent it slowly, and watch as your eyeballs pop while you roll around on the floor twitching, bleeding from your ears and rectum, and vomiting your entrails all over the deck." It wasn't pretty. But it was, to Max at any rate, intensely gratifying.

"Then we shove your carcass out into space and you get to spend eternity dancing with the stars."

The Krag moved its head to its left and slightly down, a tiny, almost imperceptible shift of which it was almost certainly not aware. The interrogation reports Max had read said that this was an unconscious sign of submission or resignation. More rodent noises. "I have answered all your questions. I have told you everything that I know."

"Bullshit. You were on board a freighter bound for Krag space carrying tons of gold, but you say you don't know about any other shipments, the recognition protocols, rendezvous points, payment arrangements, and who else you are dealing with. You insult my intelligence."

It made little barking noises, the Krag equivalent of laughter. "Any accurate reference to your mental capacity would be an insult to your intelligence, I am afraid. Perhaps with your chattering primate sociability, your species is in the habit of spreading important tactical information beyond those who have a need to know it, but that is not our practice. With us, information of this kind is rigidly compartmentalized. I was given only the information strictly necessary to complete my mission. I have given that to you, as I could not help doing with the interrogation drug you gave me.

"Kill me, if that is what you prefer to do. Or not. I no longer care. I have told you all that I know. I can tell you no more. If I am to die, that is my lot as a member of the Warrior Swarm. If I am to live, that is my lot as well, and I will carry on with the shame of failure, of giving information to monkey-blasphemer-deceivers and not striking back at you for cloaking your evil souls in misshapen, crude mimicry of the Creator-God's True Handiwork."

"Don't push your luck, Jerry. I could have you in that airlock in two minutes."

"Gloat in your power over me while you can. The Creator-God will erase you and your kind from His holy creation. The galaxy shall be cleansed."

"Maybe so. But not today. Rat." He turned to Futrell.

"Lance Corporal, opacify. I don't want to see that thing any more."

The wall went black and the Marine deactivated the translator. Max took a few steps toward the exit, then stopped.

"Lance Corporal?"

"Yes, Skipper."

"I've heard that some Marines on some ships can 'forget' to provide food and water to Krag prisoners. Make sure the detachment understands that I won't tolerate any memory lapses like that on my ship. Whiskers gets as much water as it wants and the standard Krag ration at the prescribed times. Understood?"

"Understood, sir. I'll take care of it. No memory problems on this ship, sir."

"Thank you. Carry on."

Leaving the brig, Max was not in the best of moods. He hated every time he had to come face to face with a Krag. Seeing their beady little eyes, watching the twitchy way they moved their arms and their noses, hearing their squeaking and chittering speech, all triggered too many truly horrific memories for him to be able to experience such an encounter with equanimity.

He was lost in his own thoughts, trying to bury even more deeply the sights and sounds that kept on trying to surface in his mind, and was not paying attention to his surroundings. So, it was not with perfect amiability that he responded to an ordinary spacer third who, when Max was passing in front of the ship's store on the way back to his quarters, bawled a little too loudly, "Hey, Skipper. You gotta see this."

Every warship has a ship's store. This is where personnel obtain items such as stationery, toiletries other than the basics issued to them, gum, candy bars, sundries, book and periodical download codes, and trid vid cubes.

But most of the business in ship's stores was in ship's souvenirs: T-shirts, caps, jackets, coffee mugs, and patches that said "Navy" or that displayed the name of the ship or the ship's emblem. The men bought these items not just for themselves but also to give to family members and sweethearts. Most ships did a particularly brisk business in children's items such as child-sized T-shirts and baby pajamas, all with the ship's emblem so that everyone could see where their fathers or grandfathers or uncles served and that they were "children of the ship."

The *Cumberland*'s store had done very little of that sort of business, as there was little demand for these items and no one had ever taken the trouble to design an emblem for the vessel.

Max was probably not wearing the most receptive-looking face when he looked around to see who had called for him, but his expression rapidly turned to surprise. The spacer who had yelled at his skipper was pointing to the line in front of the ship's store. The line that had twenty men standing in it. Max had never seen so many as two people in line before. Careful to stand slightly to the side to make it clear that he was not cutting in front of twenty men who were waiting patiently for something, he stepped up to the store's window, a roughly one-by-two-meter opening set chest high in the wall of the corridor, opening into a small shop behind that was manned by a clerk who sold the items and handed them over the counter to his customers.

The clerk visibly brightened when he saw Max, and he began to talk breathlessly. "Captain, sir, we just got these out of the FabriFax half an hour ago, and we done more business in them thirty minutes than in the last ninety days put together.

"We got the T-shirts, the ball caps, the pins, the coffee mugs, and the pillow cases right now, and by tomorrow we gonna have the pendants, charms for the wives' and sweethearts' charm bracelets, polo shirts, shot glasses, T-shirts in kids sizes, and workout shorts, all with the new emblem thing. It's gonna be a few days on the throw pillows and Christmas tree ornaments, but there's no rush on them ornaments, it being only February and all—"

"Petrone," Max broke in, clueless, "what 'emblem thing'?"

"This." Wearing the biggest grin that Max had ever seen on this ship, Ordinary Spacer Third Class Walter Petrone held up a T-shirt with an enormous emblem on it that Max had never seen before. But after looking at it for a few seconds, Max found himself grinning even more widely than Petrone.

The emblem covered the entire front of the T-shirt and was almost twice as large as such things were customarily printed. The whole thing was encircled by a gold ring, two or three fingers wide, into which was inscribed along the top in Navy blue, "USS *Cumberland* DPA-0004." Below that, inside the circle, was depicted a deep cleft in a range of green-forested mountains, presumably the Cumberland Gap on Earth. Beyond the Gap, one could discern a tiny image of the destroyer herself, leaving a stylized "swoosh" in her wake from having flown level through the Gap, her bow now pointed almost straight up at a cluster of stars in the sky high above her.

Perhaps the best part, and Max's rudimentary grasp of Latin let him instantly understand what the men must have just made the ship's new motto, was inscribed in the bottom of the gold ring: *"Per laboram ad victoriam."* Through hardship to victory.

Right on.

A few minutes later, having been rebuffed in an effort to buy a T-shirt and a ball cap by Petrone, who informed him (quite correctly) that, under immemorial naval custom, the captain never pays for anything with his ship's name on it, so long as it is for his personal use, Max had stowed his new shirt and cap and was in his day cabin, sitting at the coffee table, sipping some truly outstanding coffee with the doctor and Jones.

"Have you decided what to do with the Krag?" Sahin asked. "I ask purely out of academic interest, because if you intend to kill him, I was hoping you would do so in such a way that would preserve as many of his tissues as possible in undamaged condition and cause minimum biochemical change. An air embolism perhaps? I have never gotten to dissect a Krag, and after having repaired this one's arm, I am very curious about many of the details of his finer anatomy."

"Doctor, I'm afraid that you will have to do without the dissection. I am planning to let it live."

"Really?" Jones smiled enigmatically, like someone who has heard something he wants to hear but is very surprised nonetheless. "Why is that?"

"I generally kill only when I have good reason, and I don't have any good reason to kill it. This particular Krag has committed no crime for which I am required to execute it. Since there are no other Krag on board, I can't use the death of this one to threaten the others. There's just no benefit in killing the thing, and letting it live doesn't do any harm that I can see. Maybe someone at an interrogation center can get more out of it than we have. This one has basically had its incisors pulled. It's got no bite left."

"For what it's worth, I concur," said Jones. "It was a low-level operative possessing a tiny sliver of compartmentalized knowledge, which we have successfully extracted. It may prove useful in the future if we can break it to voluntary cooperation and we capture another Krag that it knows. Then it might help us break the second Krag, who might possess some knowledge that is more valuable. Not a likely scenario, but in total war you don't throw away any tool, no matter how small or apparently limited its usefulness."

The doctor shook his head. "You two offer the most cold-blooded reasons for an act of generosity, mercy, and humanitarianism that I have ever heard."

"Doctor," said Max, "for all you know, all I told you was a tiny portion of my true reasoning on the issue. Perhaps I am sparing the Krag primarily because the Sermon on the Mount says, 'Blessed are the merciful, for they shall obtain mercy.'"

"I would feel better if that were your true reason, but if you do not open your mind to me, I will never know."

"Then you will never know. Besides, we have bigger fish to fry now. The first transponder shows that one of your art dealer friend's freighters carrying Krag cargo left Rashid IV several hours ago. According to the schedule, it will be jumping into the S'regor system at 00:14 tomorrow and rendezvousing with another freighter to transfer its cargo at 05:52. There's only one jump point in that system that leads to anywhere near Krag space. It goes to Keldof. It will take the freighter at least fifteen hours to get from the rendezvous point to the jump point. We're already on our way to Keldof following a different route. We'll get there a few hours ahead of him and lie in wait, then either take or destroy the freighter, depending on what kind of ship it is and what kind of escort it has, if any."

"If that's all you have for me, Captain, I have a report to write," said Jones, thoroughly uninterested in the business of attacking and taking freighters. He left.

"I heard that the crew has finally come up with a coat of arms, as it were, for the ship," said the doctor.

"Indeed, they have. Take a look." Max retrieved the T-shirt and unfolded it on the table in front of the doctor.

"Very, very interesting," he remarked. "This is good news, indeed."

"How so?"

"Max, whatever your drills and efficiency ratings are telling you, this emblem that you hold in your hands right now says that you have already won the most important battle—the one for the hearts of the crew. You have turned these men around. You have given them back their pride, their honor, and their self-respect. Experience shows that once you have done that for a group of men, they will follow you to the very gates of Hell."

CHAPTER 22

00:12Z Hours, 8 February 2315

The freighter turned out not to have any escort at all. When the ship carrying the Krag-purchased cargo arrived in the Keldof system, the *Cumberland* was already doing its now well-rehearsed imitation of a Romanovan Revenue and Inspection cutter. Because it had documentation showing its cargo to be entirely legitimate, the Igandii freighter *Frenkung-Tan* had no reluctance whatsoever about heaving to for inspection by the representatives of the Romanovan Imperium.

When the appropriately costumed doctor and Marine boarding party went aboard her, they were not surprised to see the vessel crewed by humans, as the Igandii rarely ventured into space themselves and usually crewed their ships with humans from one of the neutral systems. "May I see your ID cube please," the doctor asked the freighter captain, who identified himself as Brigham Johnson.

As the man fished the cube out of his pocket, the doctor noticed that the front zipper of the uniform, a utilitarian jumpsuit that had one zipper running from the crotch to the neck, was pulled down to roughly the middle of the man's sternum, revealing a bare and distinctly hairy chest. The man was not wearing any kind of undershirt, which was nothing unusual for a freighter rat. A quick scan of the bridge showed two other crew members at their stations, one of whom was drinking hot coffee from a mug. A glance at the mug sitting at the Captain's Station showed that he was drinking coffee as well. One of the crew, a hard-looking sixtyish woman at the Maneuvering Station, appeared to have just noticed that a pack of cigarettes was protruding from a stack of personal items in a rack near her seat and was trying to cover it up without drawing notice to herself.

The reader showed that the ID cube was a forgery that Romanovan equipment would read as the genuine article. The captain's entirely false biography appeared on the screen, including his date and place of birth, residence history, piloting certificates, and so on.

"So," the doctor said, in a conversational tone, "you are from New Zarahemla."

"Yes, I am. We all are."

That too was nothing out of the ordinary. A lot of people from New Zarahemla became freighter rats. The local economy had been struggling for the past several years; the planet had a strong space-faring tradition; and transit companies liked to hire from there because the people of that world had a reputation for being honest, hard working, reliable, and family oriented, and for being less prone than most to abusing alcohol and drugs on long, lonely freighter runs.

"Raised there?"

"Yes. We all grew up there together. We're old friends and we like to ship out on the same crew."

"Yes, many freighter crew do that. I envy you, coming from such a world. I've always wanted to visit New Zarahemla. Especially the beaches. I hear they are beautiful."

"Yes," the captain responded, with the rest of his crew nodding their support. "Absolutely beautiful. I love them. In fact, I was born and raised close to the water, right there on a bay. Practically lived on the beach. Went fishing every day. I love fishing. Are you a fisherman, Captain?"

The doctor shook his head.

"Anyways, I remember my father telling me over and over again about how he had this little cypress skiff that he would row out to his favorite fishing spot, an oyster shell reef in a shallow, muddy bay that he would find by lining up a wind turbine with a gap between some trees. He'd catch redfish and speckled trout and a really tasty but hard-fighting little fish that we called a 'croaker' because of the noise it made. He'd bring the fish back and his mother would fry them up in this little cottage we had right on the water—beautiful place with a screen porch where we used to sit in rocking chairs and enjoy the breeze off the water. I've got a holocube of it right here. You'll see that it was really quite quaint the way they built them back then."

As the captain was droning on, he opened a small locker near the Commander's Station as if to pull out a holocube. What came out of the locker, though, was decidedly not an image of a beach cottage. Just as he accelerated his motion to bring the object to bear, two sharp reports rang out, accompanied by the sudden appearance of two roughly eleven-and-a-half-millimeter circles in the center of the captain's forehead and an explosion of bone and brain matter from the back of his skull. As the man fell to the floor, all eyes turned in the direction of the two shots.

There, in his garish faux uniform, stood Dr. Ibrahim Sahin, holding a smoking M-1911 in a two-handed combat grip, with a look on his face that could almost be characterized as embarrassment. By this time the Marines had the other crew members covered with shotguns, and Major Kraft was taking a small black pistol from the dead man's hand.

"CZ 535, nine millimeter, made on Bravo. Good little pistol, actually. Good thing you had the drop on him, Doctor." He peered at the dead man's forehead. "Nice grouping, by the way. You could cover both entry wounds with a one-credit coin."

"Without meaning any insult to you, Major, I decline to accept the compliment, I'm afraid. I take pride in saving lives, not taking them."

"No insult taken. Merely admiring a thing done well." He turned to two of his men.

"Bind these two, and take them across to the *Cumberland*."

To two others: "Zamora and Ulmer, you two search the rest of the ship. Be careful." He turned back to the dead man.

"Doctor, what was it that tipped you off? I had a vague feeling that these people were not what they said they were, but I can tell you were certain they were lying."

"Quite simple, really. His ID cube said he was from New Zarahemla. What do you know about that world? Do you recognize the significance of the name?"

"Only that a lot of freighter crews come from there and that if a man from there is under your command in the corps, you generally don't have to worry about him being a drunk or a tranker. I have no idea where the name comes from."

"Aaah. Well, it appears that you and our friends here share the same—apparently quite widespread—ignorance. Zarahemla is the name of a city and a republic mentioned in the Book of Mormon. New Zarahemla takes its name from there, as it was settled by an expedition funded by the Mormon, or LDS Church as they call themselves, and to this day virtually every resident of the planet is an adherent of that faith. The first name 'Brigham' is also very rare except among Mormons. Do you know anything about the Mormons, Major?"

"Very little, I'm afraid. I suspect I'm about to learn, though."

The doctor smiled. "I will try to keep my exposition short. First, their beliefs include a requirement that they wear at all times a highly characteristic type of undergarment as a constant reminder of their promises to God, somewhat akin to the wearing of a *yarmulke*, or *kippah*, by orthodox Jews, although the precise theological bases for the two are distinct. Our late captain here, as I could see from the way he was wearing his uniform, was clearly not wearing those garments. I am quite familiar with their appearance, as a physician who, from time to time, examines members of that faith.

"Second, the Latter Day Saints strictly avoid consumption of coffee or other stimulants. As you can see, there are two cups of coffee on this bridge. Third, their religion teaches them, quite accurately I might add from a purely secular perspective, that tobacco is not fit for human consumption. The woman had a pack of cigarettes among her effects.

"On top of that, not only did they not know the tenets of the faith to which they purported to adhere, but they were profoundly ignorant of the very world from which they said they came. Our supposed captain waxed eloquent about all the time he spent on the beautiful beaches of his planet when, according to every text and guidebook, their unfortunate geology is such that the land masses rise from the ocean so steeply that continent and sea generally meet in towering cliffs and jagged rocks.

"All of their seaports are either artificial harbors created by building jetties and wharfs that extend from the land or by dredging rivers far inland to where the water level is closer to the elevation of the land mass, which makes him a liar, and a bad one at that. I am afraid that my recognition of that fact must have shown on my face, so Mr. Johnson—or whatever his name really is—was reaching for his pistol, thinking he might be able to take the boarding party hostage and convince our people to let him go. Remember, he thought I was the captain and accordingly believed that if he held me, he might have some bargaining power."

Kraft nodded his head in admiration. "At any rate, Doctor, you thwarted that plan. Let us see what Zamora and Ulmer found in their search and let our real captain know that the vessel is secure so that he can send over a prize crew."

"Major Kraft says you double-tapped that freighter captain like a Special Forces commando, Doctor," Max said admiringly.

"Traders often go to dangerous places and deal with unsavory individuals. Accordingly, most are almost always armed. I have used the Model 1911 since boyhood. I believe it to be the best fighting handgun ever fashioned by human hands, and I am very comfortable with it, which is why I had it with me, instead of the usual sidearm for the Romanovans. I did a bit of research and found that some Romanovan officers carry that weapon, so I decided to bring with me what I knew."

"Always a wise decision when it comes to something on which you may be staking your life."

The two men were sharing another companionable dinner in Max's day cabin, this one decidedly tastier than the last. The entrée had been shrimp étouffée, served alongside various fresh-frozen vegetables and the usual fresh bread. All topped off with apple pie made with fresh apples.

"What of those other two we took off the freighter, the younger man and the cigarette-smoking woman?" asked Sahin.

"They are both neutrals, it turns out. The whole crew was from Hibernia. I put them aboard the prize and sent it back to Lovell Station. Since they aren't our citizens, we don't have jurisdiction over them, although we do get the ship. They will be turned over to the Igandii authorities, who Major Kraft tells me *do* have authority to try them under something called 'Jurisdiction by Estoppel.'"

"I'm certain I have never heard of it."

"It's a great thing—perfect justice all the way around," Max said. "You see, if that ship had actually been Igandii, those two would have been under Igandii jurisdiction, pure and simple."

"That is fundamental. But the ship wasn't Igandii, in reality. It had no true registry."

"Exactly. Here's the part I really like. When they get hauled before an Igandii court, they are not permitted to argue that the Igandii lack jurisdiction, because they earlier masqueraded as an Igandii freighter. The are, essentially, forced to stick with their first lie instead of being able to argue the truth. Sometimes, the law can be a glorious thing. Not usually, you understand, not usually at all, but in this case, glorious.

"In any event, the Igandii take a dim view of those who falsely claim to be navigating under their flag. These two won't be executed, but they will spend several years in an Igandii prison, and the Igandii don't provide much in the way of luxuries in their correctional facilities."

"What do the Igandii regard as a luxury, pray tell?" asked the doctor.

"Oh, things like…beds."

"Alas, it can be a brutal galaxy."

"It sure can. Although a good dinner can take the edge off the brutality. And there is at least some good news about the capture."

"You are speaking on the subject of prize money?"

"One of my favorite subjects. This little freighter wasn't carrying gold, but she wasn't carrying potting soil, either."

"And what exactly was the cargo?"

"Bearings."

"Bearings? You mean those little metal balls that they used to put in machinery before suspensive magnetic interfaces?"

"There's no 'used to' about it in the Navy, Bram. If you fill a spacecraft full of suspensive magnetic interfaces, you fill a spacecraft full of electromagnetic fields—fields that radiate into the surrounding space, where they can be detected by the enemy. Naval vessels still use bearings. Lots and lots of bearings. There are probably half a million bearings of fifteen or twenty different sizes on this ship alone, maybe more. Wernher could tell you exactly.

"Not only do we use lots of bearings, but they are precision-manufactured, super hard, temperature resistant, low friction, antimagnetic, static dissipating, and have all sorts of other exotic properties. All of our bearings come from a small number of factories on Earth, Bravo, and Neue Bayern. God only knows where the Krag make theirs, but there are a few worlds in the Free Corridor that manufacture bearings to naval specifications, and one of them is Rashid V C, a moon in the same system as Rashid IV. Started as a mining colony, easy access to the rare earths and special metals used in these things—you know the drill.

"So, this freighter is stuffed to the brim with the highest quality precision bearings made to naval specifications. Worth a small fortune. Our share of their value will be a nice bit of change, as will the value of the freighter. The loss of those bearings will cut into Krag warship production in a big way. We captured enough bearings to equip dozens of vessels. Maybe as many as a hundred. This is almost as big a blow to them as seizing all that gold."

"I never thought I would say something like this," Sahin said, "but I am deriving a great deal of satisfaction from my small role in setting back the enemy's war effort."

"It's a good feeling, no doubt about it. And your role is not small either. Like how you figured out those freighter rats were lying to you. There's not a man on board who would have sniffed out that lie the way you did. Major Kraft says it was a very nice piece of observation and deduction."

"Thank you. It helps that I have a rather broad knowledge of the beliefs of many different faiths. It put me right onto the deception. It was clear to me that these people were by no means Mormons."

"I don't know much about them, save what was in your report. But right now, I wish we had a ship full of them."

"Why is that?" the doctor asked.

"Not only would it leave more coffee for you and me, but we wouldn't have to deal with this stinking drug problem, at least to this degree. How are we doing on that?"

"Much better. Most of the men who had the worst addictions and the worst reactions are through the most severe of their symptoms. Everyone is now completely detoxified—that is, the drugs are out of their bodies. They will still need medication and observation for some weeks, but very few experienced the really acute symptoms. It helps that these men are in prime physical condition, all well nourished and hydrated, and that none of them are what we medically consider long-term users, that is, those who have been using these drugs for a period of years.

"There are some who have underlying psychological issues that predisposed them to drug addiction, who I am counseling. At the end of this cruise, I may recommend that two or three be put into some more intensive treatment for a period of weeks before they are returned to duty, but then again, I may not. It depends on how they are doing at the time. There is substantial therapeutic benefit to serving on this ship, which is becoming a very supportive environment."

"Outstanding. A happy ship is the best medicine for everyone. It is the cure to virtually every naval ill."

"I am beginning to believe it."

"It's a good thing, because I may need this crew to be at their best very soon. There was something aboard that freighter that was much more interesting than its cargo of bearings."

"There is something more interesting to you than another small fortune in prize money?"

"Very much so. It seems that our freighter rats' Krag masters had a schedule for them to keep—a very precise schedule. They were to deliver their cargo to their rat-faced customers, take on a standard type two freight container from the Krag cruiser they were meeting—no telling what's inside—and then go to the Pfelung system, coming through the jump within a three-minute window.

"Then, they were ordered to synchronize their arrivals at the main freight transfer facility near the Charlie jump point to all occur as close as possible to 08:23 tomorrow. I plan to be there. We've already altered course. I need to see what happens when they bring all those freighters together."

"Why? You certainly cannot intend to blow up all those freighters right there in Pfelung space. It would be a gross violation of their neutrality."

"I know that. But we are stealthy enough that we can sneak into the system unobserved, see what's going on, and then sneak right back out with no one the wiser. I just want to watch. Every instinct is telling me that this is important."

"How can anything involving that system be important? The Pfelung are just another alien neutral power in the Free Corridor, and a fairly minor one at that."

"They're more important than you think. Sure, their Navy isn't nearly the size of ours, or even the Romanovans', but it is nothing to disregard either. The Pfelung Association contains eleven systems: there's Pfelung itself, which is more populous than Earth and has a higher industrial capacity, and then they have ten other worlds, all very populous and productive. Imagine ten worlds all like Alphacen or Bravo, with a strong industrial base and most with shipyards capable of producing warships.

"And their navy is substantial—enough to make up three or four well-rounded battle groups. They've got four carriers, seven heavy battlecruisers, about two dozen cruisers, and more than fifty frigates and destroyers, plus some truly amazing battle stations to cover their jump points. If you know something of Earth history, think of Switzerland, a small independent neutral power more than strong enough to be safe from invasion.

"And there's one more thing to remember about their navy. They have, by far, the best fighter pilots in the Known Galaxy."

Sahin laughed. "Surely not. The idea is almost comical. I have never seen a species that looked less likely to be able to pilot nimble little fighter ships in my life. The adults must weigh a hundred and seventy kilos if they weigh a gram, lumbering about on those great limbs of theirs; they can scarcely move unless they're in the water, and even then they are slow and ponderous."

"And yet, they are undoubtedly the best. They make the Blue Angels look like drunk greenies flying Gemini space capsules. It's the smaller, nimble adolescents who fly the fighters, not the lumbering adults you're used to seeing. In the wild, they had the job of defending both the young and the little hatchlings from predators. A lot like bottle-nosed dolphins on Earth: a meter and a half long, about fifty kilos, accustomed to moving in a three-dimensional environment, fast, agile, incredibly brave on a fundamental and instinctual level. Natural fighter pilots. A squadron of them could mop the deck with the fighter wings from two fleet carriers and maybe a third, easy. I'd love to have them as allies."

"Sure, that would be a help. No doubt."

"But that doesn't touch the real issue with the Pfelung. It isn't evident from most maps, but they stand on the best invasion route from Krag space toward the Core Systems. It's all in the jump points. The way the jump points lie, if the Krag take Pfelung itself, then they can just jump around the current lines of defense and plunge right into the heart of our space. If they do that, they can cut off the main body of our fleet from its source of fuel and provisions, outflank and destroy it, and then they're free to turn to the Core Systems.

"To make things worse, the forces sent to do it would have a clear, straight line of communications and supply back to Krag space. Complete disaster. The war would effectively be over. It would still take years for the Krag to work their way through each system and move up their heavy forces jump by jump, but we would have no hope of stopping them."

"But surely, adequate provision has been made for this eventuality."

"The Pfelung themselves can read a star projection as well as anyone. They know they're on a natural invasion route, and they have no wish to be invaded. So, the jump point into their system that the Krag would use is covered by the most powerful battle station in Known Space. I can't pronounce the name in their language, but it means 'That Which Cannot Be Moved.' It's got twenty pulse cannons, powered by half a dozen huge fusion reactors with a twenty-five hundred gigawatt rating. Each. Nothing could get past it. Even if you could push a dozen *Battleax* class battleships through the jump without any warning, the Pfelung would have space wiped clean of the lot in under a minute.

"Plus, they have most of their not-inconsiderable fleet patrolling the outskirts of their system to deal with anything of the limited size and power that could come up on them from the outside, using compression drive.

"There's no way past them. Crossing interstellar space on compression drive, the Krag have too far to go. Any force with enough firepower to break through the Pfelung fleet and defensive installations would be so large and slow that it would be spotted two months out. The Pfelung would subject it to continual hit-and-run attrition attacks for the whole two months and wear them down to nothing. Any force fast enough to cross the distance before it's spotted and attacked wouldn't have the necessary firepower. If the Krag were to try to get around that problem by jumping into the system, when they fail to send the right IFF, 'That Which Cannot Be Moved' pounds them to dust before they can squeak. There's just no way in."

"Like Gibraltar."

"Hmm?" Max's attention, having wandered off to turn over the problem in his mind, snapped back.

"Gibraltar. I'm quite certain you must have heard of it. It was a British fortress guarding a strategically important maritime choke point at the entrance to the Mediterranean Sea on Earth, formerly known as the Pillars of Her—"

"Oh my God!" Max suddenly felt as though his stomach had been filled with cold lead. The deck seemed to move under his feet.

"What's wrong?"

"I've just had the most horrible thought. Sweet Jesus, I can't believe this. Have you ever heard of the 'Gibraltar of the East'?"

"No, I cannot say that I have."

"Singapore. It was a British base on an island at the tip of the Malay Peninsula: the 'Gibraltar of the East,' supposedly impregnable. Two shore batteries, brilliantly made 380-millimeter guns, expertly served, vast supply of ammunition, protected by reasonably good troops under a competent commander. It was an impossible nut to crack from the sea. Yet, the Japanese took it with ease early in Earth's Second World War."

"But if it was so impregnable, how did the Japanese take it?"

"They attacked from the land."

CHAPTER 23

06:09Z Hours, 9 February, 2315: The Battle of Pfelung

Max was frustrated. Frustrated enough to punch holes through bulkheads, chew through reactor shielding, and insult a fully grown Vaaach forest victor to his face. No, he was more frustrated than that. He could see the whole thing. He knew exactly what the Krag were doing, as well as when, where, and how they were going to do it. He knew that if they did it, it would be an unmitigated catastrophe for the human race and for just about everyone else in this part of the galaxy.

And there didn't seem to be a damn thing he could do about it.

Comms had tried all the Pfelung voice and data channels, but the main Pfelung OutSystem Communications Relay and Exchange had automatically rejected the incoming signal because it came from a Union warship and, under their strict neutrality laws, the Pfelung did not communicate with the warships of any of the belligerent powers in the current war. Comms tried spoofing the OSCoRE by changing the source origination code for the signal to make it appear that it did not come from a Union warship, but the Pfelung computer had already associated the ship's location in space with the original code and saw through the ruse.

Comms tried bypassing the OSCoRE by signaling some of the larger entities on the planet that had their own comm networks and channels, but all had rejected the signal as soon as the recipient figured out who the sender was. A very helpful female with the Pfelung Astronomical, Astrophysical, Astrometric, and Astrocartographic Administration had, however, suggested that the communication should be directed through standard diplomatic channels.

Standard diplomatic channels. Brilliant. Only, as part of their strict neutrality, the Pfelung would not allow the Union to maintain an embassy or a consulate or even so much as a GT&T branch office in their space. When the Pfelung said "strict neutrality," they weren't kidding.

Accordingly, "standard diplomatic channels" would consist of a long chain of transmissions across hundreds of light years of space involving the also-neutral Tri-Nin as intermediaries and requiring at least three and a half days. The Krag would be halfway to Bravo by then.

However, Max was not above bypassing official channels. He had low level, unofficial contacts with virtually every military establishment in Known Space. Except, of course, with the Pfelung. So, he had Comms and his back room root through every database and sigint intercept for every known Pfelung voice channel, comm frequency, data network, or any other means by which someone could get any sort of voice message, electronic mail message, text message, digital image protocol facsimile message, video call, tachyon semaphore, or carrier pigeon with a jet pack and a pressure suit through to the Pfelung Comprehensive Authority for the Harmonious Swimming Together of the Warriors, which is what they called their high command or joint chiefs, to let them know that their continued survival as a species was in jeopardy.

All to no avail. Naturally, Max had notified Admiral Hornmeyer, who had sent a Priority Flash dispatch off to the chief of naval operations, who in turn, as soon as he got the message fourteen hours later, would frantically throw as many forces as he could in the path of the anticipated Krag thrust.

But it didn't take a vice admiral in Strategic Plans to know that it would be far too little, and vastly too late. It would be like what the Germans did to the French in 1940. Disaster. The place to stop the Krag was at Pfelung, not Tarsind, or Virkandum, or—God forbid—Stein 2051.

Admiral Hornmeyer had dispatched a combat group at maximum speed. It would arrive in ten days.

Having no help to send, Max had to go himself. In his one puny destroyer. To stop the whole Krag navy. It was suicide, with the added drama of bringing 214 men and boys along for company.

They might die before even reaching their battlefield. The *Cumberland* was courting destruction from within by pushing its compression drive beyond the "red line" to propel the ship at the lunatic velocity of 2200 c, about 80 c beyond the vessel's rated maximum. Lieutenant Brown made his obligatory, ritual protest, but he took one look at Max's face and decided not to press the matter. The engineer was unable to make further impassioned pleas on behalf of his engines; he was too busy trying to keep them from blowing up and the ship from flying apart.

Even at this speed, the two light years between Zoleft and Pfelung was nearly an eight-hour trip. And unless Max could convince them not to fire in a great burning hurry, the ship could not jump into the system because the Pfelung defensive installations covering the jump point would vaporize his destroyer in a few seconds.

"Captain," Garcia said, "as the ship's legal compliance officer, it is my duty to inform you that we will be crossing into Pfelung territorial space in approximately two minutes and that doing so will be in express contravention of our orders. I will be required to note that fact in my log."

"Understood, XO. And will your log also show a protest of my action?" Garcia had the right to log an official protest of any action he thought to be illegal or outside of the commander's authority.

"No, sir. It will show that the action was taken with my full concurrence and support." Then, so that only Max could hear: "If we live through this, I'll stand right beside you at the court martial."

"I appreciate your loyalty."

"Any time, sir. Far better to hang together—"

"Than to hang separately."

Indeed, living long enough just to get past the Pfelung defenses, much less dealing with the coming Krag attack, was by no means certain. Already, as the *Cumberland* streaked into the outskirts of their system and penetrated their defensive sensor net, the Pfelung were warning him off, telling him in great detail that he was violating their sovereign territorial space and that if he did not turn about and leave, he would be intercepted and destroyed.

"Mr. Kasparov, some information on what is going on in that system would be very helpful about now," Max prompted.

"Sorry, sir, we have every sensor on active scan, maximum intensity, focused on the area in question, but at this speed the sensor beams aren't moving much faster than we are. I am getting lateral sensor returns from the patrol ships in this part of the outer solar system now, and I should be receiving data on any vessels at intermediate ranges on intercept courses in about a minute. But as for what's going on near Pfelung, we won't have much in the way of readings until we are almost there ourselves."

"Receiving the transponder codes listed in the freighter's data base," Comms chimed in. As each ship continually broadcast its transponder ID, the signal was there to be picked up as soon as the *Cumberland* was in range.

"Eight of the ten expected freighters are already in place at the freight facility; one is in the traffic pattern to enter it; and one is about a tenth of an AU out, just getting inserted into the traffic pattern. The last ship is still at least two hours from being docked with the other ships, maybe as long as four or five, depending on the Pfelung traffic control system."

"Tactical, how are we doing?"

"At this speed, we've already blown past the Pfelung system perimeter defense," Bartoli said. "We're moving so fast that by the time they detected us, the interception geometry was hopeless for them. They're far behind us now. They have two cruisers about twenty-five AU from the primary that are moving to intercept—they won't be able to catch us. But we'll pass through the outer weapons range of one in just over a minute, and of the other one about two minutes after that. Again, given our present speed, and the firing angles, it would be almost impossible to get a hit on us. After that, it gets more interesting. We'll have to reduce speed, and they have other ships moving into position that will have a much more favorable interception geometry."

"Understood. Comms, any luck opening a direct channel to that pulse cannon battery?

"Negative, Skipper. Cold shoulder all the way. Oh, and sir, one of the Marine sentries is on the comm saying that the doctor wishes permission to enter CIC." *That's odd.*

"Permission granted." Max decided that if he lived through this battle, he would give the doctor CIC access status. One of the

Marines opened the hatch to admit the doctor. Just as the hatch was about to close, Clouseau darted in, zoomed past the doctor's feet, and scampered onto the command island, where he stood, apparently waiting for something.

"Come on in, Doctor. If you would like to have a seat, use the Commodore's Station."

"Thank you. When I was play acting the part of the cutter captain, I got to like knowing what was going on. None of the Casualty Station consoles tie into any of the tactical displays."

He took a seat at the Commodore's Station. Clouseau immediately leaped in his lap and sat up, watching that station's displays with great interest. The doctor spoke to the animal, "I gather you like to be where the action is, just as I do. How unfortunate that I do not like cats." Clouseau curled up on the doctor's lap, still keeping his eyes on the display, while the doctor absently stroked his fur. Clouseau began purring.

"Both of you are welcome in CIC, of course," Max said, before turning to Garcia.

"XO, I think it's time for you to get on your way."

"Aye sir. And Skipper, good luck to you."

"Thanks, XO, to us all." They shook hands, and the XO strode out of CIC. "Weapons, confirm missile tube load out."

"Sir, current missile tube load out is: Raven in tube one, missile is unarmed, warhead is unarmed; Raven in tube two, missile is unarmed, warhead is unarmed; Talon in Tube three, missile is unarmed, warhead is unarmed."

"Very well. Weapons Officer, this is a Nuclear Weapons Arming Order. Arm missile and warhead in tube one; arm missile and warhead in tube two. Do not—repeat, do *not*—set target at this time."

"Nuclear Weapons Arming Order confirmed and logged. Missile and warhead in tube one armed. Missile and warhead in tube two armed. Targets not set at this time."

"Sir," Bartoli said, "we are coming in missile range of the first Pfelung cruiser." He paused slightly. "He has fired a superluminal antiship missile." Pause. "Missile has gone to active homing mode." Yet another pause. "Missile is locked onto us and is homing. Based on the active homing pulse characteristics, am classifying this missile as code name 'Minnow.' Interception geometry is poor, and it is overtaking us very slowly. Point defense batteries locking on. Firing. Missile destroyed."

CIC was virtually silent for about half a minute. Bartoli picked up the narration again from the Tactical Station. "Coming into range of the second cruiser. Second cruiser firing. Missile is superluminal and has gone to active homing. Locked and tracking. Classifying as Minnow. Point defense batteries locking on. Firing. Miss. Missile still tracking. Point defense batteries reengaging. Miss. Point defense second layer engaging—rail gun going to continuous firing. Missile range now ten thousand meters. Nine thousand. Eight thousand. Seven thousand. Six thousand. Five thousand. Four thousand. Hit. Missile destroyed."

Bartoli shook his head. "I don't think we'll be so lucky next time, sir. There is a screen of eight cruisers and twelve destroyers in what looks like the Pfelung version of a Zhou Matrix, right in our path and about sixteen AU from our destination. With their superluminal missiles and with the other missile installations and pulse cannon battle stations they've got in this part of the system, there is no way around them, sir. Not if we want to get where we're going in enough time to do any good."

"Then, we'll have to go through them," Max said, his fists clenched with determination. "Alert all decks and prepare to accept incoming fire. We'll pass through the screen and then see what we can do about those freighters. Comms, keep broadcasting the same message. Maybe someone will get the idea that we're not trying to hurt them, and maybe that will convince them not to shoot." *And maybe Santa Claus will come by in his sleigh and act as a missile decoy.*

WHAM! A bone-jarring shock shook the ship.

"Stealthed mine," said Tactical. "Intel *said* that the Pfelung are in the process of developing them, but they're *supposed* to not be deployed yet." He sounded annoyed, as though Intel had let him down, personally.

WHAM! WHAM!

"It appears that their information is not entirely up to date," Max observed. "Damage?"

"Damage to several of the amidships sensor arrays, antennas, and fairings—complete list on your DC subdisplay in about two minutes, Skipper." DC had the answer right away. Minor damage. The way things were going, that wouldn't last long.

WHAM! One of the Environmental consoles went dark. In less than ten seconds, one man and a mid had the access panel open and were replacing the overloaded module.

"Captain," Bartoli said, "based on my assessment of the number and location of the Pfelung defending vessels and the known capability of their missiles, if each ship fires a full salvo, and if our countermeasures and point defense systems perform as predicted, we will be overwhelmed. Our likelihood of survival is very low."

"Very low? Be more specific. How low? Give me an approximate percent."

"An approximate percent chance of survival? Zero."

Zero. That's low.

"How long until they launch?" Heads turned. The question came from the doctor.

Max nodded to Bartoli, giving him leave to answer. "Just over a minute."

Sahin thought about something for about half a second. Making up his mind, he squinted at the unfamiliar commodore's console, managed to configure it to allow him to key in message text, and started typing furiously.

He said to Comms, "Two days ago, I saved four images to my personal database. My password is 'Harun1453.' You need to broadcast this message and those images to those ships, on every frequency and band and however else you can."

Max didn't have time to ask what the text was or what the images were. Max didn't have time to ask the doctor to explain. If the doctor's idea, whatever it may be, was going to be implemented in time to do any good, Max had to give the order in the next two or three seconds. He had to make the call: run the gauntlet of Pfelung warships or trust his life, his ship, and the lives of 214 men to a Hail Mary pass being thrown by a man Max had known for only twenty-two days.

Easy call. "Comms. Do it."

Ensign Chin's fingers flew over his console, capturing the text message, accessing and capturing the image files, bundling them in a message packet, and broadcasting them by every means the *Cumberland* had.

"Pfelung missile targeting scanners engaging and locking. They are preparing to fire." *Tactical was a veritable fountain of good news today.*

It was only after the message and images were sent that Max saw exactly what kind of pass the doctor had thrown. The message read: "DO NOT FIRE STOP THIS SHIP CARRIES PRICELESS PFELUNG VITREUM SCULPTURAL VASE KNOWN AS BIRTH OF THE WATERS STOP SEE ATTACHED IMAGES STOP DESTRUCTION OF THIS VESSEL WILL DESTROY IRREPLACEABLE PART OF PFELUNG ARTISTIC HERITAGE STOP PLEASE LISTEN TO US STOP WE ARE NOT YOUR ENEMIES STOP MESSAGE ENDS." Four images of the piece were attached.

"Sir, the cruisers just shut down their targeting scanners."
Well, maybe Tactical did have good news every now and then.

"Skipper, incoming from the Pfelung force commander," Comms said. "Text only."

"Let's see it."

"TRANSMIT NAME OF OBJECT OWNER STOP MESSAGE ENDS."

"Comms," said Max, "send 'Dr. Ibrahim Sahin.'"

"Sending." Ten-second pause. "Receiving."

"IDENTITY OF OWNER CONSISTENT WITH OUR RECORDS STOP PLEASE RETRANSMIT EARLIER MESSAGE STOP MESSAGE ENDS."

"Quick, Chin, send the earlier message again. Tack on the tactical projection of the expected Krag attack we prepared for the follow-up message. And tell the hangar deck to launch the cutter."

"Cutter away," Tactical announced. The cutter was launched with the XO and ten men aboard. It immediately set course for the last of the ten freighters. The idea was for the cutter crew to board and take the last freighter, then use the freighter's comm equipment and codes to attempt to induce the other freighters not to do what they planned to do.

"Maneuvering, reduce to fifteen c and steer for jump point Charlie." That was the jump point that led in the direction of Krag space. The one the Krag would come through. "Put us fifty thousand kills away from the jump point and from the cargo facility."

Maneuvering confirmed the order, and the ship began to slow.

"Incoming message."

"THIS IS ADMIRAL CENRUU-MAA 114 STOP HAVE RECEIVED YOUR WARNING AND PROVISIONALLY EVALUATE ITS CONTENT AS TRUTHFUL STOP HAVE FORWARDED MESSAGE TO BATTERY COMMANDERS AND

HIGHER AUTHORITY STOP HAVE ALSO RECALLED ON MY AUTHORITY PERIMETER DEFENSE FORCE TO MEET THIS THREAT STOP INNER SYSTEM DEFENSE FORCE UNDER MY COMMAND IS NOW CLOSING JUMP POINT ETA ONE POINT THREE STANDARD HOURS STOP YOU ARE DIRECTED TO NULL DRIVES AND AWAIT PILOT VESSEL THAT WILL ESCORT YOU TO HOLDING AREA STOP MESSAGE ENDS."

"Damnit," said Max. "We've got to neutralize those freighters. If they figure out that we're onto them, I'm sure there's a Krag paying close attention on one of those ships with a remote triggering device, or somewhere in the system, who—"

Max never got to finish his sentence, as what the closely attentive Krag would do manifested itself in the most obvious manner. All ten of the freighters mentioned in the captured Krag data exploded in the blue-white glare of matter–antimatter annihilation. Max had never seen an antimatter explosion, as antimatter weapons had never been used by any power in Known Space. Until now.

The explosion instantly vaporized all the affected ships as well as much of the cargo transshipment facility and about half of the thirty or so ships docked there, while turning the rest into sharp-edged shreds of metal debris, some the size of ground cars and weighing almost three tons, embedded in the shock wave. Travelling at an appreciable fraction of lightspeed, the shock wave and debris reached the pulse cannon battery covering jump point Charlie a quarter of a second later.

Unfortunately, as its designers had thought the battery would face attack only from the direction of the jump point, the side facing the depot was unarmored. The debris tore through the battery's rear hull in a dozen places like a shotgun blast through cardboard, destroying the advanced fusion reactors that provided plasma for the pulse cannons. Unleashed from magnetic confinement in the reactors' cores, superheated plasma flashed out in all directions, consuming virtually everything it touched.

When the fireball faded, all that was left of the "impregnable" battle station was the 5.3-meter-thick, heavily armored, and ultimately useless glacis plate that formed the battery's hull on the side that had once faced the jump point. Like the British fortifications at Singapore, when the enemy came, the battle station's defenses were facing in the wrong direction.

The door to the heart of the Union was now wide open. The Krag would walk through it any second.

"Maneuvering," Max almost shouted, adrenalin getting the better of him, "head straight for the jump point, bring us to one thousand kills. I want to see the whites of their eyes. Weapons, disable warhead safeties in missiles one and two. Prepare to target designated ships emerging from jump. Pulse cannons one, two, and three to Prefire. Same with the Stinger."

Weapons confirmed the order.

"Skipper, the cutter is hailing and requesting instructions."

"Signal that it appears he won't need to board that freighter and that I need him to close to within five thousand kills of the jump point, then go to station keeping and stand by." Max turned to his sensor officer.

"Okay, Kasparov, when the Krag come through, I'm going to need IDs fast, so we know who to target first. Quick and dirty—just give me types."

Then, to everyone. "When they come out of jump, remember that they'll be blind, deaf, paralyzed, and stupid for a few seconds. They aren't expecting anyone to be here ready to shoot. We've got to get our licks in fast. Kasparov?"

"Aye, sir, ID by types only, quick and dirty."

So, in about a minute a whole Krag task force was going to come through the jump point, with nothing but a *Khyber* class destroyer and a Type 16 cutter to stand in its way. Max thought of the three hundred defiant Spartans at Thermopylae. Persians who outnumbered them over a hundred to one demanded that the Spartans lay down their weapons. Leonidas, the Spartan king, responded, "Come and take them."

Today, there was no chance to hurl defiant words at the Krag. There was nothing to do now but stand and fight.

"Reading a polarization shift at the jump point," Kasparov announced. "Flux differential increasing. Estimating transposition in seven seconds from"—pause—"MARK." Everyone counted the seven seconds silently. "Transposition. Contacts! Six vessels."

Damn the Krag for that trick of being able to push more than one ship through a jump point at a time.

"One vessel just jumped back," Kasparov said.

"That would be the scout," Max said. "He went back to let the Krag know that the battery was destroyed. More will be coming in a few minutes, once the metaspacial boundary becomes stable enough for penetration in this direction again."

"All targets classified as hostile—classification is circumstantial only." Kasparov was, quite properly, jumping to the conclusion that the ships were Krag because they jumped in where and when Krag vessels were expected to jump in, rather than based on any evaluation of the targets' characteristics.

"Based on mass signatures only, five remaining targets are as follows: Hotel One is classified as corvette; Hotel Two is classified as destroyer; Hotel Three is classified as...light cruiser; Hotel Four is classified as heavy destroyer—maybe a very light cruiser; Hotel Five is classified as destroyer."

The Krag didn't send their heavies through with the scout ship, in case the battery was not destroyed.

"Weapons, target missile one on Hotel Three. Target missile two on Hotel Four. Open missile doors on tubes one and two."

"Targeting missile one on Hotel Three and two on Hotel Four, opening missile doors one and two."

"This is a Nuclear Weapons Firing Order. Fire one and two." The small ship shuddered as the launch tubes ejected the missiles at nearly two-thirds of the speed of light.

"One and two away."

At such close range, the flight time was short. The two Krag ships flashed and were gone, transformed into disassociated atomic nuclei and electrons by the ignition of two 1.5-megaton thermonuclear weapons, miniature suns flaring and dying as hundreds of intelligent beings suddenly were no more.

"Weapons, reload with Talons. Maneuvering, execute a flap-jack. Weapons, abbreviated firing procedure, rear tube only. Make missile in tube three ready to fire in all respects, target on Hotel Five and open tube door."

"Yield, sir?"

"Maximum."

Again, both men acknowledged the orders simultaneously, while Maneuvering gave the orders to execute the "flapjack," the maneuver in which the ship pitched end over end, rapidly swapping bow for stern. Now the stern tube was pointed at the jump point.

"Fire when ready."

"Firing."

The ship shuddered in a slightly different manner as the stern tube fired. Again, the flight time was short, and the 150-kiloton warhead dispatched the Krag destroyer, its point defense systems not yet recovered from the jump.

"Maneuvering, another flapjack, close the remaining targets at flank. Weapons, bring pulse cannon to ready."

"Sir," Kasparov talked over the other men acknowledging their orders, "it's hard to read through the hash from the three nukes, but it appears that Hotel One and Hotel Two have their drives working and are clearing the datum. They also appear to be arming weapons. Signal strength is fading. Sir, I've lost Hotels One and Two. They've engaged their stealth systems and with the radiation and debris from the nukes, I can't get a fix on them. And sir, before I lost them, I think I got a hint of a gamma signature."

That meant that they were carrying more antimatter weapons. Could this day get any worse? "Tactical, what's the status on our friends' defense fleet?"

"Skipper, the group that was trying to interdict us is closing the jump point at flank, but since they are limited to subluminal velocities in-system they are well over an hour away. By the time they get here, the Krag will have jumped in enough heavies to cut them to pieces. As for the perimeter fleet, they were in four groups in a rough arc facing Krag space about ninety AU out. They are burning back at high sublight, but the first ones won't be back here for nearly fifteen hours. That's enough time for the whole Krag navy to get jumped in. The Pfelung won't have a chance."

Yes, it could get worse. "Any other forces in system?"

"There are several system patrol vessels converging on this location, but none are close and none of them would last three minutes against that Krag destroyer." *Tactical was back to a bad-news-only diet.*

Max stood at his station, talking to CIC at large. "Okay, people, we need to find those two ships. They are probably carrying antimatter warheads. That will be genocide for the Pfelung and the end of their fleet as a fighting force. Kasparov, active sensor sweeps and optimize for stealthed Krag vessels. Maneuvering, lay in a search pattern; cover the area between here and our friends' homeworld, because if the Krag have AM bombs, that's where they're going. Comms, see if any of the Pfelung will talk to us now. Fill them in on what is going on and see if they can activate their system defense sensor grid. Try to get them to blanket the system with sensor sweeps. Remember, people, stealth is never 100 percent effective. Hit a target with a high enough signal level and put a sensitive enough detector close enough to it, and you *will* pick it up."

The doctor was shaking his head as the skipper's orders were acknowledged. "Genocide? How? How can two small ships with bombs, no matter how powerful, destroy a race, or even most of a race, and destroy their fleet as a fighting force? It is not as though they can actually destroy the planet, can they?"

"No, but they can basically destroy the species and wipe out their navy."

"I don't see how."

"Basic Pfelung biology, Doctor. You really should read your briefing materials. The capital ships in the Pfelung navy are crewed entirely with sexually mature, fully adult, already pair-mated, males—they are the only ones believed to be stable and mature enough. The adolescents are allowed only to fly the fighters. An adult pair-mated male *must* return to the river in which he first mated, and only that river, and couple with his mate, and only his mate, every thirty-one and three-quarter standard days—that's a Pfelung lunar month—or he dies.

"That's why every one of their ships has two crews that swap out every four weeks, like the old Blue-Gold system for United States strategic missile submarines. Anyway, all the mating takes place in the fifteen or so suitable rivers. All the Krag have to do is blow up the critical portions of those rivers... hell, they don't even have to do that. They just need to detonate the damn warheads in the upper atmosphere, and the gamma rays will kill everything within the line of sight. With the plants and fish in the river killed, the water chemistry will change, and the Pfelungs' bodies won't know they're in the right river. The proper chemical receptors won't be triggered. Even if they know intellectually that they are in the right location, the females won't ovulate, and the males won't be able to inseminate the eggs. Practically every adult male on the planet and most of the males in their fleet, since most of their navy crews come from the homeworld, will die. Billions. Worst genocide in history. Makes Hitler, Stalin, and Xang Cho look like half-assed amateurs."

"Sir," Tactical interrupted, "but what about the jump point? The next wave of Krag will be coming through in about ten minutes. They'll put through the maximum number this time—eight ships. If they adhere to their tactical doctrine, they'll be mostly heavies—battleships, battlecruisers, and cruisers."

What about the jump point, indeed? Damn. Max was getting to that. It had never been far from his mind. Ever since last night, Max had been afraid he would have to give the order he was about to have to give.

"Comm, give me a secure voice link to the cutter. My headset only."

"Aye, sir."

Max put on his headset. "Channel open."

"Cutter, Garcia here."

"XO, this is the captain. I'm going to have to give you a difficult order."

The voice channel communicated a pause—ever so brief—an even briefer sigh, then a sharp intake of breath as Garcia made a decision. "No, sir. You aren't. I know what has to be done. I'll see it through."

"I knew I could count on you. Thank you."

"Good luck to you, Captain. We will meet again."

"Yes, we will, my friend. In that place where warriors go to take their rest." He closed the channel.

On the cutter, Garcia heard the destroyer's carrier signal cut off. He looked over at the ordinary spacer second at Maneuvering, a truly brilliant auxiliary craft pilot, but barely seventeen years old. That would not do at all. He took off the headset, stood, and scanned the men in the bench seats that lined the sides of the vessel. His eyes settled on the craggy face of the oldest man present. "Mother Goose, front and center."

Chief Amborsky stood and went to where the XO was standing, near the cutter's one-man Maneuvering Station. "Yes, sir?"

"Chief, you think you remember how to pilot a cutter, or am I going to have to take away your Comet and use it as a Christmas tree ornament?" Officers had been threatening to use enlisted men's Comets as Christmas tree ornaments for well over a century.

"I expect that I can get her to go where you need her to go, sir."

The lieutenant lowered his voice. "Amborsky, I need you to execute a synchronous jump point infarction maneuver with the incoming Krag ships. Can you do that?"

He started to repeat the order reflexively. "Execute a synchronous jump point infarction—" and then it hit him. He paled ever so slightly. "Sir? You want...you want me to rendezvous with the *Texas*?"

"Yes, Chief." Garcia allowed himself a rueful smile at the chief's poetic rephrasing of his technically couched order. "If we don't, the whole fucking Krag navy is going to come through that jump point in about eight minutes, with nothing between it and the Core Systems but the *Cumberland* and a couple of worn-out Reserve Battle Groups. So, Mother Goose, we are called upon to 'rendezvous with the *Texas*.' Can you do that?"

The older man's face saddened for a moment, then hardened into determination. He nodded slowly. "Yes, sir. I reckon I can do that."

"I thought so. Take Maneuvering."

"Aye, aye, sir." Amborsky stepped purposefully to the Maneuvering Station.

"I'm your relief, son," he said, placing his hand on the shoulder of the man at the controls. Not expecting to be relieved, the spacer looked back at the XO, who nodded. He relinquished the controls to the chief, who settled into the seat and made a few small adjustments to the course, regaining the feel of controls he had not held in his hands for years, but that were still as familiar as old shoes.

The XO took the main sensor console, pulled up the data channel for the metaspacial flux at the jump point, and configured the system to read the flux polarization and flux differential, which would warn him of a ship on the other side of the jump point powering up its drive and preparing to jump.

"Maneuvering, bring us to within ten thousand meters of the jump point, and then go to station keeping. Program an acceleration profile to bring us through the point five seconds after my mark."

"Sir, if it's all the same to you, I'd prefer to do it manually. With my own hands."

"Are you sure you can time it right?"

"Been a Navy man for thirty-six years, Lieutenant. I've never missed my mark or my tick yet."

A sharp nod. "Manual it is."

"Thank you, sir."

A murmur went through the men seated in the personnel area. The tactical displays and the course plot were right there on the screens for everyone to see. Someone had figured out what was happening and told the others. The XO, hearing their voices, turned to meet the eyes of each of the nine men. Each met his gaze without flinching. They needed no words.

He returned his attention to his console. A minute. Then two. Then a few more. There. The scope showed clearly a rotation in the plane of the flux polarization, meaning that someone on the other side had engaged a jump drive that was tuning itself to the correct superstring harmonics. There. The polarization was locked in place. Now, the flux differential would start to change in amplitude, indicating that the ships on the other side were storing the energy that would tear through the fabric of space-time and deposit them at a spot ten thousand meters right in front of him. He waited for the amplitude to increase to just the right level.

"Coming through in seven seconds, six, FIVE."

On "Five," Mother Goose nudged the drive to just the right point, a hair past the third notch on the scale, and felt the acceleration kick in.

One spacer began to recite the Twenty-Third Psalm. In the moment's overwhelming emotional tumult, all the XO heard were the words "green pastures" and "still waters." He liked that. Suddenly, the internal cacophony quieted, leaving peace. And resolve.

Garcia looked at the chief. The chief looked at him. Lips compressed to a thin, gray line, knuckles white from his grip on the hand railing in front of him, Garcia turned back to his console, his eyes locked on the trajectory plot, making sure Mother Goose was steering the tiny ship true. At three seconds, he said, "To glory we steer."

At one, the chief answered, "Steady, boys, steady."

Right on his mark and on his tick, the chief piloted the cutter into the precise location in four-dimensional space-time at which an aperture opened from n-dimensional space and spat out eight Krag warships. As one of the Krag ships and the cutter suddenly occupied the same place at the same time, right down to the subatomic level, and as this fundamental violation of the laws of physics of both spatial domains took place precisely at the boundary between them, all the vessels occupying the boundary were instantaneously converted into pure energy, disrupting the boundary between the two kinds of space so radically that the jump point was rendered useless for at least sixty days.

The massive explosion showered the Pfelung system with a powerful flux of gamma rays, white light, tachyons, radio waves, ultraviolet, infrared, X-rays, and Cherenkov-Heaviside radiation. It flooded so much radiation, of so many types, at so many frequencies and polarizations and phases, that even the most heavily stealthed vessel could not help but catch and reflect some of it back in the direction of the sensitive detectors on board the USS *Cumberland*, which had its electronic eyes peeled for just such an event.

"Contact," said Kasparov. "Consistent with previous contacts Hotel One and Hotel Two, bearings two-eight-two mark one-zero-four and two-eight-two mark one-zero-three, both heading two-seven-eight mark one-one-zero, straight for Pfelung, range 12,529 kills, speed 18,757 meters per second. Repeat *meters* per second—that's maneuvering thrusters only; they're trying to creep away, sir."

"Get every active sensor beam we've got focused on them, Kasparov. Narrowest possible beam, maximum intensity. Light the bastards up."

Kasparov keyed in the commands with speed and proficiency that seemed almost double what they had been just three weeks ago. "Target illuminated, sir. Any kid with an Ensign Sensor from the Navy Play Set within ten parsecs is picking them up right now."

Not exactly standard CIC protocol, but given what this crew had been through, Max would let it pass for now. "Comms, hail the Pfelung. Ask them if they have any system defense batteries left, and if so, do they want the honor of vaporizing the rat-faced, shit-eating bastards who tried to commit genocide on them." He paused a moment to consider exactly what he had said and added, "But try to word it diplomatically."

"Sir, you might not need to send that message," said Bartoli. "One of their secondary missile platforms just went active and launched four large antiship missiles, two at each Krag vessel. Missiles have just gone superluminal." Almost inaudibly, he said, "Man, I wish we had some of those." Then, to the CIC at large, "Missiles are seeking." Short pause. "Missiles have acquired targets and are homing. Closing on targets. They've just gone to Terminal Intercept Mode." Two bright spots flared on several visual monitors around CIC. "Got 'em."

"Maneuvering, bring us to a stop and null the drives. Let's talk to the Pfelung and figure out what we're doing before we go anywhere."

Maneuvering executed the order. Max looked around at the men in CIC, all of whom seemed to have made a decision at that same instant to look up from their stations and meet the eyes of their shipmates. Without saying a word, they all knew they were sharing the same thoughts. They were alive. They had stopped the Krag. They had won the battle. The *Cumberland* Gap was closed.

Chin broke the spell. "Incoming message. It's Admiral Cenruu-Maa 114. Text only. Displaying now."

"WE OFFER THANKS AND APOLOGIES STOP WE SHARE YOUR SADNESS AT BRAVE PASSING OF THOSE WITH WHOM YOU SWAM STOP IMPERATIVE THAT WE TASTE

THE SAME MUD AS ACCREDITED REPRESENTATIVE OF YOUR GOVERNMENT AT EARLIEST POSSIBLE TIDE STOP PLEASE ADVISE IF THIS IS POSSIBLE STOP MESSAGE ENDS."

"It's a pity that we don't have an accredited diplomat on board," said the doctor. "We could conclude a Mutual Defense and Cooperation of Forces Treaty right now."

Max smiled. "Funny you should say that."

CHAPTER 24

13:42Z Hours (07:19 Local Time—High Tide), 10 February 2315

As several of the space-faring species of the Orion-Cygnus arm of the Milky Way Galaxy almost simultaneously developed interstellar travel and started to encounter one another in the early twenty-second century, customary rules and processes of diplomacy gradually and cautiously evolved. By an accident of history, some would say a *very unfortunate* accident, Earth's unique recent history of being divided into dozens of semi-hostile nation-states meant that humans were one of the few species with any extensive diplomatic experience and a readily available set of sophisticated rules for dealings between independent governments. Accordingly, the forms of diplomacy used among the three dozen or so cultures that interacted with one another in Known Space tended to follow, at least generally, those that evolved on Earth.

So, it was in accordance with those usages, that the captain of the USS *Cumberland*, as the commanding officer of a Rated Warship on Detached Service with an accredited diplomat on board, exchanged several messages with the Pfelung Commissariat for Communications with Creatures Who Live Beyond the Waters to negotiate the precise time at which the new acting Union ambassador would present his credentials. The result of those communications was that Max, in full dress whites, and the doctor, also in full dress whites augmented by the bright turquoise sash worn by a Union naval officer serving as an ambassador to a foreign power, were standing on a ceremonial polished stone platform at the edge of a shallow tidal pool, its gentle waves lapping quietly at the edge.

In the pool was no less a dignitary than the Pfelung Commissar for Communications with Creatures Who Live Beyond the Waters, a finely formed adult male of 185 kilograms, looking a bit like a giant catfish with crocodile legs and wise, patient eyes the size of grapefruits, accompanied by his adjutant, a somewhat smaller male of similar shape, and three females about half their size. The females were present in the capacity of witnesses from the Ruling Hatchery, which was the Pfelung's female-only legislative branch. Although evolution had left the Pfelung only semi-aquatic, and they performed a lot of business on dry land and from time to time even in buildings, they preferred to conduct high ceremony from shallow muddy pools. This one was their favorite for major diplomacy, as the mud was particularly full of delicious segmented worms.

The large male made a long string of noises that sounded like, and had in fact evolved from, the sounds one would make blowing air into soupy mud. The sounds reminded Max of a child playing with his oatmeal by using a drinking straw to make bubbles. The translator modules in the men's unobtrusive ear pieces translated the blops and bloops into Standard.

"On behalf of the Pfelung people, we welcome you, the representatives of the Terran Union, to our world, to our waters, and to taste our mud with us. Let both our peoples remember this day.

So that our people could survive, some of those with whom you swam gave their lives. Their blood has entered the stream to be carried to the Great Sea. We grieve with you for their loss.

"Our common enemy has spilled the blood of our people as well. Their blood has entered the stream, been carried to the Great Sea, and now mingles with that of your people. That blood now ties us together. Its scent in the water enrages us. We can no longer remain neutral. Your struggle is now our struggle. Your enemy is now our enemy. The Krag shall now be food for the lesser fish. They shall be a portion for the worms. That is all I have to say on this subject. The prospective ambassador may now present his credentials."

At this point, on most worlds the prospective ambassador would hand a document known as a "Letter of Credence" to the relevant official. But as one does not hand a piece of paper to a Pfelung almost eyeball deep in a muddy pool (the document is delivered to an aide, who appears near the end of the ceremony to put it in a file), the doctor read the document out loud in his somewhat stilted but cultured voice.

"To the Commissar for Communication with Creatures Who Live Beyond the Waters, The Political and Economic Association of the Pfelung Worlds, greetings. Pursuant to the Fourth Revised and Supplemental Articles of War of 9 September 2312, under the authority vested in me as vice admiral and senior officer in this theater, I do hereby name, constitute, and appoint Ibrahim Sahin, BA, BS, MA, MD, as Acting Ambassador and Minister Plenipotentiary from the Union of Earth and Terran Settled Worlds, to the Pfelung Association with all the rights, privileges, and duties appertaining thereto under Union law and the usages of interstellar diplomacy, to serve until such time as a regularly appointed ambassador shall arrive at the Pfelung seat of government and have his or her credentials accepted by proper authority. Thus given under my hand and seal this twentieth day of January in the year 2315, Louis G. Hornmeyer, Vice Admiral, Commanding, Task Force Tango Delta."

The commissar listened to the translation coming over a seashell-looking device that he held in one gill, apparently against a hearing organ located there, then made more bubbling noises. The translator rendered his words quickly in its neutral, machine voice.

"I hereby accept your credentials and recognize you, Dr. Ibrahim Sahin, as Ambassador and Minister Plenipotentiary of the government of the Union of Earth and Terran Settled Worlds. On behalf of the people of the Pfelung Association, please accept my hope that you enjoy both the purity and the temperature of the streams in which you swim, that you find our ponds to your liking, and that your gills remain free of parasites." At that, he promptly submerged and swam away, the universal Pfelung sign that the audience was at an end.

At that moment, another Pfelung male waddled his way up to the two men and said through their translators, "Ambassador, I am Herm-Mekk 943, Assistant Subcommissar. May I please take your Letter of Credence?"

The doctor gave him the document, which he grasped between two of his dozen or so finger-like prehensile mouth parts, and he slipped it into a satchel worn around his midriff.

"Now, if you gentlemen will follow me to the Commissariat building, I will show you to your meeting with Subcommissar Huugah-Han 134 and Admiral Cenruu-Maa 114 for discussions regarding the proposed Mutual Defense and Cooperation of Forces Treaty."

Max and the doctor followed the young Pfelung along a worn but somewhat muddy path—apparently the kind the Pfelung like—toward a building a few hundred meters away.

"If I may ask," said the doctor, "what are the intentions of the subcommissar and the admiral?"

"It is a proper question," responded Herm-Mekk, "although some species prefer a great deal of circumlocution and prevarication before discussing and deciding the meaningful issues. We Pfelung find that, as compared to other species, we are direct. Firm, even stubborn, but direct."

Max laughed out loud. "Direct diplomats. You must be unique in all the galaxy. You will get on famously with us. My friend and I are not diplomats at heart: he is a healer and I am a military man."

"That is good. We do not enjoy indirect and imprecise communications. They flow too closely to the current of deception and outright falsehood. On the issues covered by this treaty, we are strongly disposed to be in accord with you. We are with your people because your strategic interests and ours are two currents flowing in the same river bed. And with you, Captain, for your heroism on our behalf and with you, Ambassador, for your obvious understanding of the importance that things of beauty have to the Pfelung soul.

"A team of staff diplomats, led by myself, labored through the night, without mud between their toes or worms in their mouth parts for so much as a moment, to prepare a draft treaty, with the object of making it so equitable and reasonable that you would accept it with little negotiation, allowing it to be concluded within the next few tides. The plan is to present that draft to you at this meeting. We hope we are not being presumptuous."

"Not at all," said the doctor, nearly overcome with relief that he would not be called upon to do any diplomatic heavy lifting. "We wish to conclude discussions as soon as possible so that our respective military establishments can begin to work out joint arrangements for the defense of this area. In particular, we need to work out with you how to protect the critical jump points in your system until you get those new battle stations constructed."

"Those new battle stations that will, we strongly hope, be protected from attack from all sides," Max added.

"Yes. That is certain. The Commissariat for the Design of Installations for the Repulsion of Those Who Would Disturb Our Hatcheries is already well along in that regard."

The draft treaty proved to be exceptionally reasonable. The doctor needed to propose only a few changes, one relating to exactly when the treaty became effective and one—suggested by Max—a minor amendment regarding the command structure to be employed in Union–Pfelung joint operations. The text of the treaty, with the proposed amendments, was transmitted to the admiral's legal staff for review and approval (the matter being deemed too urgent to wait for the transmission delays involving a message to Earth), resulting in the approval of the lawyers and the blessings of the admiral.

The Pfelung speedily accepted both proposed amendments and, indeed, apologized for not including the requested language in the first draft, stating that they should have thought of those matters themselves.

In fact, the only wrinkle in the whole affair was a sudden insistence by the Ruling Hatchery (four members of which bustled into the meeting room unannounced and apparently in something of a lather) that no further business could be transacted until the Union delegation provided to the Pfelung holographic images, of a certain size and resolution, of Lieutenant Garcia, Chief Amborsky, and the nine other men who died on the cutter, as well as the nonconfidential portions of their service records. Max immediately contacted the ship on his percom, and the requisite data was transmitted on the prescribed channel within five minutes.

Once the proceedings were concluded, the negotiators, following the Pfelung custom, sat together in a muddy, shallow pool (the new acting ambassador and Max in bathing suits) and spoke at some length about various rivers, lakes, and bays each had visited, including the clarity of the water, the salinity, whether the bottom was muddy or sandy or rocky, and the amplitude of the tides. Max had very little to contribute in this regard, having spent most of his life in space, but he was able to relate a few drunken shore leave frolics in and around bodies of water.

That ritual completed, the doctor signed and the commissar himself stained the treaty the very afternoon of the day on which discussions began. The commissar's "staining" of the treaty was accomplished in the standard Pfelung manner by producing a small quantity of the dye the Pfelung squirted into the water to help them evade predators, coating his left ventral fin with the ink, and then leaving a print of the inked fin on the document.

The diplomatic proceedings concluded, Max and Sahin returned to the ship.

"I'm certainly very pleased that we obtained this treaty and very gratified at the most complimentary signal sent by the admiral, but I think that people are making a planet out of a meteoroid," the doctor said over dinner with Max in the captain's day cabin. Tonight's dinner was private; the ship's official celebratory dinner would be the following night, to give the cooks time to lay on something special. Another larger dinner would be held once the admiral and an element of the Task Force arrived in several days.

"I know all about the Pfelung's nice little navy and their staggeringly brilliant fighter pilots and their strategic location, but the admiral's uncustomarily effusive praise and all of the hoopla makes it seem as though this treaty may actually be the key to winning the war."

Max had to swallow another bite of a truly splendid black-berry cobbler before he could answer. "Old Hit 'em Hard did pen some very kind words—about you and the treaty at any rate," said Max. "Of course, he also pointed out that by entering the Pfelung system without their consent, I directly violated my orders to 'respect all recognized territorial space claims,' and that the judge advocate was going to have to conduct a formal inquiry to determine whether I am to go before a court martial."

"I am quite certain that the inquiry will find you utterly blameless," said Sahin with a knowing smile. "Given that you won what is likely to become a famous victory and that you did so on the heels of destroying an enemy heavy battlecruiser and two smaller warships, and taking or destroying three freighters and their valuable cargo, they can hardly do anything else."

"You don't know Admiral Hornmeyer. He once court martialed a captain—a full captain by rank, mind you—for crossing the boundary of his designated patrol area to pursue a possible enemy contact. The court busted him down two grades. Last I heard, he was overseeing a fuel depot in the Groombridge 34 system. No, my friend, I would not put it past the admiral to haul me before a court martial and then see that I get busted down to ensign and get sent to the basement of the E Ring of the run-down Old Pentagon on Earth to work in the Department for the Production of Zippers, Buttons, Snaps, Hooks, and Other Clothing Fasteners."

"You are practicing on my credulous simplicity. Tell me truly: there is no such department, is there?"

"Well, I must admit that I've never heard of such a department and that I made that name up. But I know enough about the military bureaucracy that there is a department very much like it somewhere. I guarantee it, even if the name may be somewhat different."

"I thought so. Anyway, as we were saying, I think your worries are exaggerated. By my reading of the situation, you are a naval hero, and I cannot imagine bringing a hero up on charges."

"Time will tell. My mind will not be at ease, though, until the inquiry is complete and I have a formal exoneration in writing. Going back to the admiral's remarks, though, I must disagree with you. I don't think that he overstated the case even to the slightest degree. In fact, I am increasingly convinced that you do not appreciate the strategic value of what just happened here."

"You now how obtuse I can be about strategy. Perhaps you could enlighten me."

"First, you understand that we have had very few allies in this war. Most of the independent human powers have stayed out, even though the Krag have promised to exterminate them too, eventually. And until now, none of the nonhumans have allied with us. You know, being pushy, upstart monkeys and all that, we're not terribly popular out here in the wider galaxy. So, the Pfelung have opened the door to more nonhumans, especially since the galactic community holds the Pfelung in generally high esteem, in contrast to us."

"So, the Pfelung may help sway galactic opinion."

"Precisely, Doctor. We need allies, and the Pfelung are a good start. And then there is the immediate tactical benefit. Our finned friends declare war against the Krag, which the Ruling Hatchery did about an hour ago, and—as an Associated Power under the treaty—they take over the defense of five whole border sectors, freeing up more than five dozen destroyers; eleven or twelve cruisers; six or so battleships; and at least two, if not three, carriers to stiffen our defenses elsewhere or to use offensively. The ships are in motion as we speak.

And the Pfelung forces not needed for defense can supplement operational maneuver groups operating with a radius of a 150 light years, maybe 300, depending on how much of a safety margin they insist on for getting home in time to mate."

"I can see where that might make a difference. Absolutely."

"I know that you said you understood the strategic location of this system, but I suspect you were seeing it only defensively. Think of the offensive possibilities." Ways of taking the war to the Krag were always foremost in Max's mind.

"Just as this system represented a shortcut for them around our defenses and directly into the heart of our space, it's a shortcut for us in the other direction. The jump point from this system that our cutter blocked, when it repairs itself, reaches to a point on their coreward flank—a flank that intelligence tells us is very poorly provided with battle stations, cannon platforms, system missile batteries, or other fixed defenses because it faces the hitherto neutral Pfelung Association.

"Of course, seventy or so days is plenty of time to get ships in there, but it's a lot easier to punch through defensive formations of ships alone than to punch through a defensive formation of ships integrated with a network of heavy defensive installations. We take the forces freed up, combine them with the additional forces our allies can supply, and use this system as the invasion route, and that lets us go on the offensive in this theater. We can start pushing them back for a change."

"You seem excited at the prospect."

"Damn straight, I am. And here's the kicker. That offensive has a chance to finally succeed because we now have a forward source for fuel that we don't have to haul all the way from the Core Systems or produce with separation ships. Two-thirds of our logistics capability is devoted to fuel, you know. If we had a fuel source close to this front, it would cure the bottleneck in transporting munitions, food, medical supplies, spares—everything.

"Then, over time, the Pfelung industrial capacity can become an asset. Given several months to retool, they could make spare parts, missiles, ammunition, and so on. Finally, don't forget that they have some of the best shipyards in Known Space. There's no reason they couldn't repair or even build Union warships out here. As you recall, that's an option under the treaty to be negotiated at a later date. If we could increase ship production 10 or 20 percent, it could make a huge difference."

"Well, then, things are starting to make a bit more sense to me. But I must be missing something. I can see how all of these facts mean that this treaty is very, very important. But if I am any judge of official language—and I like to think that I am—the admiral attributes to this pact greater significance than can be explained by these things. I am becoming increasingly convinced that there is something important that I do not know."

"What you do not know, Doctor, is that we are losing the war."

The statement, delivered in a calm, matter-of-fact tone, struck Dr. Sahin like a punch to the solar plexus. The words hung in silence. For once, the doctor was aware of the sounds of the ship: the ever-present hum of the life-support systems, the minute vibration imparted by the fusion reactor's coolant pumps, the almost subliminal babble of the ship's main internal comm channel, which Max kept turned on in his cabin day and night, at this moment summoning the perpetually late-for-duty Ensign Friedrichs to his station in Auxiliary Fire Control. He perceived keenly the sounds of life in space, in the way that a pleasing background music that has always been present leaps into relief after the sounding of a funeral dirge's dark, jarring, opening chord.

Knowing that disbelief was evident on his face, the doctor struggled to find words to give it voice. After several seconds, he managed. "But Max, the news reports! I hear them daily. I see the headlines on the NewsWeb: broad offenses meeting victory, enemy attacks stopped and turned back with heavy loss, war production surging beyond expectation, new ship and weapons designs being introduced continually."

"Lies," Max said bitterly. "Well, maybe not *lies* exactly, but propaganda, clever 'information management,' the selective transmission of some facts combined with the selective withholding of others. If not blatant untruths, then they are at the least misleading. Even with the level of command access and the security clearance I have as the captain of a rated warship, I have to read between the lines, look at the raw data, locate the engagements on a star plot, and watch as they inch closer and closer to the Core Systems week after week."

"I still don't believe you."

"All right. I'll prove it to you with evidence that you have already gathered, facts you already know. Set aside the 'victories' that you've heard of from outside sources. Think only of the fleet engagements of which you have some more direct knowledge— what people said around Travis Station about battles that were fought in this theater. You know, where people who had seen the battle or fought in it or received unfiltered reports about it were talking. In the years that you have been posted to this area, how many of *those* battles were victories for the Union? You're a trained scientist—evaluate objectively the best data you have at your disposal. What's your conclusion?"

The doctor thought carefully for at least half a minute. "I recall there being general talk of thirteen fleet actions. Of those, my impression is that we won two."

While the doctor was thinking, Max was ticking off the battles in his mind. He nodded at the doctor's answer. "I'm impressed, Bram. We might make a real Navy man out of you yet. Yes. That is exactly right. Two of those eleven defeats could, arguably, be scored for the Union as strategic victories, as we turned back Krag attacks and remained in possession of the battle area, though losing more ships as measured by tonnage than we destroyed, but that's a fine point. So, as far as we can verify from our own experience, we are losing the war in this theater of operations."

The doctor was not ready to concede the point. "But speaking as a scientist, I must point out that our sample might not be representative. Things might be going less well here than in other areas. I know that I have heard the former commander, 'By the Book' Bushinko, spoken of in unflattering terms. Other commanders in other areas might be having more success."

"Bushinko was better than a lot of people think. Some of the other theatres have had worse than him by far, although I think the current crop is pretty good all around. No, from what I can tell from unfiltered reports, things here are going about as well here as they are everywhere else. Although we are putting up stubborn resistance and imposing huge losses on the enemy, and although we haven't had anything like the lightning series of defeats we suffered early in the war, we are slowly and inexorably falling back, losing system after system. The enemy had nearly a hundred years to build up a huge reserve of ships, to stockpile immense caches of ammunition, fuel, and supplies, and to plan his campaigns and diplomatic maneuvers step by step.

"We, on the other hand, were caught entirely with our pants down. Our forces were out of position, our economy wasn't on a war footing, and we had no training infrastructure or reserve of skilled manpower adequate for total war. We were caught by surprise and have been improvising from the very first hour. Sure, we've made great strides, but with the systems we've lost, with the casualties we've already suffered, with what the Gynophage did to our population and birthrate, and based on our estimates of the enemy's industrial capacity and his rate of population increase, they will eventually overwhelm us."

"What about the victory we just won? Will that not make a difference?

"Some. Not enough. I don't have access to the highest level information, but what I can access is close enough for some rough calculations—I've spent enough time doing rotations as an Intel officer to know how to turn the raw data into estimates. The Krag have a roughly 15 to 18 percent industrial advantage and somewhere between a 50 and 100 percent population growth advantage. Remember, they don't just look like rats, they breed like rats too. Our best intel from prisoners is that they give birth to litters of six after a fifty-two day gestation period. Having the Pfelung on our side will—in maybe a year or so—make up almost a quarter of the difference in industrial capacity. The only way we can win, absent some miracle, is to acquire some more allies."

"But if they have had such a decided advantage from the beginning, why have they not been able to win the war in more than thirty years?"

"Time and distance. When they attacked, the border between the Krag and the Union was seventeen hundred light years from the Core Systems. Now, it's just over a thousand. You can't just go zipping through space any which way you feel like. You need to take and hold star systems—star systems with jump points. And you can't just jump into a defended system with a jump point because—since a jump point is a fixed point in space—it can be defended with heavy pulse cannon batteries and massive missile emplacements, all zeroed in on the jump point and ready to fire on thirty seconds notice. You jump into a defended system, you're dead.

"So, if you want to take that system, you have to take months to send heavy ships, using compression drive across interstellar space at low c multiples to take the jump point. And very often, you are detected a good way out, and a task force is sent to intercept you in deep space. That's where those famous battles out in interstellar space come from.

"Say you win. Once you've taken the system, it takes more months to get the infrastructure jumped into that system and set up to get those ships fueled and repaired and reinforced and provisioned so they can cross to the next system, and more months to cross space to get to the next system, and so on. Step by step. Even when the enemy is kicking your ass, it takes a year, maybe two, for him to advance twenty parsecs.

"We've held him to far less than that. We do have *some* advantages: mainly, they didn't have as much success as they expected early in the war because the War of the Fenestrian Succession left us better prepared than they expected. That invalidated a considerable portion of their war plan, and the Krag are not good at improvising. We are; it's one of our strengths. So, we have been playing for time, trying to stave off defeat until we can convince enough other powers to declare war against the Krag to turn the tide. If nothing changes, my estimate is that we have another four to six years before the disparity of forces becomes so overwhelming that our defense will collapse."

"And then?"

"We won't have enough forces to defend all the necessary jump points, and the Krag will find a direct route to the Core Systems. Once that happens, they will be exterminating all life on Earth and Alphacen and Bravo and Nouvelle Acadiana and all the rest in a matter of days. I've heard rumors of a contingency plan involving sending a small core of survivors in fast ships to plant a new human civilization beyond the reach of the Krag somewhere in another part of the galaxy, but I don't hold out much hope of that working. I've been hunted by them, you know. The Krag are relentless. These people would be found and killed like all the rest. The human race would die."

"Not if I can help it."

"Excuse me?"

"I said: Not if I can help it. I won't let it happen."

Max was amused. "You? *You* won't let it happen? And just what do *you* think *you* are going to do about it?"

"I am a diplomat—I have a Masters degree in Interstellar Relations, you know. I have connections on dozens of independent human worlds and even on a few alien ones. I know people. I will make the necessary alliances. I am a very determined man. I have always accomplished what I set out to accomplish. I will accomplish this as well."

Unconvinced, Max nevertheless decided that it would be a futile enterprise to try to explain to Dr. Sahin the difficulties involved in a twenty-six-year-old *acting* ambassador concluding interstellar alliances with somewhere between six and fifteen discrete foreign powers. So, he turned the discussion to other matters.

"Yes, you are a diplomat. For at least the next several weeks, you will be the Union's acting ambassador to the Pfelung Association. There are several other agreements to negotiate—I have just forwarded to your pending file a memo from the admiral's legal staff outlining what they think is needed. Also, I see that the Pfelung have several ceremonies for you to attend, including a dedication of some new facility at one of their hatcheries to which they invited not just you but also me and as many of the ship's company as are available at the time. It is rather a strongly worded invitation, so I plan to turn out about 130 men. I wonder what is so important about a hatchery."

"I have no idea, but it is fortunate indeed that the admiral saw fit to provide you with that appointment for you to 'fish' out of your safe at the opportune moment. 'Fish.' What a wit I am!" Max rolled his eyes. "I am astonished at the admiral's foresight. It is beyond amazing to me that he foresaw that things would unfold as they did and require the appointment of an ambassador to the Pfelung. He is truly an amazing gentleman. I hope to make his better acquaintance someday."

"He certainly is a man of considerable ability," Max replied. "Don't expect that you will ever get chummy with him, though. You should be aware, my friend, that he may not be quite what you think he is."

He rose from his chair, walked over to the safe, entered the combination, removed two envelopes, and returned to his seat. He held in his hand the same two envelopes he had pulled from the safe back at Navbuoy JAH 1939 three weeks before.

He opened the cream-colored one and pulled out several sheets of paper covered with dense, flowing script. "This is a handwritten, confidential note from Admiral Hornmeyer. I don't think he'd mind if I shared with you this paragraph: 'I have personally assigned as your chief medical officer one Ibrahim Sahin. When you meet the gentleman, you may think I am doing you no favor, but I expect by the end of this commission you will be very thankful to have him on board. He is not officer-like to even the slightest degree, I'm afraid, and does not know a parsec from a parsnip. But he has unusual gifts in several other areas, including, I strongly suspect, an underdeveloped talent for diplomacy. Should you discover you have need of an accredited diplomat and cannot wait for one to be furnished from the Core Systems, I have made rather liberal use of my authority under the Articles of War to issue appointments of him as ambassador to each and every independent power in the Free Corridor and vicinity. I need to appoint someone, and God knows I'm not making *you* ambassador to anyone or anything. I am trusting you to pull out only the appointment(s) necessary to the occasion and to keep the others locked in your safe. Kindly destroy the remaining ones or return them to me at the conclusion of your mission.'

"So, in this envelope," Max said, indicating the larger envelope, the one that had contained his orders, "are to be found your appointment as Union Ambassador and Minister Plenipotentiary to the governments of . . ."—he pulled them out and sorted through the documents, reading the names one by one—"the Vaaach, the Ghiftee, Romanova, New Zarahemla, the Unified Kingdom of Rashid, Allied Emirates, and Protected Islamic Worlds, and four or five others. There are also two that are signed in blank that I have permission to fill in as needed. Rather clever, in my book, and quite the vote of confidence in you."

"I'm quite sure I have no idea what to say."

"From my point of view, the only thing to say is that the admiral was right about you, and then move on. I rather like that part about not knowing a parsec from a parsnip. Sometimes the old bastard comes up with a very clever turn of phrase. He seems to be right about the talent for diplomacy part. Speaking of which, I wish you would clear up one mystery for me. After meeting with the Pfelung, we have learned how important their art and their artistic heritage is to them, but however did you know that fact during the battle? It was not in the briefing materials, which—by the way—I know you did not even read. Shame, shame."

"It was obvious. No people who could fashion a work of art like the one in my quarters could be anything but fanatic about the creation and preservation of things of beauty. The dealer who gave it to me sent along a data file about the art form. It isn't made of glass, you know, but a material carefully refined from molten quartz and given a higher index of refraction by including traces of silver and lead and several exotic rare earths and metals. It's known in Standard as vitreum. The colors come not from mineral pigments or organic stains, but from microscopic particles of ground gemstones suspended in the vitreum in such number and so uniformly that it looks as though the material itself has been stained. That is why the colors are so vivid, catch the light the way they do, and never fade. The different colors come from streams of these gemstones that are swirled into the vitreum while it is still molten, layer by tiny layer.

"Some colors are the colors of one type of gemstone, and others are made by mixing as many as seven different shades of gemstone. *Birth of the Waters* consists of some seventeen thousand differently colored vitreum layers, each blown meticulously by hand, one inside the other, some only a few microns thick. It took more than a year to make. I found it impossible to imagine that any people who would go to those staggering lengths to create an object of that kind of beauty could bear to be a part of destroying it absent the most compelling necessity. And even then, they would strive greatly to find a way to preserve it. That's what I was betting on, at any rate. Have you seen it?"

"Not in person."

"Then you simply must. Immediately." They set down their coffee and went through the short series of corridors and access ladders that led to the doctor's cabin. They stood quietly in the day cabin, where the sculpture was displayed.

Max regarded the ethereal yet seductive assemblage of curves and swirling radiances and was speechless for nearly a minute, until he finally whispered, "*Regardez donc.*"

"*Je concours.*"

CHAPTER 25

02:27Z Hours, 21 February 2315

When the Task Force, or that portion of it sent to help cement the new agreement with the Pfelung, began to arrive, everyone on the *Cumberland* expected the first ships through the jump point to be scouts and escorts, followed only at great length by the more powerful vessels. It was to Max's surprise and consternation that the first vessel to appear was the *Halsey*, Admiral Hornmeyer's immense flagship.

Within minutes of coming through the jump point, the carrier had launched two fighter elements as combat area patrol and established a digital laser com-link with the *Cumberland* to enable rapid and secure exchange of data between the two ships. In only a few seconds, the *Cumberland* was able to update all of her tactical and other databases to conform with the most recent information available to the flagship, while transferring to the flag all of her logs and status reports. Personal electronic mail was also exchanged, allowing many of the *Cumberland*'s crew to receive messages from distant relatives as well as wives or sweethearts. And in some cases, wives and sweethearts.

Also received by the *Cumberland* was a one line message. CDR AND CMO REPORT TO FLAG. The "immediately" part was understood. Max and the doctor, having both been wakened from deep slumber, fortified with coffee, and attired in Working Uniforms with Arms (the everyday uniform jumpsuit plus side-arms, determined by Comms to be the Uniform of the Day on board the flagship) were in the *Cumberland*'s five-man launch, crossing the few thousand meters that separated the destroyer from the carrier. Max's stomach was in knots. This was going to be a skinning. You rousted a destroyer captain out of bed between two and three in the morning because you wanted to rip him a new one, not because you wanted to sip coffee with him and hand him a medal.

Guided by the carrier's traffic controllers, the launch maneuvered its way beneath the great ship's underbelly to settle into one of its many landing decks on the starboard side. A docking tube extended from a nearby hatch and sealed itself around the launch's hatch. Max, the doctor, and the able spacer first who had piloted the launch crossed through the tube, through an airlock, and into a small compartment set up as a salute deck for lesser captains. The age-old boatswain's whistle sounded as Max stepped onto the deck, and six Marines came to present arms. The boatswain then barked out "*Cumberland*, arriving." Max turned to his left, saluted the Union and Admiralty flags, and then pivoted back to his right to salute the officer standing in front of him. "Permission to come aboard, sir."

"Permission granted," said the lieutenant commander who greeted him, returning the salute. The doctor and the launch pilot followed, similarly saluting the flags and the officer.

Welcome aboard, Captain, Doctor. I'm Jackson, part of the admiral's staff. He's expecting both of you. Please follow me. Spacer, follow the chief here and he'll show you to the enlisted pilots lounge."

Max had been stationed on the *Halsey* for a few months but had never been into the sacred realm of the exalted admiral, so he followed the other officer almost blindly for what seemed like hours, certain that he was walking toward an unpleasant fate. The flagship seemed as big as a continent after the confined spaces aboard the *Cumberland*. The three men wound their way through several confusing twists and turns and finally arrived in the admiral's outer office, there to be greeted by the full commander who served as the admiral's flag secretary, a very responsible job in its own right. The officers exchanged salutes. "Captain, Doctor, the admiral is expecting you. Go right in."

Max took a deep breath, stepped up to a real wooden door, turned the knob, and went in. The admiral was glowering at the comm panel on his desk. Although Max could not hear what the poor fellow on the other end of the circuit was saying, there was no mistaking a certain pleading, penitent tone.

The admiral listened for about twenty seconds, then cut the other man off at the knees. "Goddamn it, Captain, that sounds like a personal problem to me. This is a forward area in wartime, son. Do you fucking understand what it means to be one thousand light years from the Core Systems? I don't think that you do. *Everyone* has personnel problems. You have fewer than most. Your ship has a full complement; many do not, and I have provided you with the best roster of officers available given other requirements.

"Now, Captain, if you can't get your shit together, reach down to whatever level this crew is at, and pull them up by their fucking bootstraps to an acceptable level of training and performance, there are lots of destroyer captains hungry to command a frigate like yours. I'll give the job to one of them and give you something to do more suited to your talents—maybe commanding a deuterium tanker on the Europa run."

The admiral listened for a few seconds to sounds of acquies-
cence. "Good. Now go train. Hard." A few more words over the
comm. "No, dumbass. Harder than that." Some pleading sounds
emerged. "No, absolutely not. I don't fucking have a week. I need
that ship on the line, killing the Krag. You have four days. Get it
done. Flag out."

He stabbed the comm button with brutal force, breaking the
connection, if not the whole comm panel, then looked up at Max
and the doctor, standing in front of his desk at painfully rigid
attention. As soon as his eyes met Max's, the admiral snapped,
"And just who the fuck are you two?"

So nice to see that the admiral is in such a good mood. They
both saluted. Max snapped out, "Lieutenant Commander
Maxime Robichaux and Lieutenant Doctor Ibrahim Sahin of the
Cumberland, reporting as ordered, sir."

The admiral returned the salute so briskly that his fingernails were in danger of being flung off, and glanced at his chrono.
"Sweet Jesus, Robichaux, you took your own goddamn time getting here, didn't you? When I summon a commander to report to
the flag, I expect him to appear with celerity." Then he moderated
slightly.

"But I suppose Jackson kept you held up with all those damn
ritual theatrics on the salute deck. Nothing gets past that man
quickly. I'm going to have to start calling him 'Stonewall.'" Max
couldn't help but smile at the joke. "And it *is* about a two–light
year walk from the salute deck to here.

"Have a seat, gentlemen." He turned his head slightly in the
approximate direction of a door in the bulkhead to the right of the
one through which Max and the doctor had entered. "Bushman!"
he bellowed loud enough to fracture hull metal.

The door flew open and a sixty-ish chief petty officer third
stuck his gray hair and severe, lined face into the compartment.

"Yes, Admiral?" The man managed somehow to sound both respectful and put out.

"Bushman, you old burned-out thruster nozzle, it's oh-three-fucking-hundred hours and I'm meeting with these officers. How the *hell* are we supposed to get jackshit done at this godforsaken hour without *coffee*? That's COFFEE, Bushman. I'm sure you've heard of it. How long have you been my steward, man?"

"Nineteen *wonderful* years, Admiral."

"And in that amount of time I'd have thought that a man of your worldly wisdom would have figured out some of the basics of the job. Now what do I have to do to get something in here that's hot and black and crammed to the fucking gunwales with caffeine?"

The man stepped all the way into the office. Max could see that, even given the limited degree to which decorations were worn on the Working Uniform, Bushman had more awards for valor than most cruiser captains. Maybe when Hornmeyer was a dashing young captain, this man was at his side in some hard-fought boarding actions. He sure hadn't earned all that fruit salad serving coffee. "If the admiral would just take a whiff, he would smell that I started a fresh pot as soon as Captain Robichaux was piped aboard." And then, after waiting just a split second too long, he added, "Sir."

"Very well, then, Bushman. When you bring it in, try not to slosh it all over these officers, will you?"

"I'll do my best, sir." He smiled briefly at Max and backed out of the room.

"Goddamn surly old Bushman. One of these days I'm going to have to bust him back to mid to show him who's the fucking boss around here. Now. Robichaux. Right. I've read your reports. God knows you've been a busy little fucker. First thing, your prisoner roster. Been locking them up left and right haven't you? First man—who's that wormy little shit with the portable drug factory? Green. Right. It seems that Spacer Green has signed a formal waiver of all right to appeal your conviction by order of him for trafficking. So, I get to sentence him on my own authority. I'm sending him to a medium-security penal facility for five years. Then, he'll serve out the rest of his enlistment. Maybe he'll go straight and maybe he won't. His choice, either way. Maybe Daddy's kicking him out the airlock will be the best thing that ever happened to the slimy little bastard. He has a chance to turn his life into something if he wants, and maybe someday he'll amount to more than a puddle of poodle piss. Or not. His choice.

"Okay, getting to your other prisoners, there's those three snake-shit sneaky chiefs of yours who tried to sabotage your atmosphere manifold. If that isn't a stab in the back, I don't fucking know what is. Those dirty sons of bitches are going to get a straight-up, full-dress, formal fucking court martial. The judge advocate has passed on outright treason—I always knew he was a goddamn pussy—and is prosecuting for attempted sabotage. I'm betting on a conviction and that they'll be sentenced to something like seven to ten years on a penal asteroid. Then desk jobs for the rest of their terms of service—you and I know, no skipper will ever let those cocksuckers serve on his ship. It would likely be twenty-five on that asteroid instead of seven to ten, but I'm sure that the court will put some of the blame on that one-man squirrel convention of a CO these men used to have."

He shook his head grimly. "Oscar. One of these days, I'd like to get my hands on that loopy son of a bitch and make him answer for what he's done to some fine officers and men in this command. He's the worst thing since Philip Francis Queeg. Ever heard of Philip Francis Queeg?"

Max and Ibrahim shook their heads.

"Fucking shame. No one reads the goddamn classics any more. Every CO in the whole fucking Navy should take a few hours off from writing all those goddamn reports that don't amount to jackshit and read *The Caine Mutiny*. If a few more people had known who Philip Francis Queeg was, it would have been plain as black sky that Captain Oscar and Captain Queeg bought their bloody ball bearings from the same gag-and-gift shop, and someone would have sent Oscar off to the nut plantation where he belonged.

"Next subject. I've also read a stack of communications from the Pfelung stating that they think you're the best thing since indoor egg incubation. They want to be sure that you're one of the officers that they get to work with because they say they like the way you swim or that you navigate the currents skillfully or some such fishy bullshit like that. You know how they talk. I told them not to worry—they'll be seeing plenty of you, Robichaux. Maybe after they get to know you, they may lose some of their enthusiasm. They'll start saying you swim into rocks or shit where the eggs are laid or something like that.

"You've always been something of a loose cannon, young man, but there's no denying that you got results this time out, and that's what counts in warfare—results. Victory in combat against the enemy will obtain for you the remission of many sins, a great many sins indeed. The Admiralty loves a winner. Not real keen on losers, though.

"And Robichaux, condolences for the loss of your XO and those men in the cutter. Damn good man, that Garcia. Damn shame to lose him. I had him pegged to have a command of his own in a year or two. I'm pulling to get the Navy Cross for him, Amborsky, and the rest.

"But you, young man, *you* are the only destroyer skipper in this *whole fucking war* to take down a Krag battlecruiser without assistance from another warship. There's gonna be some publicity from this, but I'm tempted to keep classified how you did it, just so it doesn't tempt every half-assed destroyer skipper into bolting a brace of Raven missiles onto the side of his cutter. Very dangerous stunt. Unless the pilot is a fucking genius, it's a good way to destroy the cutter and kill the pilot. With all that mass near the bow, it must have taken a brilliant goddamn pilot to manage the thing."

"My man Mori is, I think, the best small craft pilot in the Navy," Max said.

"Maybe he is. At any rate, way to kick ass. I wish I could have been there. Goddamn! I miss the real thing. Instead, I'm sitting on my fat ass two or three parsecs away from the battle, moving little electronic icons around in a fucking tactical projection. That's not leadership, it's a goddamn trideo game.

"All right, next. On this Pfelung thing, half of my Intel people tell me that there is no way they would have seen through that stunt the Krag were pulling with those freighters the way you did. Congratulations. Of course, there's the half that don't say that and are telling me 'Oh, hell, yes, it was right there all the time, and if we had known what Robichaux knew, we would have seen it in a heartbeat.' What a steaming crock of grade-A bullshit. It took a real genuine Black Sky Out the Viewport combat officer to see that plan, not some electron-pushing Intel weenies—goddamn sneaky little bastards.

"And speaking of sneaky, how'd you manage to get all those transfer requests pulled? That was a neat trick."

"What are you talking about, Admiral?"

"As of 21 January 2315, there were seventy-three pending requests for transfer from personnel assigned to the *Cumberland*. As of today, there are none. Somehow, they were all withdrawn."

"But, sir," Max asked, "can't the men withdraw them on their own?"

"Of course they can, dumbass. It's the right of every man to request a transfer and his right to withdraw that request. That's a sacred spacer right that goes back to the Saltwater Navy. But no one has ever had seventy-three transfer requests withdrawn at almost the same time. It's too much of a coincidence. Just doesn't goddamn happen."

"The reasons for wanting a transfer went away, so maybe the requests did too, sir."

"You might be right. It's just a helluva lot to swallow. If it's genuine, you might just be one of those great leaders of men, like Patton and Halsey and Litvinoff and Wong and Middleton. Like *that's* fucking likely. Humph. Speaking of leadership, I know Admiral Middleton has a soft spot for you, so I sent him a signal about how your first cruise as a skipper came out. He sent this—he's a long way off, so it came by tachyon Morse and it's pretty terse. But I thought you'd want to have it." He handed over a slip of paper, evidently torn right out of the decrypt printer.

It said: "HORNEY PLEASE TELL CAPTAIN ROBICHAUX THAT HE DID AN OUTSTANDING JOB STOP I COULD NOT BE MORE PROUD OF HIM THAN IF HE WERE MY OWN SON STOP MESSAGE ENDS."

Despite the lump in his throat, Max could not help asking, "'Horney,' sir?"

"Um, old nickname. Very old. Goes back to my mid days on the *John Houbolt*. People didn't start calling me 'Hit 'em Hard' until I got my first command. Enough about that. Put that slip of paper in your scrapbook or wherever you keep things like that. You'll be wanting that twenty years from now, unless you get your reckless ass killed first, that is." Max folded it carefully and put it in one of the chest pockets of his uniform.

"You know what probably prompted that signal? It wasn't bagging that battlecruiser or even what happened at the Battle of Pfelung. I told him about your CAPE scores."

Sahin broke in. "Cape? What's a cape?"

"Acronym, Doctor. Computerized Automatic Performance Evaluation. Your ship's computer, arrogant little fucker that it is, constantly measures every kind of job performance on the ship that can possibly be measured by computer: how long it takes your sensor people to identify a contact, how long between a system reporting trouble to when it is fixed, and hundreds of other things, and turns them into a scaled index, updated daily, with 100 representing the most perfect crew imaginable. I told Admiral Middleton that the *Cumberland*'s CAPE went up from 21.7, the lowest in the Task Force, to 71.4, which is considered to be in the average range. *Low* average, I might add, but still average. So, Robichaux, Middleton sends me back a personal signal saying how that score improvement shows you to be some kind of diamond in the rough.

Well, I'll tell you something, son, Fleet Admiral Charles L. Middleton can say that all he likes—you're not under *his* command, in the Big Chair on one of *his* ships, while *he* has to sit in a fucking swivel chair behind a fucking desk and yell into a goddamn comm panel, trusting his carefully laid strategic plans to the judgment of a twenty-eight-year-old Coonass who doesn't know when to keep his goddamn pants zipped and his goddamn mouth shut. Saying things like that from where he sits is like betting with someone else's money. I ought to transfer you to his Task Force and see how he likes the crazy shit you pull in *his* nice, orderly command.

"Your men, though, that's something different. Different thing entirely. First they put up with that bandicoot Oscar; then they go through that wild ride with you, and they still perform the way they did at the Battle of Pfelung. The ship stood and fought—not just fought but fought well—against an enemy that was superior both in numbers and in firepower. Good men. Damn good men. Been through hell. Gave 'em hell. So, in tomorrow's Orders of the Day, I'm issuing to the *Cumberland* a Bronze Battle Star.

"Light *that* big, bright fucker up the next time some shit-for-brains jerkoff fighter pilot calls your ship the *Cumberland* Gap. Getting in your comebacks by blinker is too goddamn slow."

How had the admiral heard about that? "I am also authorizing your vessel to display an 'E' for Excellence for the next thirty days. Keep this up and I wouldn't be surprised to see your CAPE at about eighty-one or eighty-two in ninety days, which would put you in the top third."

"I would," said the doctor.

"*You'd be surprised?* You don't think they will improve that much?" asked the admiral, scowling. Dr. Sahin's remark smacked of disloyalty to his crew, something of which Louis G. Hornmeyer took a very dim view.

"Actually, sir, I expect them to do substantially better. I would bet that in ninety days their score will be at least ninety."

"Doctor, I'm not sure you understand how this works. These scores are indexed against the past performance of other crews—the amount of improvement required to get from the twenties to the seventies is actually less than what it would take get the *Cumberland* from where it is now to a ninety. There is a very strong law of diminishing returns." Amazing how the admiral's legendary profanity abated when he talked to the doctor.

"I understand it perfectly. I have spent some time familiarizing myself with the subject."

"All right then. You said 'bet,' Doctor. Do you mean that literally?"

"Yes, I suppose that I do."

"It's well known that I like to put down a wager or two from time to time. I know you're flush with prize money right now, so do you want to put some of that money at risk?"

"It will not be at the slightest risk, with all due respect, Admiral. What do you propose as the size of the wager? How much can you afford to lose?"

"I think a thousand is reasonable. Agreed?"

"Agreed."

"BUSHMAN!" Max expected the ceiling tiles to fall. Bushman stuck his head in. "Bushman, get the book. The doctor here wishes to make a wager."

The man bobbed his head and ducked back out. He reappeared less than five seconds later, carrying an old, tatty, antique-style ledger book, and sat at a side table, picking up a pen to write.

"Bushman, the doctor and I have a bet that the CAPE scores for the *Cumberland* as of ninety days from this date will be ninety or higher. He is pro; I am con. The amount of the wager is one thousand credits to be paid in hard cash. Is that acceptable, Doctor?"

"Perfectly."

"Bushman, you can go." The man wrote for a few seconds, then got up and left.

"As for you, Robichaux, you are one lucky son of a bitch. Ordinarily, the judge advocate would be up my ass to beat you down hard for barging into Pfelung space, violating your orders to respect all neutral territorial rights. Sanctimonious goddamn paper pushers. Fucking lawyers care more about where to put a fucking semicolon than about where to put a carrier—but they have a lot of pull, and it's awfully damn hard to tell them to go get fucked. Thanks to your crafty friend here, I can send them an engraved invitation to take a long walk down a short boarding tube. I love this shit."

Max's face showed incomprehension.

"You don't know? Goddamn, son, you should pay closer attention to treaties you help negotiate. It's right here." He pulled the information out of his workstation as deftly as a crack CIC officer on a battleship.

"'Article XXXVII, Paragraph 19. Entry Into Effect: The provisions of this treaty shall take full force and effect *nunc pro tunc* as of the outset of hostilities between the Krag Hegemony and the Pfelung Association, which outset of hostilities shall be deemed to have occurred when Krag forces first surreptitiously entered Pfelung territorial space for the purpose of engaging in hostile acts against the Pfelung.'"

"I'm afraid I still don't understand, Admiral."

"I'll let your friend, the ambassador, explain it to you."

Max turned to the doctor, who smiled innocently and said, "*Nunc pro tunc* means 'now for then' in Latin—as long as both parties agree to do it, it is perfectly legal for both to consent as a sort of amiable fraud that the document they signed this morning actually went into effect at noon on yesterday. So, the treaty says that the Union and the Pfelung became Associated Powers when the Krag committed the first Act of War against them—sending those bomb-rigged freighters into their space."

The admiral smiled broadly. "Don't you see, Robichaux? Laughed my fat ass off when I first figured this out. That means when you went barging into their territorial space, with the Pfelung screaming that you were violating their sovereignty and that you needed to get the fuck out before they blasted you to kingdom come, technically, under this treaty, they are deemed to have already been our bosom buddies for several hours, and you weren't violating their neutrality at all! Skated over that problem slicker than owl shit. How hard was it to get this in the treaty?"

"Not at all," the doctor answered. "When I explained privately how such a provision would protect the captain from any unfortunate consequences resulting from his technical violation of their neutrality, they concurred enthusiastically."

He turned to Max. "You are liked by them exceedingly, you know. I understand, in fact, that they intend to name after you their new pulse cannon battle station and a very large egg insemination pond that they are currently excavating."

The coffee arrived at this point, Bushman expertly placing on the front of the admiral's desk the tray, containing three steaming mugs, a server containing a white slightly viscous liquid laughingly referred to as "cream," and a small bowl of the granular, allegedly sweet, factory-synthesized substance that the Navy insisted be used in coffee and tea in place of sugar. He made a discrete exit. Everyone paused for a few moments to take a few sips of his coffee. It was hot and strong and good. Bushman had that part of his job down pat.

The admiral chuckled. "An egg insemination pond? I think that's a fitting tribute to you, Robichaux. Anyway, the acting ambassador here saved me from having to haul your sorry ass in front of a board of inquiry, for which I am thankful, because it would have made this part here very, very awkward. SINKINESH!"

Did the man ever use the comm panel for anything other than ship to ship? The doctor toyed with the idea of checking himself and Max for hearing damage when they got back to the *Cumberland.*

The flag secretary came in carrying two small hinged boxes, handed them to the admiral, and left. "Frankly, I've never seen the commissioners of the Admiralty do anything so goddamn fast. I think the Pfelung leaned on them. Hard. And if they hadn't, I would have. Anyway, you both need to stand up for this."

They stood. The admiral stood as well and produced a sheet of paper from a desk drawer. Max was struck by how the man standing before him was both ordinary and extraordinary. He was barely above average height for a man in the twenty-fourth century, maybe 1.9 meters, with a full head of thick, silver hair; a square jaw with a large dimple in the center; piercing gray eyes; and an animated mouth that seemed to flow rapidly from lopsided grin to fearsome scowl with no effort at all. His build was nothing unusual, maybe a little more muscular than was common for a man of his age in a time when most heavy work was done by machine, and maybe a little trimmer around the waist than usual for a man just on the far side of sixty.

What was most striking about him was that he seemed to exude confidence, determination, and energy, as though he could take on the whole Krag fleet single-handedly, armed only with the Model 1911 pistol on his hip. The man presented himself as a winner, someone who would lead men to victory. One got the feeling that the "with Arms" part of the Uniform of the Day was because the admiral liked having a weapon at his side to remind him that he was in the business of killing the enemy.

The admiral put on a pair of reading glasses. "There's a lengthy citation here, talking about quick thinking, intuitive problem solving, and lots of other things to give you swelled heads. You can read it yourselves later, but then it goes on to say—where is it? blah, blah, blah, yadda, yadda—oh yes, here. 'And therefore, for courageous resourcefulness and conspicuous gallantry in the highest traditions of the Union Space Navy above and beyond the call of duty, the High Commissioners of the Admiralty are pleased to confer upon Maxime Tindall Robichaux and Ibrahim Abdul Sahin the Commissioners' Medal of Honor, with all the rights, privileges, and emoluments pertaining thereto.'"

The toughest flag officer in Known Space was conferring upon two rather junior officers serving on an inconsequential ship the highest military honor that the Union could bestow, an honor that came with a number of legal and traditional privileges of which Max was certain Dr. Sahin was entirely ignorant.

"Anyway, here you are." He handed over the medals in their velvet-lined boxes and shook their hands with what seemed to be genuine affection.

"In a few months, we'll confiscate those so we can hand them back to you in front of a lot of people with bands playing, long speeches, and all sorts of other back-slapping bullshit in one of the big fleet award ceremonies we have four times a year. But I wanted you to have these now. I like to hand out decorations as soon as possible. Besides, I've never gotten to award one of these, much less two.

"Well, that's everything I needed you two for. *Cumberland* will be staying in the system for about three more weeks. It will take that long for the regularly appointed ambassador to arrive from Earth, and the Pfelung want to engage in some joint exercises with you, Robichaux. Like the doctor here says, seems you're something of a hero to them.

"After that, I think I have something interesting in mind for you. I bet on horses every now and again, and one of the ways I win is by putting my money on winners. Right now, Robichaux, you're winning, so that's where my money goes. Well, haul your sorry butts back to your ship. Even a crotchety old bastard like me needs to get some sleep every now and then. You're dismissed."

EPILOGUE

12:22Z Hours (08:36 Local Time—High Tide), 21 February 2315

Hatchery Number 1817 was immense. A vast, low building enclosing nearly a square kilometer, it contained secluded, muddy pools where recently fertilized eggs progressed through the early stages of their maturation cycle; another area where the fertilized eggs incubated to maturity and hatched in warm, still water; yet another where the hatchlings swam in a series of ever larger tanks of rapidly circulating water as they grew; and the enormous, dimly lit area where Max and the doctor, along with more than a hundred of their shipmates, Admiral Hornmeyer (whom Max could hear from eighty meters away) and a contingent from the Task Force; and about two hundred Pfelung, both male and female, stood. They all lined the edge of what Max would have thought of as a swimming pool, if it were not that the now empty basin was at least twenty times the size of any pool he had ever seen.

As the two had spent very little time alone since meeting with the admiral, mainly due to the doctor's busy schedule as acting union ambassador, Max was filling him in on the meaning of some of what transpired. Sahin was particularly puzzled by the meaning of the 'E.'

"All that means," said Max, "is that when we aren't stealthed, we get to turn on a four-meter-tall letter 'E' that we made with temporary running lights—we've already installed those—to tell everyone who can see us that the admiral has found the performance of the ship to be 'Excellent.' He doesn't do it all that often. Right now, the *Kranz* is showing one, and a few cruisers on detached service. I don't think he has ever given it to a destroyer. It's right next to the big Bronze Battle Star, which we'll light up every chance we get between now and when *Cumberland* goes into the boneyard."

Once that was cleared up, the doctor explained the operation of the hatchery to Max. He apparently had something of the professor in him, as when he started to talk about this kind of subject, it usually wound up sounding like an academic lecture.

"All of this used to be done in natural ponds, rivers, and lakes, but once the Pfelung became a technological civilization, they found it intolerable having more than half of their hatchlings eaten by wild predators, so they brought the process indoors to keep the little ones safe. This huge tank is where the young juveniles, akin to our toddlers I suppose, swim until they are old enough to fend for themselves in the ocean. They are released from here to the sea, where they spend five years swimming free and wild, eating what they catch. Then, when they reach adolescence, they instinctively swim back to where they were released, where they are reclaimed, by smell, by their families and reared and educated. They spend three years in this tank. It is here that they form the earliest memories that they will still have as adults. I hear that memories formed at this stage are particularly clear."

"How deep is the tank?" Max asked. "It's so dark, I can hardly see the inside at all."

"Quite deep. When the Pfelung are in their preadolescent, or Pelagic, Stage, they don't keep to the shallows the way the hatchlings or the adults do. They need to hunt for food at several different levels in the water column. They make this tank deep so that the ones at this stage, which I think they call the Lake Dwelling Stage, can become accustomed to diving down into the deep water before going out into the ocean."

A murmur among the humans and a bubbling sound among the Pfelung indicated that something was afoot. Five females, distinguished from the males by their smaller size, their slightly lighter color, and the camouflaging pattern of spots, swirls, and splotches on their backs, were making their way up a ramp to a meter-and-a-half-tall platform. The largest of the females, flanked on each side by two others, moved to the front of the platform and began speaking into the microphone, which, as was customary for the Pfelung, was mounted in a protective mound about the size of a man's head, resting on the floor of the platform. Her remarks were swiftly translated by the devices each human wore in his ear.

"Fellow Guardians of the Ruling Hatchery, ministers and keepers, and human guests, welcome to this ceremony. As the humans present do not know me, I identify myself as Brekluk-Tamm 191. It was only a few tens of tides ago that humans from the Union, who had neither swum in our waters nor tasted mud with us, fought at our sides against an enemy who would prey on us both, who would foul the Quiet Ponds Where Eggs Are Laid and who would eat the hatchlings before they attain the Age of Reason. Although many of those with whom we were hatched, with whom we have swum, and with whom we have tasted mud and shared the waters will swim and taste and share no more, with shared sacrifice we defeated that enemy.

"In doing so, eleven brave humans were carried to the Great Ocean. We can never repay our debt to them and to their mates and hatchlings, but there is one thing we can do. We can remember them."

Her dorsal fin waved back and forth, apparently some kind of signal. At that moment, four rows of lights in the pool, one running down each corner, sprang into life, illuminating it from its top to its bottom, which Max and the doctor could now see was more than a thousand meters deep.

The ever-artistic Pfelung had decorated the tank. The sides were the color of the sky. Not the light blue of the daytime sky, or the pitch black of space, but the deepest purple of the latest twilight at that last moment before the light fades to true night, pricked with stars. And framed by the twilight, in the center of each wall, was an image, a different one for each wall. On the north wall was a depiction of the freighter explosion destroying the battle station that had defended the jump point. The painting was quite realistic, yet somehow, not photographic, managing to capture through some subtle emphasis on the reds and orange hues of the explosion the shock, horror, and fear it must have inflicted upon the Pfelung who saw it.

On the east wall was an image of the *Cumberland*. Genius-level artistic talent had turned her utilitarian, inelegant lines into something stirring and graceful by inspired use of light and shadow and by the technique of framing the ship with the sickle crescent of Pfelung's enormous moon. On the south wall, the squat, stubby shape painted to convey an impression that reminded the human observers of a defiant bulldog, was the cutter, shown with her engines blazing as she accelerated toward her destiny at the jump point. And finally, on the west wall, were arrayed the images of Garcia, Amborsky, and the other men sacrificed to close the jump point and stop the invasion. They were painted full length, standing, wearing their SCUs, as they were on the cutter that day.

The obviously brilliant Pfelung artist, informed by each man's service record, had managed to capture the essence of each: Garcia's friendly competence, Amborsky's gruff exterior and warm heart, and all the rest—some part of the spirit that had once burned within them shining forth from the images.

After letting what they were seeing sink into the minds of her audience, Brekluk went on. "As these young grow, adults swim with them so that they will remember the shapes and faces of adults as those of friends and protectors. So, now, these young will remember the shapes and faces of humans as friends and protectors as well. There are 285 such swimming places for the young throughout our worlds. These images are being placed in each. This is the highest honor we know how to bestow. That is all I have to say on this subject. Let the tank be filled."

A floodgate twenty meters across opened near the bottom of the tank, admitting water through an aqueduct bored through solid rock to a point under the ocean several miles from shore, to admit the purest sea water. It poured in rapidly, filling the tank in less than two minutes.

"Let the young be admitted," Brekluk said, and a sluice opened to pour tiny Pfelung by the thousands, each about the size of a man's hand, into the tank. In a few moments, the torrent of young had run out, and the tank was full of splashing, milling, swirling, enthusiastically swimming creatures, filling the room with a sense of playful, joyful, exuberant life. "This ceremony is concluded."

"HEARTS OF STEEL"

Official Version: Revised as Per General Order 98-153, 9 July 2298
[The Official Anthem and March of the Union Space Navy, with new verses for the current war, sung to the tune of the "Heart of Oak," the official Anthem and March of the Royal Navy of the United Kingdom of Great Britain and Northern Ireland.]

To stations my lads, 'tis to glory we steer,
Oh, sons of the Union, we fight without fear;
'Tis to Honor you call us, for Honor we stand;
We brothers in valor await fame's command.

(Chorus)

Hearts of steel, that's our ships; hearts of steel, that's our men.
We always are ready; steady, boys, steady!
We'll fight, not surrender, again and again.

We'll take payment in blood for the debt Krag must pay,
And carve them with cutlass when they come to play;

Our courage defiant ennobles the stars,
Stalwart sons of Ares, strong offspring of Mars.

(Chorus)

We still make them bleed and we still make them die,
And shout mighty cheers as they fall from the sky;
So, to stations, me lads, and let's sing with one heart,
We will win this war if we all do our part.

(Chorus)

GLOSSARY AND GUIDE TO ABBREVIATIONS

Alphacen Alpha Centauri.

AU Astronomical unit. The mean distance between Earth and the sun, approximately 150 million kilometers, or 93 million statute miles.

AuxCon Auxiliary Control.

Bravo The second letter of the Union Forces Voicecom Alphabet; a colloquial name for Epsilon Indi III (*see*).

BuDes (pronounced "bew-dess") Bureau of Design.

BuPers (pronounced "bew-perz") Bureau of Personnel. The naval department responsible for managing naval personnel assignments, recruiting, and similar matters.

c The speed of light in a vacuum, commonly stated as "light-speed," 299,792,458 meters per second, or 186,282 miles per second.

Ça c'est bon (Cajun French) That's good. Equivalent to *c'est bon* in Parisian French.

Cajun A person descended from the French-speaking Roman Catholic residents of Nova Scotia (which they called Acadia) who

were exiled by the British at the end of the French and Indian
War because of concerns regarding their loyalty to the British
crown and who settled in what was then the French Territory of
Louisiana. Most Cajuns spoke their own version of French well
into the twentieth century and maintain a distinctive culture to
this day.

C'est pas rien (Cajun French) It's nothing, think nothing of it.
Equivalent to *de rien* in Parisian French.

CDR Comprehensive disciplinary record. A complete compendium of all disciplinary actions of any kind taken with respect
to a particular naval personnel.

Cherenkov-Heaviside radiation The burst of radiation
emitted as an object emerges from a jump (*see* jump drive).

Chief of the Boat The senior noncommissioned officer on
board any naval vessel. He is considered a department head and is
the liaison between the captain and the noncommissioned ranks
Sometimes referred to as COB (pronounced "cobb") and informally known as the "Goat."

CIC Combat Information Center.

CIG Change in grade. Promotion or demotion.

class A production series of warships of highly similar or
identical design, designated by the name of the first ship of the
series.

class (Krag vessels) The Krag apparently have a class system
similar to the Union's, producing warships of similar design in
series. Because Krag vessel names are, however, unknown, difficult to pronounce, or impossible to remember, the Navy uses a
system of "reporting names" for Krag vessel classes. Essentially,
when a new class of Krag vessel is identified, a name is assigned to
that class by Naval Intelligence. Class names generally start with
the same letter or group of letters as the name of the vessel type,
with the exception of battlecruisers, the class names of which

begin with "Bar" to distinguish them from battleships. In this way, a ship's type can immediately be determined from its class name, even if the name is not familiar. Examples of class names for each major warship type follow:

Battleships: Batwing, Battalion, Battleax, Baton.
Battlecruisers: Barnacle, Barnyard, Barrister, Barsoom, Barmaid
Carriers: Carousel, Carnivore, Carpetbagger, Cardigan
Cruisers: Crusader, Crucible, Crustacean, Crumpet
Frigates: Freelancer, Frogleg, Frycook, Frigid
Destroyers: Deckhand, Delver, Dervish, Debris
Corvettes: Corpuscle, Cormorant, Cornhusker, Corsican, Cordwood

clear the datum As a "datum" or "datum point" is a location from which a vessel has been observed, to "clear the datum" is for a ship to move away from a point in space where it (1) has been observed or (2) it did something that might have allowed it to be observed.

Comet Colloquial term for the Warship Qualification Badge, a medal—shaped like a comet with a curved tail—indicating that the wearer has passed either a Warship Crew Qualification Examination or a Warship Officer Qualification Examination, showing that he can competently operate every crew or officer station on the ship, perform basic damage control, engage in close order battle with sidearm and boarding cutlass, use a pulse rifle, and fight hand to hand.

compression drive One of the two known technologies that allow ships to travel faster than lightspeed (the other being the jump drive). The compression drive permits violation of Einsteinian physics by selectively compressing and expanding the fabric of the space-time continuum. The drive creates around the vessel a bubble of distorted space-time with a diameter approximately thirty-four times the length of the ship. This bubble, in turn, contains a smaller bubble of undistorted space-time just large enough to enclose the ship itself. The density of space-time is compressed along the ship's planned line of travel and expanded behind it (hence the term "compression drive," which was thought to sound better than "expansion drive" or "warp drive"), creating a propulsive force that moves the ship forward faster than the speed of light as viewed from the perspective of a distant observer. This superluminal motion does not violate Einsteinian physics because the ship is stationary relative to the fabric of space-time inside the bubble and therefore, from the point of view of an observer located there, does not exceed the speed of light. Because the volume of distorted space rises as a geometric function as ship size goes up under the familiar $V = \pi r^2$ formula multiplied by thirty-four (pi times half the length of the ship squared times thirty-four), even a small increase in the ship's dimensions results in substantial increases in the energy required to propel it through compressed space. Accordingly, only smaller ship types can move at high speeds or for any appreciable distance using compression drive, which means, in turn, that major fleet operations and planetary conquests require the taking and holding of jump points so that carriers, battleships, tankers, and other larger or slower vessels can be brought into the system.

compression shear A dangerous phenomenon caused by a compression drive experiencing poor speed regulation, a common occurrence at speeds of less than about 80 c. Compression shear occurs when radical fluctuations in the degree of space–time distortion caused by a poorly regulated drive exert variable and rapidly fluctuating force against the "bubble" of normal space-time surrounding the ship. As the small undistorted bubble around the ship must exist in precise equilibrium with the larger zone of differentially compressed and expanded space that surrounds the smaller one, sharp variations, or "shear," along the boundary rupture the bubble and destroy the ship.

Core Systems The fifty star systems located near the astrographic center of the Union, which, although constituting only about 10 percent by number of the Union's inhabited worlds, are home to 42 percent of its population and 67 percent of its heavy industrial capacity.

DC Damage control.

Egg Scrambler A device fired from a missile tube that, when exploded, scrambles the interface between normal space and metaspace such that for nearly an hour it is impossible for a ship in the vicinity to operate its compression drive (*see*) or to cause a comm signal to cross the interface to allow faster than light communications.

EM Electromagnetic. Usually short for the term "electromagnetic radiation," meaning visible light, radio waves, ultraviolet, infrared, and similar forms of energy forming a part of the familiar electromagnetic spectrum.

EMCON Emissions Control. A security and deception measure in which a warship not only operates under what twenty-first century readers would call "radio silence" but also without navigation beacons, active sensor beams, or any other emissions that could be used to track the ship.

Epsilon Indi III The second planet colonized by humans outside of the Sol system, also known as Bravo. A major industrial and cultural center.

FabriFax The brand name of an industrial-grade, computerized machine fabricator that uses advanced numeric, microrobotic manufacturing techniques to construct machine parts rapidly from a set of digital specifications—the distant descendant of the three-dimensional printers of the twenty-first century.

fils de putain (Cajun French) Son, or sons, of a whore. Used as an insult when an English speaker would say "son of a bitch" or "bastard." It is not, however, appropriate to use this expression in those places where an English speaker uses "son of a bitch" as an impersonal expletive as in, "Son of a bitch, I left my wallet at home."

finum nuntiante (Terranovan Latin) End of message, terminate communications.

flamer A particularly scathing Report of Disciplinary Action that becomes a part of a man's Comprehensive Disciplinary Record.

frame A vertical cross section of a warship, numbered from bow to stern for the purpose of describing the location of damage the ship's structure or to large areas. A destroyer might have as few as eight frames, whereas a carrier has hundreds.

FTL Faster than light. Superluminal.

FUBAR Fucked up beyond all recognition.

genau (German) Exactly, precisely. Often used to express agreement.

greenie Colloquial term for a recruit spacer. So called because the Working Uniform for that grade is light green in color.

goat Informal name for the Chief of the Boat (*see*).

Gynophage An extremely virulent viral disease launched by the Krag against the Union in 2295. The disease organism is highly infectious to all humans, but a gene sequence unique to the human "Y" chromosome prevents disease symptoms from manifesting in all but a tiny fraction of males, thereby keeping infected males contagious but asymptomatic. It is believed that left to itself, the disease would have proved fatal to virtually all human females in the galaxy. It was disseminated by thousands of stealthed compression drive drone vessels launched by the Krag in the early days of the war, each of which launched thousands of submunitions that exploded in the atmosphere of human-inhabited planets. The disease kills in a manner similar to Ebola, by breaking down the tissues of the internal organs, but operates at a much higher rate. Once the disease begins to manifest, the subject is dead within minutes. The disease is currently treated or prevented by the Moro Treatment, a combination vaccine and antibody devised by a team led by the brilliant Dr. Emeka Moro (*see*).

HASG *See* M-22.

hypergolic Of or pertaining to two substances that, when combined, will ignite and combust without need of an ignition source, a term used in the Navy primarily to describe fuels for missiles and thrusters.

IFF Identification, friend or foe.

inertial compensator The system on a space vessel that negates the inertial effect of acceleration on the crew and vessel contents (known as "G forces"), enabling the ship to accelerate, turn, and decelerate rapidly without killing the crew and ripping the fixtures from the deck.

jawohl (German) "Yes, indeed"; emphatically yes.

je concours (Cajun French) "I agree."

jump drive One of the two systems that allow a space vessel to cross interstellar distances in less time than it would take to travel at sublight speed (the other being compression drive [*see*]). The jump drive transfers the vessel in a single Planck interval from one point in space, known as a jump point, to another jump point in a nearby star system, and never less than 3.4 or more than 12.7 light years away. Jump points are generally located between 20 to 30 AU from a star, and almost always lie at least 45 degrees away from the star's equator. For some unknown reason, systems either have no jump points, three, or a multiple of three—but most commonly three—usually located several dozen AU from each other. Jumping is always more energy efficient and much faster than traversing the same distance with compression drive.

Khyber class A class of destroyer, the first of which, the USS *Khyber*, was commissioned on 24 April 2311, making these vessels a "new" class in 2315. The *Khybers* are exceptionally fast and maneuverable, even for destroyers. The thrust-to-mass ratio of these ships is in the same range as those of many fighter designs; accordingly, it is said that they handle more like large fighters than escort vessels. They are equipped with pulse cannon as powerful as those on many capital ships (although they have only three of these and a smaller rear-firing unit whereas a capital ship might have a dozen or more). Ships in this class are extremely stealthy, possess a sophisticated ability to mimic the electronic and drive emissions of other ships, and have a highly effective sensor suite. They are also equipped with SWACS (*see*). The trade-offs made to optimize these characteristics include highly Spartan crew accommodations— even as compared to other destroyers; a radically reduced number of reloads for her missile tubes (twenty Talons and five Ravens versus a typical destroyer loadout of sixty and twelve); a small crew, making for a heavy workload for all personnel; modest fuel capacity; and a reduced cargo hold. Unsupported endurance is rated at 75 days (as compared to 180 days for most destroyers) but in practice is somewhat shorter. It is believed that the class was designed to make quick stealthy raids into enemy space and destroy supply lines and means of communication, thereby disrupting enemy logistics and command/control/communications. Mass: 16,200 metric tons. Top sublight speed: .963 c. Compression drive: 1575 c cruise, 2120 c emergency. Weapons: three forward-firing Krupp-BAE Mark XXXIV pulse cannon, 150-gigawatt rating, one rear-firing Krupp-BAE Mark XXII pulse cannon (colloquially known as the "stinger"), 75-gigawatt rating. Two forward and one rear-firing missile tubes. Standard missile loadout of twenty Talon (*see*) and five Raven (*see*) antiship missiles. Ships in this class are named after historically significant mountain passes and ocean straits. Length: ninety-seven meters; beam: nine and a half meters. Commissioned ships in this class as of 21 January 2315 are *Khyber, Gibraltar, Messina, Cumberland, Hormuz*, and *Khardung La*. The projected size of the class is eighty-five ships.

kill Military slang for "kilometer." Replaced the former term "klick" beginning in the 2150s, when humans encountered and fought a brief war against a race of aliens known as the "Khlihk," at which point the similarity in pronunciation between the two words became confusing, as it was sometimes ambiguous whether "fifty klicks" was a distance or a moderate body of enemy troops.

Kuiper belt (rhymes with "piper") A belt of bodies, made mainly of frozen volatiles such as water ice, methane, and ammonia, found in the outer regions of many star systems.

lentement (Cajun French) Slowly.

LumaTite® A registered trade mark of APG-Owens-Corning Corporation for its transparent armored viewport material for spacecraft, consisting of a titanium-silicon nanocrystalline matrix microlaminated with frequency-specific EM-rejecting polymer films. The resulting material is as durable as warship hull material and is opaque to all forms of EM except visible light. It is, however, more expensive, kilogram for kilogram, than gold.

M-22 (Model 2222) Also known as the HASG (pronounced "haz-gee"), the Naval-Military Systems, Inc., heavy automatic shotgun is an "eight-gauge," belt-fed, swivel-mounted, fully automatic shotgun designed specifically to repel enemy boarders at the close ranges and in the confined spaces found on board a warship.

M-62 Model 2162 Pistol. One of the two sidearms approved for use by Union Space Navy Personnel (the other being the M-1911), the M-62 is a ten-millimeter, semiautomatic, magazine-fed handgun with a fourteen-round magazine. It is manufactured by the Beretta-Browning Military Arms Corporation.

M-72 Model 2072 Close-Order Battle Shotgun. The Winchester-Mossberg Arms Company Model 2072 is a semiautomatic, twelve-gauge shotgun designed for close-order battle against boarding parties or for use by boarders.

M-88 Model 2288 Pulse Rifle. The Colt-Ruger Naval Arms Corporation Model 2288 is a 7.62 × 51 millimeter, select-fire, magazine-fed battle rifle issued to Navy personnel for boarding actions, ship defense, and ground combat. It is similar in form and function to the M-14 battle rifle issued by the United States of America in the mid-twentieth century. It is called a "pulse rifle" because coaxially mounted below the rifle barrel is a launcher, from which can be fired the MMD ("Make my day") pulse grenade, a thirty-five-millimeter, self-propelled short-range projectile containing a shaped charge–equipped pulse slug capable of penetrating the armor on a Krag fighting suit at a range of fifty meters and then exploding, killing the occupant. The MMD is also effective against lightly armored ground vehicles.

M-1911 Model 1911 Pistol. One of the two sidearms approved for use by Union Space Navy Personnel (the other being the M-62), the M-1911 is an 11.48 millimeter (sometimes referred to by the archaic designation ".45 caliber") semiautomatic, magazine-fed handgun invented by perhaps the most brilliant firearms designer in the Known Galaxy, John Moses Browning, who was active in the United States of America on Earth in the late nineteenth and early twentieth centuries.

mais (Cajun French) Literally, "but." Often used to intensify or to give emphasis to the expression that follows. Accordingly, "*mais* yeah," is an enthusiastic or emphatic "yeah."

midshipman A boy, between the ages of eight and seventeen, taken on board ship both to perform certain limited duties and to be trained to serve in the enlisted or officer ranks. Midshipmen are commonly referred to as "mids."

midshipman trainer A senior noncommissioned officer, typically the second most senior chief petty officer on the ship, in charge of the training, housing, discipline, and welfare of all midshipmen on board. A well-liked midshipman trainer is generally known by the nickname "Mother Goose."

MMD *See* M-88.

moi aussi (Cajun) French for "me too."

Moro, Emeka Physician and medical researcher born in Mombassa, Kenya, Earth, on 28 March 2241. Winner of the Nobel Prize for Medicine in 2295. Perhaps the foremost expert in human infectious diseases in the galaxy, Dr. Moro headed the effort to devise a treatment or preventative for the Gynophage (*see*), an effort that involved more than a million physicians and researchers on more than four hundred planets, at its peak consuming 43 percent of the interstellar communications bandwidth and 15 percent of the computing capacity available to the human race, and costing more than 300 trillion credits. When early research work began to indicate that neither a vaccine nor an antibody-based treatment would be more than 25 percent effective, it was Dr. Moro who personally had the insight to combine a vaccine with a set of broad-spectrum antibodies synthesized not only to match the current disease organism but also the nine most probable mutation-induced alternate phenotypes of its external protein coat, thereby creating a combination inoculation that prevents infection in those who are not infected and prevents manifestation of the disease in those who are infected but asymptomatic. It is believed that the vaccine also provides some protection to asymptomatic individuals above and beyond that provided by the antibodies alone. (For the ship, *see Emeka Moro*. The USS *Emeka Moro*, an *Edward Jenner* class frigate commissioned on December 8, 2295, is named after Dr. Moro.)

Mother Goose The semiofficial title for the midshipman trainer (*see*).

officer rank abbreviations:

GADM: Grand Admiral (five stars)
FADM: Fleet Admiral (four stars)
VADM: Vice Admiral (three stars)
RADM: Rear Admiral (two stars)
CMRE: Commodore (one star)
CAPT: Captain
CMDR: Commander
LCDR: Lieutenant Commander
LT: Lieutenant
LTJG: Lieutenant junior grade
ENSN: Ensign

PC-4 Patrol Craft, Type 4. A sublight only, high-speed patrol and light attack craft used for system and planetary defense as well as for light intrasystem escort duties. Length: twenty-seven meters. Beam: three and a half meters. Crew: one officer, eight enlisted. Armament: one 75-gigawatt pulse cannon, five Raytheon-Hughes Talon (*see*) ship-to-ship missiles. Top speed .97 c.

percom A wrist-carried communication, computing, and control device worn by all naval personnel when on duty.

point defense Weapons, or integrated systems of weapons and sensors, designed to destroy incoming weapons and attacking ships at close range. All warships from destroyer on up are equipped with sophisticated, multilayer point defense systems that must be penetrated by any incoming missile in order to reach the ship.

poo yai An inarticulate exclamation of amazement used by Cajuns and occasionally by Creoles, roughly equivalent to "my goodness" or "wow."

posident POSitive IDENTification. The identification of a contact as hostile, neutral, or friendly by at least two different phenomenologies from two different sensors.

pulse cannon A ship-mounted weapon that fires a pulse of plasma diverted from the ship's main fusion reactor and accelerated to between .85 and .95 c by magnetic coils. The plasma is held in a concentrated "bolt" by a magnetic field generated by a compact, liquid helium–cooled, fusion cell–powered emitter unit inserted in the bolt just as it is about to leave the cannon tube. When the emitter stops generating the field, either because it has consumed its coolant and is vaporized by the plasma, because the timer/fuse turns the emitter off at a set range, or because the bolt strikes a target destroying the emitter, the bolt loses cohesion and expands explosively with the force of a small nuclear munition.

Queeg, Phillip Francis, Lieutenant Commander Fictional commander of the destroyer-mine sweeper (DMS) USS *Caine* during World War II in Herman Wouk's classic novel *The Caine Mutiny*. The book was made into an equally classic film, with Humphrey Bogart playing Queeg. Queeg suffered from paranoid personality disorder, progressing during the course of the novel to paranoid psychosis, which caused him to give increasingly bizarre and erratic orders to his crew. He had a compulsive habit of rolling two ball bearings around in his left hand and suffered a breakdown while commanding the ship in a storm. This resulted in the executive officer relieving him of command, for which act the XO was charged with and tried for mutiny.

Raven A large antiship missile carried by Union Warships. Much larger than the Talon (*see*) and with a higher top speed, the Raven accelerates more slowly, is less nimble, and is more vulnerable to point defense systems and countermeasures than the Talon, due to its larger size. Manufactured by Gould-Martin-Marietta Naval Aerospace Corporation, the Raven finds its target with both passive and active multimodal sensor homing and then inflicts its damage with a 1.5 megaton fixed-yield fusion warhead powerful enough to destroy all but the largest enemy vessels and to cripple any known enemy ship. Ravens are equipped with an innovative system known as Cooperative Interactive Logic Mode (CILM—pronounced "Kill 'em"). When more than one Raven is launched against the same target, CILM causes the missiles to communicate with one another and attack the target jointly, closing on the enemy from multiple vectors, to render defense more difficult, and exploding at the same instant to inflict the most damage.

regardez donc (Cajun French) An expression of awe and amazement, roughly equivalent to an extremely emphatic "Wow!" Literally translates as "look at that."

saltwater navy: a navy comprised of ocean-going ships as opposed to one comprised of ships that travel in space.

Schweinhund (German) An insult that does not translate very well into Standard. The word literally means "pig-dog" but has connotations that go well beyond the translation. It is best understood as meaning that the person to whom it is applied is vile, disgusting, and utterly devoid of decency. It is a fitting insult for someone who steals little old ladies' pensions, runs a child prostitution ring, or sells out his shipmates.

Scotty The traditional nickname for a warship's chief of engineering, irrespective of the national origin of his ancestors. The term is of great antiquity and uncertain origin.

SDMF Self-destruct mechanism, fusion. A fusion munition carried on all Union warships prior to the Battle of Han VII, for the purpose of destroying the vessel as a last resort to prevent it from falling into enemy hands.

SIGINT (also SigInt) Signals Intelligence—the branch of Intelligence that attempts to determine the dispositions, intentions, and capabilities of the enemy by intercepting its communications, sensor emissions, navigation beams, and other signals.

six Shorthand for "six o'clock position," or directly astern.

SOP Standard operating procedure.

squeaker a particularly young or puny midshipman. Also "squeekie," "deck dodger," "panel puppy," and "hatch hanger" (the last for their habit of standing in the hatches while holding the rim, thereby blocking the way).

SSR Staff Support Room. A compartment, sometimes called a "back room," located in the general vicinity of the CIC, containing between three and twenty-four men whose duty it is to provide support to one CIC department by performing detailed monitoring and analysis at a level impossible for one or two people assigned that function in CIC. For example, in the Sensors SSR, one man would be monitoring graviton emissions; one man, the output from optical scanners; another man, neutrino flux; yet another, a given portion of the EM spectrum, and so on. The CIC officer communicates with the senior officer in the SSR, who in turn assigns tasks to the other personnel in that room and then communicates their observations and conclusions to CIC. The SSR has the capability to communicate with CIC by voice or text and by transferring data files. Frequently, the SSR will indicate to the CIC officer which sensor display he should be reviewing, allowing the CIC officer to pull up that display on his console.

Standard The official language of the Union; also, the official language or a widely used second language on virtually every non-Union human world. Standard is derived mostly from the English that was the most widely spoken second language on Earth and was the language of international science, commerce, shipping, and aviation when human beings first traveled to the stars in the late twenty-first and early twenty-second centuries.

SWACS Space warning and control system. An integrated sensor, computer, and command/communications/control suite placed on various spacecraft to provide an exceptionally high level of sensor coverage and detail and to coordinate the defense against attacking vessels.

Talon The primary antiship missile carried by Union warships. Manufactured by Raytheon-Hughes Space Combat Systems, the Talon is an extremely fast, stealthy, and agile missile with both passive and active multimodal sensor homing and a 5–150 kiloton variable-yield fusion warhead. The Talon is designed to elude and penetrate enemy countermeasures and point defense systems; use its on board artificial intelligence and high-resolution active sensors to find a "soft spot" on the enemy ship; and then detonate its warhead in a location designed to inflict the most damage. One Talon is capable of obliterating ships up to frigate size and of putting ships up to heavy cruiser size out of commission. Against most targets with functioning point defense systems, the Talon is a better choice than the heavier Raven (*see*).

TDY Temporary duty.

TEMPCOM Temporary command

Terran Union The common name for the Union of Earth and Terran Settled Worlds, a Federal Constitutional Republic consisting of Earth and (as of January 2315) 518 of the total 611 worlds known to be settled by human beings. Often simply referred to as the "Union." Formed in 2155 upon the collapse of the Earth and Colonial Confederation (commonly referred to as the "Earth Confederation" or simply the "Confederation") resulting from the Revolt of the Estates, which began in 2154. The territorial space controlled by the Union has an ellipsoidal shape (roughly like that of a watermelon) 2500 light-years long and 800 light-years wide, aligned lengthwise through the Orion-Cygnus arm of the Milky Way Galaxy. Population: approximately 205 billion. With the possible exception of the Krag Hegemony, the Union is the most populous and largest political entity in Known Space.

TF Task force. A group of warships assembled for a particular mission or "task."

type When applied to warships, this term refers to the general category and function of the vessel, as opposed to its class, which refers to a specific design or production run of vessels within a type. The most common types of warship, in decreasing order of size, are carrier, battleship, battlecruiser, cruiser, frigate, destroyer, corvette, and patrol vessel. There are, of course, other types of naval vessel that are not categorized as warships, including tanker, tender, tug, hospital ship, troop carrier, landing ship, cargo vessel, and so on.

UESF United Earth Space Forces. The international military arm formed in 2034 by United States and Canada, the European Union, and the China–Japan Alliance to retake the Earth's moon from the Ning-Braha who had occupied it, presumably as a prelude to a planned invasion of Earth. The UESF is the institutional successor of the armies, navies, and air forces of the founding powers, but drew its personnel primarily from their navies and air forces and drew its command structure, regulations, traditions, and other institutional foundations mainly from their "saltwater navies." The Ning-Braha technology captured by the UESF in this campaign was the catalyst for mankind's colonization of the stars.

Union *See* Terran Union.

UNREP UNderway REPlenishment.

USNGS (Uniform Sierra Nebula Galaxy Sierra) Union Space Navy Galactic Survey. The most important star catalog in Known Space—used universally by the Union Space Navy as well as by the Union Merchant Naval Service, most human navigators even outside of the Union, and many alien species.

watch The period of time that a member of the crew who is designated as a "watch stander" mans his assigned "watch station." Also, the designation of the section of the crew to which the watch stander belongs. On Union warships, there are three watches, usually known as Blue, Gold, and White. They stand watch on the following schedule:

First Watch: 2000–0000 (1 Blue) (2 Gold) (3 White)
Middle Watch: 0000–0400 (1 Gold) (2 White) (3 Blue)
Morning Watch: 0400–0800 (1 White) (2 Blue (3 Gold)
Forenoon Watch: 0800–1200 (1 Blue) (2 Gold) (3 White)
Afternoon Watch: 1200–1600 (1 Gold) (2 White) (3 Blue)
First Dog Watch: 1600–1800 (1 White) (2 Blue) (3 Gold)
Second Dog Watch: 1800–2000 (1Blue) (2 Gold) (3 White)

The captain and the XO do not stand a watch. Rather, all officers other than the CO, XO, and the CMO serve as Officer of the Deck, serving as the officer in charge of minute-to-minute operations in CIC when neither the CO nor the XO is in CIC. Officers of the Deck stand watch for eight hour shifts on a rotating basis.

XO Executive officer. The second in command of any warship.

Z (when appended to a time notation) Zulu Time. Standard Union Coordinated Time. So that all USN vessels can conduct coordinated operations, they all operate on Zulu Time, which is, for all intents and purposes, the same as Greenwich Mean Time—mean solar time as measured from the Prime Meridian in Greenwich, England, on Earth in the Sol system.

Zhou Matrix A standard fleet static defensive formation in which ships are arrayed in a plane perpendicular to the threat axis with more powerful ships interspersed with less powerful ones to provide mutual fire support and to avoid giving the enemy a "weak zone" to exploit. Named for Rear Admiral Zhou Chou Dong, who first proposed it in a lecture on hypothetical future space combat tactics in the former People's Republic of China in 2022. The Zhou Matrix can also be used offensively as the "anvil" portion of the "hammer and anvil" formation invented by Admiral Kathleen "Killer Kate" Phillips at the Battle of Sirius B on 22 August 2164.

ACKNOWLEDGMENTS

To some degree, every book is a distillation of everything an author has learned and experienced in his lifetime. Naturally, that legacy cannot be articulated in a few paragraphs. There are, however, a few individuals whose contribution to my learning and experiences is so related to the contents of this volume that they deserve particular recognition.

The author is indebted to Charles Murray and Catherine Bly Cox for their outstanding nonfiction book, *Apollo: The Race to the Moon*, which I believe to be the best single book ever written about the American space program, bar none. Readers familiar with that work's clear and evocative description of the inner workings of the Mission Operations Control Room and the Staff Support Rooms during the Gemini and Apollo Programs will be able to discern the shape of those rooms in these pages. Any resemblance between the brilliant Mission Control teams of those years and the CIC of the USS *Cumberland* is entirely by design.

Readers who know well the history of those endeavors may recognize several names in this book, scattered throughout as respectful nods to some brilliant individuals who made largely unsung contributions to what has been, thus far, mankind's greatest adventure. With one exception, mentioned below, the similarity of any other names to those of any persons, living or dead, is entirely coincidental.

I also acknowledge a profound debt to Gene Roddenberry and to the many writers, producers, and other creative people involved in the *Star Trek* franchise over the decades. Despite a few remarks directed in these pages at some aspects of those programs and many, many deliberate choices to make the ships, weapons, tactics, and procedures of the Union Navy radically different from those of Roddenberry's Starfleet, any modern author of military fiction set on a starship must deal in some way, overtly or covertly, with Mr. Roddenberry's creation. I hope my approach was original, respectful, and humorous. The original *Star Trek* series, watched so avidly during its first run on NBC, triggered my first crude efforts to imagine and write about brave men fighting on powerful starships to preserve mankind against deadly enemies. This book is a direct product of those imaginings, begun in that bygone era that we now know as "the Sixties."

Also, I offer a tip of the hat to early pioneers and modern masters of the genre that we call science fiction, whose imaginings helped shape and encourage my own: Isaac Asimov, Arthur C. Clark, Robert Heinlein, Ray Bradbury, Robert Silverberg, Poul Anderson, Keith Laumer, Norman Spinrad, Harlan Ellison, Ursula K. LeGuin, Frederick Pohl, Larry Niven, Doris Lessing, Jerry Pournelle, Greg Bear, David Weber, Joe Haldeman, Timothy Zahn, Robert L. Forward, and many, many others whose works have so entertained and inspired me over the years. I ask that they and their many fans forgive my temerity in aspiring to follow in their footsteps.

More thanks to Ronald D. Moore and David Eick and all of those involved in the production of the excellent television series *Battlestar Galactica*, which, in addition to captivating me for many hours, taught me that one can tell inspiring and uplifting, yet gritty and realistic, stories about warriors among the stars—and that there might be a market for more such stories.

My thanks also to the originators and the many contributors to Wikipedia.org. Were it not for the ready availability of this site to tell me the diameter of our solar system as measured in astronomical units; the density of gold in tons per cubic meter; whether the element mercury has multiple isotopes and is used in ion propulsion; the names of the twenty star systems closest to Earth and their distances in light years and parsecs; the status of the evolutionary development of rats on Earth eleven million years ago; and hundreds of other facts that a conscientious author of "hard science fiction" must verify, this book would have been incalculably more difficult to write.

For many lessons taught and the outstanding example provided by the late Dr. George Middleton, educator, psychologist, mentor, and leader, I extend my heartfelt thanks. The Commodore/Admiral Middleton mentioned in these pages is a poor and grossly inadequate tribute to Dr. Middleton, though the fictitious admiral is not a depiction or even a parody of the real doctor, who was so gentle a spirit that he could never have made warfare his life's work. The respect and esteem that my characters have for the fictitious "Uncle Middy" in this book are, however, designed to be a reflection of the respect that the real, and ever so profoundly missed, "Uncle Middy" enjoyed in life. *Ab illo cui multum datur multum requiritur.*

On Cajun French: I grew up in Lake Charles, Louisiana; my mother's family is from the heart of Acadiana and Cajun to the marrow, and my maternal grandmother's first language was Cajun French. Unfortunately, although I grew up hearing a fair amount of Cajun French from time to time, from relatives and neighbors, I did not grow up speaking it, much less writing it. Every Cajun expression in these pages is one that I remember hearing from my youth; nevertheless, I would have been clueless, left to myself, about how to put those expressions into writing. Therefore, it is with sincere thanks that I gratefully acknowledge the essential role served by the *Dictionary of Louisiana French: As Spoken in Cajun, Creole, and American Indian Communities*, University of Mississippi Press (2010), in the writing of this book, as a source for spelling, and to verify the accuracy of my recollection. This dictionary is an astonishingly thorough and authoritative work of scholarship, eminently usable and beautifully printed. I could not recommend it more highly.

And finally, I humbly offer my eternal gratitude to Patrick O'Brian, whose splendid "Aubry/Maturin" series of seafaring novels set in the Napoleonic Wars is the most direct inspiration for this book and for the volumes that I hope will follow. In September 2012, when I sat down to begin writing, my ultimate goal was to pen a series of tales that realized in space some of the adventure, wonder, excitement, and vivid realism that O'Brian's novels realized at sea. If this book has transported the reader to far reaches of space one-tenth as compellingly as O'Brian carried his readers to the Far Side of the World, I will have succeeded beyond my wildest expectations.

"All hands to make sail."

H. Paul Honsinger
Lake Havasu City, Arizona
17 May 2013

ABOUT THE AUTHOR

Kathleen Honsinger 2013

H. Paul Honsinger is a retired attorney with lifelong interests in space exploration, astronomy, the history of science, military history, firearms, and international relations. He was born and raised in Lake Charles, Louisiana, and is a graduate of Lake Charles High School, The University of Michigan in Ann Arbor, and Louisiana State University Law School in Baton Rouge. Honsinger has practiced law with major firms on the Gulf Coast and in Phoenix, Arizona, and most recently had his own law office in Lake Havasu City, Arizona. He currently lives in Lake Havasu City with his beloved wife, Kathleen, and his daughter and stepson, as well as a 185-pound English Mastiff and two highly eccentric cats.

This is his first novel.

Stay up to date on future "Robichaux/Sahin novels" as well as other developments in the Honsinger Publications universe by visiting Paul Honsinger's blog at: http://paulhonsinger.blogspot.com/. Follow him on Facebook as well: https://www.facebook.com/honsingerscifi.

Contact the author at: honsingermilitaryscifi@gmail.com.